2004

D0059894

By Kristin Hannah
Published by Ballantine Books

A Handful of Heaven

The Enchantment

Once in Every Lifetime

If You Believe

When Lightning Strikes

Waiting for the Moon

Home Again

On Mystic Lake

Angel Falls

Summer Island

Distant Shores

Between Sisters

The Things We Do for Love

THE THINGS WE DO FOR LOVE

THE THINGS WE DO FOR LOVE

KRISTIN HANNAH

BALLANTINE BOOKS
NEW YORK

A Ballantine Book
Published by The Random House Publishing Group

ISBN 0-345-46750-7

Text design by Susan Turner

Manufactured in the United States of America

Once again, for Benjamin and Tucker

For good friends: Holly and Gerald, Mark and Monica, Tom and Lori, Megan and Kany, and Steve and Jill

And finally, a special thanks to Linda Marrow, for an effort that was above and beyond the call of duty

Things do not change; we change.
—Henry David Thoreau

THE THINGS WE DO FOR LOVE

ONE

THE STREETS OF WEST END WERE CROWDED ON THIS UNEX-
pectedly sunny day. All across town mothers stood in
open doorways, with hands tented across their eyes,
watching their children play. Everyone knew that soon—probably tomorrow—a soapy haze would creep across the sky, covering the blue, obliterating the delicate sun, and once more the rain
would fall.

It was May, after all, in the Pacific Northwest. Rain came to
this month as surely as ghosts took to the streets on the thirty-
first of October and salmon came home from the sea.

"It sure is hot," Conlan said from the driver's seat of the sleek
black BMW convertible. It was the first thing he'd said in almost
an hour.

He was trying to make conversation; that was all. Angie
should return the volley, perhaps mention the beautiful haw-

thorn trees that were in bloom. But even as she had the thought, she was exhausted by it. In a few short months, those tiny green leaves would curl and blacken; the color would be drawn out of them by cold nights, and they would fall to the ground, unnoticed.

When you looked at it that way, what was the point in noticing so fleeting a moment?

She stared out the window at her hometown. It was the first time she'd been back in months. Although West End was only one hundred twenty miles from Seattle, that distance had seemed to swell lately in her mind. As much as she loved her family, she'd found it difficult to leave her own house. Out in the world, there were babies everywhere.

They drove into the old part of town, where Victorian houses had been built one after another on tiny patches of lawn. Huge, leafy maple trees shaded the street, cast an intricate lacework pattern of light on the asphalt. In the seventies, this neighborhood had been the town's heart. Kids had been everywhere back then, riding their Big Wheels and Schwinn bicycles from one house to the next. There had been block parties every Sunday after church, and games of Red Rover played in every backyard.

In the years between then and now, this part of the state had changed, and the old neighborhoods had fallen into silence and disrepair. Salmon runs had diminished and the timber industry had been hit hard. People who had once made their living from the land and the sea had been pushed aside, forgotten; new residents built their houses in clusters, in subdivisions named after the very trees they cut down.

But here, on this small patch of Maple Drive, time had stood still. The last house on the block looked exactly as it had for forty years. The white paint was pure and perfect; the emerald green trim glistened. No weed had ever been allowed to flourish in the lawn. Angie's father had tended to this house for four decades; it had been his pride and joy. Every Monday, after a weekend of hard work at the family's restaurant, he'd devoted a full twelve-hour day to home and garden maintenance. Since his death, Angie's mother had tried to follow that routine. It had become her solace, her way of connecting with the man she'd loved for almost fifty years, and when she tired of the hard work, someone was always ready to lend a hand. Such help, Mama often reminded them, was the advantage to having three daughters. Her payoff, she claimed, for surviving their teen years.

Conlan pulled up to the curb and parked. As the convertible top shushed mechanically into place, he turned to Angie. "Are you sure you're okay with this?"

"I'm here, aren't I?" She turned to look at him finally. He was exhausted; she saw the glint of it in his blue eyes but knew he wouldn't say more, wouldn't say anything that might remind her of the baby they'd lost a few months ago.

They sat there, side by side in silence. The air-conditioner made a soft whooshing noise.

The old Conlan would have leaned over and kissed her now, would have told her he loved her, and those few and tender words would have saved her, but they were past such comfort these days. The love they'd once shared felt far, far away, as faded and lost as her childhood.

"We could leave right now. Say the car broke down," he said, trying to be the man he used to be, the man who could tease his wife into smiling.

She didn't look at him. "Are you kidding? They all think we paid too much for this car. Besides, Mama already knows we're here. She might talk to dead people, but she has the hearing of a bat."

"She's in the kitchen making ten thousand cannoli for twenty people. And your sisters haven't stopped talking since they walked in the door. We could escape in the confusion." He smiled. For a moment everything felt normal between them, as if there were no ghosts in the car. She wished it were an ease that could last.

"Livvy cooked three casseroles," she muttered. "Mira probably crocheted a new tablecloth and made us all matching aprons."

"Last week you had two pitch meetings and a commercial shoot. It's hardly worth your time to cook."

Poor Conlan. Fourteen years of marriage and he still didn't understand the dynamics of the DeSaria family. Cooking was more than a job or a hobby; it was a kind of currency, and Angie was broke. Her papa, whom she'd idolized, had loved that she couldn't cook. He took it as a badge of success. An immigrant who'd come to this country with four dollars in his pocket and made a living feeding other immigrant families, he'd been proud that his youngest daughter made money using her head, rather than her hands.

"Let's go," she said, not wanting to think about Papa.

Angie got out of the car and went around to the trunk. It opened silently, revealing a narrow cardboard box. Inside was an extravagantly rich chocolate cake made by the Pacific Dessert Company and a to-die-for lemon tart. She reached down for it, knowing some comment would be made about her inability to cook. As the youngest daughter—"the princess"—she'd been allowed to color or talk on the phone or watch TV while her sisters worked in the kitchen. None of her sisters ever let her forget that Papa had spoiled her mercilessly. As adults, her sisters still worked in the family restaurant. That was *real* work, they always said, unlike Angie's career in advertising.

"Come on," Conlan said, taking her arm.

They walked up the concrete walkway, past the fountain of the Virgin Mary, and up the steps. A statue of Christ stood by the door, his hands outstretched in greeting. Someone had hung an umbrella from his wrist.

Conlan knocked perfunctorily and opened the door.

The house rattled with noise—loud voices, kids running up and down the stairs, ice buckets being refilled, laughter. Every piece of furniture in the foyer was buried beneath a layer of coats and shoes and empty food boxes.

The family room was full of children playing games. Candy Land for the younger kids; crazy eights for the older. Her eldest nephew, Jason, and her niece Sarah were playing Nintendo on the television. At Angie's entrance, the kids squealed and flocked to her, all talking at once, vying for her attention. From their earliest memories, she was the aunt who would get down on the floor and play with whatever toy was "in" at the moment. She never turned down their music or said that a movie was unsuitable. When asked, they all said Aunt Angie was "way cool."

She heard Conlan behind her, talking to Mira's husband, Vince. A drink was being poured. She eased through the crowd of kids and walked down the hallway toward the kitchen.

In the doorway, she paused. Mama stood at the oversized butcher block in the center of the room, rolling out the sweet dough. Flour obscured half of her face and dusted her hair. Her eyeglasses—a holdover from the seventies—had lenses the size of saucers and magnified her brown eyes. Tiny beads of sweat collected along her brow and slid down her floury cheeks, landing on her bosom in little blobs of dough. In the five months since Papa's passing, she'd lost too much weight and stopped dyeing her hair. It was snow white now.

Mira stood at the stove, dropping gnocchi into a pot of boiling water. From behind, she looked like a girl. Even after bearing four children, she was still tiny, almost birdlike, and since she often wore her teenage daughter's clothes, she appeared ten years younger than her forty-one years. Tonight, her long black hair was held back in a braid that snaked almost to her waist. She wore a pair of low-rise, flare-legged black pants and a cable-knit red sweater. She was talking now—there was no surprise in that; she was always talking. Papa had always joked that his eldest daughter sounded like a blender on high speed.

Livvy was standing off to the left, slicing fresh mozzarella. She looked like a Bic pen in her black silk sheath. The only thing higher than her heels was the puffiness of her teased hair. Long ago, Livvy had left West End in a rush, certain that she could become a model. She'd stayed in Los Angeles until the sentence "Could you please undress now?" started to accompany every job interview. Five years ago, just after her thirty-fourth birthday, she'd come home, bitter at her lack of success, defeated by the effort, dragging with her two young sons who had been fathered by a man none of the family had ever seen or met. She'd gone to work at the family restaurant, but she didn't like it. She saw herself as a big-city girl trapped in a small town. Now she was married—again; it had been a quickie ceremony last week at the Chapel of Love in Las Vegas. Everyone hoped that Salvatore Traina—lucky choice number three—would finally make her happy.

Angie smiled. So much of her time had been spent in this kitchen with these three women; no matter how old she got or what direction her life took, this would always be home. In Mama's kitchen, you were safe and warm and well loved. Though she and her sisters had chosen different lives and tended to meddle too often in one another's choices, they were like strands of a single rope. When they came together, they were unbreakable. She needed to be a part of that again; she'd been grieving alone for too long.

She stepped into the kitchen and put the box down on the table. "Hey, guys."

Livvy and Mira surged forward, enfolded her in a hug that smelled of Italian spices and drugstore perfume. They held her tightly; Angie felt the wetness of tears on her neck, but nothing was said except "It's good to have you home."

"Thanks." She gave her sisters one last tight hug, then went to

Mama, who opened her arms. Angie stepped into the warmth of that embrace. As always, Mama smelled of thyme, Tabu perfume, and Aqua Net hair spray. The scents of Angie's youth.

Mama hugged her so tightly that Angie had to draw in a gulp of air. Laughing, she tried to step back, but Mama held on.

Angie stiffened instinctively. The last time Mama had held Angie this tightly, Mama had whispered, *You'll try again. God will give you another baby.*

Angie pulled out of the embrace. "Don't," she said, trying to smile.

That did it—just the quietly voiced plea. Mama reached for the Parmesan grater and said, "Dinner's ready. Mira, get the kids to the table."

The dining room held fourteen people comfortably and fifteen tonight. An ancient mahogany table, brought here from the old country, held center stage in a big, windowless room papered in rose and burgundy. An ornate wooden crucifix hung on the wall beside a portrait of Jesus. Adults and children were crammed around the table. Dean Martin sang in the other room.

"Let us pray," Mama said as soon as everyone was seated. When silence didn't fall instantly, she reached over and thwopped Uncle Francis on the head.

Francis dropped his chin and closed his eyes. Everyone followed suit and began the prayer. Their voices joined as one: "Bless us, O Lord, and these thy gifts which we are about to receive from thy bounty through Christ our Lord. Amen."

When the prayer ended, Mama stood up quickly, raised her wineglass. "We drink a toast now to Sal and Olivia." Her voice vibrated; her mouth trembled. "I do not know what to say. Toasting is a man's job." She abruptly sat down.

Mira touched Mama's shoulder and stood up. "We welcome Sal to our family. May you two find the kind of love that Mama and Papa had. May you have full cupboards and warm bedrooms and—" She paused. Her voice softened. "—many healthy babies."

Instead of laughter and clapping and clanking glasses, there was silence.

Angie drew a sharp breath and looked up at her sisters.

"I'm not pregnant," Livvy said quickly. "But . . . we're trying."

Angie managed to smile, although it was wobbly and weak and fooled no one. Everyone was looking at her, wondering how she would handle another baby in the family. They all tried so hard not to bruise her.

She raised her glass. "To Sal and Livvy." She spoke quickly, hoping her tears would pass for joy. "May you have many healthy babies."

Conversations started up again. The table became a frenzy of clanging forks and knives scratching on porcelain and laughter. Although this family gathered for every holiday and two Monday nights a month, they never ran out of things to say.

Angie glanced around the table. Mira was talking animatedly to Mama about a school fund-raiser that needed to be catered; Vince and Uncle Francis were arguing about last week's Huskies–Ducks game; Sal and Livvy were kissing every now and then; the younger kids were spitting peas at one another; and the older ones were arguing about whether Xbox or PlayStation was better. Conlan was asking Aunt Giulia about her upcoming hip replacement surgery.

Angie couldn't concentrate on any of it. She certainly couldn't make idle conversation. Her sister wanted a baby, and so it would happen. Livvy would probably get pregnant between Leno and the news. *Oops, I forgot my diaphragm.* That was how it happened for her sisters.

After dinner, as Angie washed the dishes, no one spoke to her, but everyone who walked past the sink squeezed her shoulder or kissed her cheek. Everyone knew there were no more words to say. Hopes and prayers had been offered so many times over the years, they'd lost their sheen. Mama had kept a candle burning at St. Cecilia's for almost a decade now, and still it would be Angie and Conlan alone in the car tonight, a couple who'd never multiplied into a family.

Finally, she couldn't stand it anymore. She tossed the dishrag on the table and went up to her old bedroom. The pretty little room, still wallpapered in roses and white baskets, held twin beds ruffled in pink bedding. She sat down on the end of her bed.

Ironically, she'd once knelt on this very floor and prayed not to be pregnant. She'd been seventeen at the time, dating Tommy Matucci. Her first love.

The door opened and Conlan walked in. Her big, black-haired Irishman husband looked ridiculously out of place in her little girl's room.

"I'm fine," she said.

"Yeah, right."

She heard the bitterness in his voice, felt stung by it. There was nothing she could do, though. He couldn't comfort her; God knew that had been proven often enough.

"You need help." He said it tiredly, and no wonder. The words were old.

"I'm fine."

He stared at her for a long time. The blue eyes that had once looked at her with adoration now held an almost unbearable defeat. With a sigh, he turned and left the room, closing the door behind him.

A few moments later it opened again. Mama stood in the doorway, her fists planted on her narrow hips. The shoulder pads on her Sunday dress were *Blade Runner* big and practically touched the door frame on either side. "You always did run to your room when you were sad. Or angry."

Angie scooted sideways to make room. "And you always came running up after me."

"Your father made me. You never knew that, did you?" Mama sat down beside Angie. The old mattress sagged beneath their weight. "He could not stand to see you cry. Poor Livvy could shriek her lungs out and he never noticed. But you . . . you were his princess. One tear could break his heart." She sighed. It was a heavy sound, full of disappointment and empathy. "You're thirty-eight years old, Angela," Mama said. "It's time to grow up. Your papa—God rest his soul—would have agreed with me on this."

"I don't even know what that means."

Mama slipped an arm around her, pulled her close. "God has given you an answer to your prayers, Angela. It is not the answer you wanted, so you don't hear. It's time to listen."

ANGIE WOKE WITH A START. THE COOLNESS ON HER CHEEKS WAS from tears.

She'd had the baby dream again; the one in which she and Conlan stood on opposite shores. Between them, on the shimmering expanse of blue sea, was a tiny pink-swaddled bundle. Inch by inch, it floated away and disappeared. When it was gone, they were left alone, she and Conlan, standing too far apart.

It was the same dream she'd been having for years, as she and her husband trudged from doctor's office to doctor's office, trying one procedure after another. Supposedly she was one of the lucky ones; in eight years, she'd conceived three children. Two had ended in miscarriage; one—her daughter, Sophia—had lived for only a few short days. That had been the end of it. Neither she nor Conlan had the heart to try again.

She eased away from her husband, grabbed her pink chenille robe off the floor, and left the bedroom.

The shadowy hallway waited for her. To her right, dozens of family photographs, all framed in thick mahogany, covered the wall. Portraits of five generations of DeSarias and Malones.

She looked down the long hallway at the last, closed door. The brass knob glinted in moonlight from the nearby window.

When was the last time she'd dared to enter that room?

God has given you an answer. . . . It's time to listen.

She walked slowly past the stairs and the vacant guest room to the final door.

There she drew in a deep breath and exhaled it. Her hands were trembling as she opened the door and went inside. The air felt heavy in here, old and musty.

She turned on the light and closed the door behind her.

The room was so perfect.

She closed her eyes, as if darkness could help. The sweet notes of *Beauty and the Beast* filled her mind, took her back to the first time she'd closed the door on this room, so many years ago. It was after they'd decided on adoption.

We have a baby, Mrs. Malone. The mother—a teenager—chose you and Conlan. Come down to my office and meet her.

It had taken Angie the full four hours until their appointment to choose the outfit and do her makeup. When she and Conlan finally met Sarah Dekker in the lawyer's office, the three of them had bonded instantly. *We'll love your child,* Angie had promised the girl. *You can trust us.*

For six wonderful months Angie and Conlan had given up trying to get pregnant. Sex had become fun again; they'd fallen effortlessly back in love. Life had been good. There had been hope in this house. They'd celebrated with their families. They'd brought Sarah into their home and shared their hearts with her. They'd accompanied her to every OB appointment. Two weeks before her due date, Sarah had come home with some stencils and paint. She and Angie had decorated this room. A sky blue ceiling and walls, crowded by puffy white clouds. White picket fencing entwined with bright flowers, their colorful faces attended to by bees and butterflies and fairies.

The first sign of disaster had come on the day Sarah went into labor. Angie and Conlan had been at work. They'd come home to an empty, too-quiet house, with no message on the answering machine and no note on the kitchen table. They'd been home less than an hour when the phone rang.

They'd huddled by the phone together, holding hands, crying with happiness when they heard of the birth. It had taken a moment for the other words to register. Even now, Angie only remembered bits and pieces of the conversation.

I'm sorry—
changed her mind
back with her boyfriend
keeping the baby

They'd shut the door to this room and kept it closed. Once a week, their cleaning woman ventured inside, but Angie and Conlan never did. For well over a year, this room had stood empty, a shrine to their dream of someday. They'd given up on all of it—the doctors, the treatments, the injections, and the procedures. Then, miraculously, Angie had conceived again. By the time she was five months pregnant, they'd dared once more to enter this room and fill it with their dreams. They should have known better.

She went to the closet and pulled out a big cardboard box. One by one, she began to put things into it, trying not to attach memories to every piece she touched.

"Hey."

She hadn't even heard the door open, and yet here he was, in the room with her.

She knew how crazy it must seem to him, to find his wife sitting in the middle of the room, with a big cardboard box beside her. Inside it were all of her precious knickknacks—the Winnie-the-Pooh bedside lamp, the Aladdin picture frame, the crisp new collection of Dr. Seuss books. The only piece of furniture left was the crib. The bedding was on the floor beside it, a neat little stack of pale pink flannel.

She turned to look up at him. There were tears in her eyes, blurring her vision, but she hadn't noticed until now. She wanted to tell him how sorry she was; it had all gone wrong between them. She picked up a small pink stack of sheets, stroking the fabric. "It made me crazy" was all she could say.

He sat down beside her.

She waited for him to speak, but he just sat there, watching her. She understood. The past had taught him caution. He was like an animal that had adapted to its dangerous environment by being still and quiet. Between the fertility drugs and the broken dreams, Angie's emotions were unpredictable. "I forgot about us," she said.

"There is no us, Angie." The gentle way he said it broke her heart.

Finally. One of them had dared to say it. "I know."

"I wanted a baby, too."

She swallowed hard, trying to keep her tears under control. She'd forgotten that in the last few years; Conlan had dreamed of fatherhood just as she wanted motherhood. Somewhere along the way, it had all become about her. She'd focused so much on her own grief that his had become incidental. It was one of those realizations that would haunt her, she knew. She had always been dedicated to success in her life—her family called her obsessive—and becoming a mother had been one more goal to attain. She should have remembered that it was a team sport.

"I'm sorry," she said again.

He took her in his arms and kissed her. It was the kind of kiss they hadn't shared in years.

They sat that way, entwined, for a long time.

She wished his love could have been enough for her. It should have been. But her need for a child had been like a high tide, an overwhelming force that had drowned them. Maybe a year ago she could have kicked to the surface. Not now. "I loved you. . . ."

"I know."

"We should have been more careful."

Later that night, when she was alone in the bed they'd bought together, she tried to remember the hows and whys of it, the things they'd said to each other at the end of their love, but none of it came back to her. All she could really remember was the smell of baby powder and the sound of his voice when he said good-bye.

TWO

IT WAS AMAZING HOW MUCH TIME IT TOOK TO DISMANTLE A LIFE. Once Angie and Conlan had decided to end their marriage, details became what mattered. How to divide everything in half, especially the indivisible things like houses and cars and hearts. They spent months on the details of divorce, and by late September it was done.

Her house—no, it was the Pedersons' house now—was empty. Instead of bedrooms and a designer living room and a granite-layered kitchen, she had a sizeable amount of money in the bank, a storage facility filled with fifty percent of their furniture, and a car trunk full of suitcases.

Angie sat on the brick hearth, staring out across the gleaming gold of her hardwood floors.

There had been blue carpeting in here on the day she and Conlan had moved in.

Hardwood, they'd said to each other, smiling at the ease of their agreement and the power of their dream. *Kids are so hard on carpet*.

So long ago . . .

Ten years in this house. It felt like a lifetime.

The doorbell rang.

She immediately tensed.

But it couldn't be Con. He'd have a key. Besides, he wasn't scheduled to come by today. This was her day to pack up the last of her things. After fourteen years of marriage, they now had to schedule separate time in the house they'd shared.

She got to her feet and crossed the living room, opening the door.

Mama, Mira, and Livvy stood there, huddled together beneath the entry roof, trying to keep out of the rain. They were trying to smile, too; neither effort was entirely successful.

"A day like this," Mama said, "is for family." They surged forward in a pack. The aroma of garlic wafted up from a picnic basket on Mira's arm.

"Focaccia," Mira said at Angie's look. "You *know* that food eases every trouble."

Angie found herself smiling. How many times in her life had she come home from school, devastated by some social slight, only to hear Mama say, *Eat something. You'll feel better.*

Livvy sidled up to her. In a black sweater and skintight jeans she looked like Lara Flynn Boyle on Big Hair Day. "I've been through two divorces. Food *so* doesn't help. I tried to get her to put tequila in the basket, but you know Mama." She leaned closer. "I have some Zoloft in my purse if you need it."

"Come, come," Mama said, taking charge. She herded her chicks to the empty living room.

Angie felt the full weight of it then: failure. Here was her family, looking for places to sit in an empty house that yesterday had been a home.

Angie sat down on the hard, cold floor. The room was quiet now. They were waiting for her to start talking. They'd follow her lead. That was what family did. The problem was, Angie had nowhere to go and nothing to say. Her sisters would have laughed about that on any other day. Now it was hardly funny.

Mira sat down beside Angie and scooted close. The rivets on her faded jeans made a scraping noise on the floor. Mama followed, sat down on the brick hearth; Livvy sat beside her.

Angie looked around at their sad, knowing faces, wanting to explain it for them. "If Sophie had lived—"

"Don't go there," Livvy said sharply. "It can't help."

Angie's eyes stung. She almost gave in to her pain right there, let it overwhelm her. Then she rallied. It wouldn't do any good to cry. Hell, she'd spent most of the last year in tears and where had it gotten her? "You're right," she said.

Mira took her in her arms.

It was exactly what Angie needed. When she drew back, feeling somehow shakier and steadier at the same time, all three women were looking at her.

"Can I be honest here?" Livvy said, opening the basket and pulling out a bottle of red wine.

"Absolutely not," Angie said.

Livvy ignored her. "You and Con have been at odds too long. Believe me, I know about love that goes bad. It was time to give up." She began pouring the wine into glasses. "Now you should go somewhere. Take some time off."

"Running away won't help," Mira said.

"Bullshit," Livvy responded, offering Angie a glass of wine. "You've got money. Go to Rio de Janeiro. The beaches are supposed to be great. And practically nude."

Angie smiled. The pinched feeling in her chest eased a little. "So I should buy a thong and show off my rapidly dropping ass?"

Livvy laughed. "Honey, it wouldn't hurt."

For the next hour, they sat in the empty living room, drinking red wine and eating, talking about ordinary things. The weather. Life in West End. Aunt Giulia's recent surgery.

Angie tried to follow the conversation, but she kept wondering how she'd ended up here, alone and childless at thirty-eight. The early years of her marriage had been so good. . . .

"That's because business is bad," Livvy said, pouring herself another glass of wine. "What else can we do?"

Angie drifted back to the here and now, surprised to realize that she'd left for a few minutes. She looked up. "What are you guys talking about?"

"Mama wants to sell the restaurant," Mira said.

Angie straightened. *"What?"* The restaurant was the hub of their family, the center of everything.

"We were not going to speak of it today," Mama said, shooting Mira an angry look.

Angie looked from face to face. "What in the hell is going on?"

"Don't you swear, Angela," Mama said. She sounded tired. "Business at the restaurant is bad. I don't see how we can keep going."

"But . . . Papa loved it," Angie said.

Tears sprang into her mother's dark eyes. "You hardly need to tell me this."

Angie looked at Livvy. "What's wrong with the business?"

Livvy shrugged. "The economy is bad."

"DeSaria's has been doing well for thirty years. It can't be—"

"I can't *believe* you're going to tell us how to run a restaurant," Livvy snapped, lighting up a cigarette. "What would a copywriter know about it?"

"Creative director. And it's running a restaurant, not performing brain surgery. You just give people good food at good prices. How hard can—"

"Stop it, you two," Mira said. "Mama doesn't need this."

Angie looked at her mother, but didn't know what to say. A family that only moments before had been the bedrock of her life felt suddenly cracked.

They fell into silence. Angie was thinking about the restaurant . . . about her papa, who had always been able to make her laugh, even when her heart had felt close to rending . . . and about the safe world where they'd all grown up together.

The restaurant was the anchor of their family; without it, they might drift away from one another. And that, the floating on one's own tide, was a lonely way to live. Angie knew.

"Angie could help," Mama said.

Livvy made a sound of disbelief. "She doesn't know anything about the business. Papa's princess never had—"

"Hush, Livvy," Mama said, staring at Angie.

Angie understood everything in that one look. Mama was offering her a place to hide out away from the painful memories in this city. To Mama, coming home was the answer to every question. "Livvy is right," Angie said slowly. "I don't know anything about the business."

"You helped that restaurant in Olympia. The success of your campaign made the newspapers," Mira said, studying her. "Papa made us read all the clippings."

"Which Angie mailed to him," Livvy said, exhaling smoke.

Angie *had* helped put that restaurant back on the map. But

all it had taken was a good ad campaign and some money for marketing.

"Maybe you *could* help us," Mira said at last.

"I don't know," Angie said. She'd left West End so long ago, certain that the whole world awaited her. How would it feel to be back?

"You could live in the beach house," Mama said.

The beach house.

Angie thought about the tiny cottage on the wild, windswept coast, and a dozen treasured memories came to her, one after another.

She'd always felt safe and loved there. Protected.

Maybe she could learn to smile again there, in that place where, as a girl, she'd laughed easily and often.

She looked around her, at this too-empty house that was so full of sadness; it sat on a block in a city that held too many bad memories. Maybe going home *was* the answer, for a while at least, until she figured out where she belonged now.

She wouldn't feel alone at the cottage; not like she did in Seattle.

"Yeah," she said slowly, looking up. "I could help out for a little while." She didn't know which emotion was sharper just then—relief or disappointment. All she knew was this: She wouldn't be alone.

Mama smiled. "Papa told me you would come back to us someday."

Livvy rolled her eyes. "Oh, great. The princess is coming back to help us poor country bumpkins run the restaurant."

A WEEK LATER ANGIE WAS ON HER WAY. SHE'D SET OFF FOR WEST End in the way she started every project—full speed ahead. First, she'd called her boss at the advertising agency and asked for a leave of absence.

Her boss had stumbled around a bit, sputtering in surprise. There had been no indication at all that she was unhappy, none at all. *If it's a promotion you want—*

She'd laughed at that, explaining simply that she was tired.

Tired?

She needed time off. And she had no idea how much. By the time the conversation had wound around to its end, she had simply quit. Why not? She needed to find a new life, and she could hardly do that clinging to the hemline of the old one. She had plenty of money in the bank and lots of marketable skills. When she was ready to merge back into the traffic of real life, she could always find another job.

She tried not to think about how often Conlan had begged her to do this very thing. *It's killing you*, he always said. *How can we relax if you're always in overdrive? The doctors say . . .*

She cranked up the music—something old and sweet—and pressed her foot down on the accelerator.

The miles sped past, each one taking her farther from Seattle and closer to the town of her youth.

Finally, she turned off the interstate and followed the green *Washington Beaches* signs to West End.

The tiny town welcomed her. Light glinted off streets and leaves that were still wet with rain. The storefronts, long ago painted in bright blues and greens and pale pinks to reflect the Victorian fishing village theme, had, in time, weathered to a silvery softness. As she drove down Front Street, she remembered the Fourth of July parades. Every year the family had dressed up and carried a *DeSaria's Restaurant* banner. They'd tossed candies to the crowd. Angie had hated every moment, but now . . . now it made her smile sadly and remember her father's booming laugh. *You are part of this family, Angela. You march.*

She rolled down her window and immediately smelled the salty tang of sea air mixed with pine. Somewhere a bakery had opened its doors. There was the merest hint of cinnamon on the breeze.

The street was busy but not crowded on this late September afternoon. No matter where she looked, people were talking animatedly to one another. She saw Mr. Peterson, the local pharmacist, standing on the street outside his store. He waved at her, and she waved back. She knew that within minutes he would walk next door to the hardware store and tell Mr. Tannen that Angie DeSaria was back. He'd lower his voice when he'd say, *Poor thing. Divorce, you know.*

She came to a stoplight—one of four in town—and slowed. She was about to turn left, toward her parents' house, but the ocean sang its siren call and she found herself answering. Besides, she wasn't ready for the family thing yet.

She turned right and followed the long, winding road out of town. To her left, the Pacific Ocean was a windblown gray sail that stretched to forever. Dunes and sea grass waved and fluttered in the wind.

Only a mile or so from town it became a different world. There were very few houses out here. Every now and then there were signs for a so-called resort or a collection of rental cabins perched above the sea, but even then there was nothing to be seen from the road. This stretch of shoreline, hidden amid the towering trees in an out-of-the-way town between Seattle and Portland, hadn't been "discovered" yet by the yuppies, and most of the locals couldn't afford beach property. And so it was wild here. Primitive. The ocean roared its presence and reminded passersby that once, not so very long ago, people believed dragons lived in the uncharted waters. It could be quiet sometimes, deceptively so, and in those times tourists were lulled into a false sense of safety. They took their rented kayaks out into the rolling water and paddled back and forth. Every year some of those tourists were simply lost; only the bright borrowed kayaks returned.

Finally she came to an old, rusted mailbox that read: *De-Saria.*

She turned onto the rutted dirt driveway. Giant trees hemmed her in on either side, blocked out most of the sky and all of the sun. The property was covered in fallen pine needles and oversized ferns. Mist coated the ground and rose upward, gave the world an impossibly softened look. She'd forgotten the mist, how it came every morning in the autumn, breathing up from the earth like a sigh made visible. Sometimes, on early morning walks, you could look down and not see your own feet. As children, they'd gone in search of that mist in the mornings, made a game out of kicking through it.

She pulled up to the cottage and parked.

The homecoming was so sweet and sharp she swallowed a sudden lump in her throat. The house her father had built by hand sat in a tiny clearing, surrounded by trees that had been old when Lewis and Clark passed through this territory.

The shingles, once a cedar red, had aged to the color of driftwood, silvery soft. The white trim was barely a contrast at all.

When she got out of the car, she heard the symphony of her childhood summers—the sound of surf below, the whistling of the wind through the trees. Someone somewhere was flying a kite. The fluttery thwop-thwop sent her back in time.

Come on over here, princess. Help Papa trim these bushes back. . . .

Hey, Livvy, wait up! I can't run that fast. . . .

Mama, tell Mira to give me my marshmallows back. . . .

It was here, all those funny, angry, bittersweet moments that made up their family's history. She stood there in the watery sunlight, surrounded by trees, and soaked them all in, the memories she'd forgotten.

Over there by the giant nurse log that sprouted a dozen smaller plants was where Tommy had first kissed Angie . . . and tried to feel her up. There by the well house was the best ever hiding place for hide-and-go-seek.

And there, hidden in the dark shade of two gigantic cedar trees, was the fern grotto. Two summers ago, she and Conlan had brought all the nieces and nephews out here for a campout. They'd built a fort amid the huge ferns and pretended to be pirates. They'd told elaborate ghost stories that night, all of them gathered around a bonfire, roasting marshmallows and making s'mores.

Back then, she'd still believed that someday she'd bring her own children here. . . .

With a sigh, she carried her luggage into the house. The downstairs was one big room—a kitchen off to the left, with butter yellow cabinets and white tile countertops; a small dining area tucked into the corner (somehow all five of them had eaten at that tiny table); and a living room that took up the rest of the space. A giant river rock fireplace dominated the north-facing wall. Around it were clustered a pair of overstuffed blue sofas, a battered pine coffee table, and Papa's worn leather chair. There was no television at the cottage. Never had been.

We talk, Papa had always said when his daughters complained.

"Hey, Papa," she whispered.

The only answer was wind on the windowpanes.

Tap. Tap. Tap.

It was the sound a rocking chair made, on a hardwood floor, in an unused room. . . .

She tried to outrun the memories, but they were too fast. She felt her control slipping away. With every breath she took, it seemed that time marched on, moved away from her. Her youth was leaving her, as impossible to grasp as the air she breathed in her lonely bed at night.

She let out a heavy breath. She'd been a fool to think things would be different here. Why would they? Memories didn't live on streets or in cities. They flowed in the blood, pulsed with your heartbeat. She'd brought it all with her, every loss and heartache. The weight of it bowed her back, exhausted her.

She climbed the stairs and went into her parents' old bedroom. The sheets and blankets were off the bed, of course, no doubt stored in a box in the closet, and the mattress was dusty, but Angie didn't care. She crawled up onto the bed and curled into a ball.

This hadn't been a good idea, after all, coming home. She closed her eyes, listening to the bees buzzing outside her window, and tried to fall asleep.

THE NEXT MORNING, ANGIE WOKE WITH THE SUN. SHE STARED UP AT the ceiling, watching a fat black wolf spider spinning its web.

Her eyes felt gritty and swollen.

Once again she'd watered her mattress with memories.

Enough was enough.

It was a decision she'd made hundreds of times in the last year. This time she was determined to mean it.

She opened the suitcase, found a change of clothes, and headed for the bathroom. After a hot shower, she felt human again. She brushed her hair into a ponytail, dressed in a pair of faded jeans and a red turtleneck sweater, and grabbed her purse off the kitchen table. She was just about to leave for town when she happened to glance out the window.

Outside, Mama sat on a fallen log at the edge of the property. She was talking to someone, moving her hands in those wild gestures that had so embarrassed Angie in her youth.

No doubt the whole family was arguing about whether Angie could be of any use at the restaurant. After last night, she questioned it herself.

She knew that when she stepped out onto the porch, all those voices raised in disagreement would sound like a lawn mower. They would spend an hour arguing over the pros and cons of Angie's return.

Her opinion would hardly matter.

She paused at the back door, gathering courage. Forcing a smile, she opened the door and went outside, looking for the crowd.

There was no one here except Mama.

Angie crossed the yard and sat down on the log.

"We knew you'd come out sooner or later," Mama said.

"We?"

"Your papa and me."

Angie sighed. So her mother was still talking to Papa. Grief was something Angie knew well. She could hardly blame her mother for refusing to let go. Still, she couldn't help wondering if this was something to worry about. She touched her mother's hand. The skin was loose and soft. "So what does he have to say about my being home?"

Mama sighed in obvious relief. "Your sisters ask me to see a doctor. You ask me what Papa has to say. Oh, Angela, I'm glad you're home." She pulled Angie into a hug.

For the first time, Mama wasn't dressed to the nines and layered in clothes. She wore only a cable-knit sweater and an old pair of Jordache jeans. Angie could feel how thin she'd gotten and it worried her. "You've lost more weight," she said, drawing back.

"Of course. For forty-seven years I eat dinner with my husband. Alone is hard."

"Then you and I will eat together. I'm alone, too."

"Are you staying?"

"What do you mean?"

"Mira thinks you need someone to take care of you and a place to hide out for a few days. Running a restaurant in trouble is not easy. She thinks you'll be gone in a day or two."

Angie could tell that Mira spoke for others in the family, and she wasn't surprised. Her sister didn't understand the kind of dreams that sent a girl in search of a different life . . . or the heartache that could turn her around and send her home again. The family had always worried that Angie's ambition was too sharp somehow, that it would cut her. "What do you think?"

Mama bit down on her lip, worried it in a gesture as familiar as the sound of the sea. "Papa says he's waited twenty years for you to take over his baby—his restaurant—and he doesn't want anyone to get in your way."

Angie smiled. That sounded so much like Papa. For a second, she almost believed he was here with them, standing in the shadows of his beloved trees.

She sighed, wishing she could hear his voice again, but there was only the sound of the ocean, roaring up to the sand. She couldn't help thinking about last night and all the tears she'd shed. "I don't know if I'm strong enough yet to help you."

"He loved to sit here and watch the ocean," Mama said, leaning against her. "*We have to fix those stairs, Maria.* That's what he said first thing every summer."

"Did you hear me? Last night . . . was hard."

"We made a lot of changes every summer. This place never looked the same two years in a row."

"I know, but—"

"It always started with the one thing. Just fixing the stairs."

"Just the stairs, huh?" Angie said, finally smiling. "The longest journey begins with a single step and all that."

"Some sayings are simply true."

"But what if I don't know where to start?"

"You will."

Mama put an arm around her. They sat that way a long time, leaning against each other, staring out to sea. Finally, Angie said, "How did you know I was here, by the way?"

"Mr. Peterson saw you drive through town."

"And so it begins." Angie smiled, remembering the web that connected the residents in this town. Once, at the homecoming dance, she'd let Tommy Matucci put his hands on her butt; the news had reached Mama before the dance was over. As a girl, Angie had hated that small town feeling. Now, it felt good to know that people were looking out for her.

She heard a car drive up. She glanced back at the house. A forest green minivan pulled into the yard.

Mira got out of the car. She was wearing a faded pair of denim overalls and an old Metallica T-shirt. In her arms were a pile of account books. "No time like the present to get started," she said. "But you better read 'em fast—before Livvy realizes they're gone."

"You see?" Mama said, smiling at Angie. "Family will always show you where to begin."

THREE

A DRIZZLY RAIN FELL ON THE BRICK COURTYARD OF FIRCREST Academy, giving everything a shiny, lacquered appear-ance.

Standing beneath the flagpole, Lauren Ribido looked at her watch for at least the tenth time in as many minutes.

It was six-fifteen.

Her mother had promised to be here for the college fair by five-thirty.

She couldn't believe she'd fallen for the pretty promises again. She knew better. Happy hour at the Tides tavern didn't end until six-thirty.

So why did it still hurt, after all these years? You'd think a heart would grow calluses at some point.

She turned away from the empty road and headed toward

the gymnasium. She was almost to the doors when she heard a male voice call her name.

David.

She spun around, already smiling. He got out of the passenger side of a new black Cadillac Escalade and slammed the door shut with his hip. He was dressed up, wearing blue Dockers and a yellow cashmere sweater. Even with his blond hair plastered wetly to his head, he was the best-looking guy in school. "I thought you'd be inside already," he said, running up to her.

"My mom didn't show."

"Again?"

She hated the tears that burned her eyes. "It's no big deal."

He pulled her into a bear hug, and for those few moments, her world was okay.

"How about your dad?" she asked gently, hoping just this once Mr. Haynes had come through for David.

"Nope. Someone has to denude the rainforest."

She heard the bitterness in his voice and started to say *I love you*; the sound of high heels on concrete stopped her.

"Hello, Lauren."

She eased out of David's arms and looked up at his mother, who was trying not to frown. "Hello, Mrs. Haynes."

"Where is your mother?" she asked, settling an expensive brown handbag over her shoulder as she glanced around.

Lauren flashed on an image of her mother's most likely location: slumped on a barstool in the Tides, smoking a bummed cigarette. "She had to work late."

"On college fair night?"

Lauren hated the way Mrs. Haynes looked at her then. It was the *poor Lauren, so pathetic* look. She'd seen it her whole life. Adults—especially women—were always wanting to mother her. In the beginning, at least; sooner or later they moved on to their own lives, their own families, leaving Lauren somehow more alone than she'd been before. "She can't help it," Lauren said.

"That's more than I can say for Dad," David said to his mother.

"Now, David," Mrs. Haynes said with a heavy sigh, "you know your father would be here if he could."

"Yeah, right." He hooked an arm around Lauren's shoulders and drew her close. She let herself be swept across the wet courtyard and into the gymnasium. Every step of the way she focused on positive thoughts. She refused to let her mother's absence impact her self-confidence. Tonight of all nights she had to keep her eye on the goalpost, and a college scholarship to the same school David chose was the touchdown. A field goal was a school nearby.

She was committed to achieving this goal, and when she was committed, she could move mountains. She was here, wasn't she? A senior at one of the best private schools in Washington state, and on a full scholarship, to boot. She'd made her choice in fourth grade when she moved to West End from Los Angeles. Back then, she'd been a shy girl, too embarrassed by her horn-rimmed charity eyeglasses and secondhand clothes to say much. Once, long ago, she'd made the mistake of asking her mother for help. *I can't wear these shoes anymore, Mommy. Rain is getting in the holes.*

If you're like me, you'll get used to it had been Mom's response. Those four words—*if you're like me*—had been enough to change the course of Lauren's life.

The next day she set about changing herself and her life. Project Geek No More had begun. She did chores for all the neighbors in the rundown apartment complex in which she and her mother lived. Feeding the cats for old Mrs. Teabody in 4A, cleaning the kitchen for Mrs. Mauk, carrying packages upstairs for Mrs. Parmeter in 6C. One dollar at a time, she saved up money for contact lenses and new clothes. *My,* the optometrist had said on the big day, *you have the most gorgeous brown eyes I've ever seen.* Once she looked like everyone else, Lauren set about acting correctly. She started with smiles, and then graduated to waves and finally hellos. She volunteered for everything, as long as a parent contact wasn't required. By the time she started junior high, her hard work had begun to pay off. She'd earned her full ride to Fircrest Academy—a Catholic school with a strict uniform code. There, she worked even harder. She was voted class secretary in ninth grade and had retained an office every year since. In high school, she organized every school dance, took photos for the annual, ran the student body as senior class president, and lettered in both gymnastics and volleyball. She'd fallen in love with David on their first date, almost four years ago now. They'd been inseparable ever since.

She stared into the gym, which was packed with people.

To Lauren, it looked as if she were the only student here without a parent. It was a feeling she was used to; nonetheless, it made her smile falter. She couldn't help looking back at the flag-pole. Her mother still wasn't there.

David squeezed her hand. "Well, Trixie, are we ready?"

It made her smile, that little nickname. He knew how nervous she was right now. She leaned into him. "Let's go, Speed Racer."

Mrs. Haynes came up beside them. "Do you have a pen, Lauren, and some paper?"

"Yes, ma'am," she answered. It embarrassed her, how much that simple question meant to her.

"I don't have a pen," David said, grinning.

Mrs. Haynes handed him a pen and led the way forward. They merged into the stream of traffic. As always, the crowd parted for them. They were the senior couple, the pair voted most likely to stay in love. Dozens of friends waved or said hi.

They went from booth to booth, picking up literature and talking to the representatives. As always, David did everything he could to help Lauren. He told everyone he saw about her stellar grades and achievements. He was certain she'd be offered countless scholarships. In his world, things came easily, and in that world, it was easy to believe in happy endings.

He stopped at the Ivy League schools.

When Lauren looked at pictures of those venerable campuses, she felt queasy. She prayed he didn't decide to go to Harvard or Princeton. She could never fit in there, even if she *could* get accepted; not there, in those halls where the girls were named after food products and everyone had parents who believed in education. Still, she smiled her prettiest smile and took the brochures. A girl like her needed to make a good impression at all times. There was no room for error in her life.

At last, they headed for the Holy Grail.

The Stanford booth.

Lauren heard Mrs. Haynes's trailing voice as she marched ahead of them. ". . . the wing named after your grandfather . . ."

Lauren stumbled. It took pure willpower to keep her posture good and her smile in place.

David would probably go to Stanford, where his parents had gone, and his grandfather, too. The one school on the West Coast that matched the Ivy League for exclusivity. Stellar grades weren't enough. Perfect SAT scores didn't guarantee admittance, either.

No way would she get a scholarship from Stanford.

David tightened his hold on her hand. He smiled down at her. *Believe*, that smile said.

She wanted to.

"This is my son, David Ryerson Haynes," Mrs. Haynes was saying now.

Of the Ryerson-Haynes Paper Company.

She hadn't added that, of course. It would have been tacky and wholly unnecessary.

"And this is Lauren Ribido," David said, squeezing Lauren's hand. "She'd be a real asset to Stanford's student body."

The recruiter smiled at David. "So, David," he said. "You're interested in following in your family's footsteps. Good for you. At Stanford, we pride ourselves on . . ."

Lauren stood there, holding David's hand so tightly her fingers started to ache. She waited patiently for the recruiter to turn his attention to her.

He never did.

THE BUS JERKED TO A STOP AT THE CORNER. LAUREN GRABBED HER backpack off the floor and hurried to the front of the bus.

"Have a nice night," Luella, the bus driver, said.

Lauren waved and headed down Main Street. Here, in the tourist hub of downtown West End, everything was sparkling and beautiful. Years ago, when the timber and commercial fishing industries had hit hard times, the town fathers had decided to play up the Victorian cuteness of the town. Half of downtown's buildings had already fit the bill; the other half were hurriedly re-modeled. A statewide advertising campaign was started (for a solid year the city government paid for nothing else—not roads or schools or services), and West End, "Victorian getaway on the coast," was born.

The campaign worked. Tourists drifted in, drawn by the bed-and-breakfasts, the sand castle competitions, the kite flying, and the sport fishing. It became a destination instead of a detour on the road from Seattle to Portland.

But the veneer went only so deep, and like all towns, West End had its forgotten places, its corners that remained unseen by visitors and unvisited by locals. *That part of town*, the place where people lived in apartments without decorations or security. Lauren's part of town.

She turned off Main Street and kept walking.

With each step, the neighborhood deteriorated; the world became darker, more rundown. There were no Victorian-inspired curliques on the buildings here, no advertisements for quaint bed-and-breakfasts or seaplane rides. This was where the old-timers lived, men who'd once worked in the timber mills or on the fishing boats. The people who'd missed the tide of change and been washed into the dark, muddy marshlands. Here, the only bright lights were neon signs that advertised booze.

Lauren walked briskly, looking straight ahead. She noticed every nuance of change, every shadow that seemed new, every noise and movement, but she wasn't afraid. This street had been her home turf for more than six years. Though most of her neighbors were down on their luck, they knew how to take care of one another, and little Lauren Ribido belonged here.

Home was a narrow, six-story apartment building that sat dead center on a lot overgrown with blackberry bushes and salal. The stucco exterior was grayed with dirt and debris. Light shone from behind several windows, giving the place its only sign of life.

Lauren hiked up the creaking steps, pushed through the front door (the lock had been broken five times last year; the property manager, Mrs. Mauk, refused to fix it again), and headed for the tired steps that led to her apartment on the fourth floor.

As she crept past the manager's door, she held her breath. She was almost to the stairs when she heard the door open, heard:

"Lauren? Is that you?"

Damn it.

She turned around, trying to smile. "Hello, Mrs. Mauk."

Mrs. Mauk—*Call me Dolores, honey*—stepped into the shadowy hallway. Light from the open doorway made her look pale, almost sinister, but her toothy smile was bright. As always, she wore a navy blue kerchief over her graying hair and a floral housedress. There was a rumpled look to her, as if she'd just been unfolded from an old suitcase. Her shoulders were hunched by a lifetime of disappointment. It was a common stance in this neighborhood. "I went to the salon today."

"Uh-huh."

"Your mom didn't show for work."

"She's sick."

Mrs. Mauk clucked sympathetically. "New boyfriend again, huh?"

Lauren couldn't answer.

"Maybe this time it'll be love. Anyhow, you're overdue on the rent. I need it by Friday."

"Okay." Lauren couldn't hold on to her smile.

Mrs. Mauk gave her The Look. "You can't be warm enough in that coat," she said, frowning. "You tell your mom—"

"I will. Bye." She ran for the stairs and went up to the fourth floor.

Their door was ajar. Light spilled between the crack, slanted butterlike across the linoleum hallway.

Lauren wasn't worried. Her mom rarely remembered to shut the front door, and when she did remember to close it, she never locked it. Lost her keys too often; that was the excuse.

Lauren went inside.

The place was a mess. An open pizza box covered one end of the counter. A collection of beer bottles stood beside it. Potato chip bags were everywhere. The room smelled of cigarettes and sweat.

Mom lay on the sofa, arms and legs akimbo. A rumbling snore came up from the tangle of blankets that covered her face.

With a sigh, Lauren went into the kitchen and cleaned everything up, then she went to the couch and knelt down. "Come on, Mom, I'll help you to bed."

"Wha? Huh?" Mom sat up, bleary-eyed. Her short, tousled hair, platinum this month, stuck out around her pale face. She reached shakily for the beer bottle on the end table. She took a long drink, then set it back down. Her aim was off, unsteady; the bottle thunked to the floor, spilling its contents.

She looked like a broken doll, with her face cocked to one side. She was porcelain pale; blue-black mascara smudged around her eyes. The faintest hint of her once-great beauty remained, like a glimmer of gold trim on a dirty china plate, peeking through. "He left me."

"Who did, Mom?"

"Cal. And he swore he loved me."

"Yeah. They always do." Lauren bent down for the beer bottle, wondering if they had any paper towels to blot up the mess. Probably not. Mom's paychecks were getting thinner lately. Supposedly it was the sagging economy. Mom swore that fewer women were coming to see her at the salon. Lauren figured that was half of the story; the other half was that the Hair Apparent Beauty Salon was four doors down from the Tides tavern.

Mom reached for her cigarettes and lit one up. "You're giving me that look again. The *fuck me, my mom's a loser* look."

Lauren sat down on the coffee table. As much as she tried not to feel the sting of disappointment, it was there. She always seemed to want too much from her mother. When would she learn? These continual letdowns were eating through her. Sometimes she imagined she could even see them as a shadow above her heart. "The college fair was today."

Mom took another drag, frowning as she exhaled. "That's on Tuesday."

"This is Tuesday, Mom."

"Aw, *shit*." Mom leaned back onto the nubby avocado-green sofa. "I'm sorry, honey. I lost track of the days." She exhaled again, scooted sideways. "Sit."

Lauren moved fast, before Mom changed her mind.

"How did it go?"

She snuggled next to her mother. "I met a great guy from USC. He thought I should try and get recommendations from alumni." She sighed. "I guess who you know helps."

"Only if who you know will pay the tab, too."

Lauren heard the hard edge come into her mother's voice, and she winced. "I'll get a scholarship, Mom. You'll see."

Mom took a long drag on her cigarette and turned slightly, studying Lauren through the filmy haze.

Lauren braced herself. She knew what was coming. *Not today. Please.*

"I thought I'd get a scholarship, too, you know."

"Please, don't. Let's talk about something else. I got an A+ on my honors history paper." Lauren tried to get up. Mom grabbed her wrist, held her in place.

"My grades were okay," Mom said, unsmiling, her brown eyes growing even darker. "I lettered in track and basketball. My test scores were damn respectable, too. And I was beautiful. They said I looked like Heather Locklear."

Lauren sighed. She edged sideways, put a tiny space between them. "I know."

"Then I went to the Sadie Hawkins dance with Thad Marlow."

"I know. Big mistake."

"A few kisses, a few shots of tequila, and there I was with my dress up around my waist. I didn't know then that I was fucked in more ways than just the one. Four months later I was a senior in high school, shopping for maternity dresses. No scholarship for me. No college, no decent job. If one of your stepfathers hadn't paid for beauty school, I'd probably be living in the street and eating other people's leftovers. So, missy, you keep your—"

"Knees shut. Believe me, Mom; I know how I ruined your life."

"*Ruined* is harsh," Mom said with a tired sigh. "I never said ruined."

"I wonder if he had other children," Lauren said. She'd asked this same question every time her father's name was mentioned. She couldn't seem to help herself, though she knew the answer by heart.

"How would I know? He ran from me like I had the plague."

"I just . . . wish I had relatives, that's all."

Mom exhaled smoke. "Believe me, family is overrated. Oh, they're fine till you screw up, but then, *wham!*, they break your heart. Don't you count on people, Lauren."

Lauren had heard all this before. "I just wish—"

"Don't. It'll only hurt you."

Lauren looked at her mother. "Yeah," she said tiredly. "I know."

FOUR

FOR THE NEXT FEW DAYS, ANGIE DID WHAT SHE DID BEST: SHE threw herself into a project. She woke long before dawn and spent all day studying. She called friends and former clients—anyone who'd ever been involved in the restaurant or food service business—and wrote down every word of their advice. Then she read and reread the account books until she understood every dollar that came in and every penny that went out. When she finished that, she went to the library. Hour after hour, she sat at the cheap Formica table with books and articles strewn out in front of her. After that, she parked herself at the microfiche machine and read the archived material.

At six o'clock, the librarian, Mrs. Martin, who'd been old when Angie got her first library card, turned off the lights.

Angie got the hint. She carried several armfuls of books to her car and drove back to the cottage, where she kept reading long into the night. She fell asleep on the sofa, which was infinitely preferable to being in bed alone.

While she was doing her research, her family called like clockwork. She answered each call politely, talked for a few moments, then gently hung up. She would, she said repeatedly, let them know when she was ready to see the restaurant. At each such call, Mama snorted and said crisply, *You cannot learn without doing, Angela.*

To which Angie replied, *I can't do without learning, Mama. I'll let you know when I'm ready.*

Always you were obsessive, Mama would reply. *We do not understand you.*

There was more than a little truth in that, Angie knew. She had always been a woman with laserlike focus. When she started something, there was no halfway, no easy beginning. It was this trait that had broken her. Quite simply, once she'd decided *I want a child*, there had been ruin on the horizon. It was the thing she couldn't have, and the search had taken everything.

She knew this, had learned it, but still she was who she was. When she undertook something, she focused on success.

And to be honest—which she was with herself only in the quiet darkness of the deepest hour of night—it was better to think about the restaurant than to dwell on the losses and failures that had brought her here.

They were with her, of course, those memories and heartaches. Sometimes, as she was reading about management techniques or special promotions, she'd flash on the past.

Sophie would have been sleeping through the night by now.

Or:

Conlan loved that song.

It was like stepping barefoot on a sharp bit of broken glass. She pulled the glass out and ran on, but the pain remained. In those moments, she redoubled her efforts at studying, perhaps poured herself a glass of wine.

By Wednesday afternoon, she was exhausted by her lack of sleep and finished with her research. There was nothing more she could learn from secondary sources. It was time to apply her learning to the restaurant.

She put her books away, took a long, hot shower, and dressed carefully. Black pants, black sweater. Nothing that would draw attention or underscore her "big city" ways.

She drove slowly to town and parked in front of the restaurant. Notepad in hand, she got out of the car.

The first thing she noticed was the bench.

"Oh," she said softly, touching the wrought-iron curled back. The metal felt cold against her fingertips . . . just as it had on the day they'd bought it.

She closed her eyes, remembering. . . .

The four of them hadn't agreed on a thing all week—not the song that should be sung at the funeral, nor who should sing it, not what his headstone should look like, nor what color roses should drape the casket. Until the bench. They'd been in the hardware store, looking for citronella candles for the celebration of Papa's life, when they'd seen this bench.

Mama had stopped first. *Papa always wanted a bench outside the restaurant.*

So folks could take a load off, Mira had said, coming up beside her.

By the next morning that bench had been secured to the sidewalk. They'd never discussed putting an In Memoriam plaque on it. That was the way of big cities. In West End, everyone knew that bench belonged to Tony DeSaria. The first week it was up, a dozen flowers appeared on it, single blossoms left by people who remembered.

She stared up at the restaurant that had been his pride and joy.

"I'll save it for you, Papa," she whispered, realizing a moment later that she was waiting for an answer. There was nothing, just the sound of traffic behind her and the distant hum of the sea.

She uncapped her pen and held the tip poised just above the paper, at the ready.

The brick facade was in need of repair. Moss grew beneath the eaves. A lot of shingles were missing. The red neon sign that read *DeSaria's* was missing the apostrophe and the *i*.

She started writing.

Roof
Exterior repair
Sidewalk dirty
Moss
Sign

She climbed the few steps to the front door and paused. A menu was posted behind glass on the wall. Spaghetti with meatballs was $7.95. A lasagna dinner, including bread and salad, was $6.95.

No wonder they were losing money.

Prices

Menu

She opened the door. A bell tinkled overhead. The pungent aromas of garlic, thyme, simmering tomatoes, and baking bread filled the air.

She was drawn back in time. Not a thing had changed in twenty years. The dimly lit room, the round tables draped in red-and-white-checked fabric, the pictures of Italy on the wall. She expected to see Papa come around the corner, grinning, wiping his hands on his apron, saying, *Bella Angelina, you're home.*

"Well. Well. You're really here. I was afraid you'd fallen down the cabin stairs and couldn't get up."

Angie blinked and wiped her eyes.

Livvy stood by the hostess table, wearing a pair of tight black jeans, a black off-the-shoulder blouse, and Barbie mules. Tension came off Livvy in waves. It was as if they were kids again, teenagers fighting over who got to use the Baby Soft spray first.

"I came to help," Angie said.

"Unfortunately, you can't cook and you haven't worked at the restaurant since you got your braces off. No. Wait. You *never* worked here."

"I don't want us to fight, Livvy."

Livvy sighed. "I know. I don't mean to be a bitch. I'm just tired of all the crap. This place is bleeding money and all Mama does is make more pans of lasagna. Mira bitches at me but when I ask for help, she says she doesn't understand business, only cooking. And who does finally offer a hand? You. Daddy's princess. I don't know whether to laugh or cry." She pulled a lighter out of her pocket and lit a cigarette.

"You aren't going to smoke in here, are you?"

Livvy paused. "You sound like Papa." She dropped the cigarette into a half full glass of water. "I'm going outside for a smoke. You tell me when you've figured out how to save the day."

Angie watched her sister leave, then she headed into the kitchen where Mama was busy layering lasagna into big metal baking pans. Mira was right next to her, arranging meatballs on a metal tray that was only slightly smaller than a twin bed. At Angie's entrance, Mira looked up and smiled. "Hey there."

"Angie!" Mama wiped her cheek, leaving a red tomato trail

behind. Sweat beaded her brow. "Are you ready to learn how to cook?"

"I'll hardly save the restaurant by cooking, Mama. I'm making notes."

Mama's smile fell a fraction. She shot a worried look at Mira, who merely shrugged. "Notes?"

"On things I think might improve the business."

"And you're starting in *my* kitchen? Your Papa—God rest his soul—loved—"

"Relax, Mama. I'm just checking things out."

"Mrs. Martin says you've read every restaurant reference book in the library," Mira said.

"Remind me not to rent any X-rated movies in this town," Angie said, smiling.

Mama snorted. "People watch out for each other here, Angela. That's a good thing."

"Don't get started, Mama. I was joking."

"I should hope so." Mama pushed her heavy glasses higher on her nose and peered at Angie through owl-sized brown eyes. "If you want to help, learn to cook."

"Papa couldn't cook."

Mama blinked, sniffed, then went back to layering the ricotta-parsley mixture over noodles.

Mira and Angie exchanged a look.

This was going to be worse than Angie thought. She was going to have to tread with extreme care. An irritated Livvy was one thing. Mama pissed off was something else entirely. Barrow, Alaska, in the winter was warmer than Mama when she got mad.

Angie looked down at her notes, feeling both pairs of eyes on her. It took her a second to gather enough courage to ask: "So, how long has the menu been the same?"

Mira grinned knowingly. "Since the summer I went to Girl Scout camp."

"Very funny," Mama snapped. "We perfected it. Our regulars love every item."

"I'm not saying otherwise. I just wondered when you last changed the menu."

"Nineteen seventy-five."

Angie underlined the word *menu* on her list. She might not know much about operating a restaurant, but she knew plenty about going out to dinner. A changing menu kept people coming back for more. "And do you offer nightly specials?"

"Everything is special. This isn't downtown Seattle, Angela. We do things our own way here. It was good enough for Papa. God rest his soul." Mama's chin tilted in the air. The temperature in the kitchen dropped several degrees. "Now we'd better get back to work." She elbowed Mira, who went back to hand-forming the meatballs.

Angie knew when she'd been dismissed. She turned and went back into the empty dining room. She saw Livvy over by the hostess desk again. Her sister was talking to Rosa, the woman who'd started waitressing in the seventies. Angie waved and went upstairs.

It was quiet in her father's office. She paused at the open doorway, letting the memories wash over her. In her mind, he was still there, sitting at the big oak desk he'd bought at a Rotary Club auction, poring over the accounts.

Angelina! Come in. I'll show you about taxes.

But I want to go to the movies, Papa.

Of course you do. Run along then. Send Olivia up here.

She sighed heavily and went to his desk. She sat in his chair, heard the springs creak beneath her weight.

For the next several hours, she studied and learned and made notes. She re-read all of the old account books and then started on tax records and her father's handwritten business notes. By the time she closed the last book, she knew that her mother was right. DeSaria's was in trouble. Their income had dropped to almost nothing. She rubbed her eyes, then went downstairs.

It was seven o'clock.

The middle of the dinner hour. There were two parties in the restaurant: Dr. and Mrs. Petrocelli and the Schmidt family.

"Is it always this slow?" she said to Livvy, who stood at the hostess table, studying her talon fingernails. The bright red polish was dotted with pink stars.

"Last Wednesday we had three customers all night. You may want to write that down. They all ordered lasagna, in case you're interested."

"Like they had a choice."

"And it begins."

"I'm not here to criticize you, Liv. I'm just trying to help."

"You want to help? Figure out how to get people through the

door. Or how to pay Rosa Contadori's salary." She glanced over at the elderly waitress who moved at a glacial pace, carrying one plate at a time.

"It'll take some changes," Angie said, trying to be as gentle as possible.

Livvy tapped a long scarlet fingernail against her tooth. "Like what?"

"Menu. Advertising. Decor. Pricing. Your payables are a mess. So is ordering. You guys are wasting a lot of food."

"You have to cook for people, even if they don't show up."

"I'm just saying—"

"That we're doing everything wrong." She raised her voice so that Mama could hear.

"What's that?" Mama said, coming out of the kitchen.

"Angie's been here half a day, Mama. Long enough to know that we don't know shit."

Mama looked down at them for a moment, then turned and headed for the corner by the window, where she started talking to the curtain.

Livvy rolled her eyes. "Oh, good. She's getting Papa's opinion. If a dead man disagrees with me, I'm outta here."

Finally, Mama returned. She didn't look happy. "Papa tells me you think the menu is bad."

Angie frowned. That *was* what she thought, but she hadn't told anyone yet. "Not bad, Mama. But change might be a good thing."

Mama bit down on her lower lip, crossed her arms. "I know," she said to the air beside her. Then she looked at Livvy. "Papa thinks we should listen to Angie. For now."

"Of *course* he does. His princess." She glared at Angie. "I don't need this crap. I have a new husband who has begged me to stay home at night and make babies."

The arrow hit its mark. Angie actually flinched.

"So that's what I'm going to do." Livvy patted Angie's back. "Good luck with the place, little sis. It's all yours. *You* work nights and weekends." She turned on her high heel and walked out.

Angie stared after her, wondering how it had gone bad so quickly. "All I said was we needed to make a few changes."

"But not to the menu," Mama said, crossing her arms. "People *love* my lasagna."

· · ·

Lauren stared down at the question in front of her.

A man walks six miles at four miles per hour. At what speed would he need to travel during the next two and a half hours to have an average speed of six miles an hour during the entire trip?

The answer choices blurred in front of her tired eyes.

She pushed back from the table. She couldn't do this anymore. SAT preparation had filled so much of her time in the last month that she'd started to get headaches. It wouldn't do her any good if she aced the test but fell asleep in all her classes.

The test is in two weeks.

With a sigh, she pulled back up to the table and picked up her pencil. She'd already taken this test last year and gotten a good score. This time, she was hoping for a perfect 1600. For a girl like her, every point mattered.

By the time the oven beeper went off an hour later, she'd completed another five pages of the practice test. Numbers and vocabulary words and geometry equations floated through her head like those giant *Star Wars* spaceships, bumping into one another.

She went into the kitchen to make dinner before work. She could choose between a bowl of Raisin Bran and an apple with peanut butter. She picked the apple. When she finished eating, she dressed in a nice pair of black pants and a heavy pink sweater. Her Rite Aid smock covered most of the sweater anyway. She grabbed her backpack—just in case she found time to finish her trigonometry homework on her dinner break—and left the apartment.

She hurried down the stairs and was just reaching for the front door knob when a voice said, "Lauren?"

Dang it. She paused, turned.

Mrs. Mauk stood in the open doorway to her apartment. A tired frown pulled the edges of her mouth downward. The wrinkles on her forehead looked painted on. "I'm still waiting for that rent check."

"I know." She had trouble keeping her voice even.

Mrs. Mauk moved toward her. "I'm sorry, Lauren. You know I am, but I need to get paid. Otherwise, it's my job on the line."

Lauren felt herself deflate. Now she'd have to ask her boss for an advance. She *hated* doing that. "I know. I'll tell Mom."

"You do that."

She headed for the door, heard Mrs. Mauk say, "You're a good kid, Lauren"; it was the same thing the manager said every time she had to ask for money. There was no answer to that, so Lauren kept walking, out into a rainy, navy blue night.

It took two bus changes to get her out toward the highway, where the neon bright Rite Aid pharmacy offered all night hours. She hurried into the store, even though she wasn't late. Even a few extra minutes on her time card helped.

"Uh, Lauren?" It was Sally Ponochek, the pharmacist. As always, she was squinting. "Mr. Landers wants to see you."

"Okay. Thanks." She went back to the employees' lunchroom and dropped off her stuff, then went upstairs to the manager's small, supply-cramped office. All the way there she practiced how she would ask it: *I've worked here for almost a year. I work every holiday—you know that. I'll work Thanksgiving and Christmas Eve this year. Is there any way I could get an advance on this week's salary?*

She forced herself to smile at him. "You wanted to see me, Mr. Landers?"

He looked up from the papers on his desk. "Oh. Lauren. Yes." He ran a hand through his thinning hair, recombed what was left of it across his head. "There's no easy way to say this. We need to let you go. You've seen how slow business is. Word is corporate is thinking of shutting this location down. The locals simply won't patronize a chain store. I'm sorry."

It took a second. "You're *firing* me?"

"Technically we're laying you off. If business picks up . . ." He let the inchoate promise dangle. They both knew business wouldn't pick up. He handed her a letter. "It's a glowing recommendation. I'm sorry to lose you, Lauren."

THE HOUSE WAS TOO QUIET.

Angie stood by the fireplace, staring out at the moonlit ocean. Heat radiated up her legs but somehow didn't reach her core. She crossed her arms, still cold.

It was only eight-thirty; too early for bed.

She turned away from the window and looked longingly at the stairs. If only she could turn back time a few years, become again the woman who slept easily.

It had been easier with Conlan's arms around her. She hadn't slept alone in so long she'd forgotten how big a mattress could be, how much heat a lover's body generated.

There was no way she'd sleep tonight, not the way she felt right now.

What she needed was noise. The approximation of a life.

She bent down and grabbed her keys off the coffee table, then headed for the door.

Fifteen minutes later, she was parked in Mira's driveway. The small two-story house sat tucked on a tiny lot, hemmed on both sides by houses of remarkable similarity. The front yard was littered with toys and bikes and skateboards.

Angie sat there a minute, clutching the steering wheel. She couldn't bust in on Mira's family at nine o'clock. It would be too rude.

But if she left now, where would she go? Back to the silence of her lonely cottage, to the shadowland of memories that were best left alone?

She opened the door, got out.

The night closed around her, chilled her. She smelled autumn. A bloated gray cloud floated overhead, started spitting rain on the sidewalk.

She hurried up the walk and knocked on the front door.

Mira answered almost instantly. She stood in the entry, smiling sadly, wearing an old football jersey and Grinch slippers. Her long hair was unbound; it cascaded down her sides in an unruly mass. "I wondered how long you were going to sit out there."

"You knew?"

"Are you kidding? Kim Fisk called the minute you parked. Andrea Schmidt called five seconds later. You forget what it's like to live in a neighborhood."

Angie felt like an idiot. "Oh."

"Come on in. I figured you'd be by." She led the way down a linoleum-floored hallway and turned in to the family room, where a huge brown sectional framed a big-screen television. Two glasses of red wine waited on the oak coffee table.

Angie couldn't help smiling. She sat down on the sofa and reached for the wineglass. "Where is everyone?"

"The little ones are asleep, the big ones are doing homework, and tonight is Vince's league night." Mira stretched out on the sofa, looking at Angie. "Well?"

"Well what?"

"You were just driving around in the dark?"

"Something like that."

"Come on, Ange. Livvy quit. Mama threw down the lasagna gauntlet and the restaurant is bleeding."

Angie looked up, trying to smile. "And don't forget that I'm learning to live alone."

"By the looks of it, that isn't going well."

"No." She took a sip of wine. Maybe more than a sip. She didn't really want to talk about her life. All it did was wound her. "I need to convince Livvy to come back."

Mira sighed, obviously disappointed by Angie's change in subject. "We probably should have told you that she's wanted to quit for months."

"Yeah. That would have been good to know."

"Look on the bright side. There's one less of us to piss off when you start making changes."

For some reason, the word *changes* hit Angie hard. She put down the wineglass and stood up; then she moved to the window, staring out, as if her location had been the problem.

"Angie?"

"I don't know what the hell is wrong with me lately."

Mira came up beside her, touched her shoulder. "You need to slow down."

"What do you mean?"

"Ever since you were a girl, you've been running for what you wanted. You couldn't get out of West End quickly enough. Poor Tommy Matucci asked about you for two years after you left, but you never called him. Then you rushed through college and blistered up the food chain in advertising." Her voice softened. "And when you and Conlan decided to start your family, you immediately started tracking your ovulation and working at it."

"A lot of good it did me."

"The point is, now you're lost, but you're still running full speed. Away from Seattle and your ruined marriage, toward West End and the failing restaurant. How will you ever figure out what you want when everything is a blur?"

Angie stared at her reflection in the window. Her skin looked parchment pale, her eyes seemed bruised by darkness, and her mouth was barely a strip. "What do you know about wanting?" she said, hearing the ache in her voice.

"I have four kids and a husband who loves his bowling league almost as much as he loves me, and I've never had a boss who wasn't related to me. While you were sending me postcards from

New York and London and Los Angeles, I was trying to save enough money to get my hair cut. Believe me, I know about wanting."

Angie wanted to turn and face her sister but she didn't dare. "I would have traded it all—the trips, the lifestyle, the career—for just one of those babies upstairs."

Mira touched her shoulder. "I know."

Angie finally turned and knew instantly it was a mistake.

Mira's eyes were full of tears.

"I need to go," Angie said, hearing the thickness of her voice. "Don't—"

She pushed past Mira and ran for the front door. Outside, rain slashed at her, blurred her vision. Not caring, she raced for the car. Mira's *Come back* echoed behind her.

"I can't," she said, too softly for her sister to hear.

She climbed into the car and slammed the door, starting the engine and backing out before Mira could follow her.

She drove up one street and down another, barely aware of where she was. The radio volume was turned high. Right now Cher was singing at her to "Believe."

At last she found herself in the Safeway parking lot, drawn like a moth to the bright lights.

There she sat beneath the glaring streetlamp, staring out at the rain hammering her windshield.

I would have traded it all.

She closed her eyes. Just saying those words aloud had hurt.

No.

She wouldn't sit here and stew about it. Enough was enough. This was definitely the last time she'd vow to forget what couldn't be changed.

She'd go into the store, buy some over-the-counter sleeping pills, and take just enough to get her through the night.

She got out of her car and went into the sprawling white-lit store. None of her family would be here, she knew. They patronized the locals.

She went straight to the aspirin aisle and found what she was looking for.

She was halfway to the checkout aisle when she saw them.

A bird-thin woman in dirty clothes carrying three cartons of cigarettes and a twelve-pack of beer. Four raggedly dressed children buzzed around her. One of them—the smallest—asked for a doughnut, and the mother cuffed him.

The children's hair and faces were filthy; their tennis shoes were pocked with holes.

Angie stopped; her breathing felt heavy. The pain welled up again. If it would have done any good, she would have looked up at God and begged, *Why?*

Why did some women make babies so easily, while others . . .

She dropped the box of sleeping pills and walked out of the store. Outside, rain hit her hard, mingled with her tears.

In the car, she sat perfectly still, staring through the beaded windshield. In time, the family came out of the store. They piled into a shabby car and drove off. None of the kids put on a seat belt.

Angie closed her eyes. She knew that if she sat here long enough, it would pass. Grief was like a rain cloud; sooner or later, if you were patient, it moved on. All she had to do was keep breathing. . . .

Something smacked on her windshield.

Her eyes opened.

A pink flyer was on her windshield. It read: *Work Wanted. Steady. Reliable.*

Before she could read any more, the rain pummeled the flyer, ruined the ink.

Angie leaned toward the passenger seat and rolled down the window.

A girl with red hair was planting the flyers. She moved stoically from car to car, heedless of the rain, wearing a threadbare coat and faded jeans.

Angie didn't think. She reacted. Getting out of the car, she yelled, "Hey, you!"

The girl looked up.

Angie ran toward her. "Can I help you?"

"No." The girl started to move away.

Angie reached into her coat pocket and pulled out money. "Here," she said, pressing the wad of bills into the girl's cold, wet hand.

"I can't take that," the girl whispered, shaking her head.

"Please. For me," Angie said.

They looked at each other for a long moment.

Finally, the girl nodded. Tears filled her eyes. "Thanks." Then she turned and ran into the night.

. . .

LAUREN CLIMBED THE DARK, SHADOWY STAIRS TOWARD THE APART-
ment building. Every step seemed to draw something out of her,
until, by the time she reached Mrs. Mauk's front door, Lauren
was certain she'd grown smaller somehow. She was so tired of
feeling vulnerable and alone.

She paused, staring down at the damp wad of bills in her
hand. One hundred twenty-five dollars.

For me, the woman in the parking lot had said, as if she were
the one in need.

Yeah, right. Lauren knew charity when she saw it. She'd
wanted to turn it down, maybe laugh lightly and say *You've got me
all wrong*. Instead, she'd run all the way home.

She wiped the leftover tears from her eyes and knocked on
the door.

Mrs. Mauk answered. When she saw Lauren, her smile faded.
"You're soaking wet."

"I'm fine," Lauren said. "Here."

Mrs. Mauk took the money, counted it. There was a small
pause, then the woman said, "I'll just take one hundred of it,
okay? You go buy yourself something decent to eat."

Lauren almost started to cry again. Before the tears could fill
her eyes, she turned away and ran for the stairway.

In her apartment, she called out for her mother.

Silence answered her.

With a sigh, she tossed her backpack onto the sofa and went
to the refrigerator. It was practically empty. She was just reaching
for a half-eaten sandwich when someone knocked.

She crossed the small, messy apartment and opened the door.

David stood there, holding a big cardboard box. "Hey, Trix,"
he said.

"What—"

"I called the pharmacy. They said you didn't work there anymore."

"Oh." She bit her lip. The softness of his voice and the understanding in his eyes was almost more than she could take right
now.

"So I cleaned out the fridge at home. Mom had a dinner party
last night and there were killer leftovers." He reached into the
box and pulled out a videotape. "And I brought my *Speed Racer*
tapes."

She forced a smile. "Did you bring the one where Trixie saves
his ass?"

He gazed down at her. In that single look, she saw everything. Love. Understanding. Caring. "Of course."

"Thank you" was all she could say.

"You should have called me, you know. When you lost your job."

He didn't know how it felt, to lose something you needed so desperately. But he was right. She should have called him. Even at seventeen, as young and immature as he could sometimes be, he was the steadiest person in her life. When she was with him, her future—their future—seemed as pure and shimmering as a pearl. "I know."

"Now, come on, let's get something to eat and watch a movie. I have to be home by midnight."

FIVE

M R. LUNDBERG DRONED ON AND ON, FLITTERING FROM ONE
contemporary social issue to another like a child chas-
ing soap bubbles.

Lauren tried to pay attention; she really did. But she was
more than exhausted.

"Lauren. Lauren?"

She blinked awake, realizing a second too late that she'd
fallen asleep.

Mr. Lundberg was staring at her. He did not look happy.

She felt her cheeks grow hot. That was the problem with being a redhead. Pale skin blushed easily. "Yes, Mr. Lundberg?"

"I *asked* you for your position on capital punishment."

"Prone," someone called out. Everyone laughed.

Lauren tried to suppress a giggle. "I'm against the death
penalty. At least until we can ensure that it's being fairly and uni-

formly carried out. No. Wait. I'm against it anyway. The state should not be in the business of killing people to preserve the notion that killing is morally wrong."

Mr. Lundberg nodded, then turned back to the television he'd set up in the middle of the room. "In the past weeks we've discussed justice—or its lack—in America. I think sometimes we forget how fortunate we are to be *able* to have such discussions. Things are very different in other parts of the world. In Sierra Leone, for example . . ."

He pushed a tape into the VCR and hit play.

Halfway through the documentary, the bell rang. Lauren gathered her books and notebooks and left the classroom. In the halls, the noise was amped up; the laughing, hey-dude soundtrack of day's end.

She moved through the crowd, too tired to do much more than wave at passing friends.

David came up behind her, pulled her into his arms. She twisted around and clung to him, staring up into his blue, blue eyes. The noise in the hallway faded to a buzzing whine. The memories of last night came to her all at once, made her smile. He had saved her; it was as simple as that.

"My parents have to 'dash off' to New York tonight," he whispered. "They won't be home till Saturday."

"Really?"

"Football is out at five-thirty. You want me to pick you up?"

"No. I need to look for a new job after school."

"Oh. Right." She heard the disappointment in his voice.

She pressed onto her toes and kissed him, tasting the fruity residue of his daily Snapple. "I could be to your house by seven."

He grinned. "Great. Do you need a ride?"

"No. I'll be fine. Should I bring anything?"

He grinned. "Mom left me two hundred bucks. We'll order pizza."

Two hundred dollars. That was the amount of back rent they still owed. And David could spend it on pizza.

LAUREN WAS READY TO GO JOB HUNTING. SHE'D GONE TO THE school library and printed off fifteen copies of her résumé and her recommendation letter.

She was just about ready to leave when her mother tore into the house; the front door cracked against the wall.

Mom ran to the sofa and threw the cushions aside, looking for something. There was nothing there. Wild-eyed, she looked up. "Did you say I looked fat?"

"You don't weigh a hundred pounds, Mom. I didn't say you were fat. If anything, you're too thin. There's food—"

Mom held up a hand. A cigarette wobbled between her fingers, spewed ash. "Don't start with me. I know you think I drink too much and don't eat enough. Like I need a *kid* policing me." She glanced around the room again, frowning, then raced off to the kitchen. In two minutes, she was back. "I need money."

Some nights Lauren remembered that her mother was sick, that alcoholism was a disease. On those nights, she felt sorry for her.

This wasn't one of those times. "We're broke, Mom. It would help if you went to work." She tossed her backpack on the kitchen table and bent to pick up the fallen cushions.

"*You* work. All I need is a few bucks. Please, baby." Mom sidled close, placing a hand on Lauren's back. The touch reminded Lauren that they were a team, she and Mom. Dysfunctional, certainly, but a family nonetheless.

Mom's hand slid up Lauren's arm and closed around her shoulder; the hold was pure desperation. "Come on," she said, her voice trembling. "Ten bucks will do it."

Lauren reached into her pocket and pulled out a wadded-up five. Thank God she'd hidden the twenty under her pillow. "I won't have lunch money tomorrow."

Mom grabbed the bill. "Pack yourself something. There's pb and j and crackers in the fridge."

"Cracker sandwiches. Perfect." Thank God for the leftovers David had brought over.

Mom was already moving to the door. When she opened it, she stopped and turned around. Her green eyes looked sad; the lines on her face made her appear a decade older than thirty-four. She ran a hand through her spiked, unkempt white hair. "Where'd you get that suit?"

"Mrs. Mauk. It's her daughter's."

"Suzie Mauk died six years ago."

Lauren shrugged, unable to think of a response.

"She kept her daughter's clothes all those years. Wow."

"Some mothers would find it painful to throw their child's clothes away."

"Whatever. Why are you dressed in a dead girl's suit?"

"I . . . need a job."

"You work at the drugstore."

"I got laid off. Times are bad."

"I've been trying to tell you that. I'm sure they'll hire you back for the holidays."

"We need money now. The rent is late."

Her mom seemed to still, and in the sadness of her look, Lauren saw a glimpse of the beauty her mother had once had. "Yeah. I know."

They stared at each other. Lauren found herself leaning forward, waiting. *Say you'll go to work tomorrow.*

"I gotta go," Mom said at last. Without a backward glance, she left the apartment.

Lauren tucked away the ridiculous disappointment she felt and followed her mother out. By the time she reached the picturesque heart of West End, the rain had stopped. It was only five o'clock, but at this time of year night came early. The sky was a pale purple.

Her first stop was the Sea Side, a booming tourist stop that featured microbrews and local oysters.

A little over an hour later, she had made her way from one end of downtown to the other. Three restaurants had politely taken her résumé and promised to call her if a job came up. Another two had not bothered with false hopes. All four of the retail shops had told her to come back after Thanksgiving.

Now she stood in front of the last restaurant on the block. DeSaria's.

She glanced at her watch. It was six-twelve. She was going to be late to David's house.

With a sigh, she climbed the few steps to the front door, noticing that they were rickety. Not a good sign. At the door, she paused to look at the menu. The highest priced item was manicotti at $8.95. That was not a good sign, either.

Still, she opened the door and went inside.

It was a small place. The walls were brick. An archway separated the space into two equal-sized rooms, each of which held five or six tables that were draped in red-and-white fabric. An oak-manteled fireplace dominated one room. Pictures hung in wooden frames on the rough walls. Family pictures, by the look of them. There were also framed prints of Italy and of grapes and olives. Music was playing. An instrumental version of "I Left My Heart in San Francisco." The aroma was pure heaven.

There was one family having dinner. One.

Not much of a crowd for a Thursday night.

There was no point in applying here for a job. She might as well give up for tonight. Maybe, if she hurried, she could get home, change her clothes, and make it to David's by seven o'clock. She turned and headed back outside.

As she walked to the bus stop, it started to rain again. A cold wind swept off the ocean and roared through town. Her tattered coat was no shield at all, and by the time she got home, she was freezing.

The front door stood open, but even worse, the dining room window was open, too, and the apartment was freezing.

"Shit," Lauren muttered, rubbing her cold hands together as she kicked the door shut. She hurried to the window. As she reached for it, she heard her mother's voice singing, "Leavin' on a jet plane . . . don't know when I'll be back again."

Lauren paused. Anger rippled through her, made her bunch her fists. If she'd been a boy, she might have punched the wall. She hadn't found a job, she was late for her date, and now this. Her mother was drunk and communing with the stars again.

Lauren climbed through the window and up the rickety fire escape.

On the rooftop, she found her mother sitting on the ledge of the building, wearing a soaking wet cotton dress. Her feet were bare.

Lauren came up behind her, taking care not to get too close to the edge. "Mom?"

Mom twisted slightly and smiled at her. "Hey."

"You're too close to the edge, Mom. Move back."

"Sometimes you gotta remember you're alive. C'mere." She patted the ledge beside her.

Lauren hated times like this, moments where her need ran alongside fear. Her mother loved to live dangerously; she always said so. Lauren moved cautiously forward. Very slowly, she sat beside her mother.

The street below them was almost empty. A single car drove past, its headlights blinking through the rain, looking insubstantial, unreal.

Lauren could feel her mother trembling with the cold. "Where's your coat, Mom?"

"I lost it. No. I gave it to Phoebe. Traded it for a carton of smokes. The rain makes everything look beautiful, doesn't it?"

"You traded your coat for cigarettes," she said dully, knowing it was useless to be angry. "They're predicting a cold winter this year."

Mom shrugged. "I was broke."

Lauren put her arm around her mother. "Come on. You need to get warmed up. A bath would be good."

Mom looked at her. "Franco said he'd call today. Did you hear the phone ring?"

"No."

"They never come back. Not to me."

Even though Lauren had heard it a thousand times, she still felt her mother's pain. "I know. C'mon." She helped her to her feet and guided her to the fire escape. Lauren followed her mother down the iron-grate stairs and into the apartment. Once there, she convinced her mother to take a hot bath, then went into her own room and changed her clothes. By the time she was ready to leave, her mother was in bed.

Lauren went to her, sat on the edge of the bed beside her. "You'll be okay while I'm gone?"

Mom's eyes were already getting heavy. "Did the phone ring while I was in the bath?"

"No."

Slowly, Mom looked at her. "How come no one loves me, Lauren?"

The question, asked softly and with such utter despair, hurt Lauren so deeply that she gasped. *I love you,* she thought. *Why didn't that count?*

Mom turned her head into the pillow and closed her eyes.

Slowly, Lauren got to her feet and backed away from the bed. All she could think about as she made her way through the apartment and down the stairs and across town was: David.

David.

He would fill this emptiness in her heart.

THE STAID, ULTRARICH ENCLAVE CALLED MOUNTAINAIRE INHAB-ited only a few city blocks on the easternmost edge of West End, but there, behind the guarded gates and ironwork fences, another world existed. This oasis of wealth dominated a hillside over-looking the ocean. Here in David's world, the driveways were made of stone or patterned brick; the cars pulled up beneath fancy porticoes and parked in cavernous garages; dinners were eaten off china as thin and translucent as a baby's skin. On an evening like this one, streetlamps lit every corner and turned the falling rain into tiny diamonds.

Lauren felt acutely out of place as she walked up to the guardhouse at the entrance gate, a girl who didn't belong. She imagined that a notation was made on some chart that would be presented to Mr. and Mrs. Haynes on their return: Bad Element Visits Home.

"I'm here to see David Haynes," she said, forcing her hands to her side.

The guard smiled knowingly.

The gate buzzed, then swung open. She followed the winding black asphalt road past dozens of homes that looked like magazine covers. Georgian mansions, French villas, Bel-Air-style haciendas.

It was so quiet here. No honking horns, no fighting neighbors or blaring television noise.

As always, Lauren tried to imagine how it felt to belong in a place like this. No one in Mountainaire worried about back rent or how to pay the light bill. She knew that if a person started here, there was no destination that was out of reach.

She walked up the path to the front door. Fragrant, saucer-sized pink roses hemmed her in on either side, made her feel a little bit like a princess in a fairy tale. Dozens of hidden lights illuminated the landscaped yard.

She knocked on the big mahogany front door.

It was only a moment before David answered. So quickly, in fact, she thought perhaps he'd been waiting at the window.

"You're late," he said, smiling slowly. He pulled her into his arms, right there in the open doorway where all the neighbors could see. She wanted to tell him to wait, to close the door, but once he kissed her, she forgot everything else. He'd always had that effect on her. At night, when she was in bed, alone and thinking about him, missing him, she wondered about her odd amnesia. Her only explanation for it was love; what else could make a perfectly sane girl think that without her boyfriend's touch, the sun might slip out of the sky and leave the world cold and dark?

She looped her arms around his neck and smiled up at him. Their night hadn't even really begun and already her chest felt tight with anticipation.

"It's so cool that you can just *be* here. I'd have to tell my mom a dozen lies to get a night with you if they were in town."

Lauren tried to imagine a life like that, one where someone—a mom—was waiting for you, worrying about you.

No lies were needed in the Ribido apartment. Mom had spoken to Lauren about sex when she turned twelve. *You'll get talked into it*, she'd said, lighting up a cigarette. *It'll seem like a good idea at the time.* Still smoking, she'd tossed a box of condoms on the coffee table.

After that, Mom had let Lauren make her own decisions, as if handing out condoms were a mother's only responsibility. Lauren had been setting her own curfews since childhood; if she didn't come home at all, that was all right, too.

Lauren knew that if she told her friends this, they'd ooh and aah and tell her how lucky she was, but she would have traded all that freedom for a single bedtime kiss.

He stepped back, smiling, and took hold of her hand. "I have a surprise for you."

She followed him down the wide hallway. Her heels clicked on the creamy marble tiles. If his parents had been home, she would have tiptoed in silence; with only the two of them here she could be herself.

He turned, walked through the creamy stone archway that separated the hallway from the formal dining room.

It looked like a movie set. A long, brilliant wooden table flanked by sixteen ornately carved wooden chairs. In the center of the table was a huge arrangement of white roses, white lilies, and greenery.

On one end there were two place settings. Beautiful, translucent bone china rimmed in gold sat on ivory silk placemats. Gold flatware glinted in the light of a single candle.

She looked up at David, who was smiling so brightly he looked like a kid on the last day of school. "It took me forever to find all that shit. My mom has it all buried in all these blue covers."

"It's beautiful."

He led her to her seat, pulled out her chair. When she sat down, he poured sparkling cider into her wineglass. "I was going to raid the old man's wine room, but I knew you'd bitch at me and worry about getting caught."

"I love you," she said, embarrassed by the tears that stung her eyes.

"I love you, too." He grinned again. "And I'd like to formally ask you to go to the homecoming dance with me."

She laughed at that. "I'd be honored." They'd gone to every high school dance together. This would be their last homecoming. At the thought, her smile faded. Suddenly she was thinking of next year and the chance that they'd be separated. She looked up at him; she needed to convince him that they should be together at school. He believed their love could survive a separation. She wasn't willing to take that chance. He was the only person who'd ever told her *I love you*. She didn't want to live without that. Without him. "David, I—"

The doorbell rang.

She gasped. "Is it your parents? Oh, God—"

"Relax. They called from New York an hour ago. My dad was pissed off because the limo was five minutes late." He started for the door.

"Don't answer it." She didn't want anything to ruin this night for them. What if Jared and the guys had heard about the Hayneses' business trip? That was all the seed that was needed; a high school party could blossom in a second.

David laughed. "Just stay here."

She heard him walk down the hallway and open the door. Then she heard voices. A bit of laughter. The door clicked shut.

A minute later, David walked into the formal dining room, holding a pizza box. Dressed in his low-slung, baggy jeans and *Don't Be Jealous, Not Everyone Can Be Me* T-shirt, he was so handsome she had trouble breathing.

He came to the table, set the box down. "I wanted to cook for you," he said, losing his smile for just a second. "I burned the shit out of everything."

Lauren stood up slowly, moved in close to him. "This is perfect."

"Really?"

She heard the neediness in his voice and it touched her heart in a deep, deep place. She knew how that felt, wanting to please someone. "Really," she answered, pressing onto her toes to kiss him.

He pulled her into his arms, held her so close she couldn't breathe.

By the time they ate the pizza, it was cold.

SIX

Ivvy's new house was a 1970s-style split-level on a big corner lot in one of the nicer subdivisions in town. Some of the homes—the really expensive ones—looked out over the ocean. The rest had access to a kidney-shaped swimming pool and a community center that proudly offered kitchen facilities. When Angie had been in school, Havenwood had been The Place to live. She remembered sitting around the pool in the summers with her friends, watching the mothers. Most of them were in lounge chairs, wearing sexy one-piece swimming suits and wide brimmed hats; cigarettes and gin and tonics were in every adult hand. She'd thought they were so sophisticated, those white-bread suburban women. Nothing like her spicy Italian mother who had never spent a day lounging beside a community pool.

Her sister must have looked on this place with the same adolescent longing to belong.

She parked in Livvy's circular driveway behind the Subaru wagon and got out of the car. At the front door, she paused.

This had to be done carefully. Surgeon-doing-open-heart-work carefully. Angie had been awake most of last night thinking about it. Well, about that and other things. It had been another bad night in her lonely bed, and while she'd lain there, remembering what she'd longed to forget and worrying about her future, one thing had come clear: She had to get Livvy back to work. Angie had no idea how to run the restaurant by herself and no desire to do it for long.

I'm sorry, Liv.

Those were clearly the opening words. After that, she'd eat a little humble pie and cajole her sister with compliments. Whatever would work. Livvy *had* to return to the restaurant. Angie hadn't wanted to work here for life, after all; just for a month or two until she could sleep alone in her bed again.

She knocked on the door.

And waited.

Knocked again.

Finally Livvy opened the door. She wore a tight pink velour sweat suit with *J.Lo* emblazoned across her chest. "I figured you'd show up. Come on in." She backed up and turned around. There wasn't really room for both of them in the postage stamp–sized entry. Livvy went up the carpeted stairs to the formal living room, where a plastic runner lay over the carpet, showing the preferred footpath.

Pale blue velvet sofas faced each other, separated by a glossy wood table. The accent chairs were ornately gilt; the fabric was pink and blue flowers. The sculpted carpet was orange.

"We haven't gotten new carpeting yet," Livvy said. "The furniture is awesome, though. Don't you think?"

Angie noticed the taupe-colored Naugahyde La-Z-Boy, still in plastic. "Beautiful. Did you decorate yourself?"

Livvy's plank chest seemed to expand. "I did. I was going to use a decorator, but Sal said I was as good as any of those gals down at Rick's Sofa World."

"I'm sure you are."

"I was thinking maybe I'd even get a job down there. Have a seat. Coffee?"

"Sure." Angie sat down on a sofa.

Livvy went into the kitchen and came back a few minutes later with two cups of coffee. She handed one to Angie, then sat down across from her.

Angie stared into her coffee. There was no point in putting it off. "You know why I'm here."

"Of course."

"I'm sorry, Livvy. I didn't mean to insult you or criticize you or hurt your feelings."

"I know that. You've always done it accidentally."

"I'm different from you and Mira, as you've pointed out so often. Sometimes I can be too . . . focused."

"Is that what they call it in the big city? Us small-town girls say bitchy. Or obsessive-compulsive." Livvy smiled. "We watch *Oprah*, too, you know."

"Come on, Liv. You're killing me here. Accept my apology and say you'll come back to work. I need your help. I think we can really help Mama out."

Livvy took a deep breath. "Here's the thing. I've *been* helping Mama out. For five years, I've worked at that damn restaurant and listened to her opinion on everything from my haircut to my shoes. No wonder it took me so long to meet a decent guy." She leaned forward. "Now I'm a *wife*. I have a husband who loves me. I don't want to blow it. It's time for me to stop being a DeSaria first and everything else second. Sal deserves that."

Angie wanted to be angry at Livvy, to bend her sister to her will; instead, she had a fleeting, painful thought about her own marriage: Maybe at some point she should have made it more important than children. She sighed. It was too late now. "You want a new start," she said quietly, feeling an unexpected connection to her sister. They had this in common.

"Exactly."

"You're doing the right thing. I should have—"

"Don't go there, Angie. I know you flip me shit about my other husbands but I learned something from them. Life keeps going. You think it'll stop, wait for you to be done crying, but it just keeps moving. Don't spend your time looking back. You don't want to miss what's ahead."

"I guess this is what's ahead for me right now. Thanks a lot." She tried to smile. "Could you see your way to helping me, at least? Maybe give me some advice?"

"You're asking *me* for advice?"

"Just this once, and I probably won't follow it." She reached into her purse for her notepad.

Livvy laughed. "Read me your list."

"How did you know—"

"You started making lists in third grade. Remember how they used to disappear?"

"Yeah."

"I flushed them down the toilet. They made me crazy. All those things you wanted to accomplish." She smiled. "I should have made a few lists of my own."

It was as close to a compliment as Angie had ever gotten from her sister. She handed her the notepad. The list was three pages long.

Livvy flipped it open. Her lips moved as she read. A smile started, slowly at first. By the time she looked up, she was close to laughing. "You want to do all this?"

"What's wrong with it?"

"Have you met our mother? You know, the woman who has put exactly the same ornaments on her Christmas tree for more than three decades? Why? Because she likes the tree the way it is."

Angie winced. It was true. Mama was a generous, loving, giving woman . . . as long as things went exactly the way she wanted them to go. These changes would not be welcomed.

"However," Livvy went on, "your ideas could save DeSaria's . . . if that's possible. But I wouldn't want to be in your shoes."

"What would you do first?"

Livvy looked down at the list, flipped through the pages. "It's not here."

"What isn't?"

"First, you hire a new waitress. Rosa Contadori has been serving food at DeSaria's since before you were born. I could learn to play golf in the time it takes her to write down an order. I've been picking up the slack, but . . ." She shrugged. "I don't see you waitressing."

Angie couldn't disagree with that. "Any suggestions?"

Livvy grinned. "Make sure she's Italian."

"Very funny." Angie reached for her pen. "Anything else?"

"Plenty. Let's start with the basics. . . ."

ANGIE STOOD ON THE SIDEWALK, LOOKING AT THE RESTAURANT that had been so much a part of her youth. Mama and Papa had been here every evening; he at the front door, greeting guests, she in the kitchen, cooking for them. Family dinners had taken place at four-thirty, before the guests arrived. They'd all sat at a big round table in the kitchen so that they wouldn't be seen if customers arrived early. After dinner, Mira and Livvy had gone to work, waitressing and busing tables.

But not Angie.

This one is a genius, Papa always said. *She's going to college, so she needs to study.*

It had never been questioned. Once Papa spoke, a matter was ended. Angie was going to college. That was that. Night after night, she studied in the kitchen.

No wonder she'd gotten a scholarship.

Now here she was, back at the beginning of her life, preparing to save a business she knew nothing about, and tonight there would be no Livvy to help her out.

She stared down at her notes. They had filled four more pages, she and Livvy. One idea after another.

It was up to Angie to implement the changes.

She walked up the steps and went through the front door. The place was already open, of course. Mama had arrived at three-thirty, not a minute before, not a minute later, as she'd done every Friday night for three decades.

Angie heard the clatter and jangle coming from the kitchen. She went in, found her mother cursing. "Mira is late. And Rosa called in sick tonight. I know she is playing bingo at the Elks."

"Rosa is sick?" Angie heard the panic in her voice. "She's our only waitress."

"Now *you* are our waitress," Mama said. "It is not that hard, Angela. Just give people what they order." She went back to making her meatballs.

Angie left the kitchen. In the dining rooms, she went from table to table, checking every detail, making sure the salt and pepper shakers were filled, that the place settings were clean and properly placed.

Ten minutes later, Mira came rushing through the front door. "I'm sorry I'm late," she called out to Angie on her way to the kitchen. "Daniella fell off her bike."

Angie nodded and went back to the menu, studying it as if it were a CliffsNotes guide and she were cramming for a test.

At five forty-five the first customers arrived. Dr. and Mrs. Feinstein, who ran the clinic in town. Twenty minutes later, the

Giuliani family arrived. Angie greeted them all as her father would have, then showed them to their tables. For the first few minutes, she actually felt good, as if she were part of her heritage at last. Her mother beamed at her, nodded encouragingly.

By six-fifteen, she was in trouble.

How could seven people generate so much work?

More water, please.

I asked for Parmesan.

Where's our bread—

and the oil.

"You might be a great copywriter, Angela," Mama said to her at one point, "but I would not tip you well. You're too slow."

Angie couldn't disagree. She headed for the Feinsteins' table and set down the plate of cannelloni. "I'll be right back with your scampi, Mrs. Feinstein," she said, then ran for the kitchen.

"I hope Dr. Feinstein isn't finished by the time his wife is served," Mama said, clucking in disapproval. "Mira, make those meatballs bigger."

Angie backed out of the kitchen and hurried back to the Feinsteins' table.

As she was serving the scampi, she heard the front door open. A bell tinkled.

More customers. *Oh no.*

She turned slowly and saw Livvy. Her sister took one look at her and burst out laughing.

Angie straightened. "You're here to laugh at me?"

"The princess working at DeSaria's? Of course I'm here to laugh at you." Livvy touched her shoulder. "And to help you out."

BY THE END OF THE EVENING ANGIE HAD A POUNDING HEADACHE. "Okay. It's official. I'm the worst waitress in history." She looked down at her clothes. She'd spilled red wine down her apron and dragged her sleeve in the crème anglaise. A discoloration on her pants was almost certainly from the lasagna. She sat down at a table in the back corner beside Mira. "I can't believe I wore cashmere and high heels. No wonder Livvy laughs every time she looks at me."

"You'll get better," Mira promised. "Here. Fold napkins."

"Well, I damn sure can't get worse." Angie couldn't help laughing, though it wasn't funny. In truth, she hadn't expected it to be so hard. All her life, things had come easily to her. She'd

simply been good at whatever she tried. Not exceptional, perhaps, but better than average. She'd graduated from UCLA—in
four years, thank you, with a very respectable grade point—and
she'd immediately been hired by the best ad agency in Seattle.

Frankly, this whole table-waiting handicap came as a shock.
"It's humiliating."

Mira looked up from the napkins. "Don't worry. Rosa hardly
ever calls in sick. Usually she can handle the so-called crowd.
And you'll get better."

"I know, but . . ." Angie looked down at her hands. Two bright
pink burn spots marred her skin. Fortunately, she'd spilled the
hot sauce on herself and not on Mrs. Guiliani. "I don't know if I
can do this."

Mira folded the thick white napkin into a swan and pushed it
across the table.

Angie was reminded of the night Papa had taught her how to
turn a plain square of fabric into this bird. When she looked up
and saw her sister's smile, she knew the reminder had been in-
tentional.

"It took Livvy and me weeks to learn how to do that. We sat
on the floor by Papa, trying to copy his every move so he would
smile at us and say *Good job, my princesses*. We thought we were
doing so well . . . then you joined us and learned how to fold it
in three tries. *This one*, Papa said, kissing your cheek, *can do anything.*"

The memory should have made her smile, but this time she
saw more. "That must have been tough on you and Livvy."

Mira waved off the concern. "That wasn't my point. This
place—DeSaria's—it's in your blood, just as it's in ours. Not being a part of it for all those years doesn't change who you are.
You're one of us, and you can do whatever needs to be done. Papa
believed in you and so do I."

"I'm afraid."

Mira smiled gently. "That's not you."

Angie turned her head and stared through the window at the
empty street. Leaves fell to the ground, skittered across the
rough cement sidewalk. "It's who I've become." She hated to admit it.

Mira leaned forward. "Can I be honest?"

"Absolutely not." Angie tried to laugh, but when she looked
at her sister's earnest face, she couldn't do it.

"You've gotten . . . self-centered in the last few years. I don't mean selfish. Wanting a baby and then losing Sophie . . . It made you . . . quiet. Alone somehow."

Alone somehow.

It was true.

"I felt as if I were hanging on by a thread and there was a huge hole beneath me."

"Then you fell anyway."

She thought about that. She'd lost her daughter, her father, and her husband in the same year. That was certainly the fall she'd been afraid of. "Sometimes I think I'm still falling. At night it's especially bad."

"Maybe it's time to look outward."

"I have the restaurant. I'm trying."

"What about all the hours when we're closed?"

Angie swallowed. "It's hard," she admitted. "I try to study and make notes."

"A job can't be enough."

Angie wished she could argue with the veracity of the statement, but she'd learned the truth of it long ago, when she'd loved her job and longed for a baby. "No."

"Maybe it's time to reach out to someone else in need."

Angie thought about that. The first image that popped into her mind was of the teenager she'd seen in the Safeway parking lot. Angie had been helped by helping the girl. That night, she'd slept through until morning.

Maybe that was the answer. Helping someone else.

She felt herself start to smile. "My Mondays are free."

Mira smiled back. "And most of your mornings."

For the first time ever, Lauren woke up feeling completely safe. David's arms were around her, holding her close, even in sleep.

She reveled in the feel of it, smiling, imagining a married life that would always be this way.

She lay there a long time, watching him sleep. Finally, she eased away from him and rolled out of bed. She'd make him breakfast and serve it to him in bed.

At his chest of drawers, she paused and opened the top drawer. Finding a long T-shirt, she put it on and went downstairs.

The kitchen was amazing—all granite and stainless steel and mirrored surfaces. The pots and pans shone silver in the light. She scouted through the cupboards and the refrigerator, finding everything she needed to make scrambled eggs, bacon, and pancakes. When breakfast was ready, she put it all on a beautiful wooden tray and carried it upstairs.

She found David sitting up in bed, yawning. "There you are," he said, grinning at her entrance. "I was worried. . . ."

"Like I'd ever leave you." She crawled up into bed beside him and settled the tray between them.

"This looks great," he said, kissing her cheek.

As they ate breakfast, they talked about ordinary things: the upcoming SAT test, football, school gossip. David talked about the Porsche that he and his father were restoring. It was the only thing he and his dad did together, and so David obsessed about the car. He loved the hours they spent in the garage. In truth, he talked about it so often she hardly listened anymore. He launched into something about gear ratios and speed off the line, and she found her interest waning.

She glanced out the window. Sunlight flooded the glass, and suddenly she was thinking about California and their future. She'd lost track of how often she'd organized her college brochures based on scholarship feasibility. By her calculations, her best shot at a full ride was at private colleges. Of these, her favorite was the University of Southern California. It combined world-class athletics with top-drawer academics.

Unfortunately, it was almost an eight-hour drive from Stanford.

Somehow she *had* to convince David to consider USC. The second alternative was for her to choose Santa Clara. But truthfully, she'd had enough of Catholic school.

". . . totally tight. Perfect leather. Lauren? Are you listening?"

She turned to him. "Of course. You were talking about the gear ratio."

He laughed. "Yeah, about an hour ago. I knew you weren't listening."

She felt her cheeks heat up. "I'm sorry. I was thinking about college."

He picked up the tray and put it on the oversized nightstand to his left. "You're always worrying about the future."

"And you never do."

"It won't help."

Before she could answer, he leaned over and kissed her. All

thoughts of college and their uncertain future disappeared. She lost herself in his kiss, in his arms.

Hours later, when they finally pushed the blankets back and got out of bed, she'd almost forgotten her worries.

"Let's go ice-skating over in Longview," he said, burrowing through his drawers for the shirt he wanted to wear.

Ordinarily she loved it when they went ice-skating. She glanced down at her pile of clothes. Her coat's raggedness made her wince, and she knew there were holes in her socks. "I can't go today. I need to find a job."

"On Saturday?"

She looked up at him. Just then, it felt as if so much more than a few feet of floor separated them. "I know it sucks, but what can I do?"

David moved toward her. "How much?"

"How much what?"

"Your rent. How behind is she?"

Lauren felt her cheeks flush. "I never said—"

"You never do. I'm not stupid, Lo. How much do you owe?"

She wished the ground would open up and swallow her. "Two hundred. But Monday is the first."

"Two hundred. That's what I paid for my steering wheel and shift knob."

She didn't know what to say to that. For him, that amount of money was pocket change. She broke eye contact and bent down for her clothes.

"Let me—"

"No," she said, not daring to look at him. Tears burned her eyes. Her shame was almost overwhelming. It shouldn't be, she knew. He loved her; he told her that all the time, but still.

"Why not?"

She slowly straightened. Finally looked at him. "All my life," she said, "I've watched my mom take money from men. It starts out as nothing. Beer or cigarette money. Then fifty bucks for a new dress or one hundred to pay the electric bill. It . . . changes things, that money."

"I'm not like those guys and you know it."

"I *need* us to be different. Don't you see?"

He touched her face so gently she wanted to cry. "I see that you won't let me help you."

How could she explain it to him, that helping her would be

a river that would suck them under? "Just love me," she whispered, putting her arms around him and holding on tightly.

He pulled her off her feet, kissed her until she was dizzy and smiling again.

"We're going skating and that's it."

She wanted to, wanted to lose herself in the coldness, going around and around with nothing to keep her grounded except David's warm hand. "All right. But I don't have enough clothes. I'll have to stop at home." She couldn't help smiling. It felt good to give in, to take the day off from her troubles.

He took her hand and led her out of his bedroom and down the hallway toward his parents' bedroom.

"David, what are you doing?" She followed him, frowning.

He opened the door and went to the closet, opening that door as well. A light automatically came on.

The closet was bigger than Lauren's living room.

"Her coats are back there. Pick one."

Lauren moved woodenly forward until she was standing in front of Mrs. Haynes's coats. There were at least one dozen of them. Leather. Cashmere. Wool. Suede. Not one showed the slightest sign of wear.

"Pick one and let's go."

Lauren couldn't seem to move. Her heart was beating too quickly; it made her slightly breathless. She felt vulnerable suddenly, laid bare by her neediness. She backed away, turned to David. If he noticed how bright her eyes were or how brittle her smile, he gave no indication. "I just remembered. I did bring my coat. I'll be fine."

"You sure?"

"Of course. I'll just borrow one of your sweaters. Now, let's go."

SEVEN

ANGIE FOLLOWED THE COAST ROAD TO THE EDGE OF TOWN. On her left, the Pacific Ocean seemed to be gearing up for an autumn storm. White surf battered the cement-colored sand, sent trees sprawling onto land. The sky was an ominous gunmetal gray, and wind whistled through the branches along the shore and clattered against her windshield. The rain was so heavy she had her wipers set on high, and still they couldn't keep up.

At Azalea Lane, she turned left and found herself on a small, narrow street that once had been paved. Now the potholes seemed to come more often than the asphalt. Her car wobbled down the uneven road like a drunkard.

Help-Your-Neighbor House was at the very end of the this dilapidated street, in a pale blue Victorian house that stood in sharp contrast to the faded mobile homes that made up the rest of the neighborhood. While most of the other fences had *Beware of Dog* signs out front, here it simply said *Welcome.*

She pulled into the gravel parking lot, surprised to find a crowd of cars and trucks already there. It was not yet ten o'clock on a Sunday morning, yet the place was busy.

She parked next to a battered red pickup with blue doors and a gun rack in the window. Collecting her donation—canned goods, some toiletries, and several turkey gift certificates from the local grocery store—she followed the gravel path up to the brightly painted front door. A ceramic gnome grinned up at her from the corner of the porch.

Smiling, she opened the door and stepped into pandemonium.

The entire downstairs of the house was full of people talking and moving around. Several children were clustered together by the window, playing with Legos. Women with tired faces and ragged smiles sat along the wall, filling out forms on clipboards. In the far corner, a pair of men were unloading canned goods from boxes on the floor.

"May I help you?"

It took Angie a moment to realize that she was being addressed. When it sunk in, she smiled at the woman who'd spoken. "I'm sorry. It's so busy in here."

"A circus. It'll be like this through the holidays. We hope, anyway." She frowned at Angie, tapping a pen against her chin. "You look familiar."

"Hometown girls usually do." She stepped around the toys on the floor and took a seat opposite the woman's desk. "I'm Angie Malone. Used to be DeSaria."

The woman thumped her hand on the desk, rattling the fishbowl. "Of course. I graduated with Mira. Dana Herter." She offered her hand.

Angie shook it.

"What can we do for you?"

"I'm home for a while . . ."

Dana's ruddy face creased into Shar-pei-like folds. "We heard about your divorce."

Angie struggled to keep smiling. "Of course you did."

"Small town."

"Very. Anyway, I'm working at the restaurant for a while and I thought . . ." She shrugged. "As long as I'm here, maybe it would be good to do some volunteer work."

Dana nodded. "I started here when Doug left me. Doug Rhymer? Remember him? JV wrestling captain? He's living with Kelly Santos now. Bitch." She smiled, but it was shaky and didn't light her eyes. "This place has helped me."

Angie sat back in the chair, feeling strangely boneless. *I'm one of that group*, she thought. The unmarrieds. People would assume things about her because she'd failed at marriage. How had she not realized this? "What can I do to help?"

"Lots of things. Here." Dana reached into the drawer of her desk and pulled out a two-color brochure. "This outlines our services. Read it and see what appeals to you."

Angie took the brochure and flipped it open. She had just started to read when Dana said, "Could you go give your donations to Ted—over there? He'll be leaving in a few minutes."

"Oh. Sure." Angie carried her box of donations over to the two men, who took them with a smile and went back to work. She headed back to the lobby and sat down on one of the molded plastic seats in the makeshift waiting area.

She flipped through the brochure, reading about the services offered. Family counseling. A parent and child center. A domestic violence treatment program. A food bank. There was a list of fund-raising events—golf tournaments, silent auctions, bicycle races, dance marathons. *Every day the generous citizens of our community stop by with donations of food, money, clothing, or time. In this way we help ourselves and one another.*

Angie felt a shiver of something move through her just then. When she realized that it was hope, she looked up, smiling, wishing there was someone she could tell.

Her next thought was: *Conlan.* And her smile faded. It struck her that there would be lots of moments like this in the coming months. Times when—for a split second, just long enough to hurt—she'd forget that she was alone now. She forced herself to smile again, though it felt stretched, unnatural.

That was when she saw the girl. She walked through the front door, looking like a drowned puppy, dripping water from her nose, her hair, her hemline. Her long, soaking wet hair was red, although the exact hue was impossible to tell. Her skin was Nicole Kidman pale and her eyes were a deep and impenetrable brown; too big for her face, they made her look impossibly young. Freckles dotted her cheeks and the bridge of her nose.

It was the girl from the parking lot; the one who'd been posting *Work Wanted* flyers on windshields.

The girl paused at the door. She tightened her coat around her, but the thing was so ragged it was a useless gesture. The coat was too small and frayed at the sleeves. She went to the reception desk.

Dana looked up, smiled, said something.

Angie couldn't help herself. She eased to her feet and moved within earshot.

"I read about the coat drive," the girl said, crossing her arms and shivering just a little.

"We started collecting just last week. You'll need to give us your name and number. We'll call you when your size comes in."

"It's for my mother," the girl said. "She's a size small."

Dana tapped the pen against her chin and studied the girl. "What about a coat for you? That one seems . . ."

The girl laughed; it sounded sharp. Nervous. "I'm fine." She bent forward and wrote something on a piece of paper, then shoved it across the desk. "I'm Lauren Ribido. There's my number. Just call me when one comes in. Thanks." She made a beeline for the door.

Angie stood there, unmoving, staring at the closed door. Her heart was beating too quickly.

Go after her.

The idea came to her full-blown, startling her with its intensity.

It was a crazy idea. Why?

She didn't know, had no answer. All she knew was that she felt . . . connected to that poor teenage girl who was in need of a coat and yet requested one for her mother. She got up, took a step forward, then another. Before she knew it, she was outside.

Rain hammered the grass into submission, collected in brown puddles at the slightest indentation in the ground. The fire-red hedge that outlined the lot glistened with moisture and shook with wind.

Down at the end of the road, the girl was running.

Angie got into her car, turned on the lights and wipers, and backed out of the parking lot. As she drove down the bumpy street, her headlights illuminating the girl's figure, she wondered what the hell she was doing.

Stalking, her practical self said.

Helping, the dreamer responded.

She came to the corner and slowed. Stopped. She was just about to roll down the window and offer the girl a ride (no smart girl would say yes to *that*), when a number seven bus pulled up and parked. Its brakes wheezed; the doors clattered open. The girl bounded up the stairs and disappeared.

The bus drove off.

Angie followed it all the way to town. At the corner of Driftwood Way and the highway, she had a choice: turn for home or follow the bus.

For no reason that she could articulate, she followed the bus.

Finally, deep in the darklands of West End, the girl exited the bus. She walked through a neighborhood that would have scared most people and went into the remarkably misnamed Luxury Apartments. A few moments later, a light came on in a window on the fourth floor.

Angie parked at the curb and stared up at the building. It reminded her of something out of a Roald Dahl novel, all decaying wood and blank, black spaces.

No wonder the girl had been putting *Work Wanted* flyers on windshields.

You can't save them all, Conlan used to say to Angie when she'd cry at the unfairness of the world. *I can't save any of them* had always been her answer.

Then, she'd had him to hold her when she felt like this.

Now . . .

It was up to her. She couldn't save that girl, certainly; it wasn't her place to do so.

But maybe she could find a way to *help* her.

IT ALL CAME DOWN TO FATE. THAT WAS WHAT ANGIE THOUGHT ON Monday morning as she stood in front of the Clothes Line's display window.

There it was, right in front of her.

A dark green knee-length winter coat with faux fur around the collar, down the front, and encircling the cuffs. It was exactly what the girls were wearing this year. In fact, Angie had had a coat very much like this one in fourth grade.

It would look beautiful on a pale-skinned, red-haired girl with sad brown eyes.

She spent a nanosecond or two trying to talk herself out of it. After all, she didn't know the girl and this was none of Angie's business.

The arguments were weak and didn't change her mind.

Sometimes a thing just felt right, and truthfully, she was glad to have someone to think about besides herself.

She pushed open the door and went into the small store. A bell tinkled overhead at her entrance. The sound took her back in time, and for a moment she was a pencil-thin cheerleader with Brillo-pad black hair, following her sisters into the only clothing store in town.

Now, of course, there were several stores, even a J.C. Penney department store out on the highway, but back then, the Clothes Line had been the place for Jordache jeans and leg warmers.

"That can*not* be Angie DeSaria."

The familiar voice pulled Angie out of her reverie. She heard a flurry of footsteps (rubber-soled shoes on linoleum) and started smiling.

Mrs. Costanza made her way through the rounders of clothing, bobbing and weaving with a finesse that Evander Holyfield would envy. At first, all that was visible of her was a pile of teased, dyed-black hair. Then thin, drawn-on black eyebrows and finally her cherry-red smile.

"Hey, Miz Costanza," Angie said to the woman who'd fitted her for her first bra and sold her her every pair of shoes for seventeen years.

"I cannot believe it's you." She clapped her hands together, palm to palm to protect her long, heart-spangled fingernails. "I heard you were in town, of course, but I figured you would buy your clothes in the big city. Let me look at you." She latched on to Angie's shoulder and spun her around. "Jeans by Roberto Cavalli. A good Italian boy. This is good. But your shoes aren't sensible for walking in town. You'll need new ones. And I hear you're working at the restaurant. You'll need shoes for that."

Angie couldn't contain her smile. "You're right, as always."

Mrs. Costanza touched her cheek. "Your mama is so happy to have you home. It has been a bad year."

Angie's smile faltered. "For all of us."

"He was a good man. The best."

For a moment they fell silent, staring at each other, both of them thinking about her father. Finally, Angie said, "Before you sell me a pair of comfortable shoes, I'm interested in the coat in the window."

"That coat is awfully young for you, Angela. I know in the city—"

"It's not for me. It's for . . . a friend."

"Ah." She nodded. "It is what all the girls want this year. Come."

An hour later, Angie left the Clothes Line with two winter coats, two pair of angora gloves, a pair of non–name brand tennis shoes, and a pair of black flats for work. Her first stop was the packaging store in town, where she boxed up the coats.

She intended to drop them off at Help-Your-Neighbor. She really did.

But somehow she found herself parked on the girl's street, staring up at the dilapidated apartment building.

She gathered up the box and headed for the front door. Her heels caught in cracks in the paved walkway, threw her off balance. She imagined that she looked like Quasimodo, lurching forward. If anyone were watching, which, frankly, the blank, dark windows denied.

The main door was unlocked; indeed, it hung off one hinge. She opened it, stepped into a gloomy darkness. There was a bank of mailboxes to her left, with numbers on them. The only name listed was that of the manager's: Dolores Mauk, 1A.

Angie was across the hall from 1A. Hefting the box under her arm, she went to the door and knocked. When no one answered, she tried again.

"I'm comin'," someone said.

The door opened. A middle-aged woman with a hard face and soft eyes stood there. She wore a floral housedress and Converse high-top tennis shoes. A red kerchief covered most of her hair.

"Are you Ms. Mauk?" Angie asked, feeling suddenly conspicuous. She felt the woman's wariness.

"I am. Whaddaya want?"

"This package. It's for Lauren Ribido."

"Lauren," the woman said, her mouth softening into a smile. "She's a good girl." Then she frowned again. "You don't look like a delivery person." Mrs. Mauk's gaze slid pointedly down to Angie's shoes, then back up.

"It's a winter coat," Angie said. In the silence that followed, Angie felt compelled to explain. "I was at Help-Your-Neighbor when she—Lauren—came in, asking for a coat for her mother. I thought . . . why not get two? So here I am. I could leave the box with you. Would that be okay?"

"You'd best. They aren't home now."

Angie handed her the box. She had just started to turn away when the woman asked her name.

"Angela Malone. Used to be DeSaria." She always added that in town. Everyone, it seemed, knew her family.

"From the restaurant?"

Angie smiled. "That's me."

"My daughter used to love that place."

Used to. That was the problem with the restaurant. People had forgotten about it. "Bring her by again. I'll make sure she gets the royal treatment." Angie knew instantly that she'd said something wrong.

"Thanks," Ms. Mauk said in a husky voice. "I'll do that."

And the door shut.

Angie stood there, wondering what she'd done wrong. Finally, with a sigh, she turned and headed for the door.

Once in her car, she sat there, staring through the windshield at the rundown neighborhood. A bright yellow school bus pulled up to the corner and stopped. Several children spilled down the steps and jumped out onto the street. They were young—probably first or second graders.

No moms waited for them on the corner, talking to one another, sipping expensive lattes in Starbucks cups.

She felt that old wrenching in her chest, the blossoming of her familiar ache. She swallowed hard, watching the children move together in a pack, kicking a can down the sidewalk and laughing.

It wasn't until they were almost out of eyeshot that she realized what was missing.

Coats.

Not one of those kids was wearing a winter coat, even though it was cold outside. And by next month, it would be colder still.

The idea came to her right then: A coat drive at DeSaria's. For every new or gently used coat donated, they'd offer a free dinner.

It was perfect.

She jammed her key in the ignition and started the car. She couldn't wait to tell Mira.

LAUREN HURRIED ACROSS CAMPUS. COLD AIR SMACKED HER IN THE face. Her breath released in white plumes that faded fast as she walked.

David stood at the flagpole, waiting for her. At her appearance, he smiled brightly. She could tell he'd been waiting awhile; his cheeks were ruddy pink. "Damn, it's cold out here," he said, pulling her close for a long, lingering French kiss.

They walked across the commons, waving and smiling at friends, talking quietly to each other.

Outside her classroom, they stopped. David gave her another kiss, then headed to his own class. He hadn't gone more than a few feet when he stopped, turned around.

"Hey, I forgot to ask. What color tux should I get for homecoming?"

She felt the blood drain from her face. Homecoming. The dance was ten days away.

Jeez. She'd organized all of the decorations and set up the DJ and the lights.

How could she have forgotten the most important thing: a dress?

"Lauren?"

"Uh. Black," she answered, trying to smile. "Black is always safe."

"You got it," he said with an easy smile.

Things were always easy for David. He didn't have to wonder how to finance a new dress—forget about shoes and a wrap.

All through her trigonometry class she was distracted. As soon as class was over, she bolted to a quiet corner in the library and burrowed through her wallet and backpack, looking for money.

$6.12. That was all she had to her name right now.

A frown settled into place on her forehead and stayed there for the rest of the day.

After school, she skipped her decorating meeting and raced home.

The bus let her off at the corner of Apple Way and Cascade Street. It was raining hard. No longer a silvery mist, this was an onslaught that turned the world cold and gray. Raindrops hit the pavement in such rapid succession it looked as if the streets were boiling. Her canvas hood was ineffective at best. Water dripped down the sides of her face and burrowed cold and sticky against her collar. Her backpack, stuffed full of books and notebooks and handouts, seemed to weigh a ton. On top of all that, her vinyl shoes had broken a heel three blocks ago, so now she was limping down the hill toward home.

At the corner she waved at Bubba, who waved back, then returned to his tattooing. The neon sign flickered tiredly above his head. The smaller sign, posted in the window—*I Tattooed Your Parents*—was streaked with rain. She limped forward, past the now closed Hair Apparent where her mother allegedly worked, past the mini-mart run by the Chu family and the Teriyaki Takeout that the Ramirez family owned and operated.

Outside her apartment building, she stopped, loathe suddenly to go inside. She closed her eyes and imagined the home she would someday have. Buttery yellow walls, down-filled sofas, huge picture windows, a wraparound porch overgrown with flowers.

She tried to latch on to the familiar dream, but it floated past her, as insubstantial as smoke.

She forcibly changed her mind-set. Wishing and hoping had never put food on the table or brought Mom home one minute early. It certainly didn't get a girl a homecoming gown.

She walked down the cracked concrete path, past the box of garden tools that Mrs. Mauk had set outside last week in a feeble attempt to encourage tenant pride. Soon they would begin to rust. Those tools would be ruined long before someone bothered to cut back the leggy roses and runaway blackberry bushes that covered the back half of the lot.

The dark hallway greeted her.

She went upstairs and found the door to their apartment standing open.

"Mom!" she called out, pushing through the unlatched door. There was a cigarette burning in an ashtray on the coffee table. The mound of used butts was huge. Here and there, smoked-down cigarettes lay littered across the Formica table.

The apartment was empty. Mom had probably come home from work about five (if she'd even made it to work in the first place), then changed her look from white-trash beautician to biker slut and run off to her favorite bar stool.

Lauren hurried down the hallway and into her bedroom, praying all the way there. *Please please please.*

It was empty beneath her pillow.

Mom had found the money.

EIGHT

LAUREN MEANT TO MOVE. SHE MEANT TO GET UP, PUT ON fresh makeup, and borrow Suzi Mauk's suit again, but somehow she sat there, on the floor, staring at the stack of cigarette butts in the ashtray on the coffee table. How much of her twenty dollars had literally gone up in smoke?

She wished she could cry the way she once would have. The tears, she now knew, meant hope. When your eyes dried up, there was none.

The door swung open, cracked against the wall. The whole apartment shuddered at the force of it. A beer bottle rolled off the sofa cushion and thumped to the shag carpet.

Her mother stood in the doorway, wearing a pleated black miniskirt with black boots and a tight blue T-shirt. The top—which Lauren thought looked suspiciously new—made her look much too thin. The once beautiful bone structure in her face was now a collection of sharp edges and dark hollows. Booze and cigarettes and too many bad years had chiseled away at her beauty, leaving only the stunning green of her eyes. Against the harsh pallor of her face, Mom's eyes were still arresting. Once Lauren had thought her mother was the most lovely woman in the world—lots of people had back then. For years, Mom had gotten by on her looks; as her beauty had faded, so had her ability to cope.

Mom brought a cigarette to her lips and took a long drag, exhaling sharply. "You're staring at me."

Lauren sighed. So it was going to be one of those nights; the kind where Mom came home more sober than drunk and pissed off about it. Lauren got slowly to her feet, started picking up the mess in the living room. "I'm not staring."

"You should be at work," Mom said, kicking the door shut behind her.

"So should you."

Mom laughed at that and flopped down on the sofa, putting her feet up on the coffee table. "I was headed that way. You know how it is."

"Yeah. I know. You have to walk past the Tides." She heard the bitterness in her voice and wished it weren't there.

"Don't start with me."

Lauren went to the sofa and sat down on the arm. "You took the twenty bucks from under my pillow. That was *my* money."

Mom put out one cigarette and lit up another. "So?"

"The homecoming dance is less than two weeks away. I . . ." Lauren paused, hating to admit her need, but what choice did she have? "I need a dress."

Mom looked up at her. Smoke swirled in the air, seeming to exaggerate the distance between them. "I got knocked up at a school dance," Mom finally said.

Lauren fought the urge to roll her eyes. "I know."

"Fuck the dance."

Lauren couldn't believe it still hurt, after all these years. When would she stop believing that her mom might change? "Thanks, Mom. As usual, you're a big help."

"You'll see. When you're older." Mom leaned back, exhaling smoke. Her mouth trembled, and for the merest of moments, she looked sad. "None of it matters. What you want. What you dream of. You live with what's left."

If Lauren believed that, she'd never be able to get out of bed.

Or off a bar stool. She reached down, brushed the blond hair out of her mother's eyes. "It's going to be different for me, Mom."

Her mother almost smiled. "I hope so," she murmured so softly Lauren had to lean forward to hear it.

"I'll find a way to pay the rent *and* buy a dress," she said, finding her courage again. It had left her for a few moments there, and without its heat she had gone cold and numb, but now it was back. She slid off the arm of the sofa and went back to her mother's bedroom. In the overstuffed closet, she looked for something she could redo into a dress for the dance. She was holding up a black satin nightgown when the doorbell rang.

She didn't answer it, but her mother yelled out to her: "Miz Mauk's here."

Lauren swore under her breath. If only Mom hadn't opened the door. Forcing a smile, she tossed the tiny negligee on the bed and went back into the living room.

Mrs. Mauk was there, smiling. A big cardboard box was on the floor at her feet. Beside her, Mom was buttoning up a beautiful black pant coat made of the softest wool; it had a tapered waist and a shawl collar.

Lauren frowned.

"It's an old lady's coat," Mom muttered, walking down the hallway toward the bathroom.

"Mrs. Mauk?" Lauren said.

"There's one for you, too." She bent down and pulled a green coat with faux fur trim from the box.

Lauren gasped. "For me?"

It was almost exactly the coat Melissa Stonebridge wore. The richest, most popular girl at Fircrest. Lauren couldn't help reaching for it, touching the soft fur. "You shouldn't have. I mean . . . I can't . . ." She drew her hand back. Mrs. Mauk couldn't afford this.

"It's not from me," Mrs. Mauk said, her mouth forming into a sad and knowing smile. "A woman from Help-Your-Neighbor brought it by. Her name was Angela. She's one of the DeSarias— you know, from that restaurant on Driftwood. I'd say she could afford it."

Charity. The woman somehow had seen Lauren and pitied her.

"This coat is too old for me," Mom said from the other room. "What does yours look like, Lauren?"

"Take it," Mrs. Mauk said, pushing the coat toward Lauren.

She couldn't help herself. She took it, slipped it on, and suddenly she was warm. She hadn't realized until just then how long she'd been cold. "How do you say thank you for something like this?" she whispered.

Mrs. Mauk's eyes filled with understanding. "It's hard," she said quietly, "being the one who needs help."

"Yeah."

They stared at each other a moment longer. Finally, Lauren tried to smile. "I guess I'll go to the restaurant and see if I can find her . . . say thank you."

"That's a good idea."

Lauren glanced down the hallway. "I'll be back in a while, Mom."

"Bring me a better coat," Mom yelled back.

Lauren didn't dare look at Mrs. Mauk. They walked out of the apartment and down the stairs together, neither one speaking.

Outside, Lauren waved good-bye to Mrs. Mauk who, although hidden, was always at her curtains, watching what happened on her street.

In less than thirty minutes Lauren was at DeSaria's Restaurant, opening the door.

The first thing she noticed was the aroma. The place smelled heavenly. She realized how hungry she was.

"I guess you found me."

Lauren hadn't even noticed the woman's arrival, and yet they were standing almost face-to-face. The woman was only an inch or so taller than Lauren, but she was a commanding presence. First of all, she was beautiful—movie-star beautiful—with her black hair and dark eyes and big smile. And her clothes looked like something out of an expensive catalogue. Black pants with flared legs, high-heeled black boots, and a pale yellow scoop-neck sweater. There was something familiar about her.

"Are you Angela DeSaria?"

"I am. Angie, please." She looked at Lauren, and there was an almost liquid softness in her brown eyes. "And you're Lauren Ribido."

"Thank you for the coat." Her voice snagged on the sentiment, sounded thick. She realized suddenly where she'd seen this woman before. "You're the woman who gave me money."

Angie smiled, but it seemed off somehow, not quite real. "You probably think I'm stalking you. I'm not. It's just . . . I'm new in town and kind of at loose ends. I saw you and wanted to help."

"You did." Lauren felt it again, the emotion thickening her voice.

"I'm glad to hear that. Is there anything else I could do?"

"I could use a job," Lauren said quietly.

Angie seemed surprised by that. "Have you ever waitressed before?"

"Two summers at the Hidden Lake Ranch." Lauren fought the urge to squirm. She was sure that this beautiful woman saw every flaw that Lauren tried to hide—the hair that needed a trim, the shoes that leaked in the rain, the backpack worn thin.

"I don't suppose you're Italian?"

"No. At least not that I know of. Does that matter?"

"It shouldn't. . . ." Angie looked back at a closed door. "But we've always done things a certain way."

And you're not it. "I understand."

"You saving up for college?"

Lauren started to say, "Yes," but when she saw the under-standing in Angie's dark eyes, she found herself saying, "I need a dress for the homecoming dance." The minute she said it, she blushed. She couldn't believe she'd revealed something so inti-mate to a stranger.

Angie studied her for a moment longer, neither smiling nor frowning. "I'll tell you what," she finally said. "You sit down at this table, have something to eat, and then we'll talk."

"I'm not hungry," she said, just as her stomach grumbled.

Angie smiled gently. Lauren felt wounded by that smile somehow. "Eat dinner. Then we'll talk."

ANGIE FOUND MIRA STANDING OUTSIDE THE BACK DOOR, SIPPING cappuccino, both her hands curled around the porcelain mug. Steam mingled with her breath and formed a mist in front of her face. "Winter is going to come early this year," she said as Angie sidled up beside her.

"I used to hide out here as soon as it was time to do dishes," Angie said, smiling at the memory. She could almost hear Papa's booming voice come through the brick walls.

"Like I didn't know that." Mira laughed.

Angie moved a little closer, until they were shoulder to shoulder, both of them leaning against the rough wall that contained so much of their lives. They stared out at the empty parking lot. Beyond it, the street was a silvery ribbon in the darkening night. Far away, seen in slivers between the houses and trees, was the blue-gray ocean. "Remember that list Livvy helped me come up with?"

"The DeSaria destruction list, as Mama called it? How could I forget?"

"I think I'm going to make the first change."

"Which one?"

"I found a new waitress. A high school girl. I think she could work some nights and weekends."

Mira turned to her. "Mama's going to let you hire a *high school* girl?"

Angie winced. "A problem, huh?"

"Mama will have a cow; you know that. Tell me the girl is Italian at least."

"Don't think so."

Mira grinned. "This is going to be fun."

"Knock it off. Be serious. Is it a good idea to hire a new waitress?"

"Yes. Rosa is too slow to handle any more business. I guess if you're going to make some changes around here, this is a good place to start. How did you find her? Employment office?"

Angie bit her lip and looked down at the gravel.

"Angie?" This time Mira wasn't smiling. There was concern in her voice.

"I saw her at Help-Your-Neighbor when I went to volunteer. She was there, asking for a winter coat for her mother. That's how I got the idea for the coat drive."

"So you bought her a coat."

"You said I should help people."

"And offered her a job."

Angie sighed. She heard the mistrust in her sister's voice and she understood. Everyone thought Angie was so easily victimized. It was because of Sarah Dekker. When they'd been set to adopt her baby, Angie and Conlan had opened their hearts and home to the troubled teenager.

"You have so much love to give," Mira said finally. "It must hurt to hold it in all the time."

The words had tiny barbs that sank into her skin. "Is that what it's all about? *Shit.* I thought I was just hiring a kid to serve food on weekends."

"Maybe I'm wrong. Overreacting."

"And maybe I don't make the best choices."

"Don't go there, Ange," Mira said softly. "I'm sorry I brought it up. I worry too much. That's the problem with family. But you're right to hire a new waitress. Mama will simply have to understand."

Angie almost laughed. "Yeah. She's so good at that."

Mira paused, then said, "Just be careful, okay?"

Angie knew it was good advice. "Okay."

ANGIE STOOD IN THE SHADOWS, WATCHING THE GIRL EAT HER DIN-ner. She ate slowly, as if savoring every bite. There was something almost old-fashioned about her, a round softness that brought to mind the girls of another generation. Her long copper-colored hair was a tangle of curls that fell down her back. Its color was vibrant against her pale cheeks. She had a nose that turned up just a little at the tip and was dotted with freckles. But it was her eyes—unexpectedly brown and filled with an adult's knowledge—that caught Angie's attention and held it.

You won't want me, those eyes said.

You have so much love to give. It must hurt to hold it in all the time.

Mira's words came back to Angie. It had never occurred to her that she was stepping onto the merry-go-round of her old choices.

Loss was like that, she knew. She never knew when or where it would strike. The littlest thing could set her off. A baby carriage. A doll. A bit of sad music. The Happy Birthday song. A desperate teenage girl.

But this wasn't about that. It *wasn't*. She was almost certain.

The girl—Lauren—looked up, glanced around, then looked at her wristwatch. She pushed the empty plate away and crossed her arms, waiting.

It was now or never.

Either Mama was going to let Angie make changes around here or she wasn't.

Time to find out the answer.

Angie went to the kitchen, where she found Mama washing up the last of the night's dishes. Four pans of fresh lasagna lined the counter.

"The Bolognese is almost ready," Mama said. "We'll have plenty for tomorrow night."

"And the rest of the month," Angie muttered.

Mama looked up. "What does that mean?"

Angie chose her words carefully. They were like missiles; each one could start a war. "We had seven customers tonight, Mama."

"That's good for a weeknight."

"Not good enough."

Mama wrenched the faucet's handle hard. "It will get better when the holidays come."

Angie tried another tack. "I'm a mess at waitressing."

"Yes. You'll get better."

"I was still better than Rosa. I watched her the other night, Mama. I've never seen anyone move so slowly."

"She's been here a long time, Angela. Show some respect."

"We need to make some changes. That's why I'm here, isn't it?"

"You will not fire Rosa." Mama tossed down her dishrag. It hit the counter like a gauntlet.

"I would never do that."

Mama relaxed a tiny bit. "Good."

"Come with me," Angie said, reaching out for Mama's hand.

Together they walked out of the kitchen. In the shadow behind the archway, Angie paused. "You see that girl?"

"She ordered the lasagna," Mama said. "Looks like she loved it."

"I want . . . I'm going to hire her to work nights and weekends."

"She's too young."

"I'm hiring her. And she's not too young. Livvy and Mira were waitressing at a much earlier age."

Mama shifted and frowned, studying the girl. "She doesn't *look* Italian."

"She isn't."

Mama drew in a sharp breath and pulled Angie deeper into the shadows. "Now look here—"

"Do you want me to help you in the restaurant?"

"Yes, but—"

"Then let me help."

"Rosa will feel slighted."

"Honestly, Mama, I think she'll be glad. Last night she

bumped into the walls twice. She's tired. She'll welcome the help."

"High school girls never work out. Ask your papa."

"We can't ask Papa. This is for you and me to decide."

Mama seemed to deflate at the reminder about Papa. The wrinkles in her cheeks deepened. She bit down on her lower lip and peered around the corner again. "Her hair is a mess."

"It's raining out. I think she's been looking for work. The way you did, remember, in Chicago, when you and Papa were first married."

The memory seemed to soften Mama. "Her shoes have holes in them, and her blouse is too small. Poor thing. Still." She frowned. "The last redhead who worked here stole a whole night's receipts."

"She's not going to steal from us."

Mama pulled away from the wall and walked down the hallway toward the kitchen. She was talking, whispering, the whole time, gesturing wildly.

If Angie closed her eyes, she might have seen her father there, standing firm, smiling gently at his wife's theatrics even as he disagreed with her.

Mama spun around and came back to Angie. "He always thought you were the smart one. Fine. Hire this girl but don't let her use the register."

Angie almost laughed at that, it was so absurd. "Okay."

"Okay." Mama turned on her heel and left the restaurant.

Angie glanced out the window. Mama was marching down the street, arguing with a man who wasn't there.

"Thanks, Papa," Angie said, smiling as she walked through the now empty restaurant.

Lauren looked up at her. "That was delicious," she said, sounding nervous. She folded her napkin carefully and set it on the table.

"My mother can really cook." Angie sat down across from the girl. "Are you a responsible employee?"

"Completely."

"We can count on you to show up on time?"

Lauren nodded. Her dark eyes were earnest. "Always."

Angie smiled. This was the best she'd felt in months. "Okay, then. You can start tomorrow night. Say five to ten. Is that okay?"

"It's great."

Angie reached across the table and shook Lauren's warm hand. "Welcome to the family."

"Thanks." Lauren got quickly to her feet. "I'd better go home now."

Angie would have sworn she saw tears in the girl's brown eyes, but before she could comment on it, Lauren was gone. It wasn't until later, when Angie was closing out the register, that it dawned on her.

Lauren had bolted at the word *family*.

WHEN ANGIE GOT HOME, THE COTTAGE WAS QUIET AND DARK, AND in all those shadows lay loneliness.

She closed the door behind her and stood there, listening to the sound of her own breathing. It was a sound she'd grown used to, and yet here, in this house that had been loud in her youth, it wounded her. When she couldn't stand it anymore, she tossed her purse on the entry table and went to the old RCA stereo in the living room. She pushed a cassette into the tape player and turned the system on.

Tony Bennett's voice floated through the speakers, filling the room with music and memories. This was her papa's favorite tape; the one he'd made himself. Every song began late, sometimes as much as a whole stanza. Whenever he'd heard one he loved, he'd jump up from his chair and run for the stereo, yelling, "I love this one!"

She wanted to smile at the memory, but that lightness wasn't in her. In fact, it felt far away. "I hired a new waitress tonight, Papa. She's a high school girl. You can imagine Mama's reaction to *that*. Oh, and she has red hair."

She went to the window and stared outside. Moonlight dusted the waves and glistened along the dark blue sea. The next song came on. Bette Midler's "Wind Beneath My Wings."

It had played at his funeral.

The music swirled around her, threatened to pull her under.

"It is easy to talk to him, isn't it? Especially here."

Angie spun around at the sound of her mother's voice.

Mama stood behind the sofa, staring at her, obviously trying to smile. She was dressed in a ratty old flannel nightgown, one Papa had given her years ago. She crossed the room and snapped off the stereo.

"What are you doing here, Mama?"

Mama sat down on the sofa and patted the cushion. "I knew you would have a hard night."

Angie sat down beside her, close enough to lean against her mother's steady side. "How did you know?"

Mama put an arm around her. "The girl," she said at last.

Angie couldn't believe she hadn't figured it out. Of course. "I'll need to keep my distance from her, won't I?"

"You've never been good at that."

"No."

Mama tightened her hold. "Just be careful. Your heart is soft."

"It feels as if it's in pieces sometimes."

Mama made a sound, a little sigh. "We keep breathing in times like that. There's nothing else."

Angie nodded. "I know."

After that, they got out a deck of cards and played gin rummy long into the night. By the time they fell asleep side by side on the sofa, curled up beneath a quilt Mama had made years ago, Angie had found her strength again.

NINE

LAUREN SHOWED UP FOR WORK FIFTEEN MINUTES EARLY. SHE
wore her best pair of black jeans and a white cotton blouse
that she'd gotten Mrs. Mauk to iron for her.

She knocked on the door and waited for an answer. When
none came, she cautiously opened the door and peered inside.

The restaurant was dark. Tables sat in shadows. "Hello?" She
closed the door behind her.

A woman came around the corner, moving fast, her hands
coiled in the stained white apron that covered her clothing. She
saw Lauren and stopped.

Lauren felt like a bug trapped in a child's hand. That was
how this woman stared at her, narrow-eyed and frowning. Old-
fashioned eyeglasses made her eyes appear huge.

"You are the new girl?"

She nodded, feeling a slow blush creep up her cheeks. "I'm

Lauren Ribido." She stepped forward, held her hand out. They shook hands. The woman's grip was stronger than Lauren had expected.

"I am Maria DeSaria. Is this your first job?"

"No. I've been working for years. When I was little—fifth and sixth grade—I picked strawberries and raspberries at the Magruder farm. I've been working at Rite Aid since it opened last summer."

"Berries? I thought that was mostly migrant workers."

"It is. Mostly. The pay was okay for a kid."

Maria tilted her head to one side, frowning as she studied Lauren. "Are you a troubled girl? Runaway, drugs? That sort of thing?"

"No. I have a 3.9 grade point at Fircrest Academy. I've never been in any kind of trouble."

"Fircrest. Hmm. Are you Catholic?"

"Yes," Lauren answered with a nervous frown. It was a dangerous thing to admit these days. So much trouble in the church. She forced herself to stand perfectly straight. No fidgeting.

"Well. That's good, even if you do have red hair."

Lauren had no idea what to say to that, so she remained silent.

"Have you waitressed before?" Maria asked at last.

"Yes."

"So when I tell you to set up the tables and wipe down the menus, you know what I mean."

"Yes, ma'am."

"The silverware is in that chest," Maria said. "Not that it's real silver," she added quickly.

"Okay."

They stared at each other. Lauren felt like that bug again.

"Well. Get started," Maria said.

Lauren ran for the chest and pulled open the top drawer. Silverware rattled at the ferocity of the movement. She winced, knowing that already she'd done something wrong.

She glanced worriedly back at Maria, who stood there, frowning, watching Lauren fumble through the drawer.

It was not going to be easy to please that woman, Lauren thought. Not easy at all.

. . .

BY THE END OF HER SHIFT LAUREN KNEW TWO THINGS: SHE NEEDED to wear tennis shoes to work, and earning enough money for back rent and a decent dress wasn't going to happen at DeSaria's.

Still, she liked the place. The food was wonderful. She worked as hard as she could, trying to find jobs that needed to be done before someone—namely Maria—told her what to do. Now she was refilling all the olive oil decanters.

"You know," Angie said, coming up behind her, "this could be a great restaurant if people actually showed up. Here." She handed Lauren a dessert plate that held a piece of tiramisu. "Join me."

They sat down at the table by the fireplace. The flames flickered and snapped.

Lauren felt Angie's gaze on her and she looked up. In the dark eyes, she saw something. Compassion, maybe, with an edge of pity. Angie had seen Lauren that night in the parking lot, and then again at the Help-Your-Neighbor House. There were no secrets now. "It was really nice of you to give me this job. You don't need another waitress, though." She wished immediately that she'd kept silent. She *needed* this job.

"We will. I've got big plans for the place." Angie smiled. "Although I don't know much about the business. Just ask my sister Livvy. She thinks I'm going to screw up big time."

Lauren couldn't imagine that this beautiful woman failed at anything. "I'm sure you'll do great. The food is amazing."

"Yeah. My mom and Mira can really cook." Angie took another bite, then asked, "So, how long have you lived in West End? Maybe I went to school with your folks."

"I don't think so." Lauren hoped she didn't sound bitter but it was hard to tell. "We moved here when I was in fourth grade." She paused. "It's just Mom and me." She liked the way that sounded, as if they were a team, she and her mother. Still, her family—or lack thereof—was not something she wanted to talk about. "How about you? Have you always lived in West End?"

"I grew up here. But I moved away for college and got married. . . ." Angie's voice seemed to give out. She stared down at her dessert, stabbed it with her fork. "I just moved back home after a divorce." She looked up, made an attempt at smiling. "Sorry. I'm not used to saying it yet."

"Oh." Lauren had no idea how to respond. She went back to eating. The sound of their forks on porcelain seemed loud.

Finally, Angie said, "Do you need a ride home tonight?"

"No." She was surprised by the question. "My boyfriend is picking me up." As she said it, she heard a car honk outside. She shot to her feet. "There he is. I better go." She looked down at the dishes. "Should I—"

"Run along. I'll see you tomorrow night."

Lauren looked down at her. "Are you sure?"

"I'm sure. See you then."

"Bye," Lauren said, already moving. At the hostess desk, she bent down for her backpack. Slinging it over her shoulder, she headed for the door.

THE CROWD WENT WILD.

Like everyone else, Lauren was on her feet, screaming and clapping. A roar moved through the stands. The scoreboard flickered, changed, revealed the new numbers: Fircrest—28. Kelso Christian—14.

"That was *awesome*," Anna Lyons said, grabbing Lauren's sleeve and tugging it hard.

Lauren couldn't contain herself. She started laughing. David's pass had been beautiful, a perfect forty-yard spiral right into Jared's hands. She hoped his father had seen it.

"Come on," someone said. "It's almost halftime."

Lauren followed the group of girls down the aisle and onto the concrete stairs. They hurried down to the sidelines, where the various booths were being set up. She took her place at the hot dog stand, where the annual staff was already hard at work. "My turn," she said to Marci Morford, who was busy refilling the mustard jars. For the next half hour, while the marching band moved across the field, she sold hot dogs and hamburgers to the sea of people who drifted along the sidelines, congregating now and then to talk. Parents. Teachers. Students. Graduates. On Friday nights during football season, they all met at the stadium for local games. Everyone was talking about David. He was playing the game of his life.

When Lauren's shift was over, she rejoined her friends and watched the end of the game.

Fircrest kicked the other school's butt.

The stands slowly emptied out. Lauren and her friends cleaned up the mess at the booth, then went to the locker room. Outside the door, they stood in a pod, talking and laughing and waiting. One by one, the players came out, hooked up with their girlfriends, and walked away.

At last, the double doors opened and the final few players rushed out, laughing and talking and punching one another in the arms. David was in their midst and yet he stood apart some-how, the way Brad Pitt or George Clooney must have stood out in their high schools. The floodlights fell on him alone, and right then, he appeared golden, from his blond hair to his bright smile.

Lauren ran to him. He separated easily from the pack and pulled her into an embrace. "You were great," she whispered.

He grinned. "I was, wasn't I? Did you see that bomb to Jared? *Shit.* I was on fire." Laughing, he kissed her.

At the flagpole, he stopped, looked around.

Lauren knew what—or whom—he was looking for. She tensed up, slipped her arm around him, and settled in close.

The rest of the kids drifted toward their cars. They heard the distant sound of engines starting, doors slamming shut, horns honking. The party at the beach would be huge tonight. There was nothing like a big victory to get the gang going. Their last home game had been quiet; she and David had spent the hours afterward in his mom's car, talking about everything. This night would be different. She didn't care how they celebrated as long as they were together.

"Hey, David," someone called out, "are you and Lauren com-ing to the beach?"

"We'll be there," David said, waving back. His eyes were nar-rowed; he kept glancing away from the lights, toward the field. The parking lot. Finally, he said, "Did you see them?"

Before Lauren could answer, she heard his mother's voice. "David. Lauren. There you are."

Mrs. Haynes crossed the courtyard and came up to them. She hugged David fiercely, and then smiled up at him. Lauren won-dered if David saw the way that smile shook. "I'm so proud of you."

"Thanks, Mom." David looked behind her.

"Your dad had a business meeting tonight," she said slowly. "He's sorry."

David's face seemed to crumble. "Whatever."

"I'll take you guys out for pizza, if you'd like—"

"No, thanks. There's a party at Clayborne Beach. But thanks." David grabbed Lauren's hand and pulled her away.

Mrs. Haynes fell into step beside them. In silence, the three of them walked to the parking lot. David opened the car door for Lauren.

She paused for a moment, looked at his mother. "Thanks for the invitation, Mrs. Haynes," she said.

"You're welcome," she answered quietly. "Have fun." Then she looked at David. "Be home by midnight."

He walked around to his side of the car. "Sure."

Later that night, as they were huddled around the fire, sitting amid a circle of kids who were talking about the traditional grad night party, Lauren leaned against him, whispered, "I'm sure he wanted to be there."

David sighed. "Yeah. He'll be there next Friday," he said, but when he looked at her, his eyes were bright. "I love you."

"I love you, too" she said, slipping her hand into his.

Finally, he smiled.

IN THE PAST FEW DAYS, ANGIE HAD WORKED CEASELESSLY. EVERY morning, she was up before dawn and seated at the kitchen table, with notes and menus and paperwork spread out before her. In these, the quiet, pale pink hours, she put together the coat campaign and created a series of advertisements and promotions. By seven-thirty, she was at the restaurant, meeting with Mama to learn the behind-the-scenes routine.

First, they visited the suppliers. Angie watched her mother move through the boxes of fresh vegetables, choosing the same things day after day: tomatoes, green peppers, eggplants, iceberg lettuce, yellow onions, and carrots. Mama never paused to inspect the portobello or porcini mushrooms, the brightly colored array of peppers, the baby pea pods, the butter lettuce, or the rich, dark truffles.

It was the same routine at the fish and meat markets. Mama bought tiny, shell pink shrimp for cocktails and nothing else. From Alpac Brothers, she chose extra lean ground sirloin, ground pork and veal, and dozens of boneless chicken breasts. By the end of the fourth day, Angie had begun to see the missed opportunities. Finally, she hung back, told Mama to "go on home"; that Angie would be along soon. As soon as Mama left, Angie turned to the produce supervisor. "Okay," she said, "let's pretend that DeSaria's is a brand-new restaurant."

For the next few hours, he tossed information at her like a

circus performer. She caught every word and wrote it down, then did the same thing at the fish and meat markets.

She must have asked a hundred questions.

What does it mean if the fish was flash frozen?
What are the best kinds of clams? Oysters?
Why would we want to buy squid ink?
How do you pick a good cantaloupe?
Why is Dungeness crab better than snow or king?

The vendors answered each question patiently, and by the end of the week, Angie was beginning to understand how they could improve the menu. She compulsively collected recipes and menus from some of the most famous restaurants in Los Angeles, San Francisco, and New York. All of them, she noticed, used the freshest local ingredients for seasonal dishes. In addition, she read all her father's notes and records and interrogated her sisters until they begged for mercy.

For the first time in her life, she was becoming a part of the restaurant instead of a satellite in its orbit. To Angie's—and everyone's—surprise, she loved it.

On Saturday night, in between helping Lauren waitress, she read over the accounts payable, paid bills, and jotted down some notes on what supplies were running low. The day passed in a blur of activity, and by the time the last guests left, she was exhausted.

It felt great.

She said good night to Mama and Mira, then got two bowls of gelato and sat down at a table by the fireplace. She loved this time of night, in the quiet of the closed restaurant. It relaxed her, and sometimes, in the crackle of the fire or the tap of rain on the roof, she felt her father's presence.

"I'm going home now, Angie," Lauren said, walking through the dining room.

"Have some of this gelato with me. It's delicious." It had become a ritual in the past few nights: Angie and Lauren sharing dessert at the end of the evening. Angie actually looked forward to it.

Lauren grinned. "At this rate I'll have to waddle to the dance."

Angie laughed. "Funny. Sit."

Lauren sat down across from her, where Angie had already placed a bowl of the gelato and a spoon.

Angie spooned up a bit of gelato, let it melt in her mouth, "Man, this is good. Too bad we hardly had any customers tonight." She looked at Lauren. "Your tips can't be too good."

"They're not."

"The ad for the coat drive hits tomorrow. That should help."

"I hope so."

Angie heard the desperate edge in Lauren's voice. "How much does a homecoming dress cost these days?"

Lauren sighed. "Lots."

Angie studied her. "What size are you?"

"An eight."

"Same as me." The answer was there, plain as the spoon in her hand. "I could loan you a dress. Conlan—my . . . ex-husband— was a reporter for the *Seattle Times*. Every now and then we went to some event. So I have a few dresses. One of them might fit you."

The look on Lauren's face was easy to read: a combination of longing and shame. "I couldn't do that. But thanks."

Angie decided not to push the offer. Lauren could think about it. "You're going with the boy who picks you up from work?"

Lauren blushed. "David Haynes."

Angie saw the transformation, knew what it meant. *Love.* It was no surprise. Lauren was a serious girl, the kind who fell in love hard and didn't come out of it easily. A good girl, in other words. "How long have you and David been dating?"

"Almost four years."

Angie lifted her eyebrows. High school years were like those of a dog's life; four years could be a lifetime.

She wanted to say *Be careful, Lauren; love can kill you*, but of course she didn't. If Lauren was lucky, it was a lesson she'd never learn.

The thought made Angie sigh. Suddenly, she was thinking about Conlan and all the years she'd loved him. And how it had felt when it was gone.

She got up from the table quickly, before her sadness could be seen. She stood by the window, staring out at the night. The cold of autumn had come early this year; already a layer of frost was forming on the street. All over town leaves were falling from shivering trees, landing in piles on the sidewalks and along the roadsides. By this time next week, those heaps would be slippery and black. Soon there would be no leaves left.

"Are you okay?"

Angie heard the worry in Lauren's voice and it embarrassed her. "Fine." Before she could say more, apologize or perhaps explain, a car pulled up outside the restaurant and honked.

"That's David," Lauren said, popping to her feet.

Angie looked at the car out front. It was a classic Porsche Speedster, painted primer gray. The wheels shone with chrome and the tires were obviously new. "That's some car."

Lauren came up beside her. "I call him Speed Racer sometimes. You know, from the old cartoon. 'Cause he lives for that car."

"Ah. A boy and his car."

Lauren laughed. "If I have to see one more paint chip, I might scream. Of course I don't tell him that."

Angie stared down at the girl. Never had she seen such purity of emotion, such blatant adoration. First love. All at once, she remembered how consuming it was. She almost said, *You be careful, Lauren,* but it wasn't her place. Such advice was for a mother to give.

"See you Tuesday," Lauren said, leaving.

Angie watched Lauren go outside. The girl ran across the sidewalk and disappeared into the sports car.

And suddenly she was thinking of a long time ago, back when she'd been head-over-heels in love with Tommy Matucci. He'd driven an old, battered Ford Fairlane; rickety and temperamental as that car had been, he'd loved it.

Funny.

She hadn't thought of that in years.

THEY PARKED IN FRONT OF LAUREN'S BUILDING, IN THEIR USUAL spot. She gently eased herself into position. It wasn't easy in a car this small; the gear shift seemed to take up a lot of space. Still, they'd had years to perfect their technique.

David took her in his arms and kissed her. She felt herself falling into that familiar breathy darkness, that needing. Her heart-beat sped up. Within minutes the windows were fogged up and their privacy was complete.

"Lauren," he murmured, and she heard it in his voice, too;

that needing of her. His hand slid beneath her blouse. She shivered at the touch.

Then his wristwatch started to bleat.

"Shit," he groaned, pulling his hand from her body. "I can't *believe* they make me come home this early. I know eighth graders who can stay out till midnight." He crossed his arms with a dramatic flourish.

It was all Lauren could do not to smile. He had no idea how childish he looked right now. The great David Ryerson Haynes, pouting. "You're lucky," she said, snuggling up to him. "It means they love you."

"Yeah, right."

Lauren felt his heartbeat; it fluttered beneath her palm. For a second, just that, she felt older than him by years.

"Your mom doesn't give a shit what time you get home. Or even if you come home."

"My point exactly," she said, feeling a swell of the old bitterness. She and mom had tackled the issue of curfews a long time ago. *I won't be your warden*, Mom had said. *My parents tried that and it only made me more wild.* Now Lauren could come and go as she pleased.

David kissed her again, and then drew back with a sigh.

She knew instantly that something was wrong. "What's the matter?"

He leaned across her, opened the glove box. "Here," he said, handing her some papers.

"What—" She looked down. "The Stanford application."

"My dad wants me to go for early decision. It's due November fifteenth."

"Oh," Lauren said, easing back into her own seat. She knew he'd do anything to please his father.

"I thought you could do it, too."

The eagerness in his voice made her want to cry. How could he drive her home, see her apartment, and not get it? "I can't afford to do that, David. I need a scholarship. And not a few vanity bucks. I need a full ride."

His breath exhaled heavily. "I know."

They sat that way for a few long minutes, each in a separate seat, not touching, staring at the foggy windshield.

"I probably won't get in," he said at last.

"Come on, David. They have a building named after your family."

"Then you will, too." He turned to her then, gathered her into his arms, and held her, kissed her. She let herself be swept into that kiss until nothing else mattered but them.

Later, when she was alone again, walking through the sad darkness of her apartment, she couldn't help wishing she lived in his world, where everything came easy. Dreams most of all.

WHEN MIRA RETURNED FROM CARPOOL, ANGIE WAS STANDING ON her front porch.

"You're up bright and early," Mira said, walking up the path. "And you sorta look like shit."

"You should talk. Does everyone wear ripped sweatpants and rubber shoes for carpool?"

"Most of us. Come on in." Smiling, she led Angie into the house, which smelled of coffee and pancakes. Picking up toys along the way, she went to the kitchen and poured two cups of coffee. "Okay," she said, settling into a plaid, overstuffed chair in the cluttered family room. "Why are you here and why do you look like a *Survivor* contestant?"

"Very funny." Angie plopped into a chair. "I was up most of the night, working."

"Working, huh?" Mira sipped her coffee and eyed Angie over the chipped rim.

Angie handed her sister a notebook. "Here's what I want to do."

Mira set down her mug and opened the notebook. Surprise widened her eyes as she read.

Angie launched into it. "In addition to the coat promotion, I've planned for wine night on Tuesdays, where all bottles would be half off; date night on Thursdays, where dinner would come with two movie tickets; and happy hour on Fridays and Saturdays. We could open the restaurant at three o'clock and serve drinks and free hors d'oeuvres until five o'clock. You know: antipasti, bruschetta, that kind of thing. My research indicates that a few happy hours a week could almost double our weekly gross. We're wasting our liquor license by using it for a drink here and there. And how's this: *Rediscover Romance at DeSaria's.* It's my ad tagline. I thought we could hand out roses to all the couples who come in."

"Holy shit," Mira muttered.

Angie knew what that meant: Her sister had come to the Big

Item. The menu change. "I want us to double the prices and cut half the items on the current menu. We need to do more with fresh fish and seasonal vegetables."

"Holy shit," Mira said again, looking up. "Papa would have loved all this, Ange."

"I know. It's Mama I'm worried about."

Mira laughed. "As we used to say, *duh*."

"How do I pitch these ideas to her?"

"From a distance, preferably wearing body armor."

"Funny."

"Okay, princess. There are two ways to get around Mama. The first and most obvious is to use Papa. Ultimately, she's always done anything to make him happy."

"Unfortunately, she's the one he's talking to."

"Yeah, so you'll need plan B. Make her think it's her idea. I did that when I wanted to go see Wings at the Kingdome. It took almost a month, but she finally decided I wouldn't be American enough if I didn't go with my friends."

"How do I do that?"

"It starts with asking for advice."

TEN

L AUREN STOOD IN THE CENTER OF THE DINING ROOM, STARING down at the collection of salt and pepper shakers she'd gathered together.

All night she'd been trying to figure out how to ask Angie for an advance on her first paycheck. Or to borrow a dress.

Either way she'd look like a real loser. Not to mention that the DeSarias might wonder what had happened to her tip money.

Drugs, Maria would say, shaking her head. *So sad.* No doubt she'd blame it all on Lauren's red hair.

If she told the truth—that she'd had to cough up back-due rent—Maria and Angie would give each other that startled *Oh, she's poor/how pathetic* look. Lauren had seen that look a hundred times in her life, from teachers and school counselors and neighbors.

She went to the window, stared out at the foggy night.

There were moments that mattered, that changed your life. Was a homecoming dance one of those memories that should be acquired at all costs? Would she be . . . lessened somehow by a failure to attend? Perhaps she should go in a vintage dress and pretend it was a fashion statement, an airy disregard for convention, instead of a response to her penniless life. They all knew she was on scholarship anyway. No one would say anything. But Lauren would *know*. All night she'd feel a little broken inside. Was the dance worth that?

These were questions a girl should ask her mother.

"Ha," Lauren said without a trace of humor.

As usual, she had to follow her own counsel. There were two choices. She could make up a lie . . . or she could ask Angie for help.

ANGIE SAT AT THE STAINLESS STEEL COUNTER. NOTES AND PAPERS were spread out in front of her.

Mama stood with her back to the sink, her arms crossed. It didn't take an expert to read her body language. Her eyes were narrowed and her mouth was a needle-thin line of displeasure.

Angie proceeded with the utmost caution. "I've spoken with Scott Forman at the theater. He's ready to give us a fifty percent discount on tickets if we include him in our ads."

Mama sniffed. "The movies are terrible these days. So much violence. It will upset people's stomachs."

"They'll be eating before the movie."

"Exactly."

Angie pressed forward. Business had really picked up since the inception of the coat drive. It was time to implement the rest of her plan. "Do you think it's a good idea?"

Mama shrugged. "We will see, I suppose."

"And the advertising—you think that's smart?"

"How much does it cost?"

Angie laid out the pricing sheets. Mama glanced at them but didn't move from her place at the sink. "Too much."

"I'll see if I can negotiate better pricing." She gently moved her notepad, revealing a menu from Cassiopeia's, the four-star Italian restaurant in Vancouver. "Do you have any suggestions for wine night?"

Mama sniffed. "We could talk to Victoria and Casey McClellan. They own that winery in Walla Walla. What's it called— Seven Hills? And Randy Finley up at Mount Baker Vineyards makes good wines. Maybe they would give us a good rate to feature their wines. Randy loves my osso bucco."

"That's a great idea, Mama." Angie made some more notes on her list. When she finished, she nudged the Cassiopeia's menu.

Mama craned her neck forward and tilted her head. "What's that?"

"What?" Angie bit back a smile. "Now, about the fresh fish. We—"

"Angela Rose, why do you have that menu?"

Angie feigned surprise. "This? I was just interested in our competition."

Mama waved her hand airily. "They have never even been to the old country, those people."

"Their pricing is interesting."

Mama looked at her. "How so?"

"The entrées start at $14.95 and go up from there." Angie paused, shaking her head. "It's sad that so many people equate high prices with quality."

"Give me that." Mama snatched the menu from the table and whipped it open. "Herbed pancakes with wild mushroom butter and pan-fried whitefish—for $21.95. This is not Italian. My mama, God rest her soul, made a *tonno al cartoccio*—tuna baked in parchment—that melted in your mouth."

"Terry has tuna on sale this week, Mama. Ahi, too. And his calamari steaks were beautiful."

"You are remembering your papa's favorite. *Calamari ripieni.* It takes the very best tomatoes."

"Johnny from the farmer's market promises me red heaven."

"Calamari and ahi are expensive."

"We could try it for a night or two—an advertised special. If it doesn't work, we can forget about it."

There was a knock at the door.

Angie swore under her breath. Mama was close to agreeing. Any little change could send them back to square one.

Lauren walked into the kitchen, clutching her neatly folded apron.

"Good night, Lauren," Angie said. "Lock up on your way out."

Lauren didn't move. She looked confused somehow, uncertain.

"Thank you, Lauren," Mama said. "Have a nice evening."

Lauren didn't move.

"What is it?" Angie asked.

"I . . . uh . . ." Lauren frowned. "I can work tomorrow night after all."

"Great," Angie said, going back to her notes. "See you at five."

The minute Lauren left, Angie returned to the discussion. "So, Mama, what do you think about upping the prices a little and adding a daily fish special?"

"I think my daughter is trying to change the menu that has been good enough for DeSaria's for years."

"Small changes, Mama. The kind that take us forward in time." She paused, loading the big gun. "Papa would have approved."

"He loved my *calamari ripieni*, it's true." Mama pushed away from the sink and sat down beside Angie. "I remember when your papa bought me the Cadillac. He was so proud of that car."

"But you wouldn't drive it."

Mama smiled. "Your papa thought I was crazy, ignoring that beautiful car. So one day he sold my Buick and left the new car keys on the table, along with a note that read: *Meet me for lunch. I'll bring the wine.*" She smiled. "He knew I had to be pushed into change."

"I don't want to push too hard."

"Yes, you do." Mama sighed. "Your whole life has been about pushing, Angela, getting what you want." She touched Angie's cheek. "Your papa loved that about you, and he'd be so proud of you right now."

Suddenly, Angie wasn't thinking about the menu at all. She was thinking about her father and all the things that she missed about him; the way he hefted her on his shoulders to watch the Thanksgiving Day parade, the way he said prayers with her at night and told silly, meaningless jokes at the breakfast table.

"So," Mama said, her eyes misty, too. "We will try a few specials this week and then we will see."

"It'll work, Mama. You'll see. Business will really pick up when the ads start. We're the front page of the entertainment section on Sunday."

"Already more people are coming. I must admit that. It's a good thing you hired that girl. She's been a good waitress," Mama said. "When you hired her—a redhead—I was sure we were in for trouble, and when you told me about the poor thing needing a dress, I thought—"

"Oh, *no.*" Angie shot to her feet. "The dance."

"What's the matter?"

"Tomorrow night is homecoming. That's why Lauren was hanging around in the kitchen. She wanted to remind me that she needed tomorrow night off."

"Then why did she say she'd work?"

"I don't know." Angie fished her car keys out of her pocket and grabbed her coat off the hook by the door. "Bye, Mama. See you tomorrow."

Angie hurried from the restaurant. Outside, a light rain was falling.

She looked up and down the street.

No Lauren.

She ran to the parking lot and got in her car, heading north on Driftwood. There wasn't another car on the road. She was about to turn onto the highway when she noticed the bus stop.

Light from a nearby streetlamp spilled down, giving everything a soft, amber glow. Even from this distance, she could see Lauren's copper-red hair.

She pulled up in front of her.

Lauren looked up slowly. Her eyes were red and swollen.

"Oh," she said, snapping upright when she saw Angie.

Angie hit the window button. The glass slid downward. Cold air immediately whooshed into the car. She leaned toward the passenger side. "Get in."

Lauren pointed behind her. "My bus is here. But thanks."

"Tomorrow is the dance, right?" Angie said. "That's what you were trying to tell me in the kitchen."

"Don't worry about it. I'm not going."

"Why not?"

Lauren looked away. "I don't feel like it."

Angie glanced down at the girl's old, too-worn shoes. "I offered to loan you a dress, remember?"

Lauren nodded.

"Do you need one?"

"Yes." The answer was barely audible.

"Okay. You be at the restaurant at three o'clock. Have you made arrangements to get dressed at a friend's house?"

Lauren shook her head.

"Would you like to get ready at my house? It might be fun."

"Really? I'd love that."

"Okay. Call David and tell him to pick you up at my house, 7998 Miracle Mile Road. It's the first driveway after the bridge."

The bus pulled up behind them and honked.

It wasn't until much later, when Angie walked into her dark, empty house, that she wondered whether she'd made a mistake.

Getting a girl ready for a dance was a mother's job.

THE NEXT MORNING ANGIE HIT THE GROUND RUNNING. AT SEVEN o'clock she and Mama met with suppliers and delivery men. By ten they'd ordered most of the week's food, checked the vegetables and fruits for freshness, made out the payroll checks, deposited money in the restaurant's account, and dropped the tablecloths off at the laundry. When Mama went off to do her own errands, Angie headed for the printers, where she had flyers and coupons made for wine night and date night. Then she dropped off the first batch of donated coats to Help-Your-Neighbor.

It started raining when she was at the dry cleaners. By noon it was a full-on rainstorm. The streets were a cauldron of boiling water. There was nothing new in that.

The weather this time of year was predictable. From now until early May it would be gray skies and raindrops. Sunlight in the coming months would be a rare and unexpected gift that couldn't be counted on and wouldn't last. Those who couldn't stand the continual shadow world of misty gray would find themselves waking in the middle of the night, restless, unable to sleep through the sound of rain on the roof.

She pulled up to the restaurant fifteen minutes late.

Lauren stood on the sidewalk beneath the restaurant's green and white awning. There was an old blue backpack on the sidewalk at her feet.

Angie rolled down the window. "Sorry I'm late."

"I'd thought you'd forgotten."

Angie wondered if anyone kept the promises made to this girl, or if, in fact, any promises were ever made.

"Get in," she said, opening the passenger door.

"Are you sure?"

Angie smiled. "Believe me, Lauren. I'm always sure. Livvy is covering my shift. Now get in."

Lauren did as she was told, shutting the door hard. Rain hammered the car, made it shake and rattle.

They drove in silence. The metronomic thwop-thwop-thwop of the wipers was so loud it didn't make sense to talk.

When they reached the cottage, Angie parked close to the front door.

Angie turned to Lauren. "Do you think we should call your mom? Maybe she'd like to join us."

Lauren laughed. It was a bitter, humorless sound. "I don't think so." She seemed to realize how harsh she'd sounded. She smiled and shrugged. "She's not one for dances."

Angie didn't go down the road of those words. She was this girl's boss; that was all. She was loaning a dress to Lauren. Just that.

"Okay. Let's go inside and see what I have."

Lauren launched herself sideways, threw her arms around Angie. Her smile was so big it swallowed her face, made her look about eleven years old. "Thank you, Angie. Oh, thank you."

LAUREN HADN'T GROWN UP ON MAKE-BELIEVE. UNLIKE MOST OF her friends, she'd spent her childhood hours watching television shows that featured shoot-outs and hookers and women in jeopardy. *Real life*, as her mother so often pointed out. There had been no cartoons in the Ribido apartment, no Disney specials. By the tender age of seven, Lauren knew that Prince Charming was a crock. When she lay in her narrow twin bed in her apartment that smelled vaguely of cigarettes and beer, she didn't dream of being Cinderella or Snow White. She'd never seen the point in the princess-swept-off-her-feet fantasy.

Until tonight.

Angie Malone had opened a door for Lauren on this night, and the view from its porch was staggering. It was a world that seemed bathed in sunlight and possibility.

First had come the dress. No, first had come the house.

"My papa built this place," Angie had said. "When I was a kid, we spent summers out here."

The house was tucked in among towering trees. The music of the distant surf filled the air.

A wraparound porch outlined the shingled, two-story cottage. Wicker rocking chairs were positioned carefully here and there; one could imagine sitting there, sipping hot cocoa on a day like today, watching the silver-tipped ocean below.

When Lauren saw the cottage, she stopped. This was the kind of home she'd always dreamed of.

"Lauren?" Angie had said, looking back at her.

Just looking at this home sparked a well of wanting.

"Sorry," Lauren said, lurching forward.

Inside, the house was every bit as perfect as the exterior had implied. Big overstuffed denim sofas faced each other in front of a river rock fireplace. An old green trunk was the coffee table.

The kitchen was small and cheery, with butter yellow cabinets and a picture window that looked past the porch to a rose garden. Huge fir trees ringed the property, made it feel worlds away from any neighbor.

"It's beautiful," Lauren whispered.

"Thanks. We like it. So," Angie said, bending down to light a fire. "What look do you want to go for?"

"Huh?"

Angie turned to face her. "Sexy? Innocent? Princess? What do you want to be tonight?"

"Any dress is okay."

"You need *serious* help in the girlfriend department. Perhaps even send-an-aid-car help. Come on." She walked past Lauren and headed up the narrow staircase. The steps creaked along the way.

Lauren rushed up behind her. They followed a slim hallway into an airy, lived-in-looking bedroom with a high-peaked white ceiling and whitewashed wood floors. A big four-poster bed dominated the room; on either side banged-up tables held reading lamps and piles of paperbacks.

Angie went to the walk-in closet and pulled the light cord. A single bulb hung overhead, casting a swinging beam of light onto rows of clothing.

"Let's see here. I brought only a few of my gowns. I was actually going to try selling them on eBay." She moved down to one end of the closet, where several yellow-beige Nordstrom garment bags hung smashed together.

Nordstrom.

Lauren had never owned anything from that venerable Seattle landmark. Heck, she couldn't afford a cup of coffee at the kiosk outside the store. She took a step back.

Angie unzipped a bag and pulled out a long black dress, then turned to her. "What do you think?"

The dress was halter style, with rhinestones at the throat and a double band of bigger stones at the waistline. The fabric was slippery. Silk probably.

"What do I think?" Lauren couldn't borrow something like that. What if she spilled on it?

"You're right. Too mature. This is a fun night." Angie dropped the dress on the floor and went back to garment bags, burrowing through them in a frenzy.

Lauren bent down and picked up the fallen gown. The material caressed her fingers. She'd never touched fabric so soft.

"Aha!" Angie withdrew another gown; pink this time, the dainty color of a scallop shell. The fabric was heavier, some kind of knit that could expand or contract to fit a woman's—or a girl's—body. It was a single sleeveless tank front with a deeply plunging back. "It has a built-in bra. Not that seventeen-year-old breasts need a bra."

Angie pulled out another dress; this one was emerald green with long sleeves and an off-the-shoulder neckline. It was gorgeous, but Lauren's gaze returned to the pink knit.

"How much did that one cost?" she dared to ask.

Angie glanced at the pink dress and smiled. "This old thing? I got it at the Rack. No, it was at that secondhand store on Capitol Hill."

Lauren couldn't help smiling. "Yeah, right."

"So it's the pink, yes?"

"I might damage it. I couldn't—"

"The pink." Angie hung the black and green dresses back up, then slung the pink one over her arm. "Shower time."

Lauren followed behind Angie as she tossed the gown on the bed, then headed for the master bathroom.

"Do you have shoes?"

Lauren nodded.

"What color?"

"Black."

"We can make that work," Angie said as she turned the shower on. "I could knit a sweater in the amount of time it takes to heat the water around here." She started grabbing bottles and jars from the cabinet. "This is an exfoliant. You know what that is, don't you?"

At Lauren's nod, Angie reached for something else.

"This is a hydrating mask. It helps my skin. Makes me look ten years younger."

"That would make me a kindergartner."

Angie laughed and shoved the products in Lauren's arms. "Take a shower, then we'll do your hair and makeup."

Lauren took the longest, most luxurious shower of her life. There were no pinging pipes, no water that came and went and suddenly turned cold. She used all the expensive products, and when she came out she felt brand-new. She dried her hair, then wrapped herself in a thick, oversized white towel and returned to the bedroom.

Angie was sitting on the edge of the bed. There was a pile of accessories around her—hairbrushes and makeup, curling irons and handbags and wraps. "I found a beaded black shawl and a black evening bag, and this!" She held up a beautiful pink and black butterfly hair clip. "Come on, sit down. My sisters and I used to do each other's hair for hours." She tossed a pillow onto the floor in front of her.

Lauren dutifully sat down, her back to the bed.

Angie immediately started brushing her hair. It felt so good Lauren actually sighed. She couldn't remember ever having her hair brushed. Even when her mother took the time to cut Lauren's hair, there was no brushing involved.

"Okay," Angie said after a while, "now sit on the bed."

Lauren changed positions. Angie knelt in front of her. "Close your eyes."

The whisper-soft touch of eye shadow . . . a flicking of blush.

"I'm going to put some sparkle on your throat. I bought it for my niece, but Mira said it was inappropriate . . . There," she said a moment later. "All done."

Lauren stood up and slipped into the dress. Angie zipped her up.

"Perfect," Angie said, sighing. "Go look."

Slowly, Lauren walked toward the full-length mirror that hung on the back of the closed door.

She gasped. The gown fit her beautifully, made her look like a princess from one of the storybooks she'd never read. For the first time in her life, she looked like all the other girls at school.

ELEVEN

ANGIE STOOD IN FRONT OF HER DRESSER. THE TOP DRAWER was open. There, buried among the bras and panties and socks, was her camera.

To take photos of my grandbabies, Mama had said when she'd given Angie the camera.

Babies, that smile of Mama's said, grow as naturally as green buds in springtime.

Angie sighed.

For years, she had used this camera all the time, documenting every moment of her life. She was there, year after year, snapping pictures at family gatherings—birthday parties, baby showers, preschool graduations. Somewhere along the way, it had begun to cause her pain, this looking through the viewfinder at a life she wanted desperately but couldn't have. One by one, she'd stopped photographing her nieces and nephews. It simply hurt too much

to see her loss in color. She knew it was selfish of her, and childish, too, but some lines couldn't be crossed. By the time little
Dani had been born—only five years ago now; it felt like a lifetime—Angie had put the camera away for good.

She grabbed the camera, refilled the film, and went downstairs.

Lauren stood at the fireplace with her back to the flames. The
golden glow wreathed her, gave her pale, freckled skin a bronze
sheen. The shell pink gown was a little too big on her, and a little
too long, but neither flaw was noticeable. With her hair coiled
into a French twist and held back by the butterfly clip, she looked
like a princess.

"You look beautiful," Angie said, coming into the room. She
was embarrassed by how much emotion she suddenly felt. It was
a little thing—helping a teenage girl get ready for a school dance;
nothing, really—so why did she feel so much?

"I know," Lauren said. There was wonder in her voice. Surprise.

Angie needed the distance of a viewfinder suddenly. She
started snapping photographs. She kept taking them, one after
another, until Lauren laughed and said: "Wait! Save some film for
David."

Angie felt like an idiot. "You're right. Have a seat. I'll get us
tea while we wait." She went into the kitchen.

"He said he'd be here at seven o'clock. We're going to the
club for dinner."

In the kitchen, Angie made two cups of tea, then carried
them into the living room. "The club, huh? Pretty hoity-toity."

Lauren giggled. She looked impossibly young just then,
perched as she was on the very edge of the sofa. Obviously she
was afraid to wrinkle her gown. She sipped her tea with extreme
care, holding the cup with two hands.

Angie felt a surge of emotion; she was afraid of what the
world could do to a girl like this, one who seemed sometimes to
be too alone.

"You're looking at me weird. Am I holding the cup wrong?"
Lauren asked.

"No." Angie quickly took another photograph. As she lowered the camera back to her lap, she met Lauren's starry-eyed
gaze. How could a mother not want to experience this moment?
"I guess you've gone to lots of school dances," she said. That was
probably the answer.

"Yeah. Most of them." Lauren didn't seem to really be listening, though. Her voice sounded distracted. Finally, she set down her teacup and said, "Can I ask you something?"

"Generally that's a question one should say no to. Often hell no."

"Really. Can I?"

"Fire away." Angie leaned back into the sofa's denim pillows.

"Why did you do all this for me tonight?"

"I like you, Lauren. That's all. I wanted to help."

"I think it's because you feel sorry for me."

Angie sighed. She knew she couldn't deflect the question. Lauren wanted a real answer. "That was part of it, maybe. Mostly, though . . . I know how it feels not to get what you want."

"*You?*"

Angie swallowed hard. A part of her wished she hadn't opened this particular door—and yet it had felt so natural to speak. Though now that she'd begun, she didn't know quite how to move forward. "I don't have children," she said.

"Why not?"

Angie actually appreciated the directness of the question. Women her own age tended to recognize the land mine in this conversation and walk gingerly around it. "The doctors don't know, exactly. I've been pregnant three times but . . ." She thought of Sophia and closed her eyes for a second, then went on. "No luck."

"So you *liked* helping me get ready?" There was a wistfulness in Lauren's voice that matched Angie's own emotions.

"I did," she answered softly. She was about to say something else when the doorbell rang.

"It's David," Lauren said, popping to her feet, running for the door.

"Stop!" Angie called out.

"What?"

"A lady is called when the date arrives. Go upstairs. I'll answer the door."

"Really?" Lauren's voice was barely above a whisper.

"Go."

As soon as Lauren was upstairs, Angie went to the front door and opened it.

David stood on the small porch. In a flawlessly cut black tuxedo with a white shirt and silver tie, he was every teenage girl's dream.

"You must be David. I've seen you drive up to the restaurant. I'm Angie Malone."

He shook her hand so hard she swore she felt the bones clamp together. "David Ryerson Haynes," he said, smiling nervously, looking past her.

Angie stepped back, ushered him inside. "Of the timber family?"

"That's us. Is Lauren ready?"

That explained the Porsche. She called out Lauren's name. Within a second she appeared at the top of the stairs.

David gasped. "Whoa," he said softly, moving toward the stairs. "You look awesome."

Lauren hurried downstairs and went to David. She looked up at him, her smile trembling. "You think so?"

He handed her a white wrist corsage, then kissed her.

Even from across the room Angie could see the gentleness of that kiss, and it made her smile.

"Come on, you two," she said. "Photo op. Stand by the fireplace."

Angie snapped several pictures. It took an act of will to stop. "Okay," she finally said. "Have fun. Drive safely."

She wasn't even sure they heard her. Lauren and David were lost in each other's eyes.

But at the front door, Lauren threw her arms around Angie, holding on in a death-grip hug. "I'll never forget this," she whispered. "Thank you."

Angie whispered back, "You're welcome," but her throat was suddenly tight and she wasn't sure if her words carried any sound or not.

She stood there as David led Lauren to the car and opened the door for her.

In the amount of time it took to wave, they were gone.

Angie backed into the house and closed the door. The silence seemed oppressive suddenly.

She'd forgotten how quiet her life was. Lately, if she didn't turn on the stereo, she would hear nothing except her own breathing or the patter of her own footsteps on the hardwood floor.

She felt herself slipping down a slope she knew too well; at the bottom it was lonely and cold.

She didn't want to go down there again. It had taken so long to crawl up. She wished she could call Conlan right now. He'd once been so good at talking her down from the ledge. But those days were gone, too.

The phone rang. *Thank God.* She ran to answer it. "Hello?" She was surprised at how ordinary her voice sounded. A drowning woman shouldn't speak in so certain a voice.

"How did the dance preparation go?" It was Mama.

"Great. She looked beautiful." Angie made herself laugh, prayed it sounded more natural than it felt.

"Are you okay?"

She loved her mother for asking. "I'm fine. I think I'll go to bed early. We'll talk in the morning, okay?"

"I love you, Angela."

"Love you, too, Mama."

She was trembling when she hung up. She thought about doing a lot of things—listening to music, reading a book, working on the new menu. In the end, though, she was too tired for any of it. She climbed into her big king-sized bed, pulled the covers up to her chin, and closed her eyes.

Sometime later, she woke up.

Someone was calling her name. She glanced at the clock. It wasn't yet nine o'clock.

She crawled out of bed and stumbled down the stairs.

Mama stood in the kitchen, her clothes dappled with raindrops, her red-splattered apron still in place. She put her hands on her hips. "You are not fine."

"I will be."

"I will be ninety someday. That doesn't mean getting there will be easy. Come." She took Angie by the hand and led her toward the sofa. They sat down, cuddled together the way they'd done when Angie was a girl. Mama stroked her hair.

"It was fun helping her get ready for the dance. It wasn't until later . . . after she'd left . . . that I started thinking about . . ."

"I know," Mama said gently. "It made you think of your daughter."

Angie sighed. Grief was like that; both she and Mama knew it well. It would sometimes feel fresh, no matter how long she lived. Some losses ran deep, and time moved too slowly in a lifetime to heal them completely.

"I lost a son once," Mama said into the silence that fell between them.

Angie gasped. "You never told us that."

"Some things are too difficult to speak of. He would have been my first."

"Why didn't you tell me?"

"I couldn't."

Angie felt her mother's pain. It connected them, that common loss, brought them to a place that felt like friendship.

"I wanted to say only hopeful things."

Angie stared down at her own hands. For a split second she was surprised to see that her wedding ring was gone.

"Be careful with this girl, Angela," her mother said gently.

It was the second time she'd been given this advice. Angie wondered if she could follow it.

SUNSHINE ON AN AUTUMN'S MORNING WAS A GIFT FROM GOD HIMself, as rare as pink diamonds in this part of the world.

Lauren took it as a sign.

She stretched lazily, coming awake. She could hear the hum of cars on the street. Next door, the neighbors were fighting. Somewhere, a car horn honked. In the bedroom down the hall, her mother was sleeping off a late-night bender.

To the rest of the world it was an ordinary Sunday morning.

Lauren rolled onto her side. The old mattress that had been her bed for as long as she could remember squeaked at the movement.

David lay sprawled on his back, his hair a tangled mess that obscured half his face. One arm hung off the side of the bed, the other was angled across his head. She could see the red smattering of pimples that dotted his hairline and the tiny zigzag scar that traced his cheekbone. He'd gotten that in sixth grade, playing touch football.

"I bled like a stuck pig," he always said when retelling the story. There was nothing he liked more than bragging about his injuries. She always teased him that he was a hypochondriac.

She touched the scar, traced it with the tip of her finger.

Last night had been perfect. Better than perfect. She'd felt like a princess, and when David led her out onto the stage, she'd practically floated along behind him. Aerosmith's "Angel" had been playing. She wondered how long she'd remember that. Would she tell their children the story? *Come on, kids; come listen to the story of the night Mommy was crowned homecoming queen.*

"I love you," David had whispered, holding her hand as the

tiara was placed on her head. She remembered looking at him then, seeing him through a blur of tears. She loved him so much it made her chest ache. She couldn't imagine being apart from him.

If they went to different colleges . . .

That was all it took, just the *thought* of different colleges, and she felt sick to her stomach.

David came awake slowly. When he saw her, he smiled. "I'll have to tell my folks I'm at Jared's more often."

He pulled her into his arms. She fit perfectly against him; it was as if they'd been built for each other.

This was what it would be like when they were at college together, and later, when they were married. She would never feel alone again. She kissed him, touched him. "My mom never wakes up till noon on Sunday," she said, smiling slowly.

He drew back. "My uncle Peter is meeting me at home in an hour. I have an appointment with some bigwig from Stanford."

She drew back. "On Sunday? I thought—"

"He's only in town for the weekend. You can come along."

Her smile faded, along with her romantic hopes for the day. "Yeah, right." If he'd really wanted her to come along, he would have asked her before now.

"Don't be that way."

"Come on, David. Quit dreaming. I'm not going to get a scholarship at Stanford, and I don't have Mommy and Daddy to write a check. You, however, could get into USC."

It was an old discussion. His heavy sigh showed that he was tired of it. "First of all, you *can* get into Stanford. Second of all, if you're at USC, we'll see each other plenty. We love each other, Lauren. It doesn't go away because of a few miles."

"A few hundred miles." She stared up at the tattered acoustical tile ceiling. A water stain blossomed across one corner. She wished she could smile. "I have to work today, anyway."

He pulled her closer, gave her one of those slow kisses that made her heart beat faster. She felt her anger dissolve. When he finally released her and got out of bed, she felt cold.

He gathered up the tux and redressed.

She sat up in bed with the blankets pulled across her bare breasts. "I had a great time last night."

He walked around the bed and sat down beside her. "You worry too much."

"Look around you, David." She heard the throatiness of her

voice. With anyone else, it would have been embarrassing. "I've always had to worry."

"Not about me. I love you."

"I know that." And she did. She believed it with every cell in her body. She clung to him, kissed him. "Good luck."

After he'd gone, Lauren sat there a long time, alone, staring at the open door. Finally, she got out of bed and took a hot shower, then dressed and walked down the hallway. She stopped at her mother's bedroom door. She could hear snoring coming from inside.

A familiar longing filled her. She touched the door, wondering if her mother had even thought about the dance last night.

Ask her.

Sometimes, in the early morning, when the sunlight slanted just so through the dusty blinds, Mom woke up almost happy. Maybe this would be one of those days; Lauren needed it to be. She knocked quietly and opened the door. "Mom?"

Her mother lay in bed, sprawled across the top of the blankets. In a flimsy old T-shirt, she looked spindly and too thin. She wasn't eating enough lately.

Lauren paused. It was one of those rare moments when she remembered how young her mother was. "Mom?" She went into the room and sat down on the edge of the bed.

Mom rolled onto her back. Without opening her eyes, she murmured, "What time is it?"

"Not even ten." She wanted to push the hair out of her mother's eyes, but she didn't dare. It was the kind of intimacy that could ruin everything.

Mom rubbed her eyes. "I feel like shit. Phoebe and I partied pretty hard last night." She grinned sleepily. "No surprise there."

Lauren leaned forward. "I'm the homecoming queen," she said quietly, still not quite believing it. She couldn't contain her smile.

"Huh?" Mom's eyes slid shut again.

"The dance? It was last night," Lauren said, but already she knew she'd lost her mother's attention. "Never mind."

"I think I'll call in sick today. I feel like shit." Mom rolled over again. Within seconds, she was snoring.

Lauren refused to be disappointed. It had been stupid to expect anything else. Some lessons should have been learned a long time ago.

With a sigh, she got to her feet.

. . .

AN HOUR LATER LAUREN WAS ON THE BUS, HEADING THROUGH town. The sun had disappeared again, tucked itself behind a rapidly darkening bank of clouds. By the time they reached the last stoplight, it had begun to rain.

It was still early on this Sunday morning. Few cars were parked in the angled slots, but the church lots were full.

It reminded her of a time, not so long ago, really, when she used to open her bedroom window on the Sabbath, rain or snow. The weather didn't matter. She used to lean out the window and listen to those pealing bells. She'd close her eyes and imagine how it must feel to get dressed up on Sunday and go to church. Her daydream was always the same: She saw a little girl with red hair, wearing a bright green dress, hurrying along behind a beautiful blond woman. Up ahead, a family waited for them.

Come along, Lauren, her imaginary mother always said, smiling gently as she reached out to hold her hand. *We don't want to be late.*

Lauren hadn't opened that window of hers in a long time. Now when she looked out, all she saw was the broken down building next door and Mrs. Sanchez's dented blue El Camino. Now she had that dream only at night.

The bus slowed, began to ease toward the stop. Lauren looked down at the shopping bag in her lap. She should have called first—that was how it was done in polite homes. You didn't just stop by, even to return something. Unfortunately, she didn't know Angie's phone number. And—if she were honest with herself at least—she needed not to be alone.

"Miracle Mile Road," the bus driver called out.

Lauren lurched to her feet and hurried down the aisle, trying not to knock into anyone, then went down the narrow steps and exited the bus.

The doors wheezed shut behind her, clanged. The bus drove on.

She stood there, clutching the bag to her chest, trying to protect it from the rain that fell like bits of icy glass.

The road stretched out in front of her, bordered on either side by towering cedar trees whose tips reached toward the gray underbelly of clouds. Here and there, mailboxes dotted the roadside, but other than that there were no signs of life. This was the time of year that belonged to the forest itself, a dank dark few weeks in which the hikers who dared to venture into this green-and-black wilderness could be lost until spring.

By the time she reached the driveway, it was raining in earnest—fast, cold, razor cuts hit her cheeks.

The house looked empty. No light came through the windows. Rain played a thumping beat on the roof, splashed in the puddles. Fortunately, Angie's car was in the carport.

She went to the door and knocked.

There was noise coming from inside. Music.

She knocked again. With every minute that passed, she lost a little more feeling in her hands. It was freezing out here.

After one last knock, she reached for the doorknob. To her surprise, the knob turned easily. She opened the door.

"Hello?" She stepped inside, closed the door behind her.

There were no lights on. Without sunshine, the room looked a little gloomy.

She noticed a purse on the kitchen counter; a pile of car keys lay beside it on the white Formica.

"Angie?" Lauren took off her shoes and socks and set the bag on the counter beside the purse.

She walked toward the living room, calling out Angie's name as she went.

The house was empty.

"Damn it," Lauren muttered. Now she'd have to walk all the way back to the bus stop and stand there in the freezing rain. She had no idea how often the number nine bus stopped at that corner.

Oh, well.

As long as she was here, she might as well return the dress to its proper place. She went upstairs.

The steps creaked beneath her weight. She looked back and saw the wet footprints trailing behind her.

Great. Now she'd have to clean the floor on her way out.

She stopped at the closed bedroom door and knocked just in case, although there was no way Angie was still asleep at ten-thirty in the morning.

She opened the door.

The room was dark. Heavy floral-print drapery blocked the windows.

Lauren felt around for a light switch, found it, and flicked it up. Light burst from the overhead fixture.

She hurried toward the closet and put the dress away, then stepped back into the bedroom.

Angie was sitting up in bed, frowning at her in a bleary-eyed, confused way. "Lauren?"

Embarrassment rooted her to the spot. Her cheeks burned. "I—uh—I'm sorry. I knocked. I thought—"

Angie gave her a tired smile. Her eyes were swollen and rimmed in red, as if she'd been crying. Tiny pink lines crisscrossed the upper ridge of her cheeks. Her long dark hair was a mess. All in all, she didn't look good. "It's fine, kiddo."

"I should leave."

"No!" Then, more softly: "I'd like it if you stayed." She lifted her chin to indicate the foot of the huge four-poster bed. "Sit."

"I'm all wet."

Angie shrugged. "Wet dries."

Lauren looked down at her bare feet. The skin was almost scarlet colored; the blue veins seemed pronounced. She climbed up onto the bed, stretched her legs out, and leaned against the footboard.

Angie tossed her a huge chenille pillow, then tucked an unbelievably soft blanket around her feet. "Tell me about last night."

The question released something in Lauren. For the first time all day her chest didn't ache. She wanted to launch into every romantic detail but something stopped her. It was the sadness in Angie's eyes. "You've been crying," Lauren said matter-of-factly.

"I'm old. This is how I look in the morning."

"First of all, it's ten-thirty. Practically afternoon. Secondly, I know about crying in your sleep."

Angie dropped her head back against the headboard and stared up at the white tongue-in-groove planked ceiling. It was a while before she spoke. "Sometimes I have bad days. Not often, but . . . you know . . . sometimes." She sighed again, then looked at Lauren. "Sometimes your life just doesn't turn out the way you dreamed it would. You're too young to know about that. It doesn't matter, anyway."

"You think I'm too young to understand disappointment?"

Angie looked at her for a long, quiet moment, then said, "No. I don't. But some things aren't helped by talking. So tell me about the dance. I've been dying for details."

Lauren wished she knew Angie better. If she did, she'd know

whether to drop the subject or keep it up. What mattered was saying the right thing to this sad, wonderful woman.

"Please," Angie said.

"The dance was perfect," Lauren finally said. "Everyone said I looked great."

"You did," Angie said, smiling now. It was the real thing, too, not that fake I'm-okay smile of before.

It made Lauren feel good, as if she'd given Angie something. "The decorations were cool, too. The theme was Winter Wonderland, and there was fake snow everywhere and mirrors that looked like frozen ponds. Oh, and Brad Gaggiany brought this fifth of rum. It was gone in, like, a minute."

Angie frowned. "Oh, good."

Lauren wished she hadn't revealed that. She'd gotten wrapped up in the pseudo-girlfriend moment. She'd forgotten she was speaking to an adult. Truthfully, she didn't have enough experience with it. She *never* talked to her mom about school events. "I hardly drank at all," she lied quickly.

"I'm glad to hear that. Drinking can make a girl do things she shouldn't."

Lauren heard the gentleness of Angie's advice. She couldn't help thinking about her own mother and how she would have launched right now into her own regrets, chief among them being motherhood.

"And guess what?" Lauren couldn't wait for Angie to guess. She said, "I was homecoming queen."

Angie smiled and clapped her hands. "That is *so* cool. Start talking, missy. I want to know *everything*."

For the next hour, they talked about the dance. By eleven-thirty, when it was time to go to the restaurant, Angie was laughing again.

TWELVE

THE PHONES HAD BEEN RINGING OFF THE HOOK ALL DAY. IT was the third Sunday in October, and in the tiny *West End Gazette*, a full-page ad had run on the front page of the so-called entertainment section.

Rediscover Romance @ DeSaria's.

The ad had detailed the changes—date night, wine night, happy hour—and included a number of coupons. Fifty percent off a bottle of wine. Free dessert with purchase of an entrée. A two-for-one lunch special, Monday through Thursday.

People who had forgotten all about DeSaria's were reminded of times gone by, of nights when they'd gone with their parents to the tiny trattoria on Driftwood Way. Most of them, it seemed, picked up the phone to make a reservation. For the first time in as many years as anyone at DeSaria's could remember, they were booked solid. The coat donation box was full almost to overflowing. Everyone, it seemed, wanted to take this opportunity to help their neighbors.

"I do not understand," Mama said as she washed the ahi steaks and laid them out on the waxed paper. "There is no way to know how many people will want fish tonight. It is a bad idea, Angela. Too expensive. We should make more cannelloni and lasagna." She'd said the same thing at least five times in the last hour.

Angie shot a wink at Mira, who was trying not to giggle. "If there were a nuclear war, we'd have enough lasagna in the freezer for the whole town, Mama."

"Do not make fun of war, Angela. Chop the parsley finer, Mira. We do not want our guests to speak with a tree stuck between their front teeth. Smaller."

Mira laughed and kept chopping the parsley.

Mama set out the parchment paper with exquisite care, then brushed olive oil on the surface. "Mira. Hand me the shallots."

Angie backed quietly out of the kitchen and returned to the dining room.

Five-fifteen and already they were more than half full. Rosa and Lauren were busy taking orders and pouring water for the guests.

Angie went from table to table, greeting people in the way she remembered her father doing. He'd always snap to attention at every table, straightening napkins, pulling out chairs for the ladies, calling out for "More water!"

She saw people she hadn't seen for years, and each person seemed to have a story to share about her father. She'd forgotten, in the focus of her own family's loss, how big a hole his absence had left in the community. When she was certain that every table was being handled well, she went back into the kitchen.

Mama was a wreck, a whirling dervish of nerves. "Eight fish specials already, and I ruined the first batch. It cooks so fast. The parchment exploded."

Mira was standing off to the side, chopping tomatoes. Clearly, she was trying to stay invisible.

Angie went to her mother, touched her shoulder. "Take a deep breath, Mama."

Her mother stopped, puffed her chest out in a heaving sigh, then caved inward. "I am old," she muttered. "Too old for—"

The door banged open. Livvy stood there, dressed in a knee-length pleated black skirt, a white blouse, and black boots. "Well, is it true? Did Mama change the menu?"

"Who called you?" Mira asked, wiping her hands on her apron.

"Mr. Tannen from the hardware store came into the cleaners. He'd heard it from Mr. Garcia, who works at the printers."

Mama studiously ignored her daughters. Bending forward, she seasoned the fish steaks with salt and pepper, dotted the tops with fresh thyme and parsley and chopped cherry tomatoes. Then she sealed each parchment package and set them on a cookie sheet, which she placed in the oven.

"It's true," Livvy whispered. "What is it?"

"*Tonno al cartoccio,*" Mama said with a sniff. "It is not a big deal. Over there I have halibut. I am making your Papa's favorite *rombo alle capperi e pomodoro.* The tomatoes were very good this week."

The oven beeper went off. Mama pulled the cookie sheet from the oven and dished up the plates. Tonight's ahi special was served with marinated roasted bell peppers, grilled zucchini, and homemade polenta. "What are you all staring at?" Just then Lauren and Rosa came into the kitchen. Mama handed them plates. When the waitresses left, Mama said airily, "I've been thinking about changing the menu for years. Change is a good thing. Your papa—God rest his soul—always said I could do anything with the menu except take off the lasagna." She made a shooing gesture with her hands. "Now quit standing around like log bumps and go out there. Lauren could use your help. Mira, go get more tomatoes."

When Livvy and Mira left, Mama laughed. "Come here," she said to Angie, opening her arms. "Your papa," she whispered, "he would be so proud of you."

Angie held her tightly. "He'd be proud of *us.*"

Late that night, when the final burst of guests had been served, and their dinner plates cleared away to make room for tiramisu and bowls full of rich zabaglione with fresh raspberries, Mama came out of the kitchen to see how her food had been received.

The guests, most of whom had known Maria for years, clapped at her arrival. Mr. Fortense yelled out, "Fabulous food!"

Mama smiled. "Thank you. And come back soon. Tomorrow I make asparagus-potato gnocchi with fresh tomatoes. It will make you weep." She looked at Angie. "It is my brilliant baby daughter's favorite dish."

WHEN THE LAST CUSTOMERS FINALLY LEFT AT TEN-THIRTY, LAUREN was exhausted. The tables had been full all night. A couple of times there had been lines at the door, even. Poor Rosa couldn't possibly keep up. For the first hour or so, Lauren had been going so fast she felt nervous and queasy. Then Angie's sister had shown up. Like an angel, Livvy swept in on a cloud of laughter and eased Lauren's burden.

Now Lauren stood by the reservation desk. Rosa had gone home at least an hour ago and the women were all in the kitchen. For the first time all night, Lauren could draw a relaxed breath. She pulled her tip money out of her apron pocket and counted it.

Twice.

She'd earned sixty-one dollars tonight. Suddenly it didn't matter that her feet hurt, her hands ached, and she had cramps. She was rich. A few more nights like this and she'd have all her application money.

She took off her apron and headed for the kitchen. She was halfway there when the swinging door burst open.

Livvy walked out first. Mira was right behind her. Though they looked nothing alike, there was no doubt they were sisters. Their gestures mirrored each other. They both had the same husky laugh as Angie. From another room, it was hard to tell their voices apart.

A sound clicked through the restaurant. The rich, velvety voice of Frank Sinatra snapped off.

Mira and Livvy stopped in tandem, cocked their heads.

Another song started. Loud. The sound of it was so unexpected it took Lauren a second to recognize it.

Bruce Springsteen.

"Glory Days."

I had a friend was a big baseball player
back in high school

Livvy let out a whoop and pushed her hands high in the air. She immediately started to dance with Mira, who moved awkwardly, as if she were getting electroshock treatments.

"I haven't danced since . . . jeez, I can't remember the last time I danced," Mira yelled to her sister over the music.

Livvy laughed. "That's obvious, big sister. You look like Elaine in that *Seinfeld* episode. You have got to get out more."

Mira bumped her sister, hip to hip.

Lauren watched in awe. These two sisters who had barely spoken all night were like different people now. Younger. Freer.

Connected.

The door burst open again. Angie came dancing out with her mother behind her, holding her. "Conga line," someone yelled.

Livvy and Mira fell in behind, holding on to one another. The four of them danced around the empty tables, pausing now and then to kick out their heels or throw back their heads.

It was incredibly dorky. Like something off some old people's TV show.

And heartbreakingly cool.

Lauren's stomach tightened. She didn't know how to react. All she knew was that she didn't belong here. She was an employee.

This was family.

She started to back away, edge toward the door.

"Oh no, you don't," Angie cried out.

Lauren stopped in her tracks, looked up. The conga line had broken up.

Mira and Livvy were dancing together. Maria stood in the corner, watching her daughters with a smile.

Angie rushed toward Lauren. "You can't leave yet. It's a party."

"I don't—"

Angie grabbed her hand, grinned at her.

The word—*belong*—was lost.

The music changed. "Crocodile Rock" blared through the speakers.

"Elton!" Livvy yelled. "We saw him at the Tacoma Dome, remember?"

And the dancing started again.

"Dance," Angie said, and before Lauren knew it she was in the middle of the crowd of women, dancing. By the third song— Billy Joel's "Uptown Girl"—Lauren was laughing as loudly as the rest of them.

For the next half an hour or so, she was enfolded in the warm raucousness of a loving family. They laughed, they danced, they talked endlessly about how busy the restaurant had been. Lauren loved every minute of it, and when the party broke up near midnight, she honestly hated to go home.

But there was no choice, of course. She offered to take the bus—an offer that was rejected almost instantly. Angie ushered her out to the car. They talked all the way and laughed often, but finally Lauren was home.

She trudged up the gloomy stairs toward her apartment, shifting her heavy backpack from one tired shoulder to the other.

The door to the apartment was open.

Inside, gray smoke hung in strands along the stained acoustical tile ceiling. Cigarette butts lay heaped in ashtrays on the coffee table and scattered here and there across the floor. An empty bottle of gin rolled slowly back and forth on the wobbly dining table, finally clunking onto the linoleum floor.

Lauren recognized the signs: two kinds of butts, and beer bottles on the kitchen counter. It didn't take a forensic team to analyze the crime scene. It was familiar territory.

Mom had picked up some loser (they were all losers) from the tavern and brought him home.

They were in her mother's bedroom now. She recognized the thumping rhythm of her mother's old Hollywood bed frame. Clang-clang-thump. Clang-clang-thump.

She hurried into her bedroom and closed the door. Moving quietly, not wanting anyone to know she was home, she grabbed her day planner and flipped it open. On today's date she wrote: *DeSaria Party.* She didn't ever want to forget it. She wanted to be able to look down at those two words and remember how tonight had felt.

She went into the bathroom and got ready for bed in record speed. The last thing she wanted was to bump into Him in the hallway.

She ran back to her room and slammed the door shut. Crawling into bed, she pulled the covers to her chin and stared up at the ceiling.

Memories of tonight filled her mind. A strange emotion came with the images; part happiness, part loss. She couldn't untangle it.

It was just a restaurant, she reminded herself. A place of employment.

Angie was her boss, not her—

mother.

There it was, the truth of the matter, the pea under her mattress. She'd felt alone for so long, and now—irrationally—she felt as if she belonged somewhere.

Even if it was a lie, which it certainly was, it felt better than the cold emptiness that was the truth.

She tried to stop thinking about it, to stop playing and replaying their conversations in her mind, but she couldn't let it go. At the end of the night, when they'd all been crowded around the fireplace, talking and laughing, Lauren had loosened up enough to tell the one joke she knew. Mira and Angie had laughed long and hard; Maria had said, "This make no sense. Why would the man say such a thing?" The question had made them all laugh harder, and Lauren most of all.

Remembering it made her want to cry.

THIRTEEN

OCTOBER RUSHED PAST, BUT IN NOVEMBER, LIFE SEEMED to move slowly again. One day bled into the next. It rained constantly, sometimes in howling, sheeting storms that turned the ocean into a whirlpool of sound and fury. More often than not, though, the moisture fell in beaded drops from a bloated, tired-looking sky.

For the past two weeks Lauren had been home as little as possible. *That man* was always there, drinking beer and smoking cigarettes and stinking up the air with his loserdom. Of course Mom was in love with him. He was precisely her type.

Lauren made a point of working at the restaurant almost every night and all day on weekends. Even though they'd hired another waitress, Lauren tried to keep her hours steady. When she wasn't working, she was at the school library or hanging out with David.

The only downside to earning all this money and improving her already stellar grades was that she was exhausted. Right now it was taking every scrap of her determination to stay awake in class. In the front of the room, Mr. Goldman was waxing poetic about the way Jackson Pollock used color.

To Lauren, the painting looked like something an angry child would make if handed a box of paints.

Electives.

That was practically all she was taking this year. She hadn't realized earlier, when she'd poured the heat on her accelerated studies, that by her senior year she'd have almost all of her requirements out of the way. As it was, she could technically graduate at the end of this semester. Trigonometry was the only class she had that mattered, and it wasn't even required for graduation.

When the bell rang, she slapped her book shut and shot out of her seat, moving into the laughing, shoving, talking crowd of students around her.

At the flagpole, she found David playing hacky sack with the guys. When he saw her, his face lit up. He reached for her and pulled her into his arms. For the first time all day she wasn't tired.

"I'm starving," someone said.

"Me, too."

Lauren looped an arm around David as he followed the crowd down the street to the Hamburger Haven that was their regular hangout.

Marci Morford dropped some money in the jukebox. Afroman's "Crazy Rap" immediately started to play.

Everyone groaned, and then laughed. Anna Lyons launched into a story about Mrs. Fiore, the home economics teacher, which got everyone arguing about how sucky it was to have to do actual homework in a skate class.

Lauren ordered a strawberry milkshake, a bacon burger, and fries.

It felt good to have money in her pocket. For years she'd pretended never to be hungry. Now she ate all the time.

"Jeez, Lo," Irene Herman laughed. "Way to pack it down. Do you have a buck I can borrow?"

"No problem." Lauren pulled a few dollars out of her jeans and handed it to her friend. "I *know* you want a milkshake, too."

That got everyone talking about how much they could eat.

"Hey," Kim said after a while, "did you guys get the notice about the California schools?"

Lauren looked up. "What notice?"

"They're having a big thing in Portland this weekend."

Portland. An hour and a half away. Lauren's heartbeat picked up. "That's cool." She slipped her hand into David's, squeezing gently. "We can go together," she said, looking at him.

David looked crestfallen. "I'm going to my grandma's this weekend," he said. "In Indiana. There's no way I can cancel. It's their anniversary party." He looked around the table. "Can one of you guys give Lauren a ride?"

One by one they all made their excuses.

Crap. Now she'd have to ride the bus. And as if that weren't bad enough, she'd have to go to yet another college fair as the only kid without a parent.

When the food was gone, the crowd drifted away, leaving Lauren and David alone at the table.

"Can you get there by yourself? Maybe I could fake a cold—"

"No. If I had grandparents, I'd love to go visiting." She felt a tiny sting at the confession. How often had she dreamed of going to Grandma's, or meeting a cousin? She would have done almost anything to meet an honest-to-God relative.

"I'll bet Angie would take you. She seemed pretty cool."

Lauren thought about that. Was it possible? Could she ask Angie for that big a favor? "Yeah," she said, just so David wouldn't worry. "I'll ask her."

David's remark stayed with Lauren all the rest of that day and into the next. She was unused to having someone of whom she could ask a favor. It would make her look vaguely pathetic, she knew, might even prompt questions about her mother. Normally that would be reason enough to just forget the whole thing and take the bus.

But Angie was different. She seemed to really care.

By the end of the week, Lauren still hadn't made up her mind. On Friday, she worked hard, moving quickly from table to table, keeping the customers happy. Whenever she could, she caught a glimpse of Angie, tried to gauge how a request would be received, but Angie was a butterfly all night, flitting from place to place, talking to each patron. Twice Lauren had started to ask the question, but on both times, she'd lost her nerve and turned away abruptly.

"Okay," Angie said as she was closing up the register for the night. "Spill the beans, kiddo."

Lauren was filling the salt shakers. At the question she flinched. Salt went flying across the table.

"That's bad luck," Angie said. "Throw some salt over your left shoulder. Quick."

Lauren pinched some salt between her thumb and forefinger and tossed it over her shoulder.

"Whew. That was close. We could have been struck by lightning. Now, what's on your mind?"

"Mind?"

"That space between your ears. You've been staring at me all night, following me around. I know you, Lauren. You have something you want to say. You need Saturday night off? The new waitress is working out. I could spare you if you and David have a date."

This was it. Now or never.

Lauren went back to her backpack and pulled out a flyer, which she handed to Angie.

"California schools . . . question-and-answer session . . . meet with representatives. Hmm." Angie looked up. "They didn't have any of this cool stuff when I was a kid. So you want Saturday off so you can go?"

"I-want-to-go-could-you-give-me-a-ride?" Lauren said it in a rush.

Angie frowned at her.

This had been a bad idea. Angie was giving her that *poor Lauren, so pathetic* look. "Never mind. I'll just take the day off, okay?" Lauren reached down for her backpack.

"I like Portland," Angie said.

Lauren looked up. "You do?"

"Sure."

"You'll take me?" Lauren said, almost afraid to believe it.

"Of course I'll take you. And Lauren? Don't be such a chicken next time. We're friends. Doing favors for each other comes with the territory."

Lauren was embarrassed by how much that meant to her. "Sure, Angie. Friends."

THE TRAFFIC FROM VANCOUVER TO PORTLAND WAS STOP-AND-GO. It wasn't until they were halfway across the bridge that connected Washington to Oregon that they realized why. This after-noon was the big UW–UO football game. The Huskies versus the Ducks. A rivalry that had gone on for years.

"We're going to be late," Angie said for at least the third time in the last twenty minutes. It was alarming how angry that made her. She'd undertaken the obligation to get Lauren to the ap-pointment on time and now they were going to be late.

"Don't worry about it, Angie. So we miss a few minutes. It's hardly a trauma."

Angie flicked on the turn signal and veered left onto their exit. *Finally.*

Once they were on the surface streets, the traffic eased. She zipped down one street and up the other, then pulled into an empty parking stall. "We're here." She looked at the dashboard clock. "Only seven minutes late. Let's run."

They raced across the parking lot and into the building.

The place was packed.

"Damn." Angie started to walk down to the front. They could sit on the step if nothing else. Lauren grabbed her hand, led her to a seat in the back row.

On stage there were about fifteen people seated behind a long conference table. A moderator was facilitating a discussion of entrance requirements, school selectivity, in-state to out-of-state student ratios.

Lauren wrote down every word in her day planner.

Angie felt a strange sort of pride. If she'd had a daughter, she would have wanted her to be just like Lauren. Smart. Ambitious. Dedicated.

For the next hour, Angie listened to one statistic after the other. By the end of the presentation she knew one thing for sure: She wouldn't have been accepted to UCLA these days. In her era, you'd needed to be breathing without a respirator and have a 3.0 grade point average. Now to get into Stanford you bet-ter have cured some disease or won the National Science Fair. Unless, of course, you were good at throwing leather balls. Then you needed a solid 1.7 grade point.

Lauren closed her notebook. "That's it," she said.

All around them, people were rising, moving toward the exit aisles. The combined conversation was a loud roar in the room.

"So, what did you find out?" Angie asked, staying in her seat. There was no point merging into the ambulatory traffic.

"That in the public schools almost ninety percent of the students come from in-state. And tuition is on its way up."

"Well, you're definitely having one of those the-glass-is-half-empty moments. That's not like you."

Lauren sighed. "It's tough sometimes . . . going to Fircrest Academy. All my friends are picking the schools *they* like. I have to figure out how to get the schools to like me."

"It sounds like the essay is a big part of that."

"Yeah."

"And recommendations."

"Yeah. Too bad I can't get, like, Jerry Brown or Arnold Schwarzenegger to write one for me. As it is, I hope Mr. Baxter—my math teacher—can rock their socks off. Unfortunately, he forgets where the blackboard is half of the time."

Angie glanced down at the stage. The folks from Loyola-Marymount, USC, and Santa Clara were still there. They were sitting at the tables, talking to one another.

"What's your first choice?" she asked Lauren.

"USC, I guess. It's David's second-choice school."

"I am not even going to get into the conversation about following your boyfriend to school. Okay, I lied. It's a bad idea. Don't follow your boyfriend to college. Now come on." She stood up.

Lauren put her day planner in her backpack and got up. "Where are you going?" she said when Angie headed downstairs instead of up.

She grabbed Lauren's hand. "We did not drive all this way to be in the peanut gallery."

Lauren tried to draw back, but Angie was a freight train. She went down the stairs, around the orchestra pit, and onto the stage. Dragging Lauren behind her, she marched up to the man from USC.

He looked up, smiled tiredly. No doubt he was used to mothers hauling their children on stage. There was no way for him to know that Angie wasn't a mom. "Hello. How can I help you?"

"I'm Angela Malone," she said, offering her hand. When he shook it, she said, "I'm a UCLA girl myself, but Lauren here has her heart set on SC. I can't imagine why."

The man laughed. "That's a new approach. Knocking my school." He looked at Lauren. "And who are you?"

She blushed deeply. "L-Lauren Ribido. Fircrest Academy."

"Ah. Good school. That helps." He smiled at her. "Don't be nervous. Why SC?"

"Journalism."

Angie hadn't known that. She smiled, feeling like a proud parent.

"Think you're the next Woodward or Bernstein, huh?" the man said. "How are your grades?"

"Top six percent of the class. About a 3.92 with lots of honors classes."

"SAT?"

"Last year I got a 1520. I took it again, though. Those scores aren't in."

"A score of 1520 is impressive enough. You do sports and volunteer in your community?"

"Yes."

"And she works twenty to twenty-five hours a week," Angie put in.

"Impressive."

Angie made her move. "Do you know William Layton?"

"The dean of the business school? Sure. He's from around here, isn't he?"

Angie nodded. "I went to school with his daughter. What if he wrote Lauren a recommendation?"

The man looked at Lauren, then pulled a small brass carrier out of his back pocket. "Here's my card. You send your app. to me personally. I'll shepherd it through." To Angie, he said, "A recommendation from Layton would really help."

LAUREN STILL COULDN'T BELIEVE IT. SHE KEPT BREAKING INTO laughter for no reason. Somewhere around Kelso, Angie had asked her to please stop saying thank you.

But how could she? For the first time in her life, she'd been treated like Someone.

She had a chance at USC. A chance.

She looked at Angie. "Thanks. I mean it," she said again, bouncing in her seat.

"I know. I know." Angie laughed. "You act like this is the first time anyone's ever done you a favor. It was nothing."

"Oh, it was something," Lauren said, feeling her smile fade. It meant so much to her, what Angie had done. For once, Lauren hadn't been on her own.

FOURTEEN

THE HIGH SCHOOL CAMPUS WAS BUZZING WITH TALK TODAY. It was the third week of November and the college admission application process was in high gear. Everyone was obsessed with college. It was in every conversation. Lauren had filled out all her financial aid and scholarship paperwork, gotten all her transcripts together, and written all her essays. And miracle of miracles, Angie had gotten her a recommendation from Dr. Layton at USC. She was beginning to believe she had a real shot at a scholarship.

"Did you hear about Andrew Wanamaker? His grandpa got him into Yale. Early decisions aren't even out yet and he knows." Kim Heltne leaned back against a tree, sighing. "If I don't get into Swarthmore, my dad will crap. He doesn't care that I hate snow."

They were all sitting in the quad, eating lunch, the "gang" who'd been best friends since freshman year.

"I'd kill for Swarthmore," Jared said, rubbing Kim's back. "I'm supposed to go to Stone Hill. Another private Catholic school. I'm afraid I'll go postal."

Lauren lay back, rested her head in David's lap. For once, the sun was shining and the grass was thick and dry. Even though it was cold out, the sun warmed her cheeks.

"It's Mom's alma mater for me," Susan said. "Yippee. William and Mary, here I come. This high school is bigger than the college."

"How's it going for you, Lauren? Any word on scholarships?" Kim asked.

Lauren shrugged. "I keep filling out the paperwork. One more why-I-deserve-it essay and I might scream."

"She'll get a full ride," David said. "Hell, she's the smartest kid in the school."

Lauren heard the pride in David's voice as he said it; normally that would have made her smile, but now, as she stared up at his chin, all she could think about was their future. He'd applied to Stanford, and it was a foregone conclusion that he'd be accepted. The thought of being separated from him chilled her more than the November weather, and he didn't seem to worry about it at all. He was sure of their love. How did a person come by that kind of certainty?

Kim opened her pop. It snapped and hissed. "I can't wait to be done with all this application crap."

Lauren closed her eyes. The conversation swirled around her, but she didn't join in.

She wasn't sure why, but suddenly she was on edge. Maybe it was the weather: cold and clear. Storms followed days like this, when the sky was scrubbed clean by clouds that raced from west to east. Or maybe it was the college talk. All she knew was that something was not right.

A FINE SILVER MIST CLUNG TO THE MORNING-WET GRASS. ANGIE SAT on the back porch, drinking her coffee and staring out to sea. The rhythmic whoosh-whoosh of the waves seemed as familiar and constant as the beating of her own heart.

Here was the soundtrack of her youth. The rumbling roar of the tides, the sound of raindrops hitting rhododendron leaves, the creaking whine of her rocking chair on the weathered porch floor.

The only thing missing was the sound of voices; children yelling at one another and giggling. She turned to say something to her husband, realizing a second too late that she was alone.

She got up slowly, went back inside for more coffee. She was just reaching for the pot when there was a knock on the door.

"Coming." She went to the door, answered it.

Her mother stood on the porch, wearing an ankle-length flannel nightgown and green rubber gardening clogs. "He wants me to go."

Angie frowned, shook her head. It looked as if Mama had been crying. "Come in out of the rain, Mama." She put an arm around her mother, led her to a place on the sofa. "Now, what's going on?"

Mama reached into her pocket, pulled out a rumpled white envelope. "He wants me to go."

"Who?" Angie took the envelope.

"Papa."

She opened it. Inside were two tickets to *The Phantom of the Opera*. Mama and Papa had always had seats at the Fifth Avenue Theater in downtown Seattle. It had been one of her father's rare indulgences.

"I was going to just let the date go past. I missed *The Producers* in July." Mama sighed, her shoulders caving downward. "But Papa thinks you and I should go."

Angie closed her eyes for a moment, seeing her father dressed in his best black suit, heading for the door. He'd adored musicals most of all, had always come home from them singing. *West Side Story* had been his favorite, of course. Tony and Maria. *That's your mama and me*, he always said, *except we love each other forever, eh, Maria?*

She slowly opened her eyes; saw the same play of bittersweet memories on her mother's face.

"It's a good idea," Angie said. "We'll make a night of it. Dinner at Palisades and a room at the Fairmont Olympic. It'll be good for us."

"Thank you," Mama said, her voice cracking. "That is what your papa said."

THE NEXT MORNING, LAUREN GOT UP EARLY AND MADE HERSELF breakfast, but when she stared down at the eggs on her plate, the thought of eating that runny pile of yellow goo was more than

she could bear. She pushed the plate away so fast the fork fell off
and clanged on the Formica table. For a second, she thought she
was going to throw up.

"What's wrong with you?"

Startled, she looked up. Mom stood in the doorway, dressed
in an obnoxiously short pink denim skirt and an old Black Sabbath T-shirt. The dark circles under her eyes were the size of
Samsonites. She was smoking a cigarette.

"Gee, Mom. It's nice to see you again. I thought you'd died in
your bedroom. Where's Prince Charming?"

Mom leaned against the doorway. There was a dreamy, self-
satisfied smile on her face. "This one is different."

Lauren wanted to say *As in different species?* But she held
back. She was in a crappy, irritable mood. It wouldn't do any
good to tangle with her mother. "You always say that. Jerry Eck-
strand was different, all right. And that guy who drove the VW
bus—what was his name? Dirk? He was *definitely* different."

"You're being a bitch." Mom took a long drag on her cigarette. As she exhaled, she nibbled on her thumbnail. "Are you
having your period?"

"No, but we're behind in the rent again and you seem to have
retired."

"Not that it's any of your business, but I might be falling in
love."

"The last time you said that, his name was Snake. God knows
you can never go wrong with a guy named after a reptile. You
pretty much know what you're getting."

"There is definitely something wrong with you." Mom
crossed the room and sat down on the sofa. She put her feet up
on the coffee table. "I really think this guy might be The One,
Lo."

Lauren thought she heard a crack in her mother's voice, but
that wasn't possible. Men had always drifted in and out of her
mother's life. Mostly out. She'd fallen in love with dozens of
them. They never stuck around for long.

"I was havin' drinks with Phoebe, and just gettin' ready to
leave, when Jake walked in." Mom sucked in a long drag on her
cigarette, exhaled. "He looked like a gunfighter, coming in to the
bar for a shoot-out. When the light hit his face, I thought for a
second it was Brad Pitt." She laughed. "The next morning,
o' course, when I woke up with him, he didn't look much like a
movie star. But he kissed me. In the light of day. A kiss."

Lauren felt the tiniest of openings between them. Such a moment was rare, and she couldn't help moving toward it. She sat down beside her mom. "You sound . . . different when you say his name."

For once, Mom didn't ease away. "I didn't think it would happen for me." She seemed to realize what she'd said, what she'd revealed, so she smiled. "I'm sure it's nothing."

"I guess I could say hi to him."

"Yeah. He thinks you're a figment of my imagination." Mom laughed. "Like I would pretend to have a kid."

Lauren couldn't believe she'd walked into it again. Or that it still hurt. She started to get up, but her mother stopped her. Actually touched her.

"And the sex. Holy shit, it's good." She took another drag, exhaled, smiling dreamily.

Smoke swirled around Lauren's face, clogged her nostrils. She gagged at the smell and felt her stomach rise.

She ran for the bathroom, where she threw up. Afterward, still shaky, she brushed her teeth and went back to the dining room table. "How many times do I have to ask you not to exhale your smoke in my face?"

Mom stabbed out the cigarette in the overloaded ashtray and stared at Lauren. "Puking is a new response."

Lauren grabbed her plate from the table and headed for the sink. "I gotta go. David and I are studying together tonight."

"Who's David?"

Lauren rolled her eyes. "Nice. I've been dating him for almost four years."

"Oh, him. The good-looking one." Mom gazed at her through the still-lingering smoke, and then took another drink of her Coke. For once, Lauren felt as if her mother were actually *seeing* her. "You have a lot going for you, Lauren. Trust me when I tell you that a hard dick can ruin everything."

"Yeah. I think Mrs. Brady said the same thing to Marcia."

Mom didn't laugh; neither did she look away. It was a long moment before she said softly, "You know what makes a girl throw up for no reason, don't you?"

"I CAN'T BELIEVE I LET YOU TALK ME INTO THIS DRESS," ANGIE SAID, studying herself in the mirror in their hotel room.

"I didn't talk you into it," Mama said from the bathroom. "I bought it for you."

Angie turned sideways, noticed how the red silk clung to her body. The dress Mama had chosen from the sale rack at Nordstrom was one Angie never would have bought for herself. Red was such a look-at-me color. Even more outrageous was the pure sexiness of the dress. Angie usually preferred classic elegance.

Normally, she would have refused to wear it, but she and her mother had had such a wonderful day. Lunch at the Georgian, facials at Gene Juarez's downtown spa, and shopping at Nordstrom. When Mama had seen this dress, she'd screamed and made a beeline.

At first Angie had thought it was just a joke. The dress was a scarlet halter-style with a plunging back. Thousands of tiny silver bugle beads glittered along the bodice. And even at seventy percent off, the price tag was hefty.

"You've got to be kidding," she said to her mother, shaking her head. "We're going to the theater, not the Oscar ceremony."

"You are a single woman now," Mama said, coming out of the bathroom, and though she was smiling, there was a sad knowing in her eyes. *Life changes,* that look said, *whether you want it to or not.* "Mr. Tannen at the hardware store said Tommy Matucci was asking about you."

Angie decided to let that pass. Hooking up with her high school boyfriend was not at the top of her to-do list. "So you think if I dress like an expensive hooker—or a Hollywood celebrity, which is pretty much the same thing—I'll find my way to a new life." Angie meant to sound flip, but when she got to the words *new life,* her smile shook.

"What I think," Mama said slowly, "is that it's time to look forward instead of back. You're doing a great job with the restaurant. Date night is a huge success. You've collected enough coats for most of the elementary school children in town. For now, be happy."

Angie knew it was good advice. "I love you, Mama. Have I told you that recently?"

"Not enough. Now let's go. Your father says we are late."

They made it to the theater in less than fifteen minutes. They passed through the doors, showed their tickets, and stepped into the crowded but beautiful lobby.

"He loved it here," Mama said, her voice thready. "He always bought one of those expensive programs, and he never threw them away. I still have a huge stack of them in the closet."

Angie put an arm around her mother, held her tightly.

"He would have led us right to the bar."

"And so we'll follow him." Angie led the way to the small area where cocktails were served. Elbowing her way through the crowd, she ordered two white wines. Glasses in hand, she and Mama sipped the wines and walked around the lobby, appreciating the gilded, baroque decor.

At seven-fifty, the lights flickered.

They hurried to their seats in the fourth row and sat down. The theater was filled with hushed noise—footsteps, whispered voices, people moving in the orchestra pit.

Then the show began.

For the next hour, the audience sat, enthralled, as the sad and beautiful story unfurled. At intermission, when the house lights came up, Angie turned to her mother. "What do you think?"

Mama was crying.

Angie understood. This music did that to you; it released your deepest emotions.

"He would have loved this one," Mama said. "I would have grown weary of the soundtrack."

Angie touched her mother's velvety soft hand. "You'll tell him all about it."

Mama turned to her. The old-fashioned glasses magnified her dark, teary eyes. "He won't talk to me so much anymore. He says, 'It's time, Maria.' I don't know what I'll do all alone."

Angie knew about that kind of loneliness. It hurt, sometimes more than you could bear, but there was no way to avoid it. You simply kept moving until it passed. "You'll never be alone, Mama. You have children and grandchildren and friends and family."

"It's not the same."

"No."

Mama's mouth creased sadly downward. They sat there, silent and remembering, until Mama said, "Would you get me something to drink?"

"Sure."

Angie sidled down the row of seats and merged into the crowd. At the door, she paused for a moment and looked back.

Mama was the only person left in the fourth row. She looked small from here, a little hunched. And she was talking to Papa.

Angie hurried across the lobby toward the bar. There were dozens of people clustered there.

That was when she saw him.

She drew in a deep breath and exhaled slowly.

He looked good.

Take your breath away and make your heart ache good.

But then, he'd always been the most handsome man she'd ever seen. She remembered the first time she'd ever seen him, all those years ago on Huntington Beach. She'd been trying to learn to surf and doing a terrible job of it. A huge wave had tumbled over her, sucked her under, and turned her around. She'd panicked and flailed, unable to tell which way was up. Then a hand had grabbed her by the wrist and pulled her to the surface. She'd found herself looking into the bluest pair of eyes she'd ever seen. . . .

"Conlan." She said his name quietly, as if maybe he wasn't really there and she was imagining him. She moved toward him.

He saw her.

They stared at each other, started to come together for a hug, and then backed off. They were like toys stuck in the pause mode, struggling to move.

"It's good to see you," he said.

"It's good to see you, too."

An awkward pause settled between them, and suddenly Angie wished she'd never walked over here, never said hello.

"How are you doing? Still in West End?"

"I'm good. It seems I have a knack for the restaurant biz. Who knew?"

"Your dad," he said, reminding her with those two words how much he knew about her.

"Yeah. Well. How's the news?"

"Good. I'm writing a series on the freeway killer. Maybe you've read it?"

She wished she could say yes. Once, she'd been his first reader on everything. "I kind of stick with local news these days."

"Oh."

Her heart was swelling now, starting to ache. It was beginning to hurt just standing so near him. She ought to leave while her dignity was intact. Instead, she found herself asking, "Are you by yourself?"

"No."

She nodded; it was more a jerking tilt of the chin. "Of course not. Well, I better—" She turned to go.

"Wait." He grabbed her wrist.

She stopped, looked down at his strong, tanned fingers, so stark against her pale wrist.

"How are you?" he asked, moving closer to her. "Really?"

She could smell his aftershave. It was the expensive Dolce & Gabbana brand she'd bought him for Christmas last year. She looked up at him, noticed a tiny patch of black on his jaw where he'd missed shaving. He'd always had that problem, he did everything in such a hurry. Angie had had to inspect his shave every morning. She wanted to reach up and touch his face, let her fingertip trail along his jaw. "I'm okay. Better than that, really. I like being in West End again."

"You always said you'd never go home."

"I said a lot of things. And I didn't say a lot of things."

She saw the change that came over his face. A terrible sorrow seemed to pull at his mouth. "Don't, Ange—"

"I miss you." She couldn't believe she'd said it. Before he could respond (or not), she forced a smile. "I've been hanging out with my sisters and being Auntie Angela again. It's fun."

He laughed, obviously relieved by the change of subject. "Let me guess: You've promised Jason to convince Mira that an eyebrow ring is okay."

For a second it was like the old days between them. The good old days. "Very funny. I would never think an eyebrow ring is okay. Although he *has* mentioned a tattoo."

"Conlan?"

Angie saw the blond thirty-something woman who'd come up to Conlan. She wore a plain navy dress and a strand of pearls. Not a hair was out of place. She looked like the owner of a small, exclusive boutique.

"Angie, this is Lara. Lara, Angie."

Angie forced a smile. It was probably absurdly overbright, but there was nothing she could do about that. "It's nice to meet you. Well. I'd better run." She started to rush away.

Conlan pulled her gently toward him. "I'm sorry," he said quietly.

"For what?" She made herself laugh.

"Call me sometime."

She held on to a smile by force of will. "Sure, Conlan. I'd love to run into you again. Bye."

FIFTEEN

T HE WORST PART ABOUT IT WAS THAT SHE'D ALMOST FOR-
gotten. At least, she believed she had, and in the end,
that was pretty much the same thing.

"Denial" was Mira's one-word answer to Angie's long, drawn-
out explanation of how she'd handled her emotions after the divorce.

It was, she thought, as good an observation as any. In the
months between May and November, she'd allowed herself to
think about several of her losses. Particularly her father's death
and the loss of her daughter and the subsequent realization that
there would be no babies. In fact, she was proud of the way she'd
handled her grief. Every now and then it had shocked her, pulled
her under its icy surface, but in each instance, she'd swum free.

The divorce somehow had been pushed aside, a little thing in
the presence of giants.

Now she saw the whole of it and she couldn't look away.

"There's nothing wrong with denial," she said to Mira, who stood at the stainless steel counter, making pasta.

"Maybe not, but it can fill up and explode one day. That's how people find themselves in McDonald's with a loaded handgun."

"Are you suggesting there's a felony in my future?"

"I'm pointing out that you can ignore your feelings for only so long."

"And I've reached the end of my time, huh?"

"Conlan was one of the good ones," Mira said gently.

Angie went to the window, stared out at the busy street. "I think *was* is the key word in that sentence."

"Some women choose to go after men they've accidentally let go."

"You make Conlan sound like a dog that broke its leash and ran. Should I put reward posters around Volunteer Park?"

Mira came around the counter and stood beside Angie, put a hand on her shoulder. Together they stared out the window. In the silvery pane, backed by night, they became a pair of watery faces. "I remember when you met Conlan."

"Enough," Angie said. She couldn't go down memory lane right now.

"I'm just saying—"

"I *know* what you're saying."

"Do you?"

"Of course." She gave her sister a tender smile, hoping it wasn't as sad as it felt. "Some things end, Mira."

"Love shouldn't be one of those things."

Angie wished she could be that naïve again, but innocence was one of the casualties of divorce. Maybe the first one. "I know," she answered, leaning against her sister. She didn't say what they both knew: that it happened every day.

LAUREN GOT OFF THE BUS ON SHOREWOOD STREET.

There it was in front of her: a bright, sprawling Safeway.

You know what makes a girl throw up for no reason, don't you?

She flipped the hood of her sweatshirt up and tried to lose herself in the soft, cottony folds. Looking down to avoid eye contact with anyone, she marched into the store, snagged a red basket, and headed straight for the "feminine needs" aisle.

She didn't bother pricing the tests; instead, she grabbed two boxes and tossed them in her basket, then ran to the magazine aisle, where she yanked a *U.S. News & World Report* out of the stack. The cover story was "How Colleges Compare."

Perfect.

She tossed it on top of her pregnancy tests and made a beeline for the checkout.

An hour later she was home again, sitting on the edge of the bathtub. She'd locked the door, but there had been no need. The sounds that came from her mother's bedroom were unmistakable: Mom wouldn't be bothering Lauren right now.

She stared down at the box. The fine print was hard to read; her hands were trembling as she opened the box.

"Please God." She didn't voice the rest of her plea. He knew what she wanted.

Or, more precisely, what she most fervently did not want.

ANGIE STOOD AT THE HOSTESS DESK, MAKING NOTES ON THE CALendar. For the last twenty-four hours she'd worked from sunup to sundown. Anything was better than thinking about Conlan.

She looked up and saw Lauren standing by the fireplace, staring into the flames. The restaurant was full of customers, and yet there Lauren stood, doing nothing. Angie went to her, touched the girl's shoulder.

Lauren turned, looking dazed. "What? Did you say something?"

"Are you okay?"

"Fine. Fine. I just needed something for table seven." She frowned as if she couldn't remember what she'd just said.

"Zabaglione."

"Huh?"

"Table seven. Mr. and Mrs. Rex Mayberry. They're waiting for zabaglione and cappuccino. And Bonnie Schmidt ordered a tiramisu."

Lauren's smile was pathetic. Her dark eyes remained dull, even sad. "That's right." She headed for the kitchen.

"Wait," Angie said.

Lauren paused, looked back.

"Mama made some extra *panna cotta*. You know how quickly it goes bad. Stay a few minutes after work and have some with me."

"I hardly need to eat fattening foods," Lauren said, and walked away.

For the next few hours, Angie watched Lauren closely, noticing the paleness of her skin, the woodenness of her smile. Several times she tried to make Lauren laugh, all to no avail. Something was definitely wrong. Maybe it was David. Or maybe she'd been rejected by a college.

By the time Angie had ushered out the final guest, said goodbye to Mama, Mira, and Rosa, and closed out the register, she was really worried.

Lauren stood at the big picture window, staring out at the night, her arms crossed tightly against her chest. Across the street, volunteers were busily hanging turkeys and pilgrim hats from the streetlamps. Next, Angie knew, they'd string thousands of Christmas lights for the celebration that followed Thanksgiving. The annual tree lighting ceremony was an event to be remembered. Hundreds of tourists came to town for it. The first Saturday in December. Angie had rarely missed it, not even during her married years. Some family traditions were inviolable.

Angie came up behind Lauren. "It's only a week until the first lighting celebration."

"Yeah."

She could see Lauren's face in the window; the reflection was pale and indistinct. "Do you guys go to the ceremony every year?"

"You guys?" Lauren uncrossed her arms.

"You and your mom."

Lauren made a sound that might have been a laugh. "Mommie Dearest isn't one to stand in line on a cold night to watch lights turn on."

A grown-up's words, Angie realized; the explanation given to a child who longed to see the Christmas lights. Angie wanted to place a hand on the girl's shoulder to let her know that she wasn't alone, but such an intimacy felt unwelcome right now. "Maybe you'd like to come with me. I should say with *us*. The DeSarias descend on the town like locusts. We eat hot dogs and sip hot cocoa and buy roasted chestnuts from the Rotary booth. It's hokey, I know, but—"

"No, thanks."

Angie heard a defensive edge in the girl's voice; beneath that, she heard heartache. She could also tell that Lauren was ready to bolt into the night, so she chose her words carefully. "What's wrong, honey?"

At the word *honey*, Lauren seemed to shrink. She made a sound and spun away from the window. "See yah."

"Lauren Ribido, you stop right there." Angie surprised herself. She hadn't known she had the Mom voice in her.

Lauren slowly turned to face Angie. "What do you want from me?"

Angie heard a well of pain in the girl's voice. She recognized every nuance of that sound. "I care about you, Lauren. Obviously you're upset. I'd like to help."

Lauren looked stricken. "Don't. Please."

"Don't what?"

"Be nice to me. I really can't take it tonight."

It was the sort of thing Angie understood, that kind of fragility. She hated that someone so young should be in such pain, but then again, what was adolescence if not acute confusion and overwhelming emotions? The whole thing was probably over a bad test score. Unless . . . "Did you and David break up?"

Lauren almost smiled. "Thanks for reminding me it could be worse."

"Put your coat on."

"Am I going somewhere?"

"You are."

Angie took a chance. She headed back to the kitchen for her coat. When she returned, Lauren was standing by the door, wearing her new green coat. Her backpack was slung over one shoulder.

"Come on," Angie said.

They walked side by side down the dark street. Every few feet an ornate iron streetlamp tossed light down on them. Normally, these streets would be deserted at ten-thirty on a weeknight, but tonight there were people everywhere, readying downtown for the holiday festivities. The chilly air smelled of burning wood and the ocean.

Angie stopped at the corner, where women from the local Soropotomist Club were giving away cups of hot cocoa.

"Would you like marshmallows?" the woman asked brightly, her breath a feathery white plume.

Angie smiled. "Sure."

Angie cupped her hands around the insulated cup. Warmth seeped into her fingers; steam wafted toward her face. She led

Lauren into the town square. They sat on a concrete bench. Even from this distance, you could hear the ocean. It was the heartbeat of the town, steady and even.

She glanced sideways at Lauren, who was staring gloomily into the cup. "You can talk to me, Lauren. I know I'm a grown-up, and therefore the enemy, but sometimes life throws you a curveball. It can help to talk to someone about your troubles."

"Troubles." Lauren repeated the word, made it sound small somehow. But that was part of the teen years, Angie knew. Everything seemed big.

"Come on, Lauren," Angie urged. "Let me help you."

At last, Lauren turned to her. "It's about David."

Of course it was. At seventeen, almost everything was about a boy. If he didn't call often enough, it could break your heart. If he talked to Melissa Sue at lunch, it could make you cry for hours.

Angie waited. If she had spoken, it would have been to tell Lauren that she was young and that someday David would be a fond memory of first love. Not what a teenager wanted to hear.

Finally, Lauren said, "How do you tell someone bad news? If you love them, I mean?"

"The important thing is that you're honest. Always. I learned that the hard way. I tried to spare my husband's feelings by lying to him. It ruined us." She looked at Lauren. "It's college, right?" Angie softened her voice, hoping it would take the sting out of her next words. "You're afraid you and David will be separated. But you haven't even heard back from the schools yet. You need all the facts before you react."

Overhead, the moon came out from behind a bank of clouds. The silvery light fell across Lauren's face, making her look older suddenly, wiser. Her plump cheeks were planed by shadow; her eyes seemed impossibly dark and full of secrets. "College," she said dully.

"Lauren? Are you okay?"

Lauren looked away quickly, as if to hide tears. "Yes. That's it. I'm afraid we'll be . . . separated." The word seemed almost too much for her.

Angie reached out, placed a hand on Lauren's shoulder. She noticed that the girl was trembling, and she didn't believe it was from the cold. "That's perfectly normal, Lauren. When I was a senior I was in love with Tommy. He—"

Lauren jumped up suddenly, pushed Angie's hand away. Moonlight traced the tear tracks on her cheeks. "I gotta go."

"Wait. At least let me drive you home."

"No." Lauren was crying now and not trying to hide it. "Thanks for the pep talk, but I need to get home now. I'll be at work tomorrow night. Don't worry."

With that, Lauren ran into the night.

Angie stood there, listening to the girl's footsteps until they faded away. She'd done something wrong tonight, either by commission or omission; she wasn't sure which. All she knew was that it had gone badly from the start. Whatever Angie had said, it was wrong.

"Maybe it's a good thing I never had kids," she said aloud.

Then she remembered her own teen years. She and Mama had engaged in daily knockdown, drag-out fights about everything from skirt length to heel height to curfews. Nothing Mama said had ever been right. Certainly her advice about sex, love, and drugs had fallen on deaf ears.

Maybe that had been Angie's mistake. She'd wanted so much to solve Lauren's problem, but perhaps that wasn't what the teenager wanted from her.

Next time, Angie vowed, she would just listen.

SIXTEEN

DATE NIGHT WAS A HUGE SUCCESS. IT SEEMED THAT MANY of the West Enders, young and old, had been looking for an excuse to go out for dinner and a movie. The weather had probably helped. This had been a gray and dismal November, and with Thanksgiving just around the corner, it didn't look like it would improve much. There wasn't a lot to do in a town like this on a cold and rainy night.

Angie moved from table to table, talking to their guests, making sure that Rosa and the new waitress, Carla, were getting the job done. She refilled water, delivered bread, and bused many of the tables herself.

Mama's specials had been especially good tonight. They'd run out of the risotto with mussels and saffron by eight, and it looked like the salmon over angel-hair pasta with roasted tomatoes and artichoke heart aioli wouldn't last another hour. It was surprising how good this success felt.

Angie had given that some thought lately. Ever since she'd seen Conlan, in fact. After all, she had a lot of time to think. In a small town, a single woman with no children and no romantic prospects had plenty of thinking time.

Once she began to contemplate her life, she couldn't seem to stop. She thought about the choice she'd made, so long ago, before she'd even been old enough to understand what truly mattered.

At sixteen she'd decided to be Someone. Perhaps because she'd grown up in a big family in a small town, or maybe because her father's adoration and respect meant so much to her. Even now she wasn't sure what had shaped her choices. She knew only that she'd longed for a different, faster, more sophisticated life. UCLA had been the beginning. No one else in her high school class had gone to college so far away; once there, she'd studied things that set her even farther apart from her high school friends and her family. Russian literature. Art history. Eastern religions. Philosophy. All of that learning had made her aware of the bigness of the world. She'd wanted to seize it all, experience it. And once you strapped yourself into a race car and roared onto the fast track, you forgot to slow down and see the scenery. Everything was a blur except the finish line.

Then she'd met Conlan.

She'd loved him so much. Enough to vow before God that she'd love no other man in this lifetime.

She wasn't sure when it had started to be too little, that love, when exactly she'd started to judge her life by what it lacked, but that had been the end result. It was ironic, really; love had set them in search of a child, and that search had depleted their ability to stay in love.

If only loss had brought them together instead of pulling them apart.

If only they'd been stronger.

These were the things she should have said to him at the theater. Instead, she'd acted like a silly teenager with an unreciprocated crush on the quarterback.

She was still thinking about it when the restaurant closed, so she poured herself a glass of wine and sat down by the fire. It was quiet in the restaurant now that everyone had gone. She saw no reason to go home. Here, she was comfortable. There, it was too easy to go down the dark road of feeling alone.

Alone.

She took a sip of wine, told herself the shiver she'd just felt had been caused by the fire's heat.

The kitchen door swung open. Mira walked into the dining room, looking tired.

"I thought you'd gone home," Angie said, pushing a chair toward her sister.

"I walked Mama out to her car. While we were standing in the rain, she decided to tell me that my teenage daughter is dressing like a hooker." She sank into the chair. "I'll take a glass of that wine."

Angie poured a glass, handed it to her sister. "All teenagers dress like that these days."

"That's what I told Mama. Her answer was, *You better tell Sarah that she is advertising a product she is too young to sell.* Oh. And that Papa would be spinning in his grave."

"Ah. The big guns."

Mira smiled tiredly, sipped her wine. "You don't look too happy, either."

She sighed. "I'm in trouble, Mira. Ever since I saw Conlan again—"

"You've been in trouble since the day you two split up. Everybody knows that except you."

"I miss him," Angie admitted quietly.

"So what are you going to do?"

"Do?"

"To get him back."

Just the sound of it hurt. "That train has left the station, Mira. It's too late."

"It's never too late until you're dead. Remember Kent John? When he dumped you, you waged a campaign that was for the record books."

Angie laughed. It was true. The poor guy hadn't stood a chance. She'd gone after him like a cold wind. "I was fifteen years old."

"Yeah, and now you're thirty-eight. Conlan's worth more than some high school jock. If you love him . . ." Like any good fisherman—and everyone in West End knew how to fish—Mira let the bait dangle.

"He doesn't love me anymore," Angie said quickly.

Mira looked at her. "Are you sure?"

. . .

IN HER WHOLE LIFE, THIS WAS THE FIRST TIME LAUREN HAD EVER skipped a whole day of school. But Angie had been right: Lauren needed facts, not just fear.

She sat stiffly in her window seat on a Greyhound bus, watching the landscape change. When she'd paid her fare and climbed aboard, it had been dark outside, predawn. Light was just creeping over the hills when the bus drove through Fircrest. There, it made several stops. At each one she tensed up, praying no one she knew got on. Thankfully, she was safe.

She closed her eyes finally, not wanting to watch the passing of miles. Each one took her closer to her destination.

You know what makes a girl throw up for no reason, don't you?

"I'm not," Lauren whispered, praying that it was true.

Those cheapo home pregnancy tests were wrong all the time. Everyone knew that.

She *couldn't* be pregnant. It didn't matter what that little strip had shown.

"Seventh and Gallen," the driver called out as the bus rattled to a stop.

Lauren grabbed her backpack and hurried off.

The cold hit her face. Damp, freezing air wrapped around her, made her draw in a sharp breath. Unlike at home, where the air smelled of pine trees and greenery and the salty tang of the sea, here it smelled citylike, of car exhaust and trapped air.

She flipped her collar up to protect her face and checked her directions, then walked the two blocks to Chester Street.

There it was: a squat, unadorned concrete block building with a flat roof.

Planned
Parenthood

What a joke. When you broke it down, she had no business being here at all. It should be called unplanned non-parenthood.

She let out a deep breath, realizing a second too late that she'd started to cry.

Stop it.

You're not pregnant. You're just making sure.

She walked briskly up the flagstone path to the building's front door. Without daring to pause, she opened the door, went through security, and entered the waiting room.

First, she saw the women—and the girls—who had arrived

before her. Not one of them looked pleased to be here. There were no men. Next she saw the dullness of it—gray walls, gray plastic chairs, industrial gray carpeting.

Lauren strode up to the front desk, where a receptionist smiled up at her.

"May I help you?" the woman asked, pulling a pen out of her bouffant hairdo.

Lauren leaned closer and whispered, "Ribido. I called about seeing a doctor."

The woman consulted paperwork. "Oh, yes. Pregnancy test."

Lauren flinched. The woman had practically screamed the word *pregnancy*. "Yes. That's right."

"Take a seat."

Lauren carefully avoided eye contact with anyone as she hurried to a chair and sat down. She bowed her head, let her hair fall across her face, and stared down at the backpack in her lap.

An endless wait later, a woman came into the room and called out Lauren's name.

She popped up and hurried forward. "I'm Lauren."

"Come with me," the woman said. "I'm Judy." They went into a small examining room. Judy directed Lauren to sit on the paper-covered exam table, then sat in a chair opposite her, clipboard in hand. "So, Lauren," Judy said, "you want a pregnancy test?"

"I'm sure I don't need it, but . . ." She tried to smile. "Better safe than sorry." Her smile faded. She waited for Judy to point out that if Lauren had been more safe, she wouldn't be worrying about being sorry now.

"Are you sexually active?"

She felt small and much too young to be here, answering these adult questions. "Yes."

"Do you practice safe sex?"

"Yes. Absolutely. I was with David for three years before I let him . . . you know . . . and we've only done it without a condom *once*."

Judy's face was filled with a sad understanding. "It only takes once, Lauren."

"I know." Now she felt miserable and stupid as well as small. "The thing is that one time was in the first week in October. I remember because it was after the Longview game. And my period that month was right on time."

"So why are you here today?"

"My period this month is late, and . . ." She couldn't say it out loud.

"And?"

"I did one of those home pregnancy tests. It showed positive. But they're wrong all the time, right?"

"They can be wrong, certainly. How heavy was last month's period?"

"Hardly noticeable. But it was there."

Judy looked at her. "Did you know that spotting can occur while you're pregnant? Sometimes it can seem like a period."

Lauren felt a chill move through her. "Oh."

"Well, let's get you tested and see where we stand."

LAUREN SHUT THE APARTMENT DOOR BEHIND HER.

Tossing her backpack onto the sofa, she headed down the hallway toward her mother's room. All the way home she'd been trying to figure what to say. Now that she was here, in their apartment that smelled of stale smoke, standing by her mother's halfway opened bedroom door, she was nowhere near an answer.

She was about to knock when she heard voices.

Perfect. *He* was here again.

"You remember the night we met?" he said in a gravelly, timeworn voice. All of Mom's boyfriends sounded like that, as if they'd been smoking unfiltered cigarettes since boyhood.

Still, it was a romantic question, surprisingly so. Lauren found herself leaning forward, straining to hear her mother's answer through the opening.

"Of course," Mom said. "How could I forget?"

"I told you I was in town for a few weeks. It's been a month."

"Oh." There was a surprising vulnerability in her mother's voice. "I knew that. Fun while it lasted and all that."

"Don't," he said softly.

Lauren leaned closer.

"Don't what?" Mom said.

"I'm no catch, Billie. I've done some bad shit in my life. I've hurt people. Especially the three women who've married me."

"You think I'm Mother Teresa?"

Lauren heard him cross the room. The mattress pinged beneath his weight. The headboard thumped against the wall.

"You'd be stupid to come with me when I leave town," he said.

Lauren gasped, heard her mother do the same.

"Are you asking me to come with you?" Mom asked.

"I guess I am."

"Lauren graduates in June. If you could—"

"I ain't the waitin' type, Billie."

There was a long pause, then her mother said, "It's too bad, Jake. Maybe we coulda . . . I don't know. Made something."

"Yeah," he said. "Bad timing."

Lauren heard him get to his feet and walk toward the door.

She stumbled back into the living room, trying to look as if she'd just gotten home.

Jake came hurrying out of the bedroom. When he saw Lauren, he stopped. Smiled.

It was the first time Lauren had actually seen him. He was tall—maybe six foot three—with long blond hair. He was dressed in biker clothes—worn black leather pants, heavy black boots, and a concho-encrusted black leather coat. His face reminded her of the craggy mountains in the National Forest, rough and harsh. There was no softness in his face; it was all sharp angles and deep hollows. At his throat, a multicolored tattoo coiled up from the skin beneath his collar. It was a tail. Dragon or snake, probably.

If trouble had a face, this was it.

"Hey, kid," he said, nodding, already moving past her.

She watched him leave the apartment, then looked back at Mom's bedroom. She took a few steps toward the door, then paused.

Maybe this wasn't a good time.

The bedroom door cracked open. Mom came stumbling out of the room, swearing as she brushed past Lauren. "Where are my damn cigarettes?"

"On the coffee table."

"Thanks. Man, I feel like shit. Too much partying last night." Mom looked down at a pile of pizza boxes on the counter, smiling when she found her cigarettes. "You're home early. What gives?"

"I'm pregnant."

Mom looked up sharply. The cigarette dangled from her mouth, unlit. "Tell me you're kidding."

Lauren moved closer. She couldn't help herself. No matter how often she'd been disappointed in the past, she always believed—or hoped—that *this time* would be different, and right now she longed to be held and comforted, to be told, *It's okay, honey*, even though she knew it would be a lie. "I'm pregnant," she said, softer this time.

Mom slapped her across the face. Hard. They both looked stunned by the suddenness of the movement.

Lauren gasped. Her cheek stung like hell, but it was Mom who had tears in her eyes.

"Don't cry," Lauren said. "Please."

Mom stood there, staring at her, that cigarette still dangling from her mouth.

In her pink, low-rise pants and cropped white shirt, she should have looked like a teenager. Instead, she looked like a disappointed old woman. "Didn't you learn anything from me?" She leaned back against the rough stucco wall.

Lauren went to stand beside her. Their shoulders touched, but neither one reached for the other. Lauren stared dully at the messy kitchen, trying to remember what she'd even hoped her mother would say. "I need your help."

"Doing what?"

All her life Lauren had felt alone in her mother's presence, but never more than now. "I don't know."

Mom turned to her. The sadness in her makeup-smeared eyes was worse than the slap. "Get rid of it," she said tiredly. "Don't let one mistake ruin everything for you."

"Was that all I ever was? Just your mistake?"

"Look at me. Is this the life you want?"

Lauren swallowed hard, wiped her eyes. "It's a baby, not . . . nothing. What if I wanted to keep it? Would you help me?"

"No."

"No? Just like that, no?"

At last her mother touched her. It was sad and soft and hardly lasted any time at all. "I paid for my mistake. I'm not paying for yours. Trust me on this. Have an abortion. Give yourself a chance in life."

ARE YOU SURE?

The question had kept Angie wide awake last night.

"Damn you, Mira," she muttered.

"What was that?" Mama said, coming up behind her. They were in Mama's kitchen at home now, making pies for Thanksgiving.

"Nothing, Mama."

"You have been muttering since you got here. I think you have something to say. Put those pecans on neatly, Angela. No one wants to eat a pie that's a mess."

"I don't know what the hell I'm doing." Angie tossed the bag of pecans on the counter and went outside. On the deck there was dew everywhere, clinging to the rails and floorboards. The lawn was as thick and soft as a layer of Christmas velvet.

She heard the sliding door open. Close.

Mama came up beside her, stood at her side, looking down at the bare rose garden. "You weren't talking about the pecans."

Angie rubbed her eyes and sighed. "I saw Conlan in Seattle."

"It's about time you tell me."

"Mira blabbed, huh?"

"*Shared* is the word I would use. She was worried about you. As I am."

Angie put her hands on the cold wooden railing and leaned forward. For a second, she thought she heard the ocean in the distance, then she realized that it was a jet flying overhead. She sighed, wanting to ask her mother how she'd gotten to this place in her life, a thirty-eight-year-old single, childless woman. But she knew. She'd let love slip through her fingers. "I feel lost."

"So what will you do now?"

"I don't know. Mira asked me the same thing."

"She has brilliance in her genes, that girl. And?"

"Maybe I'll call him," she said, allowing herself to think it for the first time.

"That would work. Of course, if it were me, I'd want to look in his eyes. Only then can you know."

"He could just walk away."

Mama looked stunned. "You hear this, Papa? Your Angela is being a coward. This is not the child I know."

"I've taken some hits in the past few years, Mama." She tried to smile. "I'm not as strong as I used to be."

"That's not true. The old Angela was broken by her losses. This new daughter of mine isn't afraid."

Angie turned, looked into her mother's deep, dark eyes. The whole of her life was reflected back at her. She smelled Mama's Aqua Net hair spray and Tabu perfume. It was comforting suddenly to be standing here on this deck, above this yard, with this woman. It reminded her that however much life changed, a part of it stayed the same.

Family.

It was ironic. She'd run all the way to California to put distance between her and her family. She should have known that such a thing was impossible. This family was in her blood and her bones. They were with her always, even her papa who'd gone away . . . and yet would always be on this deck on a cold autumn morning.

"I'm glad I came home, Mama. I didn't even know how much I missed you all."

Mama smiled. "We knew. Now get those pies in the oven. We have a lot more baking to do."

SEVENTEEN

THE WAISTBAND OF LAUREN'S SCHOOL UNIFORM WAS AS loose as usual; still, it didn't fit somehow. She looked at herself in the mirror and tried to tell herself that no one could tell. She felt like Hester Prynne, only the letter was a scarlet P on her stomach.

She washed and dried her hands and left the bathroom.

Classes were just getting out for the day. Students rushed past her in laughing, chattering pods of red-and-black plaid. On the last school day before a holiday, it was always this loud. She lost track of how many kids called out to her. It seemed impossible they couldn't see how different she was now, how separate.

"Lo!" David called out to her, loping forward, his backpack dragging on the ground beside him. He dropped it when he reached her, pulled her into his arms for a hug.

She clung to him. When she finally drew back, she was trembling.

"Where were you?" he asked, nuzzling her throat.

"Can we go somewhere to talk?"

"You heard, didn't you? Damn it, I *told* everyone I wanted to surprise you."

She looked up at him, noticing suddenly how bright his eyes were, how broad his smile. He looked ready to start laughing at any moment. "I don't know what you're talking about."

"Really?" If possible, his smile grew. He grabbed her hand and pulled her along behind him. They ran past the cafeteria and the library, then ducked into a shadowy alcove near the music room. The marching band was practicing. The staccato notes of "Tequila" stuttered onto the cold afternoon air.

He kissed her hard, then drew back, grinning. "Here."

She stared down at the envelope in his hand. It had been ripped open. The upper edge was tattered. She took it from him and saw the return address.

Stanford University.

She barely breathed as she withdrew the letter and read the first line. *Dear Mr. Haynes: We are pleased to offer you a place of admission . . .*

Tears made it impossible to read the rest.

"Isn't it great?" he said, taking the letter from her. "Early decision rocks."

"It's so early . . . no one else knows yet."

"I guess I'm just lucky."

Lucky. Yeah. "Wow," she said, unable to look at him. There was no way she could tell him now.

"This is the beginning, Lauren. You'll get into USC or Berkeley, and we'll be on our way. We'll be together every weekend. And holidays."

She finally looked up at him. It felt as if miles separated them now, a distance as big as an ocean. Different colleges hardly seemed to matter. "You're leaving tonight, aren't you?" Even to her own ears, her voice sounded dull, wooden.

"Thanksgiving at Uncle Frederick's." He pulled her into his arms and held her tightly, whispering, "It's only through the weekend. Then we can celebrate."

She wanted to be happy for him. *Stanford.* It was what he'd dreamed of. "I'm proud of you, David."

"I love you, Lauren."

It was true. He loved her. And not in that silly high school I-just-want-to-get-laid way, either.

Yesterday that would have been enough; today she saw things differently.

It was easy to love someone when life was uncomplicated.

Last week Lauren's biggest fear—and it had seemed Incredible Hulk big—had been not getting in to Stanford. Today that was the least of her worries. Soon, she would have to tell David about the baby, and from that moment on, nothing would be easy. Love least of all.

SOMEHOW LAUREN MADE IT THROUGH HER WEDNESDAY SHIFT AT the restaurant. Truthfully, she wasn't sure how she did it. Her mind was crammed so full, it didn't seem possible that she could remember a single order, let alone dozens.

"Lauren?"

She turned, found Angie standing there, smiling at her with a worried look in her eyes.

"We want you and your mother to come to Mama's house for Thanksgiving dinner."

"Oh." Lauren hoped her longing didn't show.

Angie moved closer. "We'd really like you to be there."

All her life she'd waited for an invitation like this. "I . . ." She couldn't seem to say no. "My mom isn't one for parties." *Unless you're offering gin and pot.*

"If she's busy, come by yourself. Just think about it. Please? Everyone will get to Mama's around one o'clock." Angie handed Lauren a slip of paper. "Here's the address. It would mean a lot to us if you were there. You work at DeSaria's. That makes you family."

ON THANKSGIVING, WHEN LAUREN WOKE UP, HER VERY FIRST thought was: *You work at DeSaria's. That makes you family.*

For once, she had somewhere to go on this holiday, but how could she go there now, ruined and stupid? Angie would take one look at her and know. Lauren had been dreading that moment from the second she found out she was pregnant.

She was still pacing the apartment at eleven when the phone rang. She answered on the first ring. "Hello?"

"Lauren? It's Angie."

"Oh. Hi."

"I wondered if you needed a ride today. It looks like it might rain and I know that your mom's car isn't running."

Lauren sighed. It was a sound of pure longing. "No. Thanks."

"You'll be here at one o'clock, right?"

The question was asked so softly Lauren couldn't say no. She wanted it too much. "Sure. One o'clock." When she hung up, she went to her mom's room and stood by the door, listening. It was quiet. Finally, she knocked. "Mom?"

There was the pinging of bedsprings, then footsteps. The door opened. Mom stood there, bleary-eyed and ashen-skinned, wearing a knee-length T-shirt that advertised a tavern. The slogan was *Alcoholics serving alcoholics for 89 years.* "Yeah?"

"It's Thanksgiving, remember? We're invited to dinner."

Mom reached sideways for a pack of smokes. Lit one up. "Oh, yeah. Your boss. I thought you weren't sure."

"I . . . I'd like to go."

Mom glanced behind her—at the man in the bed, no doubt. "I think I'll hang around here."

"But—"

"You go. Have a good time. I'm not one for big to-dos, anyway. You know that."

"They invited both of us. It'll be embarrassing to show up alone."

Mom exhaled smoke and smiled. "No more embarrassing than showing up with me." She looked pointedly at Lauren's stomach. "Besides, you're not alone anymore."

The door closed.

Lauren walked back to her bedroom. By twelve-fifteen, she'd pulled out three outfits and changed her mind on each one. The truth was, she was thankful for the distraction of clothes. It kept her mind occupied, gave her something to think about beside the pregnancy.

Finally, she ran out of time and wore the outfit she had on: a flowing Indian print gauze skirt, a white T-shirt with black lace at the neckline, and the coat Angie had given her. She straightened her hair and brushed it back into a ponytail, then dabbed on a tiny amount of makeup, just enough to give her pale cheeks and even paler eyelashes some color.

She caught the twelve forty-five crosstown bus.

She was the only passenger on this Thanksgiving Day. There

was something sad in it, she supposed, the very portrait of a human being without family.

Then again, it meant she had somewhere to go. Better than the people who sat home alone today, eating dinners from tinfoil trays and watching movies that made you ache for what you didn't have. All the holiday specials were like that. The movies, the parades; they all showed families coming together, enjoying the day, enjoying each other. Mothers holding . . .

babies.

Lauren sighed heavily.

It was always right there, buoyant as a cork, ready to pop to the surface of her thoughts.

"Not today," she said aloud. Why not talk to herself? There was no one here to laugh about it and scoot nervously sideways.

This would be her first ever family Thanksgiving. She'd waited a lifetime for it. She refused to let the baby ruin it for her.

At the corner of Maple Drive and Sentinel, she exited the bus. Outside, the sky was lead pipe gray. It looked more like evening than midday. Wind scraped along the ground, swirling up blackened leaves and shaking the bare trees. It wasn't raining yet, but it soon would be. A storm was coming.

She buttoned her coat against the cold and hurried down the street, reading house numbers along the way, although she hadn't needed to. When she came to the DeSaria house, she knew it instantly. The yard was perfectly trimmed and cared for. Purple cabbagelike flowers bloomed along the walkway, created a stream of color against the winter-dead ground.

The house was a beautiful Tudor-style home with leaded glass windows and a slanting shake roof and an arching brick entrance. A statue of Jesus stood by the door, his hands outstretched in greeting.

She walked down the cement path, past a fountain of the Virgin Mary, and knocked on the door.

There was no answer, though she could hear a commotion going on inside.

She rang the bell.

Again, nothing. She was about to turn and leave when the door suddenly flew open.

A tiny, blond-haired girl stood there, looking up. She wore a pretty black velvet dress with white trim.

"Who are you?" the girl asked.

"I'm Lauren. Angie invited me to dinner."

"Oh." The girl smiled at her, then turned and ran.

Lauren stood there, confused. Cold air breezed up the back of her skirt, reminding her to shut the door.

Cautiously, she walked through the tiny foyer and paused at the edge of the living room.

It was pandemonium. There had to be at least twenty people in there. Three men stood in the corner by the picture window, drinking cocktails and talking animatedly as they watched a football game. Several teenagers sat at a game table, playing cards. They were laughing and yelling at one another. Some small kids lay on the carpet, sprawled out around the Candy Land board game like spokes on a wheel.

Afraid to walk through the crowd, she backed away from the doorway and turned around. On the other end of the small foyer was another room. In it, a few older people were watching television.

Lauren hurried through, holding her breath. No one asked who she was, and then she found herself at the doorway to the kitchen.

The aroma hit her first.

Pure heaven.

Then she saw the women. They were working together in the kitchen. Mira was peeling potatoes, Livvy was arranging antipasti on an ornate silver tray, Angie was chopping vegetables, and Maria was rolling out pasta.

They were all talking at once, and laughing often. Lauren could make out only snippets of the conversation.

"Lauren!" Angie cried out, looking up from the mound of vegetables. "You made it."

"Thanks for the invitation." She realized suddenly that she should have brought something, like a bunch of flowers.

Angie looked behind her. "Where's your mom?"

Lauren felt herself blush. "She . . . uh . . . has the flu."

"Well, we're glad you're here."

The next thing Lauren knew, she was surrounded by women. For the next hour, she worked in the kitchen. She helped Livvy set the tables, helped Mira set out the antipasto trays in the living room, and helped Angie wash dishes.

At any given time, there were at least five people in the kitchen. When they set about the task of serving, there was double that number. Everyone seemed to know exactly what to do. The women moved like synchronized swimmers, serving food and carrying platters from one room to the other. When it was finally time to sit down, Lauren found herself seated at the adult table, between Mira and Sal.

She'd never seen so much food in her life. There was the turkey, of course, and two bowls of dressing—one from inside the bird and one from outside—mounds of mashed potatoes and boats of gravy, green beans with onion, garlic and pancetta, risotto with Parmesan cheese and prosciutto, homemade pasta in capon broth, roasted stuffed vegetables, and homemade bread.

"It's obscene, isn't it?" Mira said, leaning close, laughing.

"It's beautiful," Lauren answered wistfully.

At the head of the table, Maria led them all in a prayer that ended with family blessings. Then she stood up. "It is my first Thanksgiving in Papa's chair." She paused, closed her eyes tightly. "Somewhere he is thinking how much he loves us all."

When she opened her eyes, they were full of tears. "Eat," she said, sitting down abruptly. After a moment of silence, the conversations started up again.

Mira reached for the platter of sliced turkey meat and offered it to Lauren. "Here. Youth before beauty." She laughed.

Lauren started with the turkey and didn't stop there. She filled her plate until it was heaped with food. Each bite was more delicious than the last.

"How are your college applications going?" Mira asked, taking a sip of white wine.

"I've mailed them all out." She tried to inject some enthusiasm in her voice. Only a week ago, she would have been pumped up about her applications. Scared of not getting in, perhaps, scared of being separated from David, but still excited about the future.

Not now.

"Where are you applying?"

"USC, UCLA, Pepperdine, Berkeley, UW, and Stanford," she said, sighing.

"That's an impressive list. No wonder Angie is so proud of you."

Lauren looked at Mira. "She's proud of me?"

"She says so all the time."

The thought of it was an arrow that pierced her chest. "Oh."

Mira cut her turkey into bite-sized pieces. "I wish I'd gone away to college. Maybe to Rice or Brown. But we didn't think like that in those days. At least, I didn't. Angie did. Then I met Vince and . . . you know."

"What?"

"The plan was two years at the community college in Fircrest, then two years at Western." She smiled. "In a way, it worked. I didn't count on eight years between my sophomore and junior years, but life follows its own plan." She glanced across the room at the kids' table.

"So a baby kept you out of college."

Mira frowned. "What an odd way to phrase it. No, just slowed me down, that's all."

After that, Lauren had trouble eating or talking or even smiling. She finished her meal—or pretended to—then helped with the dishes like an automaton. All she could think about was the baby inside of her, how it would grow bigger and bigger and make her world smaller.

And all around her there was talk of children and babies and friends who were having both. It stopped when Angie was in the room, but the minute she left, the women started up with the kid talk again.

Lauren wished she could leave, just slip unnoticed into the night and disappear.

But that would be rude, and she was the type of girl who followed the rules and played nicely with others.

The kind of girl who let her boyfriend convince her that one time without a condom would be fine. *I'll pull out*, he'd promised.

"Not fast enough," she muttered, taking her piece of pie into the living room.

Her mind was far away as she sat in the living room, tucked between Livvy's little boys. She stared down at her untouched pie. One of the boys kept talking to her, asking her questions about toys she'd never heard of and movies she'd never seen. She couldn't answer any of his questions. Hell, she could hardly keep remembering to nod and smile and pretend she was listening. How could she possibly concentrate on a child's questions when now, this second, a human life was taking root inside her, growing with every beat of her heart? She touched her stomach, feeling how flat it was.

"Come with me."

Lauren jerked her chin up, yanked her hand away from her belly.

Angie stood there, a plaid woolen blanket thrown over her shoulder. Without waiting for Lauren to answer, she turned and headed toward the sliding glass doors.

Lauren followed her out to the back deck. They sat side by side on a wooden bench, both of them resting their feet on the deck railing. Angie tucked the blanket around their bodies.

"Do you want to talk about it?"

The gentleness of the question was Lauren's undoing. Her resolve faded, leaving behind a pale gray desperation. She looked at Angie. "You know about love, right?"

"I was in love with Conlan for a long time, and my folks were married for almost fifty years. So, yeah, I know something about love."

"But you're divorced. So you know it ends, too."

"Yes. It can end. It can also build a family and last forever."

Lauren knew nothing about the kind of love that stayed firm in shaky years. She did know how David would react to news of their baby, though. His smile would vanish. He would try to say it didn't matter, that he loved Lauren and that they'd be okay, but neither one of them would believe it.

"Did you love your husband?" Lauren asked.

"Yes."

Lauren wished she hadn't asked the question; that was how hurt Angie looked right now. But she couldn't stop herself. "So he stopped loving you?"

"Oh, Lauren." Angie sighed. "The answers aren't always so clear when it comes to things like that. Love can get us through the hardest times. It can also *be* our hardest times." She looked down at her bare left hand. "I think he loved me for a long time."

"But your marriage didn't last."

"We had big issues, Lauren."

"Your daughter."

Angie looked up, obviously surprised. Then she smiled sadly. "Not many people dare to bring her up."

"I'm sorry—"

"Don't be. I like talking about her sometimes. Anyway, when she died, it was the beginning of the end for Con and me. But let's talk about you. Have you and David broken up?"

"No."

"So it must be college-related. You want to talk about it?"

College.

For a second she didn't understand the question. College seemed distant now, not like real life at all.

Not like a girl who was pregnant.

Or a woman who would have given anything for a child.

She looked at Angie, wanting to ask for help so badly the words tasted bitter. But she couldn't do it, couldn't bring this problem to Angie.

"Maybe it's more serious than that," Angie said slowly.

Lauren threw back the blanket and got to her feet. Walking toward the railing, she stared out at the dark backyard.

Angie came up behind her, touched her shoulder. "Is there some way I can help you?"

Lauren closed her eyes. It felt good to have someone offer.

But there was no way anyone could help. She knew that. It was up to her to take care of it.

She sighed. What choice did she have, really? She was seventeen years old. She'd just sent out college applications and paid every dime she had for the privilege.

She was a teenager. She couldn't be a mother. God knew she understood about mommies who resented their babies. She didn't want to do that to a child. It was a painful legacy that she'd hate to pass on.

And if she were going to take care of it—

Say it, her subconscious demanded. *If you can think it, identify it.*

And if she were going to have an abortion, should she tell David?

How could she not?

"Believe me," she whispered, seeing her breath in lacy white fronds, "he'd rather not know."

"What did you say?"

Lauren turned to Angie. "The truth is . . . things are bad at home. My mom is in love with yet another loser—big surprise— and she's hardly working. And we're . . . fighting about stuff."

"My mom and I went at it pretty good when I was your age. I'm sure—"

"Believe me. It's not the same thing. My mom isn't like yours." Lauren felt that loneliness well up in her throat again. She looked away before Angie could see it in her eyes. "You know how we live."

Angie moved closer. "You told me your mom is young, right?

Thirty-four? That means she was just a kid when she had you. That's a tough road to walk. I'm sure she's doing the best she can." She touched Lauren's shoulder. "Sometimes we have to forgive the people we love, even if we're mad as hell. That's just how it is."

"Yeah," Lauren said dully.

"Thanks for being honest with me," Angie said. "It's hard to talk about family problems."

And there it was—the feeling worse when you thought you'd hit the bottom. Lauren stared out at the darkness, unable to look at Angie. She tried to think of something to say but nothing came to her except a soft, thready "Thanks. It helps to talk."

Angie put an arm around her, squeezing gently. "That's what friends are for."

EIGHTEEN

S O HE STOPPED LOVING YOU?
For the whole of that night, Angie found herself thinking about Lauren's question. It stayed with her, haunted
her. By morning it was all she could think about.

So he stopped loving you?

He had never said that to Angie. In all the months it had
taken to dismantle their marriage, neither one of them had said,
"I don't love you anymore."

They'd stopped loving their life together.

That wasn't the same thing at all.

The tiny seed of *what if* took root, blossomed.

What if he still loved her? Or if he could love her again?
Once she had that thought, nothing else mattered.

She called her sister. "Hey, Livvy. I need you to work for me
today," she said without even bothering to say hello.

"It's Thanksgiving weekend. Why should I—"

"I'm going to see Conlan."

"I'll be there."

Sisters. Thank God for them.

Now it was almost noon and Angie was on the outskirts of Seattle. As always, the traffic was bumper to bumper in this city that had built its freeways too many years ago.

She took the next exit and looped into downtown. Amazingly, there was a parking spot right across the street from the *Times*'s office. She pulled in and parked.

And wondered what the hell she was doing here. She didn't even know if he'd be working today. She knew nothing about his life now.

They were separate. Divorced. What had made her think he'd want to see her?

You hear that, Papa? Your Angela is afraid.

It was true. And it was no way to live.

She flipped down the mirror and checked her face. She saw every wrinkle that time and circumstance had left on her.

"Damn."

If only there was time for a chemical peel.

Be brave, Angie.

She grabbed her purse and went inside the building.

The receptionist was new.

"I'm here to see Conlan Malone."

"Do you have an appointment?"

"No."

"Mr. Malone is busy today. I'll check—"

"I'm his wife." She winced, corrected herself. "*Ex*-wife."

"Oh. Let me—"

Henry Chase, the security guard who'd worked this building for more years than anyone could count, came around the corner. "Angie," he said grinning. "Long time no see."

She let out a relieved breath. "Hey, Henry."

"You here to see him?"

"I am."

"Come on."

She smiled back at the receptionist, who shrugged and reached for the phone.

Angie followed Henry to the bank of elevators, said goodbye, and went upstairs. On the third floor, she stepped out into the busy center of Conlan's life.

There were desks everywhere. On this holiday weekend, many of them were empty. She was glad of that. Still, there were plenty of familiar faces. People looked up, smiled nervously, and glanced toward Conlan's office.

The ex-wife's visit was worry-worthy, apparently. No doubt, word of her visit would spread from desk to desk; reporters loved to hear news and pass it on.

She tilted her chin up, clutched her purse in sweaty fingers, and kept moving.

She saw him before he saw her. He stood at the window of his corner office, talking on the phone. He was putting on his coat as he talked.

In that instant, everything she'd repressed came flooding back. She remembered how he used to kiss her first thing in the morning, every day, even when he was late for work, and how she sometimes pushed him away because she had other, more important things on her mind.

She knocked on the glass door.

Conlan turned, saw her. His smile faded slowly, his eyes narrowed. In anger? Disappointment? She wasn't sure anymore; she couldn't read his face. Maybe the look had been one of sadness.

He waved her in.

She opened the door and went inside.

He held up one finger to her, then said into the phone, "That's *not* okay, George. We're scheduled. I have the photographer ready. He's waiting in the van already."

Angie looked down at his desk. It was covered with notes and letters; a stack of newspapers dominated one side.

The pictures of her were gone. Now there was nothing personal at all, no glimpse of who he was on his off hours.

She didn't sit down, afraid that she'd start to tap her foot or squirm nervously.

"Ten minutes, George. Don't you move." Conlan hung up the phone, then turned to her. "Angie" was all he said. The *Why are you here?* was silent but unmistakable.

"I was in town. I thought we could—"

"Bad timing, Ange. That was George Stephanopoulos on the phone. I have a meeting with him in"—he looked at his watch—"seventeen minutes."

"Oh."

He reached down for his briefcase.

She took a step backward, feeling vulnerable now.

He looked at her.

Neither of them moved or spoke. The room felt full of ghosts and long lost sounds. Laughter. Crying. Whispering.

She wanted him to move toward her, give her some sign of encouragement, however small. Then she could launch into *I'm sorry* and he would know why she was here.

"I've gotta run. Sorry." He started to reach for her, probably to pat her shoulder, but drew back before making contact. They stared at each other for another long moment, and then he walked out on her.

She sank down into the chair in front of his desk.

"Angie?"

She wasn't sure how long she'd been sitting there, dazed, trying to collect the pieces of herself. She looked up and saw Diane VanDerbeek.

Angie didn't rise. She wasn't sure her legs would hold her. "Diane. It's good to see you again."

And it was. Diane had worked with Conlan for a long time. She and her husband, John, had been their friends for years. Conlan had gotten custody of the friendship in the divorce. No, that wasn't quite true. Angie had given them up without a fight. For weeks after the separation, Diane had called. Angie hadn't called her back.

"Let him be, for heaven's sake. He's finally getting his life back."

Angie frowned. "You make it sound like he fell apart after the divorce. He was a rock."

Diane stared down at her silently, as if measuring what to say. After a moment, she glanced out the window at the gray November day. Her mouth, usually so quick to smile, remained pressed in a thin line, perhaps even curled downward ever so slightly.

Angie felt herself tightening up. Diane had always had a reporter's directness. *I call 'em like I see 'em* had been her mantra. Whatever observation she was about to make, Angie was pretty sure she didn't want to hear it.

"Did you really miss so much?" Diane finally asked.

"I don't think I want to talk about this."

"Twice this year I came into his office and found him crying. Once when Sophie died and once when you'd decided to divorce." Her voice softened; so did the look in her eyes. "With Sophie, I thought: How sad that he had to come here to cry."

"Don't," Angie murmured.

"I tried to tell you this before, when it mattered, but you wouldn't listen. So why are you here now?"

"I thought . . ." Angie stood up suddenly. In about five seconds, she was going to start crying. If she started, God alone knew when she'd stop. "It doesn't matter. I need to go. I was an idiot." She ran for the door. As she rounded the corner into the hallway, she heard Diane say:

"Leave him alone, Angie. You've hurt him enough."

ANGIE HARDLY SLEPT THAT NIGHT. WHEN SHE CRAWLED INTO BED and closed her eyes, all she saw were memories flickering across the theater screen in her mind.

She and Conlan were in New York four years ago for his birthday. He'd bought her an Armani dress—her first designer garment.

"It cost more than my first car. I don't think I can wear it. We should return it, in fact. There are children starving in Africa . . ."

He came up beside her. Their reflections were framed in the perfect oval of the hotel room mirror. "Let's not worry about the starving children tonight. You look beautiful."

She turned, looped her arms around him, and looked up into his blue, blue eyes.

She should have told him she loved him more than life, more even than the babies God had withheld from them. Why hadn't she?

"The thing about silk," he said, sliding his hand down her back, "is that it slips off as easily as it slips on."

She'd felt a shiver of desire then; she remembered that clearly. But it had been the wrong time of the month for conception.

"It's the wrong time," she'd said, not noticing until later how much those words had taken from him.

Stupid woman. Stupid.

Another memory came to her. More recent. This time they were in San Francisco on business. She'd been pitching a high-concept campaign for a national account. Conlan had come along for the ride. He'd thought they could make a romantic weekend out of it, or so he'd said. She'd agreed because . . . well, their romantic weekends had become few and far between by then.

In the Promenade Bar, thirty-four stories above the busy San Francisco streets, they chose a window table. The city, in all her jeweled glory, lay glittering all around them.

Conlan excused himself and went to the restroom. Angie ordered a Cosmopolitan for herself and a Maker's Mark on the rocks for him. While she waited, she studied the company's statistics again. The waitress delivered the drinks.

Angie was stunned by the bill. "Seventeen dollars for one Cosmopolitan?"

"It's the Promenade," the waitress answered. "Magic is expensive. You want the drinks?"

"Sure, thanks."

Conlan returned a minute later. He had barely sat down when Angie leaned over and said, "I closed out the tab. Seventeen bucks for one drink."

He sighed, then smiled. Had it been forced? Then, she hadn't thought so. "None of your DeSaria economy plans for us tonight. We've got the money, Ange. We might as well spend it."

Finally, she understood. He'd come along on this trip not in search of romance, but rather in search of a different life. It was his way of dealing with a dream that hadn't come true. He wanted to remind himself—and her—that they could make a full, wonderful life without children, and that getaway weekends were the trade-off for a too-quiet house and an empty nursery.

What she should have said was "Then I'll have *three* drinks . . . and order the lobster."

It would have been so easy. He would have kissed her then, and maybe their new life would have begun.

Instead, she'd started to cry. "Don't ask me to give it up," she'd whispered. "I'm not ready."

And just like that, their new beginning had slid down into the mud of the same old middle.

Why hadn't she seen the truth when it was right beside her, sharing her bed night after night? All this time, she'd thought that the search for a baby had ruined them.

But that wasn't the whole truth. It had broken her, and she in turn had ruined them. No wonder he'd divorced her.

No wonder.

Twice I came into his office and found him crying. . . . How sad that he had to come here to cry. . . .

.   .   .

SATURDAY NIGHT AT THE RESTAURANT WAS WILD. EVERY TABLE WAS full, and a line of hopefuls waited in the corner. Angie was grateful for the business. It meant she didn't have time to think.

Thinking was the last thing she wanted to do.

At closing time, Mira showed up, running in from the cold. "Well?" she said. "Livvy said you went to see Conlan. How did it go?"

"Not well."

"Oh." Mira's plump face seemed to crumple. "I'm sorry."

"Not as sorry as I am, believe me."

LOVE CAN GET US THROUGH THE HARDEST TIMES.

It can also be *our hardest times.*

All weekend Lauren had been thinking about her conversation with Angie. Lauren kept hoping that somehow the answer was there, waiting for her to be smart enough to see it. Because as it was, she saw nothing but bad decisions in front of her.

She didn't want to be a mother.

She didn't want to have a baby and give it away.

What she *wanted* was not to be pregnant.

By Sunday she'd worried herself sick. She'd ignored Angie at work and slipped out of the restaurant without a good-bye to anyone. She walked all the way home, not bothering with the crosstown bus. No matter how much she tried to think about other things, THE BABY was always there.

Somewhere along the way it started to rain. She flipped her hood up and kept walking. The weather suited her mood. She took a perverse pleasure in the cold and chill.

She turned the corner toward home and saw him.

David stood on the sidewalk in front of her apartment, holding a bouquet of red roses. The rain pummeled him. "Hey, Trixie."

Love swept through her, hot as a flame, and consumed everything. She ran for him, threw her arms around him. He picked her up, held her so tightly that she could hardly breathe.

He loves me.

That was what she'd forgotten this weekend. She wasn't alone in this. She wasn't her mother.

She slid down to her feet again, smiled up at him, blinking through the rain. "I thought you guys were out of town until tomorrow morning."

"I missed you, so I came back early."

"Your mom couldn't have been too happy about that."

"I told her I had a chem test." He grinned. "We wouldn't want Stanford to change their mind. My future's gold, don'tcha know?"

Lauren's smile faded. His future *was* golden.

Stanford.

The loneliness came back full force, made her feel older than David and infinitely far away, even though she was in his arms. She had to tell him about the baby. It was the right thing to do.

"I love you, David." She felt herself start to cry; her tears mingled with the rain and were washed away before he could see them.

"I love you, too. Now let's get in my car before we catch pneumonia." He smiled. "There's a party at Eric's house."

She wanted to say, *No, not tonight,* and take him into her shabby apartment and close the door. But once they were alone, she'd have to tell him the truth, and she didn't want to do that. Not yet, anyway. She wanted one more night where they could be kids. Speed Racer and Trixie, laughing it up with their friends.

So when he held her hand and pulled her toward the car, she followed.

Love can get us through the hardest times.

Please, God, she thought, *let it be true.*

NINETEEN

ANGIE'S DREAMS THAT NIGHT CAME IN BLACK AND WHITE; faded images from some forgotten family album of the has-been and never-were moments. She was in Searle Park, at the merry-go-round, waving at a small dark-haired girl who had her father's blue eyes . . .

Slowly, the girl faded to gray and disappeared; it was as if a mist had swept in and veiled the world.

Then she saw Conlan on the ball field, coaching Little League.

The images were watery and uncertain because she'd never really been there in the stands, watching her husband coach his friends' sons, clapping when Billy VanDerbeek hit a line drive up the middle. She'd been at home on those days, curled in a fetal position on her bed. *It hurts too much*, she'd told her husband when he begged her to come along.

Why hadn't she thought about what *he* needed?

"I'm sorry, Con," her dream self whispered, reaching out for him.

She woke with a gasp. For the next few hours she lay in her bed, curled on her side, trying to put it all back in storage. She shouldn't have tried to go back in time; it hurt too much. Some things were simply lost. She should have known that.

Every now and again she realized that she was crying. By the time she heard a knock at the front door, her pillow was damp.

Thank God, she thought. Someone to keep her mind off the past.

She sat up, shoved the hair from her eyes. Throwing the covers aside, she climbed out of bed and stumbled downstairs. "I'm coming. Don't leave," she yelled.

The door swung open. Mama and Mira and Livvy stood there, all dressed in their Sunday best.

"It's Advent," Mama said. "You're coming to church with us."

"Maybe next Sunday," Angie said tiredly. "I was up late last night. I didn't sleep well."

"Of course you didn't sleep well," Mama said.

Angie knew when she'd hit a wall, and the DeSaria women with their minds made up were solid brick. "Fine."

It took her fifteen minutes to shower and dress and towel dry her hair. Another three minutes for makeup, and she was ready to go.

By ten o'clock, they were pulling into the church lot.

Angie stepped out into the cold December morning and felt as if she were going back in time. She was a girl again, dressed in white for her first communion . . . then a woman in white on her wedding day . . . then a woman in black, crying for her father. So much of her life had happened beneath these stained glass windows.

They went to the third row, where Vince and Sal had the children lined up by height. Angie sat next to Mama.

For the next hour, she went through the motions of her youth: rising and kneeling and rising again.

By the closing prayer, she realized that something had changed in her, shifted suddenly back into place, though she hadn't known it was out of alignment until now.

Her faith had been there all along, flowing in her veins, waiting for her return. A kind of peace overcame her, made her feel stronger, safer. When the service was over, she walked outside into the crisp, freezing air and looked across the street.

There it was: Searle Park. The merry-go-round from her dream glittered in the sharp sunlight. She'd grown up playing in this park. Her children would have loved it, too.

She walked across the street, hearing laughter that had never been: *Push me, Mommy.*

She sat down on the cold, corrugated steel and closed her eyes, thinking about the adoption that had failed, the babies who'd never been, the daughter who'd been taken too soon, and the marriage that had been broken.

She cried for it. Great heaving sobs that seemed to crack her chest and bruise her heart, but when it was over, she was dry inside. At last.

She looked up to the pale blue sky. She felt her father beside her, a warm presence in all that cold air.

"Angie!"

She wiped her eyes.

Mira was running across the street, her long skirt flapping against her legs. She was out of breath by the time she reached the park. "Are you okay?"

It was surprisingly easy to smile. "You know what? I am."

"No kidding?"

"No kidding."

Mira sat down beside her. They kicked their feet in the sand, and the merry-go-round started to turn.

Angie leaned back and stared up at the sky. She was moving again.

LAUREN SPENT ALL OF THE NEXT DAY GATHERING HER COURAGE. IT was dark by the time she reached Mountainaire. The gate was closed and the guardhouse looked deserted. A man in a tan uniform was stringing Christmas lights along the tall wrought-iron fence that protected the houses within.

She went to the guardhouse and peered through the window. An empty chair sat behind a desk cluttered with car magazines.

"Can I help you?"

It was the man with the lights. He looked irritated by her presence, or maybe it was simply the job.

"I'm here to see David Haynes."

"He expecting you?"

"No." Her voice was barely there. It wasn't surprising. Last night's party had been Thunderdome loud. She and David had had to shout at each other just to carry on a conversation. Later, after he'd gone home—just in case his folks showed up—she'd cried herself to sleep.

This wasn't a secret she could keep. It was ripping her up inside.

In front of her, the gate jerked once, and then arced inward slowly.

Lauren nodded at the guard, though she couldn't see him through the small window. In its square surface all she could see was her own reflection: a thin, frightened-looking girl with curly red hair and brown eyes that were already filling with tears.

By the time she reached David's house—she'd gone the long way, walking up and down several unfamiliar streets—it had started to rain. Not much of a rain, really—more of a mist that beaded your cheeks and made it difficult to breathe.

Finally, she came to his house. The majestic Georgian home looked like a Hallmark Christmas card. The perfect holiday house with lights everywhere, fake candles in the windows, and evergreen boughs draped above the front door.

She pushed through the gate at the perimeter of the lot and walked up the patterned stone path to the front door. When she reached the door, a light automatically came on. She rang the bell. It played a symphonic melody; Bach, maybe.

Mr. Haynes answered the door, wearing a pair of expertly creased khaki pants and a shirt as white as fresh snow. His hair was as flawless as his tan. "Hello, Lauren. This is a surprise."

"I know it's late, sir. Almost seven-thirty. I should have called. I *did* call, actually. Or I tried to, but no one answered."

"So you came anyway."

"I figured you were on long distance, and I . . . really needed to see David."

He smiled. "Don't worry about it. He's just playing that damn Xbox. I'm sure he'll be glad to see you."

"Thank you, sir." She could breathe again.

"Go on downstairs. I'll send David."

The carpet on the stairs was so thick her shoes made no sound at all. Downstairs, the room was big and perfectly decorated. Flax-colored carpeting, an oversized cream suede sectional with gold and taupe pillows, a coffee table made of pale marble.

Ornately carved wooden doors concealed a huge plasma screen television.

She perched uncomfortably on the sofa, waiting. She didn't hear footsteps on the stairs, but suddenly David was there, bounding into the room, pulling her up into his arms.

She clung to him.

She would give anything to go back in time, to have nothing more important to tell him than how much she loved him. Adults always talked about mistakes, the cost of doing the wrong thing. She wished she'd listened now.

"I love you, David." She heard the tinny, desperate edge in her voice and she winced.

He frowned down at her, drew back.

She hated that, the pulling away.

"You've been acting weird lately," he said, lying down on the sofa, pulling her on top of him.

She slid sideways, then knelt beside the sofa. "Your parents are home. We can't—"

"Only my dad. Mom's at some fund-raiser in town." He tried again to pull her on top of him.

She wanted to. Wanted to kiss him and let him touch her until she forgot all about . . .

the baby.

She gently pushed him back, then sat on her heels. "David." It seemed to take everything she had just to say his name.

"What's up? You're scaring me."

She couldn't stop herself; tears burned her eyes.

He touched her face, wiped her tears away. "I've never seen you cry before." She heard the rising panic in his voice.

She took a deep breath. "Remember the Longview game? The first home game of the year?"

His confusion was obvious. "Yeah, 21–7."

"I was thinking of a different score."

"Huh?"

"After the game we all went to Rocco's for pizza, and then to the state park."

"Yeah. What's your point, Lo?"

"You had your mom's Escalade," she said softly, remembering it all. The way he'd pushed the back seat down and brought out a pale blue blanket and a chenille pillow. Everything except the accessory that mattered most.

A condom.

They'd parked out on the edge of the beach, beneath the dark fringe of ancient cedar trees. A huge silver moon gazed down on them, giving their faces a tarnished, shiny look. Savage Garden's "Truly, Madly, Deeply" had been playing on the radio.

He remembered it, too. She saw the memories move across his face. She knew instantly when the realization dawned. Fear narrowed his eyes. He drew back, frowning. "I remember."

"I'm pregnant."

He made a sound that tore at her heart, a sigh that faded into silence. "No." He closed his eyes. "Fuck. *Fuck*."

"I guess we've pinpointed the problem." She felt him ease away from her, and it hurt more than she'd imagined. She'd tried to prepare herself for any reaction, but if he stopped loving her, she couldn't bear it.

Slowly, his eyes opened. He turned, looked at her through eyes that were dull. "Are you sure?"

"Positive."

"Oh," he said softly, and though he looked dazed and terrified, he was trying to smile, and the attempt pushed some of her despair aside. "What now?" he finally asked in a voice that was thick and tight.

She refused to look at him. She could tell that he was on the verge of tears. She couldn't see him break. "I don't know."

"Could you . . . have . . . you know?"

"An abortion." She squeezed her eyes shut, feeling as if something inside were tearing away. Tears burned again but didn't fall. It was the same thought she'd had. So why did it hurt so much to hear him say it? "That's probably the answer."

"Yeah," he said, too quickly. "I'll pay for it. And go with you."

She felt as if she were slowly falling underwater. "Okay." Even to her own ears, her voice sounded distant.

LAUREN STARED OUT THE WINDOW AT THE BLUR OF GREEN AND gold landscape and tried not to think about where she was going, what she was doing. David was beside her, his hands tight on the steering wheel. They hadn't spoken in almost an hour. What was there to say now? They were going to

take care of it.

She shivered at the thought, but what choice did she have?

The drive from West End to Vancouver seemed to take forever, and with every passing mile, her bones seemed to tighten.

She could have had this done closer to home, but David hadn't wanted to risk being seen. His family was friendly with too many local doctors.

There, through the filmy glass of the car window, was the clinic. She'd expected picketers out front carrying signs that said terrible things and showed heartbreaking pictures, but the entrance was quiet today, empty. Maybe even protesters didn't want to be out on such a bleak and freezing day.

Lauren closed her eyes, battling a suddenly rising panic.

David touched her for the first time. His hand was shaking and cold; strangely, his anxiety gave her strength. "Are you okay?"

She loved him for that, for being here and loving her. She would have said so, but her throat was tight. When they parked, the full weight of her decision pressed down on her. She wasn't taking care of something, she was having an abortion.

For a terrifying moment, she couldn't make herself move. David came around and opened her door. She clung to his hand.

Together, they walked toward the clinic. One foot in front of the other; that was all she let herself think about.

He opened the door for her.

The waiting room was full of women—girls, mostly, sitting alone, their heads bowed as if in prayer or despair, their knees clamped together. A belated gesture. Some pretended to read magazines; others didn't pretend that anything could take their minds off why they were here. David was the only boy in the room.

Lauren went to the front desk and checked in, then returned to an empty chair and filled out the paperwork she'd been handed. When she finished, she took the clipboard up to the desk and handed it to the woman, who looked it over.

"You're seventeen?" she asked, looking up.

Lauren felt a rush of panic. She'd meant to lie about her age, but she'd been too nervous to think clearly. "Almost eighteen. Do I . . ." She lowered her voice. "Do I need my mom's permission for the . . . for this?"

"Not in Washington. I just wanted to make sure it was accurate. You look younger."

She nodded weakly, relieved. "Oh."

"Have a seat. We'll call you."

Lauren went back to her seat. David sat down beside her. They held hands but didn't look at each other. Lauren was afraid she'd cry if she did. She read the pamphlet that was on the table, obviously left there by another unfortunate girl.

The procedure, it stated, *should take no more than fifteen minutes.*

. . . recovery enough for work within twenty-four to forty-eight hours . . .

. . . minimal discomfort . . .

She closed the pamphlet, set it aside. She might be young, but she knew that what mattered was not the pain or the recovery or the length of the "procedure."

What mattered was this: Could she live with it?

She pressed a hand to her still-flat stomach. There was life inside her.

Life.

It was easier not to think about her pregnancy that way, easier to pretend a procedure that lasted fifteen minutes could wash away her problem. But what if it didn't? What if she mourned this lost baby for the rest of her life? What if she felt forever tarnished by today?

She looked up at David. "Are you sure?"

He paled. "What choice do we have?"

"I don't know."

A woman walked into the waiting room. Holding a clipboard, she read off some names. "Lauren. Sally. Justine."

David squeezed her hand. "I love you."

Lauren was shaking as she got to her feet. Two other girls also stood. Lauren gave David one last, lingering look, then followed the white-clad nurse down the hallway.

"Justine, exam room two," the woman said, pausing at a closed door.

A frightened-looking teenage girl went inside, closed the door behind her.

"Lauren. Room three," the woman said a few seconds later, opening a door. "Put on that gown and cap."

This time Lauren was the frightened-looking girl who walked into the room. As she disrobed and redressed in the white cotton gown and paper cap, she couldn't help noticing the irony: cap and gown. As a senior, this was hardly the way she'd imagined it. She sat on the edge of the table.

Bright silver cabinets and countertops made her wince; they were too bright beneath the glare of an overhead light.

The door opened. An elderly man walked in, wearing a cap

and a loosened mask that flapped against his throat as he moved. He looked tired, as worn down as an old pencil. "Hello," he said, looking down at her chart. "Lauren. Go ahead and put your feet in the stirrups and lie back. Get comfortable."

Another person came in. "Hello, Lauren. I'm Martha. I'll be assisting the doctor." She patted Lauren's hand.

Lauren felt the sting of tears in her eyes; they blurred her vision.

"It'll all be over in a few minutes," the nurse said.

Over.

A few minutes.

No baby.

The procedure.

And she knew.

She sat upright. "I can't do it," she said, feeling the tears roll down her cheeks. "I can't live with it."

The doctor sighed heavily. His sad, downward-tilted eyes told her how often he'd seen this moment played out. "Are you sure?" He consulted her chart. "Your window for having the procedure—"

"Abortion," Lauren said, saying the word out loud for the first time. It seemed to cut her tongue with its sharp edges.

"Yes," he said. "The abortion can't happen after—"

"I know." For the first time in days, she was certain of something, and the sureness calmed her. "I won't change my mind." She pulled off the cap.

"Okay. Good luck to you," he said, then left the room.

"Planned Parenthood can help with adoption . . . if that's what you're interested in," the nurse said. Not waiting for an answer, she, too, left the room.

Lauren sat there, alone now. Her emotions were all tangled up. She felt good about her decision. It was the only thing she could have lived with. She believed absolutely in a woman's right to choose. But this was her choice.

She slid off the table and began to undress.

She'd done the right thing for her. She *had*. She knew it in her bones.

But what would David say?

HOURS LATER, LAUREN SAT BESIDE DAVID ON THE CREAM-COLORED sofa in his family's media room. Upstairs, perhaps, ordinary life was going on; down here, it was eerily quiet. She was holding his hand so tightly her fingers felt numb. She couldn't seem to stop crying.

"We get married, I guess," he said in a flat voice.

It hurt her as much as anything had, hearing him sound so defeated. She turned to him then, gathered him into her arms. She felt his tears on her throat; each one scalded her. She drew back a little, just enough to see him. He looked . . . broken. He was trying so hard to be grown-up, but his eyes betrayed his youth. They were wide with fear; his mouth was trembling. She touched his damp cheek. "Just because I'm pregnant doesn't mean—"

David yanked away from her. "Mom!"

Mrs. Haynes stood in the doorway, dressed in an impeccable black suit with a snowy blouse. She held a pizza box out in front of her. "Your dad called me. He thought you guys might like a pizza," she said dully, staring at David. Then she started to cry.

TWENTY

LAUREN HAD THOUGHT SHE COULDN'T FEEL ANY WORSE. THAT evening, sitting in an elegant white chair in the living room, beside a fire that should have warmed her, she realized how wrong she'd been. Seeing Mrs. Haynes cry was almost unbearable. David's reaction to his mother's tears was worse. Through all of it—the yelling, the arguing, the talking, the weeping—Lauren tried to say as little as possible.

It felt as if it were all her fault.

In her head, she knew that wasn't true. It had taken both of them to make this baby, but how many times had Mom told Lauren to keep condoms in her purse? *No man thinks straight with a hard-on*, she'd said more than once, *and it's you who'll get knocked up*. It had been the sum total of her advice on sex. Lauren should have listened.

"I have contacts in Los Angeles and San Francisco," Mr.

Haynes said, running a hand through his ruined hair. "Excellent doctors. And discreet. No one would ever have to know."

They'd been on this subject for at least ten minutes. After a lot of chest pounding and how-could-you-have-been-so-careless, they'd finally come around to the superstar of questions. What now?

"She tried," David said.

"In Vancouver," Lauren said. She could hardly hear herself.

Mrs. Haynes was staring at her. Slowly, slowly, she sat down. It was more of a crumpling, really. "We're Catholic," she said.

Lauren was grateful for even that small bit. "Yes," she answered. "And . . . there was more than that." She didn't want to say the word aloud—*baby* or *life*—but it was there anyway, as much a presence as the furniture or the music coming from another room.

"I asked Lauren to marry me," David said.

She could see how hard he was trying to be strong and she loved him for it; she also saw how close he was to breaking and she hated herself for that. He was realizing all of it now, piece by piece, the things he would have to give up. How could love demand so many sacrifices and survive?

"You're too young to get married, for God's sake. Tell them, Anita."

"We're too young to have a baby, too," David said. That sent everyone into silence again.

"There's adoption," Mrs. Haynes said.

David looked up. "That's right, Lauren. There are people who would love this baby."

The hope in his voice was her undoing. Tears stung her eyes. She wanted to disagree, to say that she could love this baby. Her baby. Their baby. But her voice had gone missing.

"I'll call Bill Talbot," Mr. Haynes said. "He's sure to give me a good contact. We'll find a couple who would provide a good home."

He made it sound like they were giving away a puppy.

Mrs. Haynes watched her husband walk out of the room, then she sighed and bowed her head.

Lauren frowned. They acted like a decision had been made.

David came over to her. She'd never known his eyes could be so sad. He took her hand, squeezed it. She waited for him to say something; her need to hear *I love you* was near desperate. But he said nothing.

What was there to say? There was no A answer out of this situation, no road that didn't lead someone—mostly Lauren—to heartache. She wasn't ready to make this decision yet.

"Let's go, Lauren," Mrs. Haynes finally said, standing.

"I can drive her home, Mom."

"I'll do it," Mrs. Haynes said in a voice that, even in its ragged state, brooked no disagreement.

"Then we'll all go," David said, taking Lauren's hand.

They turned and followed Mrs. Haynes out to the garage, where the glossy black Cadillac Escalade waited.

The scene of the crime.

David opened the front passenger side door. Lauren wanted to protest at sitting up front, but she didn't want to appear rude. With a sigh, she climbed into the seat. The CD player immediately came on. The lonely, haunting strains of "Hotel California" filled the car.

David told his mother to take the highway west; other than that, they didn't speak. With every second that passed in silence, Lauren felt her stomach tightening. She had a terrifying feeling that Mrs. Haynes wanted to see Lauren's mother, that it was the whole reason for this drive home.

What could Lauren say to that? It would be almost midnight by the time they reached the apartment.

"My mom is out of town on business." Lauren said the lie in a rush, hating how it made her feel.

"I thought she was a hairdresser," his mother said.

"She is. It's a convention. One of those things where they show them all the new products." Lauren remembered that her mother's boss had sometimes gone to conventions like that.

"I see."

"You can let me off here," Lauren said. "There's no point—"

"At the Safeway?" Mrs. Haynes frowned at her. "I don't think so."

Lauren swallowed hard. She couldn't find her voice. From the backseat, David gave directions to the apartment.

They pulled up in front of the dilapidated building. In the moonlight, it looked like something out of a Roald Dahl novel, one of those *a poor, pathetic child lives here* kind of places.

David climbed out of the car and walked around to the passenger door.

Mrs. Haynes hit the door locks, then turned, frowning.

Lauren flinched at the loud click.

"This is where you live?"

"Yes."

Amazingly, Mrs. Haynes's face seemed to soften. She sighed heavily.

David tried to open the door.

"David's the only child I could have," Mrs. Haynes said. "He was a miracle, really. Maybe I loved him too much. Mother-hood . . . changes who you are somehow. All I wanted was for him to be happy, to have all the choices I didn't have." She looked at Lauren. "If you and David get married and keep this baby . . ." Her voice broke. "Life with a baby is hard. Without money or education, it's worse than hard. I know how much you love David. I can see that. And he loves you. Enough to walk away from his future. I guess I should be proud about that." She said this last part softly, as if she wanted to feel it but couldn't.

David pounded on the glass. "Open the door, Mom!"

Lauren understood what Mrs. Haynes wasn't saying as clearly as what she was. *If you really love David, you won't make him ruin his life.*

It was the same thing Lauren had thought on her own. If he loved her enough to give it all up, didn't she need to love him enough not to let him?

"If you need to talk about any of this, anytime, you come to me," Mrs. Haynes said.

It surprised Lauren, that offer. "Thank you."

"Tell your mother I'll call her tomorrow."

Lauren didn't even want to think about *that* conversation. "Okay."

She didn't know what else to say, so she hit the door lock button and climbed out of the car.

"What the hell did she say to you?" David said, slamming the car door shut behind her.

Lauren stared at him, remembering how his mother had cried, so quietly and yet so deeply; as if her insides were breaking. "She said she loves you."

His face crumpled at that. "What are we going to do?"

"I don't know."

They stood there a long time, staring at each other. Then, fi-nally, he said, "I better go."

She nodded. When he kissed her good night, it was all she

could do not to cling to him. It took pure willpower to let him walk away.

LAUREN FOUND HER MOTHER IN THE LIVING ROOM, SITTING ON THE sofa, smoking a cigarette. She looked jittery and nervous.

Mom put her drink on the floor. "I meant to go with you to-day."

"Yeah. What happened?"

Mom reached for the drink again. There was a noticeable trembling in her hand. "I went to the mini-mart for smokes. On the way home, I ran into Neddie. The Tides was open. I thought I'd have a quick drink. I needed one to . . . you know . . . but when I looked up again it was too late." She took a drag off her cigarette, looked at Lauren through the gray haze. "You look bad. Maybe you should sit. You want an aspirin? I'll get you one."

"I'm fine."

"I'm sorry, Lauren," she said softly.

For once, Lauren heard real regret in her mother's voice. "It's okay." She bent down and started picking up pizza boxes and empty cigarette packs from the floor. "It looks like you and Jake had quite a party last night." When Lauren looked up, her mother was crying. It warmed her heart, that simple proof of emotion.

Lauren went to her, knelt beside the sofa. "I'm okay, Mom. You don't have to cry."

"He's going to leave me."

"What?"

"My whole life is nothing. And I'm getting old." Mom put out her cigarette and lit up another.

This hurt more than the slap. Even now, on this terrible day, her mother's thoughts were on herself. Lauren swallowed hard, moved away. Very slowly she went back to picking up the apart-ment. She had to hold back tears with every breath. "I didn't go through with it," she said quietly.

Her mother looked up. Her eyes were bloodshot and rimmed in blurred mascara. "What?" It took her a minute to figure out the meaning of Lauren's words. "Tell me you're kidding."

"I'm not kidding." Lauren tried to be strong, but it felt as if she were crumbling. The pain in her heart was swift and sharp. As much as she knew it was crazy—impossible—she wanted her mother to open her arms right now, to hold her as she never had, and say, *It's okay, honey.* "I couldn't do it. I'm the one who needs to pay for my mistake, not . . ." She looked down at her stomach.

"Baby," her mother said coldly. "You can't even say the word."

Lauren took a step forward. She was biting her lower lip and wringing her hands. "I'm scared, Mom. I thought—"

"You *should* be scared. Look at me. Look at this." She stood up and made a sweeping gesture with her hands as she crossed the room. "Is this the life you want? Did you study like a fool for *this*? You'll lose out on college this year—you know that, right? And if you don't go now, you'll never go." She grabbed Lauren by the shoulders and shook her. "You'll be *me*. After all your hard work. Is that what you want? Is it?"

Lauren pulled free, stumbled back. "No," she said in a small voice.

Mom sighed heavily. "If you couldn't make it through an abortion, how in God's name do you think you can handle adoption? Or worse yet, motherhood? Go back to the clinic tomorrow. This time I'll go with you. Give yourself a chance in life." The anger seemed to slide out of her then. She pushed the hair from Lauren's eyes, tucked a strand behind her ear. It was perhaps the gentlest her mother had ever been.

The tenderness was worse than being yelled at. "I can't."

Mom stared at her through eyes that were glazed with tears. "You break my heart."

"Don't say that."

"What else can I say? You've made your decision. Fine. I tried." She bent down and grabbed her purse. "I need a drink."

"Don't go. Please."

Mom headed for the door. Halfway there, she turned back around.

Lauren stood there, crying. She knew the desperate plea to stay was in her eyes.

Mom almost started to cry again. "I'm sorry." Then she left.

THE NEXT MORNING, AFTER A SLEEPLESS NIGHT, LAUREN WOKE TO the sound of music bleeding through the walls. It was the Bruce Springsteen CD.

She came upright slowly, rubbing her swollen, gritty eyes.

Mom's party had obviously turned into an all-nighter. It wasn't surprising, she supposed. When your seventeen-year-old daughter got herself knocked up, there was nothing to do but party.

With a sigh, she climbed out of bed and stumbled to the bathroom, where she took a long, hot shower. When she was finished, she stood on the frayed scrap of a towel that served as their bathmat and studied her naked body in the mirror.

Her breasts were definitely bigger. Maybe her nipples were, too; she couldn't be sure about that, her nipples never having been high on her to-notice list.

She turned sideways.

Her stomach was as flat as ever. There was no sign there of the new life that grew within.

She wrapped a towel around her and returned to her bedroom. After making her bed, she dressed in her school uniform— red crew neck sweater, plaid skirt, white tights, and black loafers. Then she turned off her bedroom light and walked down the hallway.

In the living room she stopped. Frowned.

Something was wrong.

The ashtrays on the coffee table were empty. No half filled glasses lined the kitchen counter. The ratty old purple afghan that usually draped over the back of the sofa was gone.

Gone.

No way. Even Mom wouldn't—

She heard an engine start up outside; it was the throaty, unmistakable growl of a Harley Davidson motorcycle.

Lauren rushed to the window and whipped the flimsy curtain aside.

There, down on the street below, Mom sat behind Jake on the motorcycle. She was looking up at Lauren.

Lauren touched her fingertips to the glass. "No."

Slowly, as if it hurt to move, her mother waved good-bye.

The motorcycle roared down the street, turned the corner, and disappeared from view.

Lauren stood there a long time, looking down at the empty street, waiting for them to come back.

When she finally turned away she saw the note on the coffee table.

That was when she knew.

She picked it up, opened it. A single word had been written in bold, blue ink.

There it was, the whole of their mother-daughter relation-ship reduced to a single word.

Sorry.

And the Boss sang on: *Baby, we were born to run . . .*

TWENTY-ONE

NGIE DIALED LAUREN'S HOME NUMBER FOR THE THIRD
time.

"Still no answer?" Mama asked, coming out of the
kitchen.

Angie went to the window and stared out. "No. It's not like
her to miss work. I'm worried."

"Girls of that age screw up sometimes. I'm sure it is nothing."

"Maybe I should stop by her house . . ."

"A boss doesn't just show up. She missed a night of work. So
what? Probably she's out drinking beers with her boyfriend."

"You are hardly comforting me, Mama."

Mama came up beside her. "She'll be at work tomorrow.
You'll see. Why don't you come home with me? We'll have
wine."

"I'll take a rain check, Mama. I want to get a Christmas tree."

She leaned against her mother. "In fact, I'm going to leave early, if that's okay."

"Papa . . . would be happy to see his cottage decorated again."

Angie heard the crack in her mother's voice and she understood. Mama was facing her first Christmas without Papa. She put her arm around her mother's narrow waist, drew her close. "I'll tell you what, Mama. On Wednesday, let's make a day of it. We can go shopping and have lunch, then come home and decorate the tree. You can teach me how to make tortellini."

"Tortellini is too difficult for you. We begin slowly. With tapenade, maybe. You can use a blender, yes?"

"Very funny."

Mama's smile softened. "Thank you," she said.

They stood there a moment longer, holding each other as they stared out at the night. Finally, Angie said good-bye, grabbed her coat and left the restaurant.

The town square was a beehive of activity on this cold and cloudy night. Dozens of die-hard tourists milled about, oohing and aahing over the thousands of white lights strung throughout the town. At the end of the street a group of carolers in red and green velvet Victorian clothing sang "Silent Night." More tourists and a few locals huddled around them, listening. You could recognize the locals by their lack of shopping bags. A horse-drawn carriage rumbled down the brick-paved street, bells jangling. The first tree lighting ceremony of the year had obviously been a success; next Saturday's would be even bigger. Tourists would arrive by the busload; the locals would grumble that their town had turned into Disneyland and they would stay away at all costs. The restaurant would be packed all week.

By the time she reached the Christmas Shoppe, it had begun to snow. She flipped her hood up and hurried across the street, ducking into the store.

It was a Christmas wonderland, with trees and ornaments and lights everywhere. Angie came to a stop. Directly in front of her was a thin, noble fir tree, spangled with silver and gold ornaments. Each one was stunningly unique. Angels and Santas and multi-colored glass balls.

It reminded her of the collection Conlan had started for her, all those years ago, with a tiny ornament from Holland that read: *Our First Christmas.* Every year since, he'd given her a new one.

"Hey, Angie," said a lilting female voice.

Angie looked up, wiped her eyes, just as the shop's owner,

Tillie, came out from behind the cash register. She was dressed as Mrs. Claus in a red dress that had been old when Angie was a kid.

"I hear you've shaken it up at DeSaria's," Tillie said. "Rumor is your mom is so proud, she's about to bust."

Angie tried to smile. Life in West End had always been like this. No bit of business was ever too small to keep track of—especially if it was someone else's. "She's having fun with the new recipes, that's for sure."

"Who would have thought? I'd best get over there. Maybe after the holidays. So. What can I help you find?"

Angie looked around. "I need a few ornaments."

Tillie nodded. "I heard about your divorce. I'm sorry."

"Thanks."

"I'll tell you what. Why don't you come back in ten minutes? I'll have a treeful for you. At cost."

"Oh, I couldn't—"

"You'll give me and Bill dinner in exchange."

Angie nodded. This was how her papa had done business in West End. "I'll go get my tree and be back in a flash."

An hour later, Angie was on her way home with a tree strapped to the roof of her car, a box of ornaments in the backseat, and a stack of white tree lights on the passenger seat. It took her longer than usual; the roads were slick and icy. "Jingle Bell Rock" blared from the speakers, putting her in the mood.

She needed to be coaxed into the mood, to be honest. The thought of a Christmas tree chosen by her, put up by her, decorated by her, and enjoyed by her was a bit depressing.

She parked in front of the cottage and killed the engine. Then she stood beside the tree, staring at it while snow fell like kisses on her face.

The tree looked bigger than it had in the lot.

Oh, well.

She got a pair of her father's old work gloves from the garage and set about freeing the tree. By the time she was finished, she'd fallen twice, been smacked in the nose by an obviously vengeful branch, and scratched the car's paint.

Tightening her hold on the trunk, she heaved the tree toward the house, one step at a time. She was almost to the door when a car drove up the driveway.

Headlights came at her; snow drifted lazily in the beams of light.

She dropped the tree and straightened. It was Mira. She'd come to help with the tree.

Sisters.

"Hey, you," Angie said, squinting into the too-bright light. "You're blinding me."

The lights didn't snap off. Instead, the driver's door opened. Mick Jagger's voice pulsed into the night. Someone stepped out.

"Mira?" Angie frowned, took a step backward. It struck her all at once how isolated she was out here. . . .

Someone walked toward her, boots soundless in the fresh snow.

When she saw his face, she gasped. "Conlan."

He came closer, so much so that she could feel the warmth of his breath on her face. "Hey, Ange."

She had no idea what to say to him. Once, years ago now, conversations had flowed like water between them. In recent times that river had gone dry. She remembered Diane's words.

Twice I came into his office and found him crying.

When you'd missed something like that as a wife, what could you say later?

"It's good to see you—"

"Beautiful night—"

They spoke at exactly the same time, then laughed awkwardly and fell to silence again. She waited for him to speak but he didn't. "I was just going to put up the tree."

"I can see that."

"Do you have a tree this year?"

"No."

At the look on his face, so sad, she wished she hadn't asked. "I don't suppose you want to help me carry it inside?"

"I think I'd rather watch you wrestle with it."

"You're six foot two; I'm five foot six. Get the tree inside."

He laughed, then bent down and picked up the tree.

She raced ahead to open the door for him.

Together, they put the tree in the stand.

"A little to the left," she said, pushing the tree to a straighter position.

He grunted and went back under the tree again.

She battled a sudden bout of sadness. Memories came at her hard. As soon as the tree was upright and locked into place in the stand, she said, "I'll get us some wine," and ran for the kitchen.

When she was out of the room, she let her breath out in a rush.

It hurt just looking at him.

She poured two glasses of red wine—his favorite—and went back into the living room. He stood by the fireplace, staring at her. In his black sweater and faded Levis, with his black hair that needed to be cut, he looked more like an aging rock star than an ace reporter.

"So," he said after she'd given him the wine and sat down on the sofa, "I could tell you I was out this way on a story and just stopped by."

"I could tell you I don't care why you're here."

They sat on opposite sides of the room, making cautious conversation, talking about nothing. Angie was finishing her third glass of wine by the time he got around to asking a question that mattered.

"Why did you come by the office?"

There were so many ways to answer that. The question was: How far out on the ledge did she want to go? She'd spent a lot of years telling Conlan half-truths. She'd started out protecting him from bad news, but deceit was an icy road that spun you around. She'd ended up protecting herself. The more her heart had been broken, the more she'd turned inward. Until one day, she'd realized that she was alone. "I missed you," she said at last.

"What does that mean?"

"Did you miss me?"

"I can't believe you can ask me that."

She got up, moved toward him. "Did you?"

She knelt in front of him. Their faces were so close she could see herself in his blue eyes. She'd forgotten how that felt, to see herself in him. "It made me crazy," she said, echoing the words she'd said to him in the nursery all those months ago.

"And you're sane now?"

She felt his breath on her lips; it brought back so many memories. "*Sane*'s such a grown-up word. But I'm definitely better. Mostly, I've accepted it."

"You scare me, Angie," he said quietly.

"Why?"

"You broke my heart."

She leaned the tiniest bit toward him. "Don't be afraid," she whispered, reaching for him.

TWENTY-TWO

ANGIE HAD FORGOTTEN HOW IT FELT TO BE REALLY KISSED. It made her feel young again; better than young, in fact, because there was none of the angst or fear or desperation that came with youth. There was just this feeling moving through her, electrifying her body, making her feel alive again. A tiny moan escaped her lips, disappeared.

Conlan pushed her back.

She blinked at him, feeling that edgy near-pain of desire. "Con?"

He felt it, too. She could see it in the darkness of his eyes, in the tightness around his mouth. For a moment there, he'd lost himself; now he was climbing to safer ground. "I loved you," he said.

If there had been a veil left over her memories, the past tense of that sentence would have ripped it free. In three words, he'd bared his soul and told her everything that mattered.

She grasped his arm. He flinched, tried to draw back. She wouldn't let him. In his eyes, she saw uncertainty and fear. A hint of hope was there, too, and she seized on it.

"Talk to me," she said, knowing that he'd learned *not* to talk to her. In the months after Sophie's death, she'd become so delicate that he'd learned to hold her in silence. Now he was afraid to care about her, afraid her fragility would return and, like a rising tide, drown them.

"What's different now?"

"What do you mean?"

"Our love wasn't enough for you."

"I've changed."

"Suddenly, after eight years of obsession, you just changed, huh?"

"Suddenly?" She drew back. "In the last year I've lost my father, my daughter, and my husband. Do you really think I can go through all of that unchanged? But of all of them, Con, the one that rips me apart and keeps me awake in the middle of the night is you. Papa and Sophia . . . they were meant to go. You . . ." Her voice dropped. "You, I left behind. It took me a long time to realize that. I wasn't there for you. Not the way you were there for me, and it's hard to live with that. So, sudden change? I don't think so."

"I knew how deeply you were hurting."

"And I let that be what mattered." She touched his face again, gently. "But you were hurting, too."

"Yes" was all he said.

They stared at each other in silence. Angie didn't know what else to say.

"Make love to me," she said, surprising herself. The desperation in her voice was obvious. She didn't care. The wine had made her bold.

His laughter was shaky and forced. "It's not quite that simple."

"Why not? All our lives we've followed the rules. College. Catholic wedding. Career. Kids." She paused. "That was where we got caught. We ended up like those animals in the Kalahari who get stuck in the mud and die." She leaned toward him, so close he could have kissed her if he chose. "But there's no map for us anymore. No right way. We're just a couple of people who have lived through tough times and come out in a new place. Take me to bed," she said softly.

He cursed. There was anger in his voice, and defeat.

She seized on that. "Please. Love me."

He groaned and reached for her, whispering, "Damn you," as his mouth found hers.

THE NEXT MORNING, ANGIE WOKE TO THE FAMILIAR CADENCE OF rain hammering the roof and sliding down the windowpanes.

Conlan's arms were around her, holding her close even in sleep. She backed into him, loving the feel of him against her skin. His slow, even breathing tickled the nape of her neck.

They'd slept in this position for all of their married life, spooned together. She'd forgotten how safe it made her feel.

She eased away from him just enough to roll over. She needed to see him. . . .

She touched his face, traced the lines that pain had left on him. They matched her own; every wrinkle was the residue of how they'd lived and what they'd gained and lost. Sooner or later, all of it took up residence on your face. But the young man was there, too; the man she'd fallen in love with. She saw him in the cheekbones, in the lips, in the hair that hadn't yet gone gray and needed to be trimmed.

He opened his eyes.

"Morning," she said, surprised by her scratchy voice.

Love, she thought; it touched every part of a woman, even her voice on a cold winter's morning.

"Morning." He kissed her gently and drew back. "What now?"

She couldn't help smiling. It was so Conlan-like. The whole we-have-no-road-map-anymore theory didn't work for a man who made his living looking for answers. She knew the answer for her. She'd known it the minute she saw him at the theater in Seattle, and probably long before that.

But they'd already failed once, and that failure had marked them, damaged them. "I guess we just see what happens," she said.

"We've never been too good at that sort of thing. You know us. The plan-makers."

Us.

That was enough for now. It was more than she'd had yesterday.

"We need to be different this time, don't we?" she said.

"You *have* changed."

"Loss will do that to a woman."

He sighed at the mention of their loss, and she wished she could take the words back. How did you undo years, though? Once, their love had been characterized by hope and joy and passion. They'd been young then, and full of faith. Could two grown people ever really find their way back to that?

"I have to be at work by noon."

"Call in sick. We could—"

"No." He pushed away from her and got out of the bed. He stood there, naked, staring down at her through unreadable eyes. "We were always good in bed, Ange. That was never the problem." He sighed, and in that sound was the reminder of all that had gone wrong between them; he bent down for his clothes.

While he was dressing, she tried to think of what to say to stop him from leaving. But the only words that came to her were: *Twice I came into his office and found him crying.*

She'd broken his heart. What could she say to him now that would matter? Words were such impermanent things; there and gone on a breath.

"Come back," she finally said as he walked toward the door. "Sometime. When you're ready."

He paused, turned to look at her. "I don't think I can. Goodbye, Angie."

And then he was gone.

ANGIE WAS DISTRACTED AT WORK. MAMA NOTICED HER BEHAVIOR and remarked on it more than once, but Angie knew better than to say anything. Gossip as juicy as *I slept with Conlan* would burn through the family. She didn't want to hear sixteen opinions on what had happened, and more important, their fear would taint it. She wanted to hold on to the hope that he'd come back to the cottage sooner or later.

Instead, she focused on more immediate worries. Like the fact that Lauren had missed another shift and hadn't bothered to call. Angie had left several messages, but none of them had been returned.

"Angela."

She realized that her mother was speaking to her, and put down the phone. "What, Mama?"

"How long are you going to stand there, staring at the telephone? We have customers waiting."

"I'm afraid she's in trouble. Someone needs to help her."

"She has a mother."

"But sometimes teenagers don't tell their parents everything. What if she's feeling all alone?"

Mama sighed. "Then you will rescue her. But you be careful, Angie."

It was good advice. Common sense. It had kept Angie away from Lauren's house for two days. Each day the worry had grown, though, and Angie was beginning to have a bad feeling.

"Tomorrow," she said firmly.

EVERY DAY IT WAS HARDER TO FIT INTO THE ORDINARY WORLD OF high school. Lauren felt as if she were an alien, plopped down on this planet without any skills that would allow her to survive. She couldn't concentrate on her classes, couldn't keep a conversation going, couldn't eat without throwing up. *Baby . . . baby . . . baby* ran through her thoughts constantly.

She didn't belong here anymore. Every moment felt like a lie. She expected the news to break any second and the rumors to start.

There's Lauren Ribido
poor girl
knocked up
ruined

She didn't know if her friends would rally around her or cut her loose, and the truth was she didn't know if she cared. She had nothing in common with them anymore. Who cared about the pop quiz in trig or the scene that Robin and Chris made at the dance? It all felt childish, and though Lauren felt trapped in the gray world that wasn't yet womanhood but had moved beyond childhood, she knew she'd never really be young again.

Even David treated her differently. He still loved her; she knew that without question, thank God. But sometimes she felt him pull away from her, go off in his own place to think, and she knew that in those away times he was contemplating all that their love had cost him.

He would do the right thing. Whatever the hell that was. But it would cost him Stanford and all the benefits that came from a school like that. Most of all, it would cost him his youth. The same price that she'd already paid.

"Lauren?"

She looked up, surprised to realize that she'd laid her head down. She hadn't meant to. Now her teacher, Mr. Knightsbridge, was standing by her desk, looking down at her.

"Am I boring you, Lauren?"

A ripple of laughter moved through the room.

She straightened. "No, sir."

"Good." He handed her a pink slip. "Mrs. Detlas wants to see you in her office."

Lauren frowned. "Why?"

"I don't know, but it is college time and she is the senior counselor."

Lauren couldn't have gotten an answer on her applications yet, but maybe she'd forgotten to fill something out or mailed a packet to the wrong address. Like it mattered now.

She gathered up her books and papers, put everything in her backpack, and walked across campus to the school's main office. It was icy cold outside. A residue of snow dusted the ditches and fields.

Strangely, it felt cold inside the office, too. Mary, the school secretary, barely looked up from her work when Lauren walked in, and Jan, the school nurse, looked away too quickly to be anything but rude.

Lauren walked down the hallway that was plastered with ads and coupons for colleges and academic camps and summer jobs. At Mrs. Detlas's office, she paused, drew in a deep breath, and knocked.

"Come in."

Lauren opened the door. "Hey, Mrs. D.," she said, trying not to sound nervous.

"Lauren. Sit down."

None of the usual banter and no smile.

This was going to be bad.

"I spoke to David this morning. He says he's thinking about bagging Stanford. He said—and I quote—something's come up. Do you know what that something is?"

Lauren swallowed hard. "I'm sure he won't give up Stanford. How could he?"

"How could he indeed." Mrs. Detlas tapped her pen on the desk while she eyed Lauren. "Naturally, I was concerned. The Hayneses are an important family in this school."

"Of course."

"So I called Anita."

Lauren sighed heavily.

"She wouldn't tell me anything, but I could tell she was upset. So I sent Coach Tripp to the boy's locker room. You know how close he and David are."

"Yes, ma'am."

"So you're pregnant."

Lauren closed her eyes and swore under her breath. David had *promised* not to tell anyone. By the end of the day, the word would be out, if it wasn't already. From now on, everywhere she went, she'd be the subject of gossip, of pointed fingers and whispering.

There was a long pause, then Mrs. Detlas said, "I'm sorry, Lauren. More than you can know."

"What do I do now?"

Mrs. Detlas shook her head. "I can't tell you that. I can tell you that no pregnant girl has ever graduated from Fircrest. The parents tend to throw a fit when the word gets out."

"Like with Evie Cochran?"

"Yes. Evie tried to stay, but in the end it was too difficult. I believe she's with an aunt in Lynden."

"I don't have any relatives."

The counselor wasn't listening. She opened a manila envelope, read the contents. Then she closed the folder. "I've already spoken to the principal at West End High. You can finish out the semester there and graduate in January."

"I don't understand."

"You're here on scholarship, Lauren. It can be revoked at any time, for any reason. And you've certainly given us a reason. We looked to you to be a role model. That will hardly be true in the coming months, now, will it? We think it will be better for everyone if you graduate from West End High."

"There's only six weeks left in the semester. I can handle gossip. Please. I want to graduate from Fircrest."

"I think you'll find it . . . unpleasant. Girls can be awfully cruel to one another."

Lauren knew about that. Back before Project Geek No More,

when she'd looked wrong and spoke poorly and lived in the trashy part of town, no one had wanted to be friends with her. In her naïveté, she'd thought she'd changed all that when she remade herself into a girl that fit in. Now she saw the painful truth. It had all been a veneer, a thin, clear layer of lies over who she really was. The real girl was visible now.

She wanted to be angry, to access the ambition and determination that had taken her through Fircrest's doors in the first place, but all that fire felt so far away.

And she was cold.

How could she argue with the role model stuff? She was a pregnant girl at a private Catholic school. If she was an inspiration to anyone now, it was as a warning.

Be careful or you'll end up like Lauren Ribido.

"Go to West End," Mrs. Detlas said gently. "Finish up the semester and graduate early. Thank God you have enough credits."

It's where you belong. Lauren heard the words as clearly as if they'd been spoken aloud.

But that was another lie.

The truth was she didn't belong anywhere.

LAUREN RETURNED TO CLASS AND WENT THROUGH THE MOTIONS OF high school. She took notes and filled out her daily planner with upcoming assignments and talked to her classmates. Once or twice she even smiled, but inside, she felt cold. An unfamiliar anger was spreading through her blood.

David had promised to keep their secret. He knew—they knew—it would get out sooner or later, of course, but not yet. She wasn't ready to face the questions and gossip.

By lunchtime, she'd gone beyond anger. She was pissed. She ignored their friends and strode across campus to the weight room. He was there with his football buddies. Amid the clunking of weights and the huffing of exertion, they were talking and laughing.

When she stepped into the room, it fell silent.

Damn you, David.

She felt her cheeks heat up. "Hey," she said, trying to sound normal, as if she were just another high school girl instead of a ruined one.

David slowly sat up. The way he looked at her made it difficult to breathe. "Bye, guys."

No one answered him.

In silence, she and David walked across the campus and out to the football field. It was a cold, crisp day, with a layer of frost glittering on the grass. The air smelled vaguely of apples.

"How could you do it?" she said at last. Her voice was surprisingly soft. She'd expected to scream the question at him, maybe hit him for emphasis, but now that she was here, she was icy cold and afraid.

He took her hand and led her to the bleachers. They sat down on the cold, hard seat. He didn't put his arm around her. Instead, he stared out at the grassy field and sighed.

"You *promised*," she said again, louder this time, her voice shrill. "And Coach Tripp. Everyone knows he has a big mouth. Didn't you think—"

"My dad won't talk to me anymore."

Lauren frowned. "But . . ." She didn't know how to finish her sentence.

"He said I'm a stupid idiot. No. A fucking idiot. Those were his exact words." David's breath floated out in pale clouds.

She lost her anger; just like that it was gone. Something inside her seemed to fold inward. She touched his thigh and leaned against him. For all the years she'd known him, he'd been trying to get his father's attention. It was one of the things they had in common. A parent who didn't seem to love you enough.

The Speedster was David's pride and joy not because it was the envy of other boys or because girls loved it. He cared about the car because his father loved it. What David cared about were the hours spent in the garage with his dad. There—and only there, it seemed—they'd talked.

"He won't even work on the car. He says there's no point in fixing up wheels for a kid who's going nowhere." He finally looked at Lauren. "I needed to talk to someone. A guy."

How could she not understand that? This was a time of almost unbearable loneliness. She slipped her hand in his. "It's okay. I'm sorry I yelled at you."

"I'm sorry I told him. I thought he'd keep quiet."

"I know." They fell silent again, each staring out at the field. Finally Lauren said, "At least we have each other."

Softly, in a voice that held no confidence, he said, "Yeah."

·   ·   ·

WHEN LAUREN GOT HOME, MRS. MAUK WAS WAITING FOR HER ON the front step. By the time Lauren saw her, it was too late to turn around.

"Lauren," she said, sighing heavily. "I went to see your mom at work today."

"Oh? Did you catch her?"

"You know I didn't. Her boss said she'd quit. Left town."

Lauren sagged beneath the weight of those two words. "Yeah. I'm going to get a full-time job. I promise—"

"I can't do it, kiddo," she said, and though Lauren could see she didn't like this news, she broke it anyway. "You can't afford this place by yourself. My boss is already tired of your mom's late payments. He wants me to evict you guys."

"Please, don't."

Mrs. Mauk's fleshy face folded into a sad look. "I wish I could help you. I'm so sorry." She slowly turned and went inside. The busted screen door banged shut behind her.

If one more person told Lauren they were sorry, she was going to scream.

Not that it would do any good.

She trudged up the stairs, walked into her apartment, and slammed the door shut.

"Think, Lauren," she said, searching for her old self, the girl who could climb any mountain. *"Think."*

Someone knocked.

No doubt Mrs. Mauk had forgotten to tell her that she needed to vacate the premises by tomorrow.

She went to the door, yanked it open. "I can't—"

There, standing in the gloomy darkness, was Angie.

"Oh" was all Lauren managed to say.

"Hello, Lauren." Angie smiled, and there was a gentleness in it that caused Lauren a physical pain. "Maybe you'd like to invite me in."

Lauren imagined it: Angie Malone inside, walking on the smelly shag carpeting, sitting—no, not daring to sit—on the lopsided sofa, looking around the room. Making judgments, feeling sorry for Lauren. "No. Not really." She crossed her arms, blocked the doorway with her body.

"Lauren," Angie said sternly. It was the mother voice. Lauren was helpless to resist. She stepped aside.

Angie eased past her and went inside.

Lauren stumbled along beside her. It was impossible not to see the place through Angie's eyes. Tawdry stucco walls stained from years of chain smoking; cloudy windows that revealed no view except the brick building next door. She couldn't possibly offer Angie a seat. "You . . . uh . . . want a Coke?" she offered nervously, moving from foot to foot. When she realized what she was doing—practically dancing the macarena, for heaven's sake—she forced herself to stand still.

To Lauren's utter amazement, Angie sat down on the broken sofa. Not one of those I'm-worried-about-ruining-my-clothes perches either. She sat. "I don't need a Coke, but thanks."

"About my job . . ."

"Yes?"

"I should have called."

"Yes, you should have. Why didn't you?"

Lauren twisted her hands together. "It's been a bad week for me."

"Sit down, Lauren."

She didn't dare get too close to Angie. She was afraid one touch would make her cry. So she grabbed a chair from the dinette set and dragged it into the living room, then sat down.

"I thought we were friends," Angie said.

"We are."

"You're in some kind of trouble, aren't you?"

"Yes."

"What can I do to help?"

That was all it took. Lauren burst into tears. "N-nothing. It's too late."

Angie left the sofa and went to Lauren, taking her in her arms and pulling her up from the chair. Lauren's sobs grew louder. Angie stroked her back and hair, said, "It'll be okay," about a dozen times.

"No, it won't," Lauren said miserably when the tears eased. "My mom dumped me."

"Dumped you?"

"She ran off with a guy named Jake Morrow."

"Oh, honey. She'll be back—"

"No," Lauren said quietly. The surprising thing was how much it hurt to admit. After all the years of knowing how little her mother loved her, still it wounded her. "And Mrs. Mauk says I can't stay here. How am I supposed to earn enough money to pay for my own apartment?" She looked down at the floor, then slowly up at Angie. "That's not even the worst of it."

"There's something worse than that?"

Lauren took a deep breath. She hated to say these words to Angie, but what choice did she have? "I'm pregnant."

TWENTY-THREE

GOD HELP HER, ANGIE'S FIRST REACTION WAS ENVY. IT stung her heart; she felt its poison begin to spread.

"Nine weeks," Lauren said, looking miserable, and young.

So desperately, impossibly young.

Angie pushed her feelings aside. There would be time, late at night, she supposed, when she was vulnerable and lonely, to think about why the world was sometimes so unfair. She scooted backward and sat on the coffee table. She needed some distance between them. Lauren's pain was so palpable, Angie wanted to make it go away, but this wasn't one of those times. A hug wouldn't do it.

She stared at Lauren. The girl's red hair was a tangled mess, her round, puffy cheeks were paler than usual, and her brown eyes were steeped in sadness.

If ever a girl was in need of mothering . . .

No.

"Did you tell your mother?" Angie asked.

"That's why she left. She said she raised one mistake and wouldn't do it again."

Angie sighed. It had, over the years of her infertility and losses, occurred to her often that motherhood was too random. Too many women that shouldn't raise a child were granted that gift, while others lived with arms that felt empty.

"I tried to have an abortion."

"Tried?"

"I thought I'd just take care of the problem, you know? Be mature. But I couldn't do it."

"You should have come to me, Lauren."

"How could I come to you with this? I knew it would hurt you. And I didn't want you looking at me the way you are."

"How's that?"

"Like I'm stupid."

Angie was drawn forward in spite of her best intentions. She tucked a stringy lock of hair behind Lauren's ear. "I'm not looking at you like that. I'm sad and scared for you, that's all."

Lauren's eyes filled slowly with tears. "I don't know what to do. David says he'll bag Stanford and marry me, but it won't work. He'd start to hate me. I don't think I could stand that."

Angie wished there were some string of magic words that would ease this poor child's heart, but sometimes life backed you into a corner and there was no easy way out.

Lauren wiped her eyes, sniffed, and sat up straighter. "I don't mean to dump all this on you. I'm just scared. I don't know what to do, and now I have to find a new place to live."

"It's okay, Lauren. Take a deep breath." Angie looked at her. "What do you want to do?"

"Go back to October and use a condom."

Angie laughed, but it was sad and a little strained. "Do you and David want to keep the baby?"

"How can I know something like that? I want . . ." She sagged deeper in her chair and bowed her head. Angie could tell that she was crying. She made almost no sound, as though she'd learned to keep her tears inside. "It's my mess. I got myself into it; I have to get myself out of it. Maybe Mrs. Mauk will let me stay here for a while longer."

Angie squeezed her eyes shut, feeling tears of her own.

Memories came at her hard—Lauren at Help-Your-Neighbor House, freezing cold, but asking for a coat for her mother . . . in the grocery store parking lot on a rainy night, pressing flyers on windshields . . . saying softly *I can't go* to the homecoming dance and then hugging Angie for something as simple as a borrowed dress and some makeup.

Lauren was alone in the world. She was a good, responsible girl, and she'd do the right thing or die trying, but how could a seventeen-year-old possibly find the right way on so treacherous a road? She would need help.

She's not your daughter, Angela.

You be careful with this girl.

It was good advice, and now, at this moment, Angie was terrified not to take it. She'd worked so hard to come out of the darkness of baby-wanting; how could she let herself slide backward? Could she stand by Lauren and watch her belly grow and grow? Could she survive the intimacies of another woman's pregnancy—the morning sickness, the dreams that expanded with every gained pound, the wonder in tiny words like: *She kicked me . . . he's a little gymnast . . . here, touch my stomach . . .*

And yet.

How could she turn Lauren away at a time like this?

"I'll tell you what," Angie said slowly, unable, really, to say anything else. "Why don't you come live with me?"

Lauren gasped, looked up. "You don't mean that."

"I do."

"You'll change your mind. You'll see me get fatter and you'll—"

"Have you ever trusted anyone?"

Lauren didn't answer, but the truth was in her eyes.

"Trust *me*. Come to the cottage for a while, until you figure out your future. You need to be taken care of."

"Taken care of."

Angie heard the wonder in Lauren's voice. It was such a simple thing—caring—but what a crater in the soul its absence must leave.

"I'll clean your house and do the laundry. I can cook, too, and if you'll show me what are weeds—"

"You don't need to clean my house." Angie smiled. Though the fear was still there, the nervous *can I watch this up close* tension, she felt good, too. She could make a difference in this girl's life. Maybe she'd never be a mother; that didn't mean she

couldn't act like one. "Just show up for work when you're scheduled and keep your grades up. Okay?"

Lauren threw herself into Angie's arms, holding her in a
death grip. "Okay."

LAUREN PACKED HER CLOTHES AND SCHOOL UNIFORMS (UNNECES-
sary now), her makeup and her mementos, and still there was
room left over.

The last thing she packed was a small, framed photograph
of her and her mother. In it, they looked like a pair of showgirls,
with their faces poked through painted openings. In truth, Lauren didn't remember ever posing for this picture. According to
Mom, they'd been in Vegas at a truck stop on the way west. For
years Lauren had tried to create a memory that matched the image, but one had never come.

It was the only picture of them together. She placed it safely
between the layers of clothes and closed the suitcase. On the way
downstairs, she stopped at Mrs. Mauk's apartment.

"Here are the keys," she said.

"Where are you going?"

Lauren grabbed the woman's arm and led her to the window.
Outside, on the street, Angie stood beside her car, looking up at
the building. "That's Angie Malone. I'm going to live with her."
She heard the wonder in her voice.

"I remember her."

"You'll sell the furniture for back rent, okay?"

"Okay." Mrs. Mauk looked down at the keys, then up at her.
Her smile was sad. "I'm sorry, Lauren. If there's anything I can do
to help . . ." She let the sentence trail off. They both knew it had
nowhere to go.

Lauren appreciated it all the same. "You were good to us. Letting the rent be so late and everything."

"You got a bum deal, kiddo. Your mom was a real piece of
work."

Lauren handed the manager a piece of paper. On it, she'd
written Angie's home address and phone number, as well as the
restaurant's information. "Here," she said softly. "When my mom
comes home, she'll want to know where I am." She heard the old
neediness in her voice, that raggedy edge; she couldn't help it.

"When?"

"When it falls apart with Jake—and it will fall apart—she'll be back."

"And you'll be waiting." Mrs. Mauk made the words sound pathetically sad.

What could Lauren say to that? All of her life, she'd been waiting for her mother's love. There was no way she could simply put her hope aside. It was a part of her, that faith, as ingrained as the beat of her heart or the flutter of her pulse. But it didn't hurt as much anymore; the sense of her loss was duller, almost distant.

She glanced down at Angie again, who was waiting to take her home.

Home.

Then she looked at Mrs. Mauk and said, "I'm okay now."

"You're a good kid, Lauren. I'll think good thoughts."

"Maybe I'll see you around."

"I hope not, Lauren. Once you're out of this part of town, you stay out. But I'll be here if you ever need me." With a last smile, Mrs. Mauk said good-bye.

In the hallway, Lauren grabbed her suitcase off the floor and hurried outside and down the steps.

"You want me to get the rest of it?" Angie asked, moving toward her.

"This is everything," Lauren said, patting the suitcase.

"Oh." Angie stopped. The merest of frowns darted across her brow, then she said, "Well, then. We're off."

On the drive through town and along the beach and up the hill, Lauren stared out the window, saying nothing. Every now and then the moonlight hit just right and she found herself staring into her own reflection. She couldn't help but see a smiling girl with sad eyes. She wondered if they'd always be sad now, always see the chances she'd lost. That had certainly happened to her mother.

She cast a sideways glance at Angie, who was humming along with the radio. Probably she didn't know what to say either.

Lauren closed her eyes. She tried to imagine her life with Angie as her mother. Everything would have been softer, sweeter. Angie would never slap her pregnant daughter or run out on her in the middle of the night or . . .

"Here we are. Home sweet home."

Lauren's eyes popped open. Maybe she'd fallen asleep for a minute there. It all felt like a dream, that was for sure.

Angie parked next to the house and got out. All the way to the front door and into the house, she talked over her shoulder to Lauren, who hurried along, dragging her suitcase.

". . . oven's about twenty degrees hotter than the indicator. No microwave. Sorry. These rusty old pipes . . ."

Lauren tried to take it all in. Besides the information Angie was giving her, she noticed a few other things. The windows needed to be washed, for instance, and there was a rip on the sofa's arm. These were jobs Lauren could do to help out.

Angie kept talking as they went upstairs. ". . . great water pressure. I recommend lashing yourself down or you'll fly out of the shower. The pipes ping a little at first, and definitely don't flush the toilet just before your shower." She stopped, turned. "It's okay to share a bathroom, isn't it? If not—"

"It's fine," Lauren said quickly.

Angie smiled. "I thought so. Good. Well, here's your room. All of us girls used to sleep here." She opened the door at the end of the hall.

It was a big, beautiful room with a steeply sloped ceiling and timber beams. Pink wallpaper—tiny rosebuds and vines—covered the walls. Matching bedspreads were on the two sets of bunk beds. A small oak writing desk was tucked in one corner; to its left three expansive rectangular windows looked out over the ocean. Tonight moonlight tarnished the silvery waves. "Wow," Lauren said.

"The sheets haven't been washed in a while. I can do that now—"

"No." Lauren sounded harsh. She hadn't meant to. It was just . . . overwhelming. "I can do my own sheets."

"Of course. You're an adult. I didn't mean to imply that you didn't know how to do laundry. It's just that—"

Lauren dropped the suitcase and ran to Angie, throwing her arms around her. "Thank you," she said, burying her face in the warm, sweet crook of Angie's neck.

Slowly, Angie hugged her back. When Lauren felt herself start to cry, she tried to pull back, but Angie wouldn't let her. Instead, she stroked Lauren's hair, murmured that it would be okay. Over and over, *It's okay now, Lauren. It's okay.*

All of her life Lauren had waited for a moment like this.

.   .   .

"*What?*"

The word was spoken in unison. Shouted, actually.

Angie fought the urge to step back. "Lauren moved in with me."

Her sisters and Mama stood in a line in Mama's kitchen. They were staring at Angie.

"This is you being careful with the girl?" Mama demanded, slamming her hands on her hips.

"I think it's great," Livvy said. "They'll be good for each other."

Mama waved her hand impatiently. "Be quiet. Your sister isn't thinking straight." She took a step forward. "You just don't go around inviting redheaded strangers into your home."

"She's hardly a stranger," Livvy said. "She's been working in the restaurant. She's good, too."

"Until she just didn't show up for three days," Mama said. "For all we know, she was on a crime spree."

Livvy laughed. "Right. Driving from town to town, robbing mini-marts, stopping only long enough to refill her ammo and take a math test."

Angie moved nervously from foot to foot. She hadn't expected such a reaction to the moving-in news.

What came next would be a different matter. The word *ballistic* came to mind.

"Angie," Mira said, moving closer, studying her. "There's something you're not telling us."

Angie winced.

"What? You're keeping secrets, too?" Mama made a snorting sound. "You know Papa will tell me everything."

Angie was cornered. There was nothing she could do. Pregnancy wasn't the kind of secret that stayed secret. She glanced down the row of women, then said, "There is one more thing. Lauren's pregnant."

Ballistic turned out to be an understatement.

THE ARGUMENT HAD GONE ON FOR HOURS. BY THE TIME IT CAME TO a tired, sputtering end, Mama had called in reinforcements. Both of Angie's brothers-in-law were there, along with Aunt Giulia and Uncle Francis. Everyone in the room had an opinion on whether Angie was making a mistake.

In a move that surprised everyone, Livvy voiced the lone dissent. "Let her do what she wants," she said sometime in the second hour. "None of us knows what it's like for her."

That had brought the pseudo–town meeting to a crashing halt. At the oblique reference to Angie's childlessness, everyone looked quickly away.

Angie shot Livvy a grateful look. Livvy winked and smiled back.

Then it started up again.

Angie couldn't stand it anymore. While they were arguing the pros and cons of the decision, she slipped out of the room and went upstairs.

In her old room, she closed the door. The blessed silence soothed her. She figured she had about six minutes of solitude before Mama or Mira came after her.

Less.

The door opened. Mama stood in the doorway, wearing her disappointed face. It was a look her daughters knew by heart. "Two minutes," Angie noted, scooting sideways on the bed. "That's a new record."

Mama closed the door behind her. "I sent everyone home."

"Good."

Mama sighed, then sat down on the bed beside Angie. The old springs pinged beneath their weight. "Your papa—God rest his soul—would have yelled at you tonight. Him, you would have listened to."

"Papa never yelled at us. You did."

Mama laughed. "He didn't have to yell. He let me rant and rave for a while and then he drew a line in the sand. 'That's enough, Maria,' he'd say." She paused. "It's hard now, with no lines in the sand."

Angie leaned against her mother. "I know."

Mama laid her wrinkled hand on Angie's thigh. "I worry about you, that's all. It is a mother's job."

"I know. And I love you for it."

"You will be careful, yes? I have seen your heart broken too many times already."

"I'm stronger now, Mama. Honestly, I am."

"I hope so, Angela."

TWENTY-FOUR

L AUREN WAS AWAKE LONG BEFORE THE ALARM CLOCK sounded. She'd gotten up around five to go to the bathroom, and after that, she hadn't been able to go back to sleep. She would have started cleaning, but she didn't want to wake Angie.

It was so quiet here. The only sounds were the surf whooshing against the sand and rocks and the occasional tapping of wind against the windowpane.

No car horns honking, no neighbors screaming at one another, no bottles breaking on the sidewalks.

In a bed like this, with heaping blankets and a down comforter, a girl felt safe.

She glanced over at the clock. It was six. Still dark outside. In these first weeks of winter, the days were short. If she'd been going to Fircrest on this Monday morning, she would have needed to wear her woolen tights with the uniform.

Not that it mattered anymore.

Today would be her first day at West End High. A pregnant transfer student who would be around only until the end of the semester. The popular girls were sure to love her.

She threw the covers back and got out of bed. Gathering her stuff together, she went into the bathroom and took a quick shower, then carefully dried her hair until it lay straight.

Back in the bedroom, she searched her drawers for something to wear.

Nothing seemed right for the first day at a new school.

Finally, she settled on a pair of flare-legged, low-rise jeans with a fringed suede belt and a white sweater. As she was putting the sweater on, one of her hoop earrings popped free and skittered across the floor.

David had given her those earrings for her last birthday.

She dropped to the floor and started looking, spreading her hands across the boards.

There it was.

She scooted under the bed and found the earring . . . and something else. Tucked way in the back was a long, narrow wooden box. It looked so much like the floorboards, you'd have to be this close to see it.

Lauren grabbed the box and dragged it out from underneath the bed. Opening it, she found a heap of old black-and-white family photographs. Most of them featured three little girls in pretty dresses gathered around a dark, well-dressed man with a smile that lit up his whole face. He was tall and almost elegantly thin, with eyes that closed into slits when he laughed. And he was laughing in most of the pictures. He reminded Lauren of that actor from the old days—the one who always fell in love with Grace Kelly.

Mr. DeSaria.

Absurdly, Lauren thought of him as Papa. She looked through the pictures, saw the images of a childhood she'd dreamed of: family road trips to the Grand Canyon and Disneyland; days spent at the Grays Harbor County Fair, eating cotton candy and riding the roller coaster; evenings at this very cottage, roasting marshmallows at a bonfire near the water's edge.

A knock pounded at the door. "It's six-thirty, Lauren. Rise and shine."

"I'm up." She pushed the box back under the bed, then made
her bed and picked up her room. When she left it and closed the
door behind her, there was no visible evidence that she'd even
been there.

Downstairs, she found Angie in the kitchen. "Good morning,"
Angie said, scooping scrambled eggs from a frying pan to a plate.
"You're just in time."

"You made me breakfast?"

"Was that okay? Do you mind?"

"Are you kidding? It's *great.*"

Angie smiled again. "Good. You'll need to eat well in the next
few months."

They stared at each other in a sudden, awkward silence. The
distant hum of the ocean seemed to grow louder. Lauren
couldn't help touching her stomach.

Angie winced. "Maybe I shouldn't have said that."

"I'm pregnant. There's no point pretending I'm not."

"No."

Lauren couldn't think of anything else to say. She went to the
table and sat down, scooting in close. "Breakfast smells great."

Angie handed her a plate with a couple of scrambled eggs,
two pieces of cinnamon toast, and some cantaloupe slices on it.
"That's about the only thing I can cook."

"Thank you," Lauren said softly, looking up.

Angie sat down across from her. "You're welcome." Finally,
she smiled. "So, how did you sleep?"

"Good. I'll have to get used to the quiet."

"Yeah. When I moved to Seattle, it took me forever to get
used to the noise."

"Do you miss the city?"

Angie looked surprised by the question, as if maybe she
hadn't thought of it before. "I don't, actually. I've been sleeping
amazingly well lately; that must mean something."

"It's the sea air."

"Excuse me?"

"Your mama told me that if a girl grows up smelling sea air,
she can never really breathe inland."

Angie laughed. "That sounds like my mother. But Seattle is
hardly inland."

"Your mother thinks everything except West End is inland."

They talked a bit more about this and that, then Angie stood up. "You do the dishes. I'll shower and meet you in ten minutes, then we'll go to school."

"What do you mean?"

"I'm driving you, of course. The restaurant is closed today, so carpool is no problem. Hey, by the way, I thought Fircrest had a uniform."

"They do."

"Why are you in civilian clothes?"

Lauren felt the heat on her cheeks. "They took back my scholarship. Uniforms don't come in elephant sizes, I guess."

"Are you telling me they kicked you out of school because you're pregnant?"

"It's no big deal." She hoped her voice didn't betray how she really felt.

"The hell you say."

"I don't know—"

"Do the dishes, Lauren, and put on your uniform. We're paying Fircrest Academy a little visit."

AN HOUR LATER, THEY WERE IN THE COUNSELOR'S OFFICE. LAUREN stood with her back to the wall, trying to disappear into the rough, white stucco.

Angie sat in a chair, facing Mrs. Detlas, who was behind her desk, with her hands clasped together on the metal surface.

"It's a pleasure to finally meet you, Mrs. Ribido," Mrs. Detlas said. "I guess there has been some miscommunication about Lauren's future here at Fircrest."

Lauren drew in a sharp breath and looked at Angie, who smiled.

"I'm here to discuss . . . my daughter's future," Angie said, crossing one leg over the other.

"I see. Well, you'll need to discuss that with the counselor at West End. You see—"

"What I *see*," Angie said evenly, "is a lawsuit. Or perhaps a headline: *Catholic school expels poor, perfect student for being pregnant.* I know about headlines because my ex-husband is a reporter for the *Seattle Times.* You know, he was saying just the other night that the big city papers could use a good small town scandal."

"We . . . uh . . . didn't technically expel Lauren. I merely suggested that girls could be cruel to a girl in her kind of trouble."

She frowned. "I didn't know about your husband." She started looking through Lauren's file.

Angie looked at Lauren. "You worried about the girls being mean to you?"

Lauren shook her head. If she had a voice, she couldn't find it.

Angie turned back to the counselor. "It was kind of you to think of Lauren's feelings on this, but as you can see, she's a tough kid."

Mrs. Detlas slowly closed Lauren's folder. Then she said, "I suppose she could finish the semester here and take the finals. There's only six weeks left in the term, and Christmas break cuts in the middle of it. She could take her finals in January and graduate early, but I really believe—"

Angie stood up. "Thank you, Mrs. Detlas. Lauren will graduate from Fircrest, which is as it should be."

"You're welcome," Mrs. Detlas said, obviously irritated.

"I'm sure you'll make every effort to help her. And I'll be sure and tell my uncle how well it all turned out for Lauren."

"Your uncle?"

"Oh, did I forget to mention that?" She looked right at the counselor. "Cardinal Lanza is my mother's brother."

Mrs. Detlas seemed to shrink into her chair. "Oh" was how she answered, but it could hardly be heard at all.

"Let's go, Lauren," Angie said, heading for the door.

Lauren stumbled along beside her. "That was *amazing*," she said when they got outside.

"And fun. The old bat needed a wake-up call."

"How did you know what to say?"

"Life, honey. It all comes in handy."

Lauren smiled. She felt great. Better than great. No one had ever fought for her like that, and the effort strengthened her, made her feel invincible. With Angie on her side, she could do anything.

Even attend classes when she knew people would be staring and talking.

Angie grinned. "I just hope there is a Cardinal Lanza."

At that, they both burst into laughter.

ANGIE STOOD AT THE CORNER, WATCHING LAUREN WALK ACROSS campus. She held herself back from shouting: "Bye, honey. Have

a good day at school. I'll be here at six to pick you up." She was
still young enough to know that such a scene would be the
height of uncool. And poor Lauren didn't need any extra attention to come her way. Pregnant in private school was tough
enough. A geek wannabe mother might push her over the edge.

Lauren paused at the big building's double door. Turning
slightly, she waved at Angie, then disappeared inside.

Angie's chest felt tight. "You little witches better be nice to
my girl," she said. Closing her eyes, she said a prayer for Lauren,
then she got into the car.

As she was driving home, trying not to imagine the firestorm
of gossip at Fircrest Academy, she considered going back, parking
by the flagpole, just in case. What if Lauren came out crying, broken by the kinds of petty cruelty that only teenage girls could in-
flict? She would need Angie . . .

"No," she said aloud, taking charge of her negative fantasies.
Lauren had to get through this day on her own. There was no
other way. The road she'd found herself on was dark and scary;
there was no way out except straight through.

The bleating ring of her cell phone saved her. She dug into
her purse and found it, answering on the third ring.

"Angie?"

She hadn't realized until just then, when she drew in a sharp
breath, that she'd been waiting for this. "Hey, Con," she said, trying to sound casual. To be safe, she pulled off to the side of the
road. Her heart was going a mile a minute.

"I've been thinking about the other night."

Me, too.

"We need to talk."

"That's been true for years," she said. "Do you want to come
down to the cottage?" The minute the invitation slipped out, she
thought: *Lauren.*

He would not be happy about the situation.

"Not today, I'm busy," he said. "Maybe . . ." His voice trailed
into the dark woods of uncertainty. He was reconsidering; she
could tell.

"It's Monday. The restaurant's closed. I could come up and
buy you lunch."

"Lunch?"

"It's a meal. Often characterized by sandwiches and soups."
Her joke fell flat. "Come on, Con. You need to eat lunch."

"How about Al Boccalino?"

"I can be there by eleven-thirty." She flicked her turn signal and eased back onto the road.

"See you then. Bye," he said.

"Bye." Angie wanted to smile, but all she could think about was the girl living under her roof. Conlan would not take this news well.

SHE MADE IT TO DOWNTOWN SEATTLE IN RECORD TIME, PARKED THE car, and headed for the restaurant.

Their restaurant.

At least, it had been once.

She was four blocks away when it started to pour. Raindrops the size of golf balls battered the sidewalk in front of her, formed rushing silver rivers along the curb. She popped open her umbrella and headed for Pioneer Square. In the park, dozens of homeless people huddled in pods, passing cigarettes back and forth, trying to keep dry.

Finally she reached Yesler. The viaduct—that arching concrete overpass that dared a big earthquake to crumble it—held the rain at bay.

She ducked into the restaurant. Al Boccalino was empty this early in the day. The working lunch crowd wouldn't be here for another hour at least.

Carlos, the owner of the restaurant, came around the corner. Seeing her, he smiled.

"Mrs. Malone. It's good to see you again."

"You, too." She handed him her coat and umbrella and followed him into the small, Tuscan-inspired trattoria. Immediately, she smelled the pungent combination of garlic and thyme that reminded her of home.

"You should bring your mama back some time," Carlos said with a smile.

Angie laughed. The one time she had brought her parents here, Mama had spent the whole night in the kitchen, chastising the chef for cutting tomatoes for marinara. *Crush them,* she'd muttered. *That is why God gave us hands.* "Sure, Carlos," she said, her smile fading when she saw Conlan.

He rose at her entrance.

Carlos helped her into her seat, gave them each a menu, and then disappeared.

"It feels strange to be here again," Angie said.

"I know. I haven't been here since our anniversary."

She frowned. "I thought your apartment was right around the corner."

"It is."

That silence descended again. They looked at each other.

Carlos appeared at the table, holding a bottle of champagne. "My favorite couple together again. Is good." He filled each fluted glass with glittering, bubbling liquid. He looked at Conlan. "You let me decide your lunch menu, yes?"

"Of course," Conlan answered, still looking at Angie.

She felt exposed by that look, vulnerable. She reached for her glass, needing something in her hand.

I want to tell you about this girl I met.

"Conlan," she said just as Carlos reappeared by the table, holding a plate of caprese salad. By the time they'd oohed and aahed over the food, Angie had lost her nerve. She finished her glass of champagne and poured a second.

She's really great. She's living with me. Oh, and did I mention she's pregnant?

Conlan leaned forward, put his elbows on the table. "This morning I got a call from my agent. I've been offered a book contract." He paused, then said, "And the only person I wanted to tell was you. What do you think that means?"

She knew how much it had cost him to admit that. She wanted to reach for him, take his hand in hers, and tell him that she still loved him, that she'd always loved him and always would, but it was too soon for that. Instead, she said, "I think it means we loved each other for a long time."

"Most of my life."

She touched her glass to his. The brittle clinking was the sound of beginnings. She knew she should tell him about Lauren now, but she couldn't do it. This moment felt magical somehow, full of possibility. "Tell me everything."

He launched into the story of a local man who had been convicted of raping and killing several elderly women in the late nineties. Conlan had done an investigative piece on the story and been hooked. He'd come to believe the man was innocent, and DNA tests had just proven it. "It's a Cinderella deal," he said. "They're giving me a decent amount of money to write this book and another one."

He was still talking about the story an hour later when they finished their dessert and paid the bill.

Angie got to her feet, noticing that she was more than a little tipsy.

Conlan stood beside her, steadied her with his touch.

She stared up at him. His face, creased now in a smile, made her want to cry. "I'm so proud of you, Conlan."

His smile faded. "This can't be good."

"What can't? I—"

He pulled her into his arms and kissed her, right there in the restaurant, in front of everyone. It wasn't one of those you-could-be-my-grandma kisses, either. Oh, no.

"Wow," she said when it was over. She realized she was swaying slightly. She tried to remain still. It was difficult; her heart was pounding. She wanted him with a ferocity that surprised her. "But we need to talk," she said, trying to think straight.

"Later," he said in a gravelly, desperate voice. Taking her hand, he pulled her toward the door. "We're going to my place."

She gave in. It was impossible not to. "Can we run?"

"Definitely."

Outside, Angie was surprised to see that it was still light. Then she remembered: It had been a lunch date. They ran through the rain down Yesler Street, turned on Jackson.

Conlan jammed his key in the lock.

Angie pressed up against his back and put her arms around him. She moved her hands down to his waistband.

"Damn," he muttered, trying another key.

The lock clicked open.

He pushed through the door and dragged her toward the elevator. When the doors opened, they tumbled inside, still kissing.

Angie was on fire. She touched him everywhere, kissed him until she felt dizzy.

She couldn't breathe.

The doors opened. He swept her into his arms and carried her down the hall. In minutes—seconds—they were in his bedroom.

Conlan placed her gently on the bed. She lay there, feeling dazed with the kind of desire she'd forgotten about. "Take off your clothes," she said in a husky voice, propping herself onto her elbows. He knelt at the foot of the bed, between her legs. "I can't stay away from you," he whispered. There was both wonder and disappointment in his voice.

She knew there would be a price for this moment.

Right now, she didn't care.

TWENTY-FIVE

NAKED, ANGIE STOOD AT THE WINDOW OF HER HUS-
band's—ex-husband's—apartment, staring out at El-
liott Bay. Rain gave the world a blurry, distant counte-
nance. Cars rumbled north and south on the viaduct. The
windowpanes rattled ever so softly from all that traffic, made a
sound like the chattering of teeth.

If this were a movie moment, she'd be smoking a cigarette
and frowning while a montage of images from their failed marriage and newborn reconciliation flashed across the screen. The
last image, as the movie returned to the present, would be Lauren's face.

"You look worried," Conlan said.

How well he knew her. Even when she stood in profile, with
her back slanted toward him, he could tell. Probably it was in her

stance. He always said she tilted her chin up and crossed her arms when she was upset.

She didn't turn to face him. In the window, a ghostly image of her face, blurred by rain, gazed back at her. "I wouldn't say worried. Thoughtful, maybe."

The bed springs creaked. He must be sitting up. "Ange?"

Finally, she went to the bed and sat down beside him. He touched her arm, kissed the swell of her breast.

"What is it?"

"I need to tell you something," she said.

He drew back. "That doesn't sound good."

"There's this girl."

"Oh?"

"She's a good girl. Perfect grades. Hardworking."

"And she's relevant to us how?"

"I hired her in September. She works at the restaurant about twenty hours a week. You know, after school, weekends. Mama hates to admit it, but she's the best waitress they've ever had."

Conlan eyed her. "What's her tragic flaw?"

"There isn't one."

"Angie Malone, I know you. Now what the hell are we really talking about here? And don't tell me it's a girl who is a great waitress."

"Her mother abandoned her."

"Abandoned?"

"Just walked out one day."

His gaze was steady. "Tell me you found her a place to live—"

"Gave her a place."

Conlan blew out a heavy breath. "She's living with you at the cottage?"

"Yes."

Disappointment stamped itself on his face—in his blue eyes, in his frowning mouth. "So you have a teenager living in the house."

"It's not like that. Not like before, anyway. I'm just helping her out until . . ."

"Until what?"

Angie sighed and covered her eyes with her hand. "Until the baby is born."

"Oh, *shit*," Conlan said, throwing the covers back, getting out of bed.

"Con—"

He stormed into the bathroom, slammed the door shut behind him.

Angie felt as if she'd been kicked in the gut. She'd known this would happen. But what choice did she have? With a sigh, she bent down for her clothes and got dressed. Then she sat on the bed, waiting.

He finally came out, wearing a pair of worn old Levi's and a pale blue T-shirt. His anger seemed to have gone; without it, he looked tired. His shoulders were rounded in defeat. "You said you'd changed."

"I have."

"The old Angie brought a pregnant teenager home, too." He looked at her. "That was the beginning of the end for us. I remember, even if you don't."

"Come on," she said, feeling as if something inside of her were breaking. She moved toward him. "I've hardly forgotten. Just give me a chance."

"I've given you a lifetime of chances, Ange." He looked around the room, then at the bed. "This was a mistake. I should have known better."

"It's different this time. I swear." She reached for him. He sidestepped out of her grasp.

"How? How is it different?"

"She's a seventeen-year-old with no one to take care of her and nowhere to go. I'm helping her, but I'm not crazy anymore with what I don't have. I've made peace with not having a baby. Please," she whispered. "Give me a chance to show you that this is different. Come meet her."

"*Meet* her? After what Sarah Dekker put us through—"

"This is not Sarah. The baby is Lauren's. Just come and meet her. Please. For me."

He looked down at her, long and hard, then he said, "I won't live through it all again. The highs. The lows. The obsessions."

"Conlan, believe me, I—"

"Don't you dare finish that sentence." He reached for his keys off the dresser and headed for the door.

"I'm sorry," she said.

He paused. Without looking back, he said, "You're always sorry, aren't you, Angie? That's what I should have remembered."

.   .   .

IN HER WORLD HISTORY CLASS LAST YEAR, LAUREN HAD DONE A RE-
port on Victorian London. One of her research sources had been
the film *The Elephant Man*. She remembered sitting in the library
after hours, staring at the small television screen, watching the
well-heeled Londoners taunt and ridicule poor John Merrick,
whose face and body had been twisted and tortured far beyond
what a man should have to endure. But the whispers and stares
hurt him as deeply as any of his deformities.

Lauren understood that now, how much it hurt to be the ob-
ject of gossip. In all her years at Fircrest she'd strived for the kind
of perfection that drew only positive attention. She was never late
to class, never broke the rules, never said mean things about other
kids. She'd tried, in all ways, to be like Caesar's wife: above re-
proach.

She should have known how far the mighty fall and how
hard the ground could be.

Everyone was staring at her, pointing and whispering. Even
the teachers seemed shocked and unnerved by her presence.
They acted as if she carried a lethal virus, one that could all too
easily go airborne and infect innocent passersby.

After school, she let herself be swept along by the laughing,
yelling crowd. Even in the midst of all these people—friends,
mostly—she felt infinitely different. Separate. Head down, she
tried to be invisible.

"Lauren!"

She looked up instinctively, though she immediately wished
she hadn't.

The gang was gathered around the flagpole; Susan and Kim
were seated on the bricked ledge beside it and David and Jared
were playing hacky sack.

She steeled herself for the inevitable. She'd avoided them at
lunch by hiding out in the library, but now she had no choice but
to say hi.

"Hey, guys," she said, coming up to the group. She hesitated,
saw David do the same.

They stared at each other from a distance.

The girls swarmed her, pulled at her arm. She followed them
out behind the school, to their place on the football field. The
boys followed along behind, keeping the hacky sack in motion.

"Well?" Kim asked when they were all standing around the
goalpost. "How does it feel?"

"Scary," Lauren answered. She so didn't want to talk about

this, but it was better to be talked to than talked about. And these were her best friends.

"What are you going to do?" Susan asked, scouting through her backpack for something. Finally she pulled out a Coke. Opening it, she took a drink and passed it around.

David came up behind Lauren, slipped an arm around her waist. "We don't know."

"How come you didn't have an abortion?" Kim asked. "That's what my cousin did."

Lauren shrugged. "I just couldn't." She was starting to wish she were far, far away from here. With Angie, where she felt safe . . .

"David says you're giving it up for adoption. That's cool. My aunt Sylvia adopted a baby last year. She's way happy now," Susan said, reaching for the Coke.

Lauren looked up at David.

For the first time she realized that he could walk away from this, leave it in the past along with all his high school memories. Someday it would be as forgotten as his tenth grade MVP trophy or his grade point. Why hadn't she seen that before?

She'd thought they were in this together, but suddenly all the warnings came back to her. It was the girl who got pregnant.

"Come with me," she whispered to him, pulling him aside. He followed her to a dark, quiet place beside the bleachers.

She wanted desperately to be held and kissed and reassured, but he just stood there, staring down at her, his confusion as obvious as his love.

"What?"

"I just . . . I'll miss you over the break." She wished he'd invited her along, but it was a family vacation.

"My dad set up a meeting in January. With a lawyer." He flinched, looked at her throat. "About adoption."

"Just give it away," she said, hearing the bitterness in her voice. That would be so easy for him.

"We should at least listen." David looked ready to cry, right there on the football field, with his friends only a few yards away.

And she knew: None of this was easy on him.

"Yeah," she said, "sure. We should listen."

He looked at her. She felt distant from him; older. "Maybe I'll get you a ring. Aspen has tons of cool jewelry stores."

Her heart did a little flip. "Really?"

"I love you," he said softly.

The words sounded different than before, as if he'd murmured them from far away or mouthed them underwater. By the time she got home, she couldn't remember the sound of those words at all.

ANGIE READ THE INSTRUCTIONS FOR MAKING RICOTTA GNOCCHI for at least the fourth time. She did not consider herself a stupid woman, but she couldn't figure out how the hell she was supposed to use the tines of a fork to form the gnocchis.

"Forget it." She rolled the dough into a rope and cut it in small pieces. She'd decided to learn to cook; that didn't mean she wanted to make it her life's work. "Good enough."

She then stirred the sauce. The pungent aroma of sizzling garlic and onion and simmering tomatoes filled the cottage. Not as good as Mama's, of course; you couldn't get that homemade aroma from a store-bought sauce. She only hoped that none of her family stopped by.

At least she was cooking.

It was supposed to be therapeutic. That was what her sisters always said. Angie had been desperate enough to give it a try, but now she knew. All that mixing and chopping and scraping hadn't helped at all.

I won't live through it all again. The highs, the lows, the obsessions.

Maybe she shouldn't have told Conlan about Lauren. Not yet anyway. Maybe she should have let their love take hold first.

No.

That would have been like the old days, with her in a lonely wilderness that bordered his but didn't cross over. Though he didn't see the nuances of her change, she did.

Honesty had been her only choice.

Once or twice today she'd meandered down the road of regret, almost wishing she hadn't invited Lauren home with her, but in truth, she couldn't really go there. She was glad to be helping the girl.

She washed a bunch of fresh basil leaves and began to chop them. They stuck to the knife and formed a green glob. She cut what was left into slices with her scissors.

The front door opened. Lauren walked into the house. She was soaking wet.

Angie glanced at the clock. "You're early. I was supposed to pick you up—"

"I thought I'd save you the trouble." Lauren peeled out of her coat and hung it up on the iron coat rack, then she kicked off her shoes. They thunked against the wall.

"Put your shoes away neatly, please," Angie said automatically, channeling her mother. At the realization, she laughed.

"What's funny?"

"I am. I sounded just like my mother for a second there." She tossed the basil in the sauce, stirred it once with a wooden spoon and covered the pot. "So," she said, setting the spoon down. "I thought you were going to stay after school with David."

Lauren looked miserable. "Yeah. Well."

"I'll tell you what. Go put on some dry clothes and we'll have some hot cocoa and talk."

"You're busy."

"I'm cooking. Which probably means we'll have to go out for dinner, so you might as well get dressed."

At last, a smile. "Okay."

Angie turned the heat on the stove to low, then made a pot of homemade hot cocoa. It was one of the few things she made well. By the time she was finished and had taken a seat in the living room, Lauren was coming down the stairs.

"Thanks," Lauren said, taking a cup of cocoa, sitting in the big leather chair by the window.

"I take it your day didn't go well," Angie said, trying to keep her voice gentle.

Lauren shrugged. "I feel . . . older than all my friends."

"I guess I can see that."

"They're worrying about Civil War battle dates, and I'm worrying about how to pay for day care while I go to college. Not a lot in common there." She looked up. "David said he might buy me a ring."

"Is that a proposal?"

It was exactly the wrong thing to say. Poor Lauren's face crumbled. "I didn't think so."

"Oh, honey, don't be too hard on him. Even grown men can't handle impending fatherhood. David probably feels like he's been dropped out of an airplane and the ground is rushing up to meet him. He knows he's going to hit hard. Just because he's scared doesn't mean he loves you less."

"I don't know if I could take that. Him not loving me, I mean."

"I know what you mean."

Lauren looked up sharply. She wiped her eyes and sniffed. "I'm sorry. I shouldn't have brought it up. I don't want you to be sad, too."

"What do you mean?"

"You still love your ex. I can tell by the way you talk about him."

"I'm that obvious, huh?" Angie looked down at her hands, then said slowly, "I saw him today." She didn't know what made her share that secret. The need to talk about it, maybe.

"Really? Is he still in love with you, too?"

Angie could hear the hope in Lauren's voice and she understood the girl's need to believe that a burned-out love could be rekindled. What woman didn't want to believe that? "I don't know. There's a lot of water under our bridge."

"He wouldn't like me living here."

The perceptiveness of the observation surprised Angie. "Why do you say that?"

"Come on. After what that other pregnant girl did to you guys?"

"That was different," Angie said, echoing what she'd said to Conlan only a few hours ago, wanting to believe it. "I cared about Sarah, sure. But I fell in love with the baby in her womb. I would have adopted that child and brought him into our lives and said good-bye to Sarah. She would have disappeared from our everyday lives. You're different."

"How?"

"I care about you, Lauren. You." She sighed. "And, yes, sometimes the old needs get away from me. Sometimes I lie in my bed upstairs and close eyes and pretend you're my daughter. But that doesn't make me who I was and it doesn't hurt anymore. I have to make Conlan see that." Angie looked up. She realized that she wasn't even talking to Lauren anymore. She was talking to herself.

Lauren was staring at her. "Sometimes I pretend you're my mom."

"Oh." The word was almost lost in the exhalation of breath that came with it.

"I wish you were."

Angie wanted to cry at that. They were both missing the

same piece of themselves, she and Lauren; no wonder they'd come together so easily.

"We're a team," she said softly. "You and me. Somehow God knew we needed each other." She forced a smile and wiped her eyes. "Now, enough doom and gloom. I'm going to try to boil this damn gnocchi. Why don't you set the table?"

LAUREN LAY ON HER BED, LOOKING AT PHOTOGRAPHS. THERE WERE dozens spread out in front of her. Mr. and Mrs. DeSaria. The three girls—together, separately, and in every combination. Pictures taken in spring, summer, winter, and fall. At the beach, in the mountains, even a few by the side of the road. She looked at these beautiful pictures and imagined how it would have felt, being loved like that for the whole of her life, to have a father come up to her, smiling, and reach for her hand.

Come with me, he'd say, *today we'll*—

There was a knock at the door.

Lauren jackknifed off the bed. She didn't want to get caught pawing through the family's private photographs. She opened the door just enough to see out.

Angie's left eye stared at her through the crack. "We're leaving in ten minutes."

"I know. Have a good time." Lauren closed the door, listening for footsteps.

Another knock.

She opened the door.

"What did you mean by that?" Angie asked.

"By what?"

"You said have a good time."

"Yeah. Downtown."

"It's Christmas Eve."

"I know. That's why you're going downtown. You told me all about it last night. You said the DeSarias descend on town like locusts, eating everything in their path. So, have fun."

"I see. And you're not a DeSaria."

Lauren didn't understand. "No. I'm not."

"So you assumed I'd leave you here alone on Christmas Eve and run off with my *real* family to gorge on cookies and hot mulled wine."

Lauren blushed. "Well, when you put it *that* way—"

"Get dressed. Is that clear enough for you?"

Lauren felt the smile expand across her face. "Yes, ma'am."

"Dress warmly. They're predicting a white Christmas. And please remember that I'm *much* too young to be a ma'am."

Lauren closed the door and ran to the bed. She scooped up all the photographs except for the few she'd chosen, and dumped them back in the box, which she shoved under the bed. Then she gathered up her two disposable cameras and hid them in the nightstand drawer. Once all the evidence was taken care of, she dressed in her old flare-leg Target jeans, a black wool turtleneck sweater, and her fur-trimmed coat.

Downstairs, Angie was waiting. She looked beautiful in a forest green wool dress with black boots and a black cape. Her long dark hair was the very best kind of mess. It made her look hip.

"You look great," Lauren said.

"You, too. Now come on."

They went out to the car and got in. All the way to town they chatted. Not about anything important; just ordinary life.

By the time they reached Front Street, the traffic was bumper to bumper.

"I can't believe all these people are out on Christmas Eve," Lauren said.

"It's the final tree-lighting ceremony."

"Oh," Lauren said, not quite understanding what all the hype was about. She'd lived in this town for years and never been to one of these ceremonies. She'd always had to work on weekends and holidays. David had told her it was "okay," but he hadn't been in years, either. "Too many people" was his parents' excuse.

Angie found a parking spot and pulled in.

The minute she got out of the car, Lauren heard the first sound of Christmas: Bells. Every church in town was pealing its bells. Somewhere nearby a horse-drawn carriage was moving along; she could hear the clip-clop of the hooves and the jangling of harness bells.

In the town square, dozens—maybe hundreds—of tourists were milling about, moving from one store to the next, collecting in front of the booths that sold everything from hot cocoa to rum cake to candy canes. The Rotary Club was roasting chestnuts by the flagpole.

"Angela!" Maria's voice rang out above the crowd.

The next thing Lauren knew, she was swept into the DeSaria

family. Everyone was talking at once, telling jokes, holding hands. They moved from booth to booth, eating every morsel that was offered and buying bags of whatever they couldn't eat on the spot. Lauren saw dozens of school friends moving through the crowd with their families. For once she felt as if she were a part of things instead of on the outside, looking in.

"It's time," Mira said at last. As if on cue, the family stopped. In fact, the whole town seemed to freeze.

The lights went out. Darkness clicked into place. Suddenly the stars overhead were stunning. An air of anticipation moved through the crowd. Angie took Lauren's hand in hers, squeezed it gently.

The Christmas lights came on. Hundreds of thousands of them, all at once.

Lauren gasped.

Magic.

"Pretty cool, huh?" Angie said.

"Yeah." Lauren's throat felt tight.

They spent another hour in the square, and then walked to church for midnight mass, which in this day and age took place at ten. Lauren almost started to cry when she entered the church with Angie at her side. It was just like her little girl's dream; she could easily pretend that Angie was her mother. After the service, the DeSarias split up, each going their separate ways.

Angie and Lauren walked through the crowd, pointing out things to each other along the way. By the time they reached the car, it had started to snow. They drove home slowly. The flakes were huge and airy. They fell lazily to earth.

Lauren couldn't remember the last time she'd seen a white Christmas. Rain was much more the holiday norm.

On Miracle Mile Road, the snow was sticking. It coated the tree limbs and dusted the roadside. The yard lay hidden beneath a blanket of sparkling white.

"I wonder if we'll be able to go sledding tomorrow," she said, bouncing up and down in her seat. She knew she was acting like a little kid but she couldn't help it. "Or maybe we could make snow angels. I saw that on television once. Hey, who's that?"

He was standing at the front door of Angie's house in a wedge of golden light. A veil of falling snow obscured his face.

The car stopped.

Lauren peered through the windshield.

He stepped down from the porch, came closer.

And suddenly Lauren knew. The man in the worn Levi's and black leather jacket was Conlan. She turned to Angie, whose eyes looked huge in her pale face.

"Is that him?"

Angie nodded. "That's my Conlan."

"Wow" was all Lauren could say. He looked like Pierce Brosnan. She got out of the car.

He came toward her, his shoes crunching on the gravel driveway. "You must be Lauren."

His voice was low and rumbly, as if maybe he'd smoked or drank too much when he was young.

Lauren fought the urge to flinch. He had the bluest eyes she'd ever seen and they seemed to penetrate her to the bone. He seemed angry with her. "I am."

"Conlan," Angie said breathlessly, coming up beside him.

He didn't look at Angie. His gaze was steady on Lauren. "I came to meet *you*."

TWENTY-SIX

H E WAS TRYING TO KEEP HIS DISTANCE FROM LAUREN; ANGIE could tell. He wore his reporter detachment like a suit of armor, as if a few patches of hammered together metal could protect a man's heart. He sat stiffly upright at the head of the table, shuffling cards. They'd been playing Hearts for the last hour, talking almost the whole time, although Angie wouldn't characterize it as conversation. An interrogation was more apt.

"And you've applied to colleges?" Conlan asked as he dealt the next hand. He didn't look at Lauren. It was, Angie knew, an old reporter's trick. Don't look; they'll think it's a casual question, one you don't care about.

"Yes," Lauren answered without looking up from her cards.

"Where?"

"USC. Pepperdine. Stanford. Berkeley. UW. UCLA."

"Do you still think college is an option?"

The reference to the baby made Angie look up sharply from her cards.

Lauren's gaze was surprisingly direct. It was clear that she'd decided enough was enough. "I'm going to college."

"It'll be hard," he said, pulling out cards to pass.

"I don't mean to be rude, Mr. Malone," Lauren said, her voice taking on strength, "but life is always hard. I got a scholarship to Fircrest because I never gave up. I'll get a scholarship to college for the same reason. Whatever I have to do, I'll do."

"Do you have any relatives to help?"

"Angie is helping me."

"What about your own family?"

Lauren answered quietly, "I'm alone."

Poor Conlan. Angie watched him melt, right there at the head of the table with the cards in his hands. The reporter face gave way, leaving behind the sad, lined face of a man who was worried.

Angie could tell he was trying to back away from the emotion he'd stirred up, but he was caught, trapped by the tears in a girl's eyes. He cleared his throat. "Angie tells me you're interested in journalism." There it was: higher ground.

Lauren nodded. She led with the two of diamonds. "Yes."

Conlan played the king. "Maybe you'd like to come to work with me someday. I could introduce you to some of the people there; let you see how reporters work."

When she looked back on it, Angie saw how everything had changed in that moment. The interrogation vanished, leaving in its place a mini-party. For the next hour, they talked and laughed and played cards. Conlan told a series of funny work stories about stupid criminals. Angie and Lauren relayed some of their cookie-making mishaps.

At around ten o'clock, the phone rang. It was David, calling from Aspen. Lauren took the phone upstairs.

Conlan turned to Angie. She wasn't sure, but she thought it was the first time he'd dared to look at her.

"Why are you here?" she asked.

"It's Christmas Eve. You're my family."

She wanted to lean forward and kiss him, but she felt awkward, unsure. After all those years of living and loving together, they were separate now. "Habit isn't enough," she said softly.

"No."

"Is it a start?"

Before he could answer, Lauren bounded back into the room, smiling brightly, looking like a girl with her whole life in front of her. "He misses me," she said, sliding into her seat and scooting up to the table.

Angie and Conlan immediately went back to playing cards. For the next hour, they all talked about things that didn't matter.

It was the best night Angie had had in years. So much so that when midnight came and Lauren announced that she was going to bed, Angie actually tried to talk her out of it. She didn't want this evening to end.

"Ange," Conlan said, "let the poor girl go to bed. It's late. How can Santa come if she's not asleep?"

Lauren laughed. It was a young, girlish sound full of hope. It did Angie's heart good to hear it. "Well, good night," Lauren said, surging toward Angie, hugging her. "Merry Christmas," she whispered. When she drew back she added, "This was my best Christmas Eve ever." Then she flashed a smile at Conlan and left the room.

Angie sat back in her chair. With Lauren gone, the room felt too quiet.

"How are you going to make it through her pregnancy?" Conlan asked the question gently, as if the words caused him pain. "How will you handle watching her belly grow and feeling the baby kick and shopping for onesies?"

"It will hurt."

"Yes."

Her gaze was steady, even if her voice wasn't. "Not being there for her would hurt more."

"We've been through this before."

Angie thought about that, about *them*. They'd played cards with Sarah Dekker, too, and watched television with her and bought her new clothes. But it had always been the unborn child that connected them. "No," she finally said. "Not this."

"Hope always came easily to you, Angie. It was part of what ruined us. You don't know how to give up."

"Hope was all I had."

"No. You had me."

The truth of it settled heavily on her heart. "Let's not look in the rearview mirror tonight. I love you. Can that be enough for now?"

"For tonight, you mean?"

She nodded. "Alcoholics take one day at a time. Maybe old lovers can do the same thing."

At that, he leaned toward her, put his hand around the back of her neck, and pulled her toward him. Their gazes met; hers was overbright with unshed tears, his was dark with worry.

He kissed her. It was everything she needed, that kiss, and more than she'd imagined. The next thing she knew, he had her in his arms and was carrying her up the stairs. He started to go to Angie's old bedroom.

She laughed. "The big bedroom. We're the grown-ups now."

He pivoted, pushed through the door, and kicked it shut behind him.

THE NEXT MORNING WHEN ANGIE WOKE UP, HER WHOLE BODY ached. She rolled onto her side and snuggled up to Conlan, kissing his stubbled jawline. "Merry Christmas," she murmured, moving her hand along his naked chest.

He blinked awake. "Merry Christmas."

For what seemed an eternity, she gazed at him, her nipples pressed against his chest, her body ripe with a longing so sharp and sweet it hurt. She could feel their hearts beating together again. When she kissed him, it was with everything she had, all the good times and the bad and the in-between. It was a kiss that peeled back the hard layer of years and made her feel young again, carefree and hopeful.

She touched his cheek in wonder. Perhaps this was how women felt when their men came home from war. Sad somehow, and yet more in love than they'd thought possible. "Love me," she whispered.

"I tried not to. It didn't work," he said, pulling her into his arms.

Much later, when Angie could breathe evenly again and the trembling in her body had stilled, she rolled out of bed and went in search of her robe. "Will you come to Mama's with us?"

He grinned. "That would certainly start up the old rumor mill."

"Please?"

"Where else would I be on Christmas morning?"

Angie laughed out loud. That was how good she felt. "Get dressed. We're already late." Finding her robe, she slipped into it and went down the hall to Lauren's room. She expected to find the girl dressed and awake, chomping at the bit to open presents, but she was sound asleep.

Angie went to the bed and sat down. "Wake up, honey," she said, brushing the hair from her eyes.

Lauren blinked awake. "Morning," she murmured.

"Get up, sleepyhead. It's Christmas."

"Oh. Yeah." Her eyes slid shut again.

Angie frowned. What kid didn't jackknife out of bed on Christmas morning?

The answer came fast on the question's heels: a kid who wasn't used to much of a Christmas. She couldn't help thinking of the apartment building . . . of the woman—mother—who'd walked away without a word.

She leaned down to kiss Lauren's head. "Come on, Sleeping Beauty. We have to be at Mama's in fifteen minutes. We open presents early in this family."

Lauren threw the covers back and ran for the bathroom. They both knew there would be lukewarm water for the second shower and only cold water for the poor third-place loser.

Angie returned to her bedroom. She found Conlan dressed in her father's old plaid bathrobe, standing by the window. He was holding a small silver-wrapped box. They'd always had their private Christmas before going to Mama's, but she hadn't expected him this year.

"You got me a present? I didn't—"

He came toward her, gave her the box. "It's just a little something."

She peeled the foil paper off and opened the white box. Inside lay a beautiful handblown Christmas ornament. A silvery angel with crystal highlights and impossibly faceted wings.

"I found it in Russia last month, when I was interviewing Svetlaska."

She stared down at the beautiful angel that fit in the palm of her hand, remembering another Christmas morning, so many years ago. *It's because I'm always thinking of you,* he'd said, giving her a small wooden shoe ornament he'd bought in Holland. It had been the start of a collection. A tradition. Finally, she looked up at him. "You bought this last month?"

"I missed you," he said quietly.

She went to the dresser then, pulled open the top drawer, and dug through her underwear. When she turned back to Conlan, she was holding a small blue velvet box. "I have a present for you, too," she said moving toward him.

They both knew what it was.

He took it from her, snapped it open.

Her wedding ring was inside. The diamond sparkled against the dark velvet. She wondered if he, too, was remembering the day they picked it out. Two kids in love, going from store to store, holding hands, believing in forever with all their hearts.

"You're giving this back to me?" he said.

She smiled. "I figure you'll know what to do with it sooner or later."

IT'S A WONDERFUL LIFE.

Miracle on 34th Street.

A Christmas Story.

For most of her life, Lauren had watched those famous holiday movies, and dozens of others, and thought: *Yeah, right.* Perfectly shaped Christmas trees dressed in thousands of lights, wrapped in garland and covered in hand-chosen, heirloom ornaments. Evergreen boughs that draped fireplace mantels and coiled up banisters.

It wasn't *real*, she would have said. It wasn't Christmas the way ordinary children saw it.

Then she walked through the wreath-decorated DeSaria front door and found herself in wonderland. There were decorations everywhere, on every table and windowsill and picture frame. Tiny glass reindeer and porcelain snowmen and brass sleighs full of brightly colored balls. The tree in the corner of the room was huge and so clustered with ornaments you could barely see the green of branches. A beautiful white star glittered at the top, its tip just touching the ceiling.

And the presents.

Lauren had never seen so many gifts in one room. She turned to Conlan. "Wow" was all she could say. She couldn't wait to call David tonight and describe it to him. She wouldn't leave out a single detail.

"That was my thought the first time I came for Christmas," Conlan said, smiling. "My dad used to give my mom a toaster for Christmas and not bother to wrap it."

Lauren could relate to that kind of holiday.

Angie came up beside them. "It's grotesque, I know. Wait till you see us eat. We're like piranha." She looped an arm around Lauren. "Come into the kitchen. That's where the real action is." She grinned at Conlan. "This should be good."

It took them almost half an hour to move through the living room. Every person, young or old, who saw Conlan screamed, jumped up from their seat, and tackled him. It was like being with a rock star. Lauren clung to Angie's hand and let herself be guided through the crowd. By the time she reached the kitchen, she was light-headed. At the doorway, they paused.

Maria was at the breakfast table, cutting out cookies from a sheet of green dough. Mira was arranging olives and sliced carrots onto an ornate crystal tray. Livvy was pouring a creamy white mixture into a pie shell.

"You're late," Maria said, barely looking up. "Three miles away and still you're late."

Conlan stepped into the room. "It's my fault, Maria. I kept your girl up late last night."

The women all shrieked at once and threw their hands into the air, running toward Conlan for hugs and kisses.

"They all love Con," Angie said to Lauren, stepping aside to let her sisters swarm him.

When they were finally done kissing and hugging and interrogating Conlan and Angie, the women went back to cooking. Lauren learned to cut radishes into roses and make gravy and arrange antipasti on a tray.

Then the kids started running into the room, pulling on Maria's sleeve, begging to open presents.

"All right," Maria finally said, wiping the flour from her hands. "It is time."

Angie took Lauren's arm and led her into the living room, where people were sitting on every available surface—chairs, sofa, footstools, hearth, floor.

The kids gathered around the tree, picking through the gifts, handing them out to the people scattered throughout the room.

Lauren excused herself and left the house, quietly closing the door behind her. She hurried out to the car and retrieved the one present she'd brought. Holding it close to her chest, she returned into the warm, cinnamony-scented house, and sat down beside Angie on the hearth.

Little Dani came up to her, offered her a gift.

"Oh, that's not for me," Lauren said. "Here, let me help you read—"

Angie touched her thigh. "It's for you."

Lauren didn't know what to say. She mumbled, "Thank you," and placed the gift gingerly on her lap. She couldn't help touching it, gliding her fingers across the sleek, foiled paper.

Then came another gift for her, and another. From Maria. From Livvy, from Mira.

Lauren had never had so many presents. She turned to Angie, whispered, "I didn't know. I didn't get gifts for—"

"It's not a competitive sport, honey. My family remembered you when they were shopping. That's all."

Conlan picked his way across the melee of children in the middle of the room and sat down on Lauren's other side. She scooted toward Angie to make room. "Kinda overwhelming, isn't it?" he said.

Lauren laughed shakily. "Totally."

"That's all of 'em, Nana," one of the kids yelled, and that was all it took. Everyone started opening their gifts. The sound of ripping paper was as loud as a chainsaw. People and children squealed with delight and jumped up to kiss one another.

Lauren bent down and picked up a present from her pile. It was from Mira, Vince, and the kids.

She was almost afraid to open it. Then the moment would be over. She ripped the paper along the seam and carefully folded it back up for reuse. She looked up quickly to see if anyone was watching her. Thankfully, everyone was busy with their own presents. She lifted the white box top. Inside lay a beautiful hand-embroidered peasant-style blouse. It would work as maternity wear.

The thought of it squeezed her heart. She looked up, across the room, but Mira and Vince were busy with their own gifts. Next, she opened a silver link bracelet from Livvy and her family. From Maria she received a cookbook. Her last gift was a gorgeous hand-tooled leather journal from Angie. The inscription read:

To my dear Lauren:

The newest member of our family.
Welcome.

Love,
Angie

She was staring at the inscription when Angie gasped beside her. "Oh, my."

Lauren looked to her left.

Angie had opened the gift Lauren had brought. It was a plain oak frame, seventeen inches by twenty, with ivory matting that had cutouts of different sizes for pictures. Lauren had chosen photographs from the box for most of the openings. A few held color shots she'd taken at Thanksgiving with her disposable camera.

Angie's forefinger traced the glass over the picture of her and her father. In it, Angie wore flowered bell-bottoms and a tight V-neck sweater with multicolored horizontal stripes. She was sitting on her father's lap, obviously telling him a story. The photographer had caught him laughing.

"Where did you find these pictures?" Angie said.

"They're copies. The originals are still in the box."

The room seemed to go silent by degrees. One conversation stopped, then another and another. Lauren felt everyone looking at her.

Maria was the first to rise and cross the room. She knelt in front of Angie, took the picture into her own lap, and stared down at it. When she looked up, there were tears in her eyes. "This is our trip to Yellowstone . . . and our twenty-fifth anniversary party. Where did you find these?"

"They were in a box under my bed. At the cottage. I'm sorry. I shouldn't have—"

Maria pulled Lauren into a tight hug. "Thank you." When she drew back, she was smiling brightly, even as tears streamed down her face. "This brings my Tony back to me for Christmas. It is the best gift. You will bring the photographs to me tomorrow, yes?"

"Of course." Lauren's smile seemed to be taking over her face. She couldn't rein it in. She was still grinning when Maria left and Angie squeezed her hand, saying, "This is beautiful. Thank you."

CHRISTMAS DINNER AT THE DESARIA HOUSE WAS SLIGHTLY QUIETER than a Mariners home game, but not much. There were three tables set up. Two in the living room with four chairs each and the one in the dining room that held sixteen people jammed together. One table was for the little kids and one was for the teenagers, whose job it was to look after the little kids. This was a job that was handled poorly most of the time. You couldn't take more than a few bites before someone big came in tattling on someone small, or vice versa. Of course, no one paid much attention to either and by the time the third bottle of wine had been finished, the children knew it was pointless to come into the dining room. The grown-ups were simply having too much fun.

It was not what Angie had expected for this first Christmas without Papa. All of them had expected quiet voices and sad eyes to be the order of the day.

Lauren's gift had changed all that. Those old photos, unseen for decades, had brought Papa back to them. Now, instead of talking around old memories, they were sharing them. Right now Mama was telling them all about the trip they'd taken to Yellowstone, and how they'd accidentally left Livvy at the diner. "Three little girls and a dog is a lot to keep track of." She laughed.

The only one who didn't laugh was Livvy. In fact, she'd been quiet all day. Angie frowned, wondering if her sister's marriage was already in trouble. She smiled across the table; Livvy looked away.

Angie made a mental note to talk to Livvy after dinner, then she glanced to her right. Lauren was engaged in an animated conversation with Mira.

When she turned to her left, she found Conlan staring at her.

"She's really something," he said.

"She got to you, too, huh?"

"It's dangerous, Ange. When she leaves . . ."

"I know." She leaned toward him. "You know what, Con? My heart is big enough to lose a piece now and then."

Slowly, he smiled. "I'm glad to hear that." He was about to say something else but the ping-ping-ping of a fork hitting glass stopped him.

Angie looked up.

Livvy and Sal stood up. Sal was tapping his fork against his wineglass. When silence fell around the table, he put an arm around Livvy. "We wanted to let you all know that there will be a new baby in the family for next Christmas."

No one said a word.

Livvy's eyes filled slowly with tears as she looked at Angie.

She waited for the pain to hit, stiffened in preparation. Conlan squeezed her thigh. *Steady now,* that touch said.

But she *was* steady. The realization made Angie smile. She

got to her feet and came around the table, hugging her sister tightly. "I'm happy for you."

Livvy drew back. "You mean it? I was so scared to tell you."

Angie smiled. The pain was there, of course it was, lodged in her heart like a piece of glass. And the envy. But it didn't hurt as much as before. Or maybe she'd finally learned to handle the pain. All she really knew was that she felt no urge to run to a quiet room and cry and her smile didn't have to be forced. "I mean it."

At that, conversations burst to life again.

Angie returned to her seat just as Mama began the prayer. When it was over and they'd listed and prayed for all their loved ones who'd been lost, including Papa and Sophia, Conlan leaned close to her.

"Are you really okay?"

"It's a shock, isn't it?"

He stared at her a long time, then very softly he said, "I love you, Angela Malone."

"What time is it?" Lauren asked, looking up from her magazine.

"Ten minutes later than the last time you asked," Angie answered. "He'll be here. Don't worry."

Lauren tossed down the magazine. There was no point in pretending to read it anyway. She walked over to the living room window and stared out. Night was slowly falling toward the ocean. The surf was barely visible now, just a thread of silver along the charcoal shoreline. January had come to West End on an easterly wind, its cold breath bending the trees backward.

Angie came up beside her, put an arm around her waist. Lauren leaned sideways. As always, Angie was able to calm her so easily, with just a—

mother's

—touch.

"Thanks," Lauren said, hearing the tremor in her voice. Sometimes it hit her in a breathless rush, the longing that Angie were her mother. It had always made her feel slightly guilty, that longing, but she couldn't deny its existence. These days, when she thought about her mother (usually late at night, in the darkness, when the distant surf was leading her toward the kind of deep peaceful sleep she'd never known before), she mostly felt disappointed. The sharp edge of betrayal had dimmed somehow. She felt sorry for her mother mostly, and for herself, too. She'd glimpsed what her life could have been. If she'd been raised by Angie, Lauren would have known love from her earliest day. She wouldn't have had to go looking for it.

The doorbell rang.

"He's here!" Lauren lurched away from the window and ran for the door, yanking it open. David stood there, wearing his red and white letterman's jacket and a pair of old jeans. He held a bouquet of red roses.

She threw her arms around him. When she drew back, laughing at her own desperation, her hands were trembling and tears stung her eyes. "I missed you."

"I missed you, too."

She took his hand, led him into the cottage. "Hey, Angie. You remember David."

Angie walked toward them. Lauren felt a swell of pride at the sight of her. She looked so beautiful in her black clothes, with her flowing dark hair and movie star smile. "It's good to see you again, David. Did you have a nice Christmas?"

He kept his arm around Lauren. "It was okay. Aspen's great if you wear fur and drink big martinis. I missed Lauren."

Angie smiled. "That must be why you called so much."

"Was it too much? Did I—"

"I'm just teasing you," Angie said. "You know I want Lauren home by midnight, right?"

Lauren giggled. A *curfew*. She must be the only kid in the world who was pleased by that.

He looked down at Lauren, obviously confused. "What do you want to do? Go see a movie?"

Lauren wanted to *be* with him; that was all. "Maybe we could play cards here. Or listen to music."

David frowned, glanced at Angie, who said quickly, "I've got work to do upstairs."

Lauren loved her for that. "What do you think, David?"

"Sure."

"Okay," Angie said. "There's food in the fridge and pop in the carport. Lauren, you know where the popcorn maker is." She looked pointedly at David. "I will be walking through every now and then."

Lauren should have been irritated by that, but in truth, she loved how it made her feel. Cared for. Cared about. "Okay."

Angie said good night, then went upstairs.

When they were alone, Lauren took the flowers and put them in a vase. As soon as she finished, she got his present from the kitchen and took it to him. "Merry Christmas."

They settled into the big overstuffed sofa, cuddled up to one another. "Open it," she said.

He unwrapped the small box. Inside lay a small gold St. Christopher medal.

"It'll protect you," Lauren said, hearing the catch in her voice. "When we're apart."

"You might get into Stanford," he said, but there was no conviction in his words.

He took a deep breath, then let it out.

"It's okay," she murmured. "I know we'll be apart. Our love can take it."

He looked down at her. Slowly, he reached into his pocket and pulled out a beautifully wrapped package.

It wasn't a ring box.

She took it from him, surprised at how unsteady she suddenly felt as she unwrapped the present. She hadn't known until just now—this second—that she'd expected a proposal tonight. Inside the box lay a pair of tiny diamond heart earrings, suspended from thread so delicate it looked like fishing wire. "They're beautiful," she said in a shaky voice. "I never thought I'd own diamond earrings."

"I wanted to buy you a ring."

"These are great. Really."

"My mom and dad don't think we should get married."

So they were going to have to talk about it. "What do you think?"

"I don't know. Remember that lawyer my dad wanted to talk to?"

"Yeah." It took everything she had to keep smiling.

"He says there are people who would love this baby. People who would want it."

"Our baby," she said softly.

"I can't be a father," he said, looking so sad and beaten that she wanted to cry. "I mean. I *am* one. I know that, but . . ."

She touched his face, wondering how long the pain of this moment would linger. She felt a dozen years older than him right now. It was clear suddenly that this might ruin them.

She longed to tell him *okay*, that she'd follow his parents'

plan and give the baby away and go on with all the things they'd
planned. But she didn't know if she could do it. She leaned
toward him. In the firelight, his watery eyes were hardly blue at
all. "You should go to Stanford and forget about all of this."

"Just talk to the lawyers, okay? Maybe they'll know something." His voice cracked and that tiny little sound ruined her resolve. He was almost crying.

She sighed. It was a small, tearing sound, like muscle ripping
away from the bone. "Okay."

TWENTY-SEVEN

L AUREN CLOSED HER TEXTBOOK AND LOOKED UP AT THE clock.
   2:45.
2:46.

She let her breath out in a nervous sigh. All around her kids were laughing and talking as they got their things together and headed out of the classroom. There was a lot of energy in school this week. That was to be expected. Finals began on Monday. In different—normal—times, Lauren would have been as keyed up as the rest of them. But now, in this third week of January, she had bigger worries. By this time next week, while her friends were looking for their new classrooms, she'd be done with high school. A graduate.

She reached down for her backpack and put her book and notebook away. Slinging the heavy pack in place, she headed out of the classroom. Merging into the crowded hallway, she forced herself to smile at friends, to talk and carry on as if this were any other day.

All the while she was thinking: *I should have asked Angie to come with me today.*

Why hadn't she?

Even now she wasn't sure.

She stopped at her locker and got her coat. She was just about to slam it shut when David came up behind her and tugged.

"Hey," he whispered against her neck.

She leaned into him. "Hey."

He slowly turned her around until she was facing him. His smile was irritatingly bright. This was the happiest he'd looked since she'd told him about the baby. "You look happy." She heard the bitterness in her voice and it made her wince. She sounded exactly like her mother.

"I'm sorry."

But he didn't know why he was sorry or what he'd done wrong. She wondered if from now on he'd start handling her with care. She forced another smile. "Don't be. My moods change faster than the weather. So. Where do we go?"

His relief was as obvious as the confusion had been. He smiled, but there was a new wariness in his eyes, too. "My house. Mom thought that would be more comfortable for you." He put his arm around her, tucked her against his side.

She kicked her locker shut and let herself be swept through the campus and into his car.

In the few miles between Fircrest Academy and Mountainaire, they talked about things that didn't matter. Gossip. The graduation night party. Hookups. Lauren tried to focus on that, the bits and pieces of ordinary high school life, but when David pulled up to the guardhouse, she drew in a sharp breath.

The gate swung open.

She coiled her hands together and looked out the window at the big, beautiful homes.

For the last few years, as she'd come into this enclave of the rich, she'd seen only the beauty of it. She'd dreamed of belonging in a place like this. Now she wondered why people with so much money didn't choose to live on the water, or why they wouldn't want to be in the busy neighborhood where the De-Sarias lived. There, the streets seemed alive. Here, everything was

too contained, too clipped and perfected. How could real life—
and real love—grow in so confined a space?

As they pulled up to the curb in front of the Hayneses' mam-
moth home, she found herself wondering what the three of them
did with all the empty spaces in their house.

David parked the car, then turned to her. "You ready for
this?"

"No."

"You want to cancel?"

"Absolutely not." She climbed down from the passenger seat
and headed for the house. Halfway there, David came up beside
her and took her hand in his. The support eased some of the butterflies in her stomach.

At the door, they both paused. Then David opened the door
and led her inside.

The house was quiet, as usual. The very opposite of the De-
Saria home.

"Mom? Dad?" David called out, shutting the door behind
them.

Mrs. Haynes came around the corner, wearing a winter white
wool dress. Her auburn hair had been drawn back in a tight bun.
She looked thinner than the last time Lauren had seen her, and
older.

Lauren could understand why. In the past weeks, she'd
learned how life could mark a person. "Hello, Mrs. Haynes," she
said, moving forward.

Mrs. Haynes looked at her. A sadness tugged ever so slightly
at her painted lips. "Hello, Lauren. How are you feeling?"

"Fine."

"Thank you for agreeing to come today. David has told us it's
difficult for you."

David squeezed her hand.

Lauren knew this was the time to say something, maybe state
her opinion, but when she tried, nothing came out. She nodded
instead.

Just then Mr. Haynes walked into the room. Dressed in a
navy blue double-breasted suit and pale yellow shirt, he looked
every bit the power player who was used to getting his way in the
boardroom. Beside him was a heavyset man in a black suit.

"Hello, Lauren," Mr. Haynes said, not bothering to smile. He
didn't look at his son. "I'd like you to meet Stuart Phillips. He's a
well-respected attorney who specializes in adoption."

That was all it took, just the word being spoken aloud, and Lauren started to cry.

Mrs. Haynes was beside her instantly, handing her a tissue, murmuring something about everything being okay.

But it wasn't okay.

Lauren wiped her eyes, muttered, "Sorry," and let herself be led into the living room. There, they all sat down on the expensive cream-colored furniture. She worried that her tears would stain the fabric.

There was a moment of awkward silence before the lawyer started to talk.

Lauren listened, or at least she tried to. Her heart was beating so loudly that sometimes she couldn't hear anything else. Bits and pieces drifted toward her, sticking like flotsam in the net of her mind.

> *best decision for the child*
> *another family/another mother*
> *better able to parent*
> *termination of rights*
> *college is best for you now*
> *too young*

When it was over and the lawyer had said everything he'd come to say, he sat back in his chair and smiled easily, as if those words had been sounds and breath, nothing more. "Do you have any questions, Lauren?"

She looked around the room.

Mrs. Haynes looked ready to burst into tears and David was pale. His blue eyes were narrowed with worry. Mr. Haynes was tapping his armrest.

"You all think I should do this," Lauren said slowly.

"You're too young to be parents," Mr. Haynes said. "David can't remember to feed the dog or make his bed, for God's sake."

Mrs. Haynes shot her husband a withering look, then smiled at Lauren. It was sad, that smile, and full of knowing. "There's no easy answer here, Lauren. We know that. But you and David are good kids. You deserve a chance in life. Parenthood is hard work. You need to think about the baby, too. You want to give your child every opportunity. I tried to discuss all this with your mother, but she didn't return my calls."

"Believe me, young lady," the lawyer said, "there are dozens of wonderful people who would love and adore your baby."

"That's the point," Lauren said so quietly that everyone

leaned forward to hear her. "It's my baby." She turned to David. "Our baby."

He didn't move, didn't look away. To someone who didn't know him, he might have appeared unaffected. But to Lauren, who'd loved him so long, everything in his eyes changed. His face seemed to crumple into disappointment.

"Okay," he said, as if she'd asked a question. She knew then— as she'd known before—that he'd stand by her, back up her choices.

But he didn't want this. To him it wasn't a baby, it was an accident. A mistake. If it were up to him, they'd sign a few papers, hand over the baby, and move on.

If she didn't make that choice, she'd ruin his life as much as her own. Maybe the child's, too.

She drew in a heavy breath, exhaled it slowly. She should break up with David. If she loved him enough, she'd set him free from all of this.

The thought of that, of losing him, paralyzed her with fear.

She looked around the room, saw everyone's expectation, and she was beaten.

"I'll think about it," she said.

The suddenness of David's smile broke her heart.

"ALL RIGHT," ANGIE SAID, COMING INTO THE LIVING ROOM. "DO you hear the timer on the stove?"

"It's beeping," Lauren said, pulling her knees up to her chest. She was sitting on the floor in front of the fire.

"Yes, it is, and do you know why?"

"Dinner is ready?"

Angie rolled her eyes. "I realize I'm not the best chef in the world, but even I don't take my dinner out of the oven at eleven in the morning."

"Oh. Right." Lauren stared down at her hands. She'd chewed her nails down to the quick.

Angie knelt down in front of her. "You've been moping around this house for too long. I brought home your favorite pizza last week when you graduated and you hardly touched it. Last night you went to bed at seven o'clock. I've been patient, waiting for you to talk to me, but—"

"I'll go clean my room." She started to get up.

Angie stopped her with a touch. "Honey. Your room couldn't

be any cleaner. That's all you've been doing in the last few days. Working and cleaning your room and sleeping. What's going on?"

"I can't talk about it."

"So it's the baby."

Lauren heard the tiny crack in Angie's voice when she said *baby*. "I don't want to talk to you about it."

Angie sighed. "I know. And I know why. But I'm not that fragile anymore."

"Your sisters say you are."

"My sisters talk too much."

Lauren looked at her. The understanding in Angie's eyes was her undoing. "How did you handle it? Losing Sophia, I mean."

Angie sat back on her heels. "Wow. No one ever asks me that head-on."

"I'm sorry. I shouldn't have—"

"No. We're friends. We can talk about our lives."

Angie sidled up beside Lauren, put an arm around her. Together they stared into the crackling fire. Angie felt the old grief move into her again, squeezing her chest until it hurt to breathe. "You're asking how you live with a broken heart," she finally said.

"Yeah. I guess."

Once the memories were there, Angie had no choice but to gather them close. "I held her; did I ever tell you that? She was so tiny. And so blue." She drew in a ragged breath. "When she was gone, I couldn't seem to stop crying. I missed her and the idea of her so much. I let the missing become who I was . . . then Conlan left me and I came back home and that's when the most amazing thing happened."

"What?"

"A bright, beautiful young woman came into my life, and she reminded me that there was joy in the world. I started to remember my blessings. I learned that my papa had been right when he used to say *This too shall pass*. Life has a way of going on, and you do your best and move with it. A broken heart heals. Like every wound, there's a scar, a memory, but it fades. Finally you realize that an hour has passed without your thinking about it, then a day. I don't know if that answers your question . . ."

Lauren stared at the flames. "The old 'time heals all wounds' answer, huh?"

"I know it's hard for a teenager to believe, but it's true."

"Maybe." She sighed. "Everyone wants me to think about adoption."

God help her, Angie's first thought was *Give me the baby.* She hated herself for it. She wished she could say something but her voice seemed to have gone missing. Suddenly, she was thinking about her nursery and all those old dreams. She battled the feelings, put them aside long enough to ask quietly, "What do *you* want?"

"I don't know. I don't want to ruin David's life. My life. All our lives, but I can't just give away my baby." She turned to Angie. "What do I do?"

"Oh, Lauren," Angie said, pulling her into her arms. She didn't point out the obvious: that Lauren had already made up her mind. Instead, she said, "Look at me."

Lauren drew back. Her face was ravaged by tears. "Wh-what?"

"I'm here for you." For the first time, Angie dared to touch Lauren's stomach. "And there's this little person who needs you to be strong."

"I'm afraid I can't do it alone."

"That's what I'm trying to tell you. Whatever you decide, you're not alone."

THE LAST, SHORT, GRAY JANUARY DAYS DRIPPED INTO ONE ANOTHER. The sky was always bloated with clouds; rain fell in a steady rhythm.

The citizens of West End gathered beneath the giant eaves of the Congregational Church and in the covered walkways along Driftwood Way; their conversations always came around to the weather. Every day, in every way, they were hoping to see the sun.

When January came to a close, they pinned their hopes on February.

On Valentine's Day, the clouds parted, and though no sun was visible, the rain diminished to a pearlescent mist.

The restaurant was packed. By seven o'clock, both dining rooms were full and a line of people waited along the windows.

Everyone was moving at top speed. Lauren, who had been working full-time since graduating, handled double her usual number of tables. Mama and Mira made triple the number of specials, while Angie poured wine and brought bread and bused the empty dishes wherever she could. Even Rosa was in the spirit of things—she carried two plates at a time instead of one.

The kitchen door banged open. "Angela!" Mama called out. "Artichoke hearts and ricotta."

"Right, Mama." Angie hurried downstairs and grabbed a huge jar of artichoke hearts and a container of fresh ricotta. For the next hour, she ran herself ragged. They were going to need to hire another waitress. Maybe two.

She was running to check the reservation book when she ran into Livvy. Literally. Angie laughed. "Don't tell me you came for dinner *tonight?*"

"Spend Valentine's Day at the family restaurant? Not hardly. Sal is working late."

"So why are you here?"

"I heard you were shorthanded."

"No. We're fine. Busy, but fine. Really. You should stay off your feet. Go home and—"

Someone came up behind Angie, grabbed her shoulders. Before she could turn around, Conlan swept her into his arms and carried her out of the restaurant.

The last thing Angie heard was her sister saying, "Like I said. Shorthanded."

His smile was dazzling as he deposited her in the passenger seat of his car. "Close your eyes."

She did as she was told.

"I like this new Angie. She listens to me."

"Only so far, pal." She laughed. This felt so good. It was cold out, freezing on this February night, but he had the top down anyway and the air stung her face and whipped her hair in a dozen different directions. "We're at the beach," she said, smelling it, hearing the roar of the surf.

He parked, then came around to her side. She heard the trunk whir open and thump shut.

He picked her up again, carried her forward. She could tell by the heaviness of his steps, the way he started breathing just a little harder, that he was walking in sand.

"Someone needs to visit a gym more often," she teased.

"Says the heavyweight in my arms."

He set her down. She heard the snap of a blanket and his curses as he straightened it out. Then he started a fire. The acrid smell tinged the sea air, made her think of every high school beach party she'd ever attended.

She drew in a deep breath and smelled the whole of her

youth. The sand, the sea, the driftwood that was never completely wet or completely dry.

"Open your eyes."

When she did, she was looking up at him.

"Happy Valentine's Day, Ange."

She leaned up to him. He knelt down to meet her. They
kissed like teenagers, with a desperate hunger, and then stretched
out on the blanket.

With a heaven of stars above them and a crackle of firelight
beside, they lay there, entwined, kissing and talking and kissing
some more. They thought about making love, but it was too
damned cold out, and frankly, making out was pretty fun.

In the blackest part of the night, when the stars were so
bright they hurt your eyes and moonlight glowed on the foamy
surf, Angie snuggled up alongside him and kissed his jaw, his
cheek, the corner of his mouth.

"What now?" he asked quietly; the question that was always
between them. If she hadn't been listening for it, the surf would
have wiped it away.

"We don't have to decide anything, Con. For now, this is
enough." In the weeks since Christmas they'd seen each other
now and then and talked on the phone for hours. She'd loved all
of it so much, she didn't want to risk needing more.

"The old Angie liked to set goals and achieve them. She
wasn't so good at 'let's wait and see.' "

"The old Angie was young." She kissed him, long and hard
and with every scrap of love in her heart. When she drew back,
she was trembling. In his eyes, she saw a shadow of the old fear,
the uncertainty that they could make it a second time when
they'd already failed once.

"We're acting like a couple of kids."

"We were grown-up for too long," she said. "Just love me,
Con. That's enough for now."

His hands slid down her back and slipped under her skirt. "I
can do that."

She grabbed the blanket and pulled it over them. "Good" was
all she managed to say before he kissed her.

THE DRIZZLY FEBRUARY DAYS MELTED INTO ONE ANOTHER, FORMING
a monotonous gray blur of passing time. It wasn't until the last
night of this shortest month that Angie had the baby dream

again. She woke with a start and rolled over in bed, searching in vain for her husband's strong and comforting presence. Alone, she crawled upright and switched on the bedside lamp, then sat there, with her knees drawn up, as if holding herself could somehow make her arms feel less empty.

The good news was there were no tear marks on her cheeks. She'd felt like crying, but she hadn't. Progress, she thought; it came in the tiniest increments when the sun went down.

It didn't surprise her that she'd had the dream again. Living with Lauren sometimes churned up the past. There was no way to avoid it, no way to step aside. Especially now; in the past week, the teenager had finally begun to gain weight. There was an almost imperceptible roundness to her waist. A stranger wouldn't notice it, but to a woman who'd spent so much of her adult life seeking that very thing, it shone like a neon sign. And today they had a doctor's appointment scheduled; that wouldn't be easy.

Angie finally gave up trying to sleep and reached for the pile of work on her nightstand. For the next few hours, she busied herself with payroll and accounts receivable. By the time the gentle sun tapped on her window, she'd found her peace again.

There would simply be days like this—nights like the one she'd just endured.

Now and then in the coming months, she would be pulled up short by loss and longing. She'd known that when she offered Lauren a place to live. Some dreams did not go away easily, and undreaming them could last a lifetime. This she knew.

She threw back the covers and headed for the bathroom. After a long, hot shower, she felt better again. Ready to face the difficult day ahead. And there was no doubt that it would be difficult.

For Lauren's sake, she would get through it. She was making her bed when she heard Lauren call out her name.

Angie went to the bedroom door, opened it, and yelled, "What?"

"Breakfast is ready."

She hurried downstairs and found Lauren in the kitchen, stirring oatmeal.

"Good morning," Lauren said brightly.

"You're up early."

"It's not early." Lauren looked up. "Did you have another bad night?"

"No. No," Angie answered quickly, wishing she'd never mentioned that sometimes sleep evaded her.

Lauren smiled, obviously relieved. "Good." She carried over two bowls of oatmeal and set them on the table, one on each blue placemat, then sat down opposite Angie. "Your mother told me I needed to eat more fiber and taught me how to make oatmeal."

Angie doctored her bowl in the DeSaria way—brown sugar, maple syrup, raisins, and milk—and tasted it. "Fabulous," she declared.

"Of course Mira told me to eat lots of protein and Livvy took me aside and said that carbohydrates would make the baby strong. I guess I'm supposed to eat everything."

"That's my family's answer to every question in life: Eat more."

Lauren laughed. "My doctor's appointment is at ten o'clock this morning. The bus leaves—"

"What on earth makes you imagine I'll let you take a bus to see the doctor?"

"I know this is hard for you."

Angie considered a smart-ass answer, but when she looked into Lauren's earnest face, she said, "Life is full of hard choices, Lauren. I want to go to the doctor's with you."

After that, their conversation veered back onto familiar, everyday roads. As they stood side by side, washing dishes, they talked about the restaurant, the weather, the schedule for the rest of the week. Lauren told a funny story about her latest date with David, and an even funnier one about Mama.

By the time they reached the doctor's office, Angie was tense again.

She paused at the clinic door, trying not to make this about her.

Lauren touched her arm. "Do you want to wait in the car?"

"Absolutely not." Forcing a smile, however unnatural it felt, she opened the door and stepped into the medicinal-smelling office.

Memories came at her hard. She'd been in too many rooms like this one, put on too many flimsy gowns and put her feet into too many cold stirrups. For years, it seemed like all she had done . . .

She kept moving across the room, one step at a time. At

the receptionist's desk, she held onto the Formica ledge. "Lauren Ribido," she said.

The receptionist flipped through the stack of manila-foldered charts and pulled one out. Then she handed a clipboard to Angie. "Here. Fill this out and return it to me."

Angie stared down at the familiar form. *Start date of your last period . . . number of previous pregnancies . . . gone to term . . .* Slowly, she handed it to Lauren.

"Oh," the receptionist said, frowning. "I'm sorry. I assumed—"

"Don't worry about it," Angie said quickly. She led Lauren over to the bank of chairs along the wall. They sat down side by side.

Lauren began filling out the form.

Angie heard the chicken scratch sound of the pen on paper. In some strange way, it calmed her.

When they called Lauren's name, Angie almost stood up. Then she thought: *No.* Lauren had a lot of growing up to do. This was the start of it. Angie could only be here for her afterward.

The appointment seemed to last forever. It gave Angie time to relax, to regroup. By the time Lauren came out, Angie had regained control. She was able to talk to Lauren about all of it—the symptoms, the aches and pains, the morning sickness, the Lamaze classes.

On the way home, they stopped at the grocery store for more prenatal vitamins, and then sat down on a bench out front.

"Why are we sitting out here?" Lauren asked. "It looks like it's going to rain any minute."

"It probably will."

"I'm getting cold."

"Button your coat."

A green minivan pulled up in front of them and parked.

"It's about time," Angie muttered, tossing her paper coffee cup into the trash bin beside the bench.

The van doors opened all at once. Mira, Mama, and Livvy emerged onto the street. They were all talking at the same time.

Mama and Livvy went to Lauren. Each taking one of the girl's arms, they hauled her to her feet.

"I thought the restaurant was closed today," Lauren said, frowning.

Mama stopped. "Angela said you needed some new clothes."

A pink blush spread across Lauren's creamy cheeks. The

color seemed to emphasize her freckles. "Oh. I didn't bring my money."

Livvy laughed. "Me, too, Mama. I forgot my wallet. You'll have to dust off the old credit card. I could use some maternity clothes, too."

Mama thwopped the back of Livvy's head. "Smart aleck. Come on. It's going to rain."

The three of them took off down the street, arm in arm, their voices sounding like a swarm of bees.

Mira hung back. "So," she said softly. "Are you going to be okay with this?"

Angie loved her sister for daring to ask the obvious. "I haven't been in a maternity shop for a long time."

"I know."

Angie looked down the street. The ironwork sign for Mother-and-Child hung at an angle above the sidewalk. The last time she'd been inside the store had been with her sisters. Angie had been pregnant then, and smiling had come easily. She turned to Mira. "I'll be okay," she said, realizing as she said the words that they contained the truth. It might hurt a bit, might remind her of a few of her harder times, but those feelings were part of who she was, and in the end, it was more hurtful to run away than to face them. "I want to be there for Lauren. She needs me."

Mira's smile was soft and held only the merest worry. "Good for you."

"Yeah," Angie said, smiling, "good for me."

Still, she took her sister's arm and held on to it for support.

TWENTY-EIGHT

S PRING CAME EARLY TO WEST END. A COLD, RAINY WINTER set the stage for riotous color. When the sun finally dared to peek through the gray layer of clouds, the landscape changed before your very eyes. Bright purple crocuses came first, popping up through the bleak, hard earth. Then the hillsides turned green, and trees unfurled the splendor of baby leaves. Daffodils bloomed along every roadside, created spots of color amid the runaway salal.

Lauren bloomed as well. She'd gained almost fifteen pounds already. Any day now she expected her obstetrician to start frowning at the weighing-in debacle. She moved more slowly, too. Sometimes at the restaurant she had to pause outside the kitchen door and catch her breath. Walking from table to table had become an Olympic caliber event.

And that wasn't the worst of it. Her feet hurt. She went to

the bathroom more often than a beer-drinking alcoholic, and gas seemed to be burning a permanent hole through the middle of her chest. She burped constantly.

By April she'd begun to face the question: What next?

She'd been bumping along for the last few months, looking only as far ahead as her next shift at the restaurant or her next date with David. But now—again—he'd asked her the Big Question, and she knew it was time to stop avoiding the obvious.

"Well?" David said, nudging her.

They were cuddled close on the sofa, their arms entwined. A fire crackled in the hearth.

"I don't know," she said softly. The three words were beginning to wear out their welcome.

"My mom said she talked to the lawyer again last week. He has several couples who are dying to raise it."

"Not it, David. Our baby."

He made a heavy sound. "I know, Lo. Believe me, I *know*."

She lifted her face toward his. "Could you really do it? Just walk away from our baby, I mean?"

He untangled himself from her and got to his feet. "I don't know what you want from me, Lauren." His voice cracked. She realized suddenly that he was near tears.

She went to him, stood behind him, and put her arms around his waist. She couldn't get close enough; her belly was so big. The baby kicked her, a featherlight flutter.

"What kind of parents would we be?" David asked, not turning to look at her. "If we give up college, what will we do? How will we afford—"

She slipped around to face him. This was one answer she had. "You're going to Stanford. No matter what."

"I'm supposed to just leave," he said dully.

Lauren looked up into his watery eyes. She wanted to tell him it would all work out, that their love would always see them through, but she felt too small right now to reach for the words, and the tiny tap-tap-tap in her stomach reminded her of how different this moment was for each of them.

She would lose him if she kept their child.

Hard choices, Angie had said to her once. How was it that Lauren hadn't truly understood that until this moment?

She was going to say something—she wasn't sure what—when the doorbell rang.

She sighed heavily, extricating herself from his embrace. "Coming."

She opened the door and saw Ernie, the mailman. He held several small packages and a bunch of letters.

"Here you go."

"Thanks." She put the packages on the table by the door and flipped through the letters. One was addressed to her.

"It's from USC," she said, feeling her heart lurch. She'd forgotten about her applications in all the craziness of the past few weeks.

David moved toward her. He looked as scared and nervous as she felt. "You know you got in," he said, and she loved him for that confidence.

She opened the letter and read the words she'd dreamed of. "I did it," she whispered. "I didn't think—"

He pulled her into his arms and held her. "Remember our first date? After the Aberdeen game. We sat down at the beach, by the huge bonfire. While everyone else was running around and dancing and drinking, we talked. You told me you were going to win a Pulitzer someday, and I believed you. You're the only one who doesn't see how great you are."

The Pulitzer. She couldn't help touching her swollen belly. *Give yourself a chance,* her mother had said. *Don't end up like me.*

"What should I do?" she whispered, looking up into David's blue eyes.

"Take the scholarship," he said, and though his words were harsh, there was a softness to his voice.

It was the right thing to do; she knew that. At least, she knew it in her head. Her heart was a different matter. How could she raise a baby if she had no education, no prospects? Once again she thought of her mother, on her feet, cutting hair all day and drinking all night, looking for love in dark places. She sighed heavily. The truth poked through her defenses, sharp as a tack. She *wanted* to go to college. It was her chance to be different from her mother. Slowly, she looked up at David again. "The lawyer found good people to take the baby?"

"The very best."

"Can we meet them? Choose for ourselves?"

Joy transformed his face, turned him back into the boy she'd fallen in love with. He held her so tightly she couldn't breathe, and kissed her until she was dizzy. When he drew back, he was grinning. "I love you, Lauren."

She couldn't seem to smile. His enthusiasm chilled her somehow, made her angry. "You always get what you want, don't you?"

His smile fell. "What do you mean?"

She didn't even know. All she knew was that she wanted two
things and couldn't have them both. "I don't know."

"Damn it, Lauren. What the hell is wrong with you? How am
I supposed to say the right thing when you change your mind
every ten seconds?"

"Like you've *ever* said the right thing. All you've ever wanted
is for me to get rid of it."

"Am I supposed to lie? Do you think I *want* to blow off my
whole future and be a dad?"

"And I do? You asshole." She pushed him away.

He seemed to fade at that; it was almost as if he were losing
weight before her eyes. "This whole thing blows."

"Big time."

They stood there, staring at each other. Finally, David moved
toward her. "I'm sorry. Really."

"This is ruining us," she said.

He took her hand and led her back to the couch. They sat
side by side. Still, it felt as if they were miles apart. "Let's quit
fighting and talk about it," he said quietly. "All of it."

ANGIE GOT OUT OF HER CAR AND CLOSED THE DOOR.

The storage compartment was in front of her.

C-22.

Other people's compartments were on either side. The long,
low building was one of dozens. *A-1 Storage*, the sign at the front
gate read. *Keep it safe. Keep it locked.*

Angie swallowed hard. The key felt cold and foreign in her
hand. She almost turned around then, almost decided she wasn't
strong enough to do this after all.

It was that, the fear that she hadn't come far enough to be
here, that finally made her move. She put one foot in front of the
other, and the next thing she knew she was at the lock. She fit her
key in place and clicked it open. The garage-style door clattered
up and snaked into place along the ceiling.

She flicked on the light switch.

A lone bulb in the ceiling came on, illuminating a stack of
boxes and furniture wrapped in blankets and bedding.

The leftovers from her marriage were all here. The bed she

and Conlan had purchased in Pioneer Square and slept on for so many years. The desk he'd used in graduate school and finally given up on. The sectional sofa that had been bought because a whole family could lie on it and watch television.

But she hadn't come here for those things, the reminders of who she'd been.

She'd come for Lauren.

She worked through the boxes, moving first one and then another as she made her way deeper into the storage unit. Finally, she found what she was looking for; it was tucked in the back corner. A trio of boxes marked *Nursery.*

She should simply take the boxes and put them in her car, but she couldn't. Instead, she knelt on the cold cement floor and opened the box. The Winnie-the-Pooh lamp lay on a stack of pink flannel bedding.

She'd known how it would feel to look at these items, each so carefully chosen, none of them ever used. They were like bits and pieces of her heart, lost along the way but never forgotten.

She picked up a tiny white onesie that was rolled into a ball and held it to her nose. There was no smell except that of cardboard. No baby powder or Johnson's shampoo.

Of course there wasn't. No baby had ever worn this, or wakened to the light that shone from Winnie-the-Pooh's honey bucket.

She closed her eyes, remembering every nuance of her nursery. Remembering the night she'd packed it all away.

In her mind, she saw a tiny dark-haired girl with her daddy's flashing blue eyes.

"Take care of our Sophia, Papa," she whispered, getting to her feet again.

It was time for all these things to come out of the bleak darkness of this storage unit. They were meant to be used, held, played with. They were meant for a baby's room.

One by one, she carried the boxes to her car. By the time she locked up the storage unit again, it was raining.

ANGIE COULDN'T BELIEVE HOW GOOD SHE FELT. THIS DAY HAD shadowed her horizon for years, blocking out the light.

The nursery. The baby clothes and toys. She'd known that as long as she kept those things, she was somehow stuck.

Now, finally, she was free.

She wished Conlan were here to see her now, after all the times he'd found her sitting on the nursery floor, holding some rattle or blanket or knickknack and crying. There wasn't an item in all those boxes that hadn't been watered by her tears.

In fact . . .

She hit the speed dial on her mounted cell phone.

"News desk."

"Hey, Kathy," Angie said into the speaker on her visor. "It's Angie. Is Conlan in?"

"Sure."

A minute later Conlan answered. "Hey, there. Are you in town?"

"No. I'm on my way back to West End."

"You're going the wrong direction."

She laughed. "Guess what's in my trunk."

"That's a new line."

She felt like an alcoholic who'd finally admitted to having a problem. Her AA meeting was in cardboard boxes in the trunk of her car. "The baby stuff."

There was a pause. Then, "What do you mean?"

"The crib. The clothes. Everything. I cleaned out the storage unit."

A pause crackled through the tiny black speaker. "For Lauren?"

"She'll need it."

Angie knew Conlan heard the distant echo of the other side of those words. *And we don't.*

"Are you okay?" he asked.

"That's the amazing thing, Con. I feel better than okay. Remember that time we went helicopter skiing in Whistler?"

"And you didn't sleep for three nights before?"

"Exactly. I worried myself sick, but once that chopper dropped us off, I flew down the mountain and couldn't wait to go again. That's how this feels. I'm flying down the mountain again."

"Wow."

"I know. I can't wait to give her this stuff. She's going to be so excited."

"I'm proud of you, Ange."

There it was: the reason she'd called him, though she hadn't realized it until just this second.

"We'll celebrate tomorrow night."

"I'll hold you to that."

She was smiling when she hung up. An old Billy Joel song came on the radio. "It's Still Rock & Roll to Me." She cranked up the volume and sang along. By the time she drove into West End and turned onto the beach road, she was singing as loud as she could and thumping the steering wheel in time to the music.

She felt like a kid again, driving home from a football game after a home team win.

She parked close to the house, grabbed her purse, and ran inside.

"Lauren!"

The house was quiet. A fire crackled in the hearth.

There was a pause that seemed to last forever, then a rustle of sound. "We're here."

Lauren sat up on the sofa. Her pale cheeks glistened with tears. Her eyes were swollen and red. David was beside her, holding her hand. He looked as if he'd been crying, too.

Angie felt a stab of fear. She knew about crying in the middle of a pregnancy. "What is it?"

"David and I have been talking."

"The baby is okay?"

"Fine. Perfect."

Angie felt a flood of relief. She'd overreacted, as usual. "Oh. Well, I'll let you two keep talking." She started toward the stairs.

"Wait," Lauren called out, getting awkwardly to her feet. She grabbed a piece of paper from the coffee table and handed it to Angie.

David immediately moved in close to Lauren, put an arm around her.

Angie looked down at the letter in her hands.

Dear Ms. Ribido: We are pleased to offer you admission to the University of Southern California . . . undergraduate . . . full scholarship for tuition and housing . . . respond by June 1 . . .

"I knew you could do it," Angie said gently. She wanted to throw her arms around Lauren and twirl her around, laughing, but that kind of enthusiasm was for ordinary girls in ordinary times. This was anything but.

"I didn't think I'd get in."

Angie had never heard that sad edge in Lauren's voice before. It was heartbreaking. Of all the trials Lauren had faced this year, this—the attainment of her dream—had perhaps hurt the most of all. Now a decision would have to be made, and all of them knew it. "I'm proud of you."

"This changes things," Lauren said so softly that Angie found herself leaning forward to hear.

Angie ached to hug her, but David was there, holding Lauren's hand. "It's not impossible to go to college with a baby."

"A two-month-old?" Lauren's voice sounded old and far away. It echoed and faded, as if she were throwing the ugly words down a well.

Angie closed her eyes. Any answer to that would be a lie. Angie knew already what Lauren was sure to discover: day cares that took two-month-olds were rare. And certainly expensive. She rubbed the bridge of her nose, sighing softly. This was like being on a sinking ship. She could feel the water rising. "That's a problem," she said at last. There was no point lying. "But you're a strong, smart girl—"

"A smart girl would have done things differently," Lauren said. Her eyes filled with tears again, though she was trying to smile. She looked up at David, who nodded down at her encouragingly. Then she looked expectantly at Angie.

For a moment no one spoke.

Angie felt a chill slide down her spine. All at once she was afraid.

Lauren let go of David's hand and took a step forward. "Take our baby, Angie."

The air rushed out of her. She felt her lungs shake with the force of it. "Don't," she whispered, using her hands to ward off the words.

Lauren took another step. Closer. She looked so young. So desperate. Tears swam in her eyes. "Please. We want you to adopt our baby. We've been talking about it all day. It's the only way."

Angie closed her eyes, barely hearing the tiny, mouselike sound that escaped her lips. She couldn't go back down that dream road. It had almost killed her last time. She couldn't think about filling her empty, empty arms again with . . .

a baby.

She couldn't. She wasn't strong enough.

And yet. How could she possibly walk away from this?

A baby.

She opened her eyes.

Lauren was staring at her. The girl's pale, full cheeks were streaked with tears. Her dark eyes were bloodshot and swollen. The letter from USC was right there, a piece of paper that could change lives . . .

"Please," Lauren whispered, starting to cry again.

Angie's heart seemed to cave in on itself, leaving her feeling empty inside. Lost. There was no doubt in her mind that she had to say no to this baby. And no way on God's green earth she could do it.

She couldn't say no. Not to Lauren, and not to herself. But she knew, deep in her slowly crumbling heart, that she was doing the wrong thing, even as she said softly, "Yes."

"THERE IS SOMETHING WRONG WITH YOU TODAY," MAMA SAID, pushing the glasses higher on her nose.

Angie looked away. "Nonsense. I'm fine."

"You are not fine. Jerrie Carl had to ask you for a table three times before you answered her."

"And when Mr. Costanza asked for red wine, you handed him the bottle," Mira said, wiping her hands on her apron.

Angie shouldn't have come into the kitchen. Like a pair of hyenas, Mira and Mama sensed distress, and once alerted, they tended to move together, following, waiting.

"I'm fine." She turned and left the kitchen.

Back in the busy dining room, she felt less obvious. She did her best to function. She moved slowly, perhaps, but given her state of mind, any movement at all was a triumph. She smiled blankly and tried to pretend that everything was okay.

The truth was, she couldn't feel much of anything at all. For the past twenty-four hours, she'd kept her emotions in a locked box into which she dared not peek.

It was better not to see. She didn't want to look too closely at this Faustian bargain that she and Lauren had struck. It would take them on a terrible journey, this deal; at the end of it there would be broken hearts on the side of the road. Angie felt as if she'd sealed herself into a small, dark room.

She went over to the window and stared out at the night. The bustling sounds of the busy restaurant faded behind her until she couldn't hear anything beyond the beating of her heart.

What now?

It was the query that had kept her up all last night; the first thing on her mind this morning.

Her emotions were a tangle of hope and despair. She couldn't find a place from which to begin the unraveling. A part of her kept thinking, *A baby*, and with it came a swelling in her heart that was almost unbearably sweet, but on the heels of that thought was always the other one, the darker, *Lauren won't be able to do it.*

Either way, there would be heartbreak. At the end of this road lay a terrible choice: Lauren or the baby. Angie could, at best, have one or the other. At worst, she could lose them both.

"Ange?"

She gasped and spun around. Conlan stood behind her, holding a dozen pink roses.

She'd forgotten about their date. She tried to smile, but it was weak and desperate and she saw a frown dart across his forehead. "You're early," she said, laughing a little too sharply, praying it was true. It usually was.

He was still frowning. "Only a minute or two. Are you okay?"

"Of course. Let me just get my coat and say good night." She edged past him and headed for the kitchen. She was at the swinging door when she realized she hadn't taken the flowers from him.

Damn.

"Conlan's here," she said to Mama and Mira. "Can you guys close up tonight?"

Mama and Mira exchanged knowing looks. "So that was it," Mama said. "You were thinking of him."

"I'll give Lauren a ride home," Mira said. "Have fun."

Fun.

Angie forgot to laugh or say good-bye. Instead, she headed back to the dining room. "So, where are we going?" She took the flowers from him, pretended she could smell their scent.

"You'll see." Conlan led her out to his car and helped her into the passenger seat. Within minutes they were driving south.

Angie stared out the window. In the tarnished glass, her reflection stared back at her. Her face looked long and thin, drawn out.

"Is it the baby stuff?"

She blinked, turned. "What?"

"Yesterday you cleaned out the storage room, right? Is that why you're quiet?"

There it was again, the hesitancy in Conlan's voice, the treating her with kid gloves. She hated the familiarity of it. "I was okay yesterday."

Had it really only been a day ago that she'd been there, squatting in front of the relics of her ancient hope, believing she'd moved on?

"Really?"

"I boxed everything up and brought it to the cottage for Lauren." Her voice snagged on the name and it all came rushing back.

Take our baby, Angie.

"You sounded good," he said cautiously.

"I was so happy about it." She hoped her voice didn't sound wistful. So much had happened since then.

"We're here." Conlan turned into a gravel parking lot.

Angie craned her neck and peered through the windshield.

A beautiful stone mansion stood flanked by Douglas fir trees and rimmed in rhododendrons. *The Sheldrake Inn welcomes you,* read the sign.

She looked at Conlan, giving him her first real smile of the evening. "This is more than a date."

He grinned. "You're living with a teenager now. I have to plan ahead."

She followed him out of the car and into the cozy interior of the inn.

A woman dressed in full Victorian garb greeted them at the door and showed them to the front desk.

"Mr. and Mrs. Malone," said the man behind the reservation desk. "Right on time."

Conlan filled out the paperwork, offered his credit card, then whisked her upstairs. Their room was a beautiful two-room suite with a huge four-poster bed, a river rock fireplace, a bathtub big enough for two, and a magical view of the moonlit coast.

"Ange?"

Slowly she turned around to face him.

How can I tell him?

"Come here."

She was helpless to resist the sound of his voice. She moved toward him. He pulled her into his arms, held her so tightly she felt dizzy.

She had to tell him.

Now.

If they were to have any kind of future, she had to tell him. "Conlan—"

He kissed her then, so gently. When he drew back, he looked down at her.

She felt as if she were drowning in the blue of his eyes.

"I couldn't believe you gave the baby stuff away. I'm so proud of you, Ange. I look at you now and I can breathe again. I don't think I realized until yesterday how long I'd been holding it all inside."

"Oh, Con. We need—"

Very slowly he bent on one knee. Smiling, he held out her wedding ring. "I figured out what to do with it. Marry me again."

The way Angie dropped to her knees was more like folding. "I love you, okay? Don't forget it. As Papa used to say, I love you more than all the drops of rain that fall."

He frowned. "I expected a simple yes. Then a rush to the bed."

"My yes couldn't be any simpler, but I need to tell you something first. You might change your mind."

"About wanting to marry you?"

"Yeah."

He looked at her for a long time, a slight frown creasing his brow. "Okay. Hit me."

She drew in a deep breath. "Yesterday, when I called you about the nursery, I was so excited. I couldn't wait to get home and tell Lauren." She stood up and moved away from him. She went to the window, looked out at the crashing surf. "When I got home, she'd been crying. And David was there."

Conlan stood up. She heard the creaking of the old floorboards. He probably wanted to come stand behind her but he didn't move.

"She got a full ride to USC. Her dream school."

"And?"

"It changed everything," she said softly, echoing Lauren's exact words. "Maybe if she had a toddler, she could swing it, but a two-month-old? There's no way she could handle USC, working, and raising a newborn."

It was a long time before Conlan spoke. When he did, his voice was ragged; not his voice at all. "And?"

Angie squeezed her eyes shut. "She wants to give the baby up for adoption. She thinks it will be the best thing for the baby."

"It probably will be. She's so young." He came up behind Angie, but didn't touch her.

"She said, *Take my baby.* Just like that." She sighed, felt him stiffen. "It was like being in a car wreck. That's how hard and fast it hit me."

"You said yes."

She heard the dullness in his voice. She turned to face him, thankful at least that he hadn't pulled away. "What choice did I have? I love Lauren. Maybe I never should have let her into my heart—no. No, I won't say that. I'm glad I did. She's how I came back to myself. And to you." She put her arms around his neck, held him close so that he had to look at her. "What if Sophia had asked this of us?"

"She's not Sophia," he said, and she saw how much it hurt him to say that.

"She's somebody's Sophia. She's a scared seventeen-year-old who needs someone to love her, to take care of her. How can I say no to her? Do I tell her to give her baby to strangers when I'm right here? When *we're* right here?"

"Damn you, Angie." He pushed past her, went into the other room.

She knew she shouldn't go to him, should give him time, but the thought of losing him again made her desperate. "How can we say no to this?" She crossed the room, came up beside him. "You could be his Little League coach—"

"Don't." His voice was barely recognizable.

"How can we say no?" she said again, softer this time, forcing him to face her. As she asked the question, she couldn't help thinking about the day she'd gone to his workplace, when Diane had said: *Twice I came into his office and found him crying.*

He ran a hand through his hair and sighed. "I don't think I can go through this again. I'm sorry."

She closed her eyes; those two words hurt all the way to the bone. "I know," she said, bowing her head forward. He was right. How could they—she—risk everything again? Tears burned her eyes. There was no good answer. She couldn't lose Conlan again . . . but how could she say no to Lauren? "I love you so much, Con," she whispered.

"And I love you." The way he said the words they sounded like a curse.

"This could be our chance," she said.

"We've thought that before," he reminded her dully. "Do you

know what it was like for me, always picking you up, drying your tears, listening to you cry? Worrying that it was somehow my fault?"

She touched his face. "You had tears of your own."

"Yes." His voice was harsh.

"I never dried them. How could I when I never saw you cry?"

"Your pain was so big. . . ."

"It's different this time, Con. *We're* different. We could be a team. Maybe she'll be able to go through with it, and we'll be the parents we always wanted to be. Or maybe she'll back out, and it'll be just us. Either way, we'll be okay. I swear it." She dropped down to one knee, whispered, "Marry me, Conlan."

He stared down at her, his eyes bright. "Damn you," he said, sinking slowly to his knees. "I can't live without you anymore."

"Then don't. Please . . ." She kissed him. "Trust me, Conlan. This time we'll last forever."

LAUREN HEARD DAVID'S CAR DRIVE UP. SHE RAN TO THE FRONT door and opened it, waiting for him.

For the first time in months, he was smiling.

"Are you ready for this?" he asked, taking her hand in his.

"As ready as I'll ever be."

They walked across the yard and got into his car. All the way to Mountainaire, he talked about the Porsche. Gear ratios and speed off the line and custom paint colors. She could tell how nervous he was, and strangely, his anxiety calmed her. When they reached his house, he parked the car, then let out a deep sigh and looked at her. "You're sure?"

"I am."

"Okay."

They walked up the stone path to the Hayneses' huge front door. David opened the door and led her into the cool, beige elegance of his home. "Mom? Dad?"

"Are you sure they're home?" Lauren whispered, taking his hand.

"They're home. I told them we needed to talk."

Mr. and Mrs. Haynes came into the room fast, as if they'd been waiting just around the corner.

Mrs. Haynes stared at Lauren's rounded belly.

Mr. Haynes studiously avoided looking at her. He led them

into the sunken living room, where everything was the color of heavy cream and nothing was out of place.

Unless, of course, you counted the pregnant girl.

"Well," Mr. Haynes said when they'd all sat down.

"How are you feeling?" Mrs. Haynes asked. Her voice sounded strained, and she seemed unable to meet Lauren's gaze.

"Fat but great. My doctor says everything is perfect."

"She got a full ride to USC," David said to his parents.

"That's fabulous," Mrs. Haynes said. She glanced at her husband, who leaned forward in his seat.

Lauren reached for David's hand, held it. She felt surprisingly calm. "We've decided to give the baby up for adoption."

"Thank God," Mr. Haynes said, sighing harshly. For the first time, Lauren noticed the tenseness in his jawline, the worry in his eyes. Relief changed his face. He finally smiled.

Mrs. Haynes moved to sit beside Lauren. "That couldn't have been an easy decision for you."

Lauren was grateful for that. "It wasn't."

Mrs. Haynes started to reach for her, then withdrew her hand at the last second. Lauren had the strange impression that David's mother was afraid to touch her. "I think it's for the best. You two are so young. We'll call the lawyer and—"

"We've already chosen the parents," Lauren said. "My . . . boss. Angie Malone."

Mrs. Haynes nodded. Even though she was obviously relieved, she looked sad somehow. She bent forward, picked up her purse, and pulled it onto her lap. She pulled out a checkbook, wrote a check, and ripped it out, then stood up. She handed the check to Lauren.

It was for five thousand dollars.

Lauren looked up. "I can't take this."

Mrs. Haynes gazed down at her. Lauren saw the wrinkles through her makeup for the first time. "It's for your college fund. Los Angeles is an expensive city. A scholarship won't handle everything."

"But—"

"Let me do this," she said softly. "You're a good girl, Lauren. On your way to becoming a good woman."

Lauren swallowed hard, surprised by how moved she was by that simple compliment. "Thank you."

Mrs. Haynes started to move away, then stopped and turned

back. "Maybe you could give me a photograph of my— of the baby when he's born."

It was the first time Lauren had thought of the baby as their grandchild. "Sure," she said.

Mrs. Haynes looked down at her. "Do you really think you can do this?"

"I have to. It's the right thing to do."

After that, there was nothing left to say.

TWENTY-NINE

I T WAS ALMOST MIDNIGHT WHEN LAUREN GOT HOME.

Closing the door behind her, she leaned against it, letting out a ragged sigh. She couldn't wait to climb into bed and close her eyes. This day had left her wounded.

She touched her stomach, felt a flutter-soft kick. "Hey," she murmured to the baby as she headed for the living room.

She was at the dining room table when she noticed the fire in the fireplace and the music coming through the speakers. It was something soft, Hawaiian-sounding. "Somewhere over the Rainbow" played on a ukulele.

Angie and Conlan were sitting in front of the fire.

"Oh," Lauren said in surprise. "I thought you were off on a romantic getaway."

Angie rose, walked toward Lauren. When she got closer, she

held out her left hand. A huge diamond glittered. "We're getting married again."

Lauren squealed and threw herself into Angie's arms. "That's *great*," she said, holding Angie tightly. She hadn't realized until just then how alone she'd felt all day, how much she'd missed Angie. She had trouble letting go. "Now my baby will have a daddy, too."

"Sorry," she said, finally drawing back. She felt foolish; a girl who should be a woman.

She'd said "my" baby.

"Actually, Lauren, that's what we came home to talk to you about."

It was Conlan who'd spoken.

Lauren closed her eyes for just a moment as a wave of exhaustion moved through her. She didn't know if she could talk about the baby anymore.

But she had no choice.

"Okay."

Angie took her hand, squeezed it. The touch helped. Together, hand in hand, they went to the couch and sat down.

Conlan remained sitting on the hearth. He was tilted forward, with his forearms rested on his thighs. Long black hair fell across part of his face. In the firelight, his eyes looked impossibly blue.

She felt impaled by those eyes. She shifted uncomfortably on the sofa.

"You're just a child," Conlan said, his voice surprisingly soft, "so I'm sorry about all this."

Lauren smiled. "I quit being a kid a few months ago."

"No. You had to face a grown-up thing. That's not the same thing as being a grown-up." He sighed. "The thing is . . . Angie and I are scared."

Lauren hadn't expected that. "I thought you wanted a baby."

"We do," Angie said in a tight voice. "Too much, maybe."

"So you should be happy." Lauren looked from Conlan to Angie. I'm giving you— Oh." It came to her all at once. "The other girl. The one who changed her mind."

"Yes," Angie said.

"I wouldn't do that to you guys. I promise. I mean . . . I love you. And I love my baby. *Your* baby. I want to do the right thing."

Angie touched Lauren's face. "We know that, Lauren. We just want—"

"Need," Conlan interrupted.

"—to know that you've thought about this. That you're sure. It will not be an easy thing to do."

"Will it be harder than parenting at seventeen?"

Angie's smile was as gentle as her touch had been. "That's an answer from your head. I asked a question of the heart."

"None of this is easy," Lauren said, wiping her eyes. "But I've thought and thought. This is the best answer. You can trust me."

A silence followed that statement. It was broken only by a log falling in the fireplace and a shower of hissing sparks.

"We think you should see a counselor," Conlan said at last.

"Why?"

Angie was trying to smile, as if she wanted to show that this was nothing, just another late night chat. The sadness in her eyes betrayed her. "Because I love you, Lauren, and as much as I'd love your baby to be mine, I know about where we're headed. Where *you're* headed. It's one thing to decide to give up a baby. It's another thing to do it. I want you to be *sure*."

Lauren hardly heard anything after *I love you*. Only David had ever said those words to her before. She leaned forward and pulled Angie into a fierce hug. "I'd never hurt you," she whispered throatily. "Never."

Angie drew back. "I know that."

"So you'll see the counselor?" Conlan said, sounding more than a little afraid.

"Of course." Lauren found her first genuine smile of the day. "I'd do anything for you."

Angie hugged her again. In the distance, very softly, Lauren heard Conlan say, "Then don't break her heart."

THE LAWYER'S OFFICE WAS CROWDED WITH PEOPLE. ON THE LEFT side of the room, their chairs pushed close together, were the Haynes family. On the right side, Angie sat in a chair beside Conlan. Lauren's chair was in the middle, and though there wasn't much space between her and the others, she seemed vaguely alone, separate.

Angie got up to go to her.

Just then the lawyer strode into the room. A tall, portly man in an expensive black suit, he commanded attention when he said, "Good day, all."

Angie sat back down.

"I'm Stu Phillips," the lawyer said, extending his hand to Conlan, who stood instantly.

"Conlan Malone. This is my . . . Angie Malone."

Angie shook the lawyer's hand, then sat back down. She sat very still, trying not to remember the last time they'd been in a meeting like this.

I have a baby for you, Mr. and Mrs. Malone.

A teenager.

"So, young lady," Stu said, looking gently at Lauren, "you've made up your mind?"

"Yes, sir." Her voice was barely audible.

"Okay, then. First, let's begin with the technicalities. I need to advise you all that it is sometimes problematic to share representation in an adoption. It's legal in this state, but not always advisable. If something came up—a disagreement—I wouldn't be able to represent either party."

"Nothing will come up," Lauren said. Her voice was stronger now. "I've made up my mind."

Stu looked to Conlan. "Are you two prepared for the risks of dual representation?"

"That's the least of our risk here, Stu," Conlan answered.

Stu pulled some paperwork from a manila folder and slid them across the desk. "Sign these documents and we'll proceed. They merely state that you knowingly accept the risks inherent in dual representation."

When the documents were signed, he put them away. For the next hour, he talked about the process. Who could pay for what, what needed to be signed and by whom, the ins and outs of Washington law, the home study that would need to be done, the termination of the birth parents' rights, the guardian ad litems that would be assigned, the time and expense of all of it.

Angie had heard it all before, and she knew that, in the end, the technicalities didn't add up to squat. It was emotions that mattered. Feelings. You could sign all the papers in the world and make a delivery truck full of promises, but you couldn't know how it would feel when you got there. That was why the adoption couldn't be legally finalized before the birth. Lauren would have to hold her baby and then sign her rights away.

Angie's heart ached at the very thought of it. She glanced to her left.

Lauren sat very quietly in the chair, with her hands clasped in her lap. Even with her rounded stomach, she looked young and

innocent. The girl who'd swallowed a watermelon. She was nodding earnestly at something the lawyer asked her.

Angie wanted to go to her, kneel down beside her and hold
her hand, say *You're not alone in this*, but the sad truth was that
soon Lauren *would* be alone. What could be more solitary than
giving your baby away?

And nothing Angie could do could protect Lauren from that
moment.

Angie closed her eyes. How could they get through all of this
with their hearts intact? How—

She felt a tug on her sleeve. She blinked, glanced sideways.

Conlan was staring at her. So was the attorney, Lauren, and
everyone in the room.

"Did you ask me something?" she said, feeling her cheeks
heat up.

"As I was saying," Stu said, "I like to make an adoption plan.
It makes everything go much smoother. Shall we begin?"

"Certainly," Angie said.

Stu looked from Angie to Lauren. "What kind of communication do you want to have, after the adoption?"

Lauren frowned. "What do you mean?"

"After the Malones adopt your child, you'll want some kind
of communication, I imagine. Phone calls on the baby's birthday
and perhaps Christmas. Letters and photographs at least once a
year."

Lauren drew in a sharp breath. It sounded like a gasp. She obviously hadn't thought this far ahead, hadn't realized that this
adoption would change who they all were. She turned to look at
Angie, who suddenly felt as fragile as a winter leaf.

"We'll be in touch all the time," Angie said to the attorney,
hearing the catch in her voice. "We're . . . Lauren is like family."

"I'm not sure that kind of openness is in the best interest of
the child," the lawyer said. "Clearly delineated boundaries are
most effective. We find that—"

"Oh," Lauren said, biting down on her lip. She wasn't listening to the lawyer. She was looking at Conlan and Angie. "I hadn't
thought about that. A baby needs one mother."

David leaned over and took Lauren's hand in his.

"We don't have to have an adoption like everyone else's,"
Angie said. She would have said more but her voice softened,
cracked, and she couldn't think of anything. She couldn't imag-

ine letting Lauren just walk out of their lives . . . but what other end was there to all of this?

Lauren looked at her. The sadness in the girl's dark eyes was almost unbearable. For once she looked old, ancient even. "I didn't realize . . . I should have." She tried to smile. "You're going to be the perfect mom, Angie. My baby is lucky."

"Our baby," David said softly. Lauren gave him a heartbreakingly sad smile.

Angie sat there a moment longer, unsure of what to say.

Finally, Lauren looked at the lawyer again. "Tell me how it works best?"

The meeting went on and on; words were batted back and forth and committed to paper, black marks that delineated how each of them could behave.

All the while Angie wanted to go to Lauren and take the girl in her arms and whisper that it would be all right.

But now, sitting here in this room of laws and rules, surrounded by hearts that didn't quite know what to feel, she wondered.

Would it be all right?

FOR THE FIRST TIME IN ANYONE'S MEMORY, IT DIDN'T RAIN ON Easter Sunday. Instead, the sun rose high in a clear blue sky. The sidewalks were full of people, most of them dressed in their Sunday best as they walked in all different directions to their churches.

Angie walked between Conlan and Lauren. Up ahead, the church bells started to peal. Her friends and family started toward the church, funneling inside.

Just outside the doors, Angie paused. Conlan and Lauren had no choice but to pause, too.

"We'll tell them everything later. At the Easter egg hunt, right?"

They both nodded.

Angie felt for her wedding ring, twisted it around to hide the diamond. Such a trick wouldn't fool the DeSaria women for long, but hopefully, they'd be too busy with the mass to notice. She took a step forward.

Lauren stopped her with a touch.

"What is it, honey?" There was a look in Lauren's eyes that Angie couldn't read. A kind of awe, perhaps, as if going to church with the family was a rare gift. Or maybe it was anxiety. They were all nervous about what would come next. "Here, take my hand."

"Thanks," Lauren said, looking away quickly, but not before Angie saw the girl's sudden tears. Hand in hand, they walked up the concrete steps and into the beautiful old church.

The service seemed to take forever and still not last long enough. Angie concentrated on helping Lauren rise and kneel and rise again.

When Angie got her chance to pray, she knelt on the padded riser, bowed her head, and thought: *Dear God, please show us the right way through all of this. Keep us safe. Protect and watch over Lauren. In this I pray, Amen.*

After services were over, they all went downstairs to the basement of the church, where dozens of cakes and cookies were set out on the tables. Angie kept her left hand in her pocket as she talked to family and friends.

Finally the kids streamed into the hall, all talking at once, carrying the egg-carton-and-macaroni jewelry boxes they'd made.

The congregation began moving to the doors. They walked out into the cold, bright morning, a crowd of well-dressed people with something in common. They crossed the street and went into the park.

Angie started at the empty merry-go-round. Sunlight made it glisten like sterling silver.

Conlan came up beside her, slipped an arm around her waist. She knew he was thinking of Sophie, too. How many times had they stood here together, watching other children play and dreaming of their own? Saying quietly to each other: *Someday.*

Kids jumped onto the merry-go-round, set it spinning.

"Okay, kids," said Father O'Houlihan in his lilting Irish brogue, "there are eggs hidden all 'round here. Go!"

The kids shrieked and set off in search of the hidden eggs.

Lauren went to little Dani, who stood close to Mira.

"Come on," Lauren said, attempting to kneel and then giving up. "I'll help you look." She took Dani's hand and off they went.

Within moments the whole DeSaria clan was standing together. They were like geese, Angie thought. Somehow they just floated into formation. Their conversations sounded vaguely birdlike, too, with so many voices going at once.

Angie cleared her throat.

Conlan squeezed her hand, threw her a go-for-it smile.

"I have two things to say," she said. When no one listened, she said it louder.

Mama whopped Uncle Francis in the back of the head. "Be quiet. Our Angela has something to say."

"Someday, Maria, I'm going to hit you back," Uncle Francis said, rubbing the back of his head.

Mira and Livvy moved in closer.

Angie showed off her ring.

The screams probably shattered windows all through town. The family surged forward like a wave, crashing around Angie and Conlan.

Everyone was talking at once, congratulating them and asking questions and saying they knew it all along.

When the wave receded and they were all on the shore again, it was Mama who remembered.

"What is the second thing?" she asked.

"What?" Angie said, edging toward Conlan.

"You said you had two things to tell us. What is next? You are quitting the restaurant?"

"No. Actually I think—we think—we're going to stay in West End this time. Conlan has a contract to write a book, and he's been given a weekly column for the newspaper. He can work from here."

"That's great news," Mama said.

Livvy moved closer. "So what gives, baby sis?"

Angie reached back for Conlan's hand. She held on to him, let him be her port. "We're going to adopt Lauren's baby."

This time the silence could have broken glass. Angie felt it clear to her bones.

"This is not a good idea," Mama said at last.

Angie clung to Conlan's hand. "What am I supposed to do? Say no? Watch her give the baby to strangers?"

As one, the family turned, looked at Lauren. The teenager was by the swing set, down on her hands and knees, searching through the tall grass. Little Dani was beside her, giggling and pointing. From this distance, they looked like any young mother and her daughter.

"Lauren has a big heart," Mama said, "and a sad past. It is a dangerous combination, Angela."

Livvy stepped forward. "Can you handle it?" she asked gently.

The only question that really mattered. "If she changes her mind?"

Angie looked up at Conlan, who smiled down at her and nodded. *Together,* that look said, *we can handle anything.*

"Yes," she said, finding a pretty decent smile. "I can handle it. The hardest part will be saying good-bye to Lauren."

"But you'll have a baby," Mira said.

"Maybe," Mama said. "The other time—"

"This is not up for a vote," Conlan said, and that shut them up.

They all looked at Lauren again, then, one by one, they started talking about other, more ordinary things.

Angie released her breath. The storm had been faced and survived. Oh, there would be gossip through the family, burning up the phone lines as each of them dissected this news and formed an opinion. Those opinions would be tossed back and forth on a daily basis. Some of it would filter down to Angie. Most of it would not.

It didn't matter. There was nothing they could come up with that Angie hadn't worried about and foreseen.

Some things in life, though, couldn't be gone in search of. They simply had to be waited for. Like the weather. You could look on the horizon and see a bank of black storm clouds. That didn't guarantee rain tomorrow. It might just as easily dawn bright and clear.

There was no damn way to tell.

All you could do was keep moving and live your life.

CARS HAD BEEN ARRIVING STEADILY FOR THE LAST HOUR. EVERY few minutes or so the front door cracked open and new guests streamed into the house, carrying boxes of food and presents wrapped in pretty paper. There were men in the living room, watching sports on the aged television and drinking beer. At least a dozen children were clustered in the den; some were playing board games, others had Barbies dancing with Kens, and still others played Nintendo.

But the heart of the action took place in the kitchen. Mira and Livvy were busy making the antipasto trays—provolone, roasted peppers, tuna fish, olives, bruschetta. Maria was layering homemade manicotti in porcelain baking dishes, and Angie was trying to make ricotta cream for the cannoli. In the corner, on the small kitchen table that had somehow once held the entire De-Saria family for casual meals, a three-tiered white wedding cake rose above a sea of napkins and silverware.

"Lauren," Maria said, "start setting up the buffet in the dining room."

Lauren immediately went to the little table and started picking things up. Silverware and cocktail napkins first.

She carried them into the dining room and stood there, staring at the huge table. A pale green damask tablecloth covered it. A vase full of white roses was the centerpiece.

There would be photographs taken of this table. She needed to do it right. But how?

"The silverware goes here, at the beginning," Angie said, coming up beside her. "Like this."

Lauren watched Angie arrange the silverware into a pretty pattern, and it struck her all at once, so hard that Lauren drew in a sharp breath: *I'll be leaving soon.*

"Are you okay, honey? You look like you've just lost your best friend."

Lauren forced a smile, said quickly, "I don't think you should be setting the table at your own wedding."

"That's the great thing about remarrying the same guy. What matters is the marriage, not the ceremony. We're only doing this for Mama." She leaned closer. "I told her not to bother, but you know my mother."

Angie went back to setting out the silverware.

Lauren felt her move slightly to the left, and it seemed suddenly as if there was a vast space between them. "Do you want a boy or a girl?"

Angie's hand froze in midair, a pair of knives hung suspended above the table. The moment seemed to draw out. From the other rooms, noise surrounded them, but here, in the dining room, there was only the sound of two women breathing slowly. "I don't know," she said at last, then went back to placing silverware. "Healthy is all that matters."

"That counselor you sent me to . . . she said I should feel free to ask you questions. She said it's better to have everything out in the open."

"You can talk to me about anything. You know that."

"That adoption plan we made . . ." Lauren started to ask the question that had kept her up all last night; halfway into it, she lost her nerve.

"Yes?"

Lauren swallowed hard. "Will you stick to it? Send me letters and pictures?"

"Oh, honey. Of course we will."

Something about the way she said *honey*, so gently, broke Lauren's heart. She couldn't hold it inside anymore. "You'll forget me."

Angie's face crumpled at that. Tears glistened in her eyes as she pulled Lauren into her arms and said fiercely, "Never."

Lauren was the first to draw away. Instead of comforting her, the hug had only made her feel more alone. She put a hand on her belly, felt her baby's fluttery movements. She was just about to ask Angie to touch her stomach when David walked into the living room. She ran for him, let him take her in his arms.

The loneliness that had gripped her only a moment ago released its hold. She wouldn't be alone after the baby. She'd have David.

"You look great," he said.

It made her smile, even if it was a lie. "I'm as big as a house."

He laughed. "I like houses. In fact, I'm thinking about architecture as a career."

"Smart-ass."

He looped an arm around her and headed for the food. On the way there, he told her all the gossip from school. She was laughing again by the time the music started and Maria herded everyone to the backyard, where a rented white arbor was entwined with hundreds of pink silk roses.

Conlan stood beneath the arbor, wearing a pair of black Levi's and a black crewneck sweater. Father O'Houlihan was beside him, dressed in full robes.

To the strains of Nat King Cole's "Unforgettable" Angie walked down the flagstone path. She wore a white cashmere cable-knit sweater and a gauzy white skirt. Her feet were bare and the wind whipped her long, dark hair across her back. A single white rose was her bouquet.

Lauren stared at her in awe.

As Angie passed Lauren, she smiled. Their gazes met, held for the briefest moment, and Lauren thought: *I love you, too.*

It was crazy. . . .

Angie handed Lauren the rose and kept walking.

Lauren stared down at the rose in disbelief. Even now, in this moment that was Angie's, she'd thought of Lauren.

"You see how lucky you are," she whispered to her baby, touching her swollen belly. "That's going to be your mom."

She wasn't sure why it made her want to cry.

THIRTY

O N A RAINY MONDAY IN LATE APRIL, MARIA DECIDED THAT
Angie needed to learn how to cook. She showed up
early, carrying a big cardboard box full of supplies. No
amount of arguing could change her mind. "You are a married
woman . . . again. You should cook."

Lauren stood in the doorway, trying not to laugh at Angie's
protests.

"What are you laughing about?" Maria demanded, putting
her hands on her hips. "You are learning, too. Both of you get
dressed and be back in this kitchen in ten minutes."

Lauren ran upstairs, changed out of her flannel nightgown
and into a pair of black leggings and an old Fircrest Bulldogs
T-shirt. When she skidded back into the kitchen, Maria looked
up at her.

Lauren stood there, smiling uncertainly. "What should I do?"

Maria walked over to her. Shaking her head, she made a small tsking sound. "You are too young to have such sad eyes," she said quietly.

Lauren didn't know what to say to that.

Maria grabbed an apron out of the box and handed it to Lauren. "Here. Put this on."

Lauren did as she was told.

"Now come here." Maria led the way to the counter and began pulling ingredients out of the box. By the time Angie made it back to the kitchen, dressed in jeans and a T-shirt, there was a mound of flour on the butcher block and a metal bowl full of eggs alongside it.

"Pasta," Angie said, frowning.

For the next hour, they worked side by side. Maria taught them how to scoop out the center of the flour and fill the hole with just the right amount of eggs, then to work the dough carefully so it didn't get tough. While Lauren was learning to roll the dough into sheets, Angie went into the living room and turned on the music.

"That's better," she said, dancing back into the room.

Maria handed Lauren a metal sunburst with a handle. "Now cut that pasta into strips, maybe two inches square."

Lauren frowned. "I might screw up. Maybe Angie should try."

Angie laughed at that. "Yeah. I'm certainly the better choice."

Maria touched Lauren's face gently. "You know what happens if you make a mistake?"

"What?"

"We roll it out and try again. Cut."

Lauren picked up the scalloped pastry wheel and began cutting the pasta into squares. No chemistry lab had ever been undertaken with more care.

"You see this, Angie?" Maria said. "Your girl has the gift."

Your girl.

For the rest of the morning, those two words stayed with Lauren, warmed her. As they filled the tortellini and finished the pasta, she found herself smiling. Laughing sometimes, for no reason.

She hated to see the cooking lesson come to an end.

"Well," Maria said at last, "I must go now. My garden is calling to me. I have planting to do."

Angie laughed. "Thank God." She tossed a wink at Lauren. "I think I'll stick with the restaurant's leftovers."

"Someday you will be sorry, Angela," Maria sniffed, "that you ignored your heritage."

Angie put an arm around her mother, held her close. "I'm just kidding, Mama. I appreciate the lesson. Tomorrow I'll get out a cookbook and try something on my own. How would that be?"

"Good."

Maria hugged them both, said good-bye, and left the house. Lauren went to the sink and started washing the dishes. Angie sidled up beside her. They washed and dried in the easy rhythm they'd created recently.

When the dishes were dried and put away, Angie said, "I need to run down to Help-Your-Neighbor House. I have a meeting with the director. The coat drive went so well, we're trying to come up with another promotion."

"Oh."

Lauren stood there, drying her wet hands, as Angie hurried through the house and then left. The door slammed shut; in the yard, a car started up.

Lauren went to the window and stared out, watching Angie drive away. Behind her, the CD changed. Bruce Springsteen's gravelly voice started up.

Baby, we were born to run . . .

She spun away from the window and ran for the stereo, clicking the music off hard. A sharp silence descended. It was so quiet that she thought she could hear the tapping of Conlan's fingers on the laptop upstairs, but that was impossible.

She tried not to think about her mother, but now that was impossible, too.

"I thought kids your age loved the Boss," Conlan said from behind her.

She turned around slowly. "Hey," she said.

In the weeks since the wedding, Lauren had tried to keep her distance from Conlan. They lived in the same house, of course, so it wasn't easy. But she sensed a hesitation in him, an unwillingness to get to know her.

She kept her back to the window and stared at him, twisting her hands together nervously. "Angie went to town. She'll be back in a while."

"I know."

Of course she would have told her husband. Lauren felt like an idiot for having said anything.

Conlan crossed the room, came up closer. "You're nervous around me."

"You're nervous around me."

He smiled. "Touché. I'm just worried, that's all. Angie is . . . fragile sometimes. She leads with her heart."

"And you think I'll hurt her."

"Not purposely, no."

Lauren had no answer to that, so she changed the subject. "Do you want to be a father?"

Something passed through his eyes then, a sadness, maybe, that made her wish she hadn't asked the question. "Yes."

They stared at each other. She saw the way he was trying to smile and it wounded her, made her feel closer to him. She knew about disappointment. "I'm not like that other girl, you know."

"I know." He backed up, as if he wanted to put some distance between them, and sat down on the sofa.

She went to the coffee table and sat down on it. "What kind of father would you be?"

The question seemed to jolt him. He flinched, looked down at his hands. It took him a long time to answer, and when he finally did, his voice was soft. "There, I guess. I wouldn't miss a thing. Not a game, not a school play, not a dentist appointment." He looked up. "I'd take her—or him—to the park and the beach and the movies."

Lauren's breath caught in her throat. Longing tightened her chest. She hadn't realized until just then, with that quietly spoken answer, that what she'd really been asking was: What does a father do?

He looked at her, and in his eyes, she saw that sadness again, and a new understanding.

She felt transparent suddenly, vulnerable. She stood up. "I guess I'll go read. I just started the new Stephen King book."

"We could go to the movies," he said gently. "*To Have and Have Not* is playing downtown."

She barely had a voice. "I've never heard of it."

He stood up beside her. "Bogart and Bacall? The greatest screen pair of all time? That's criminal. Come on. Let's go."

MAY ROARED ACROSS WESTERN WASHINGTON. DAY AFTER DAY dawned bright and hot. All over town roses burst into fragrant bloom. Overnight, it seemed, the baskets that hung along Driftwood Way went from spindly, gray, and unnoticeable, to riotous cascades of color. Purple lobelia, red gardenia, yellow pansies, and lavender phlox. The air smelled of fresh flowers, and salt water, and kelp baking beneath a hot sun.

People came out of their homes slowly, blinking molelike at the brightness. Kids ripped open their closets and burrowed through everything, looking for last year's cutoffs and a shirt without sleeves or a fleece lining. Later, their mothers stood in those same bedrooms, hands on hips, staring at the piles of winter clothes, hearing the whirl of bike wheels outside and the laughter of children who'd been hiding from the rain for too many months.

Soon—after Memorial Day—the town would begin to fill up with tourists. They would arrive in hordes, by car, by bus, by recreational vehicle, carrying their fishing gear, reading tide charts. The empty stretch of sandy beach would call out to them inexorably, drawing them to the sea in words so old and elemental the visitors could no longer say what had brought them here. But come they would.

To those who had lived in West End always, or to those who had survived a few wet winters, the tourists were good news/bad news. No one doubted that their money kept this town going, fixed the roads and bought the school supplies and paid the teachers. They also caused traffic and crowds and lines ten people long at the grocery checkout.

On the first Saturday in May, Lauren woke up early, unable to find a comfortable position in which to sleep. She slipped into clothes—a pair of elephant-waisted stretch leggings and a gauzy tent blouse with bell-shaped sleeves—then looked out her bedroom window.

The sky was a beautiful lavender-pink that seemed to backlight the black trees. She decided to go outside. She felt closeted-in here, too confined. She tiptoed past Angie and Conlan's closed door.

She crept downstairs, grabbed the soft angora blanket off the sofa, and went outside. The gentle, lapping sound of the surf was an instant balm to her ragged nerves. She felt herself calming down, breathing evenly again.

She stood at the porch railing for all of ten minutes before her feet started hurting.

This pregnancy was really starting to suck. Her feet hurt, her heart burned, her head ached half the time, and her baby was starting to hurl through her stomach like a gymnast. The worst part of it all was the Lamaze classes that she and Angie attended every week. The pictures were terrifying. Poor David had gone to one class and begged to be let go. In truth, she'd been glad to let him. She wanted Angie beside her when the time came. Lauren was pretty sure that breathing hard in a ha-ha-ha pattern wouldn't get her through the pain. She'd need Angie.

Last night she'd had the dream again, the one in which she was a little girl dressed in a bright green J.C. Penney dress and holding her mother's hand. She felt so safe with that strong hand wrapped around her tiny fingers. *Come on now,* her dream mother said. *We don't want to be late.*

What they were going to be late for, Lauren didn't know. Sometimes it was church, sometimes it was school, sometimes it was a dinner with Daddy. All she knew was that she would have followed that mommy anywhere. . . .

Last night, in her dream, the woman holding her hand had been Angie.

Lauren sat down in the big old oak rocker on the porch. The curved seat seemed made for her. She sighed in comfort. She'd have to tell Angie that this would be a great place to rock the baby to sleep at night. That way she (Lauren always thought of the baby as a girl) would grow up listening to the sea. Lauren believed that would have made a difference in her life, being rocked to sleep, listening to the surf instead of neighbors fighting and cigarettes being lit.

"You'd like that, wouldn't you?" she said to her unborn baby, who kicked in response.

She leaned back in the chair and closed her eyes. The gentle rocking motion was so soothing. Already today she needed that.

This was going to be a difficult day. One in which her whole life seemed to be trapped in a tiny rearview mirror. On this day last year, she'd gone to the beach with her friends. The guys had played football and hacky sack while the girls soaked up the sun, wearing tiny bikinis and sunglasses. When night fell, they built a bonfire and roasted hot dogs and marshmallows and listened to music. She'd felt so safe in David's arms that night, so certain of her place beside him in the world. She'd only just begun to worry that they'd go to different colleges. In one year she'd gone from child to woman. She hoped there was a way to go back again. When she gave her baby to Angie and Conlan, Lauren would—

She couldn't quite finish that thought. It happened that way more and more often lately, this onset of panic. It wasn't the adoption. Lauren had no doubt that she'd made the right choice and no doubt that she'd follow through with it. The problem came after that.

She was a smart girl. She'd grilled the adoption counselor and the guardian ad litem they'd appointed for her. She'd asked every question that popped into her mind. She'd even gone to the library and read about open adoptions. They were better than the old closed adoptions—from her perspective, anyway—because she could still hear about her child's growth. Pictures. Artwork. Letters. Even the occasional visit was the norm in these new adoptions.

But the one thing all adoptions had in common finally, at the end of the day, was this: The birth mother went on with her life. Alone.

This was the future that haunted Lauren. She'd found a home here with Angie and Conlan, a family in the DeSarias. The thought of losing that, of being alone in the world again, was almost more than she could bear. But sooner or later she would be alone again. David would go off to college, her mother was gone, and Angie and Conlan would hardly want Lauren hanging around once they'd adopted the baby. Some things in life had a natural order that was obvious to everyone. *Good-bye birth mother* was one of those things.

She sighed deeply, stroking her distended stomach. What mattered was her baby's happiness, and Angie's. That was what she needed to remember.

Behind her, the screen door screeched open and banged shut. "You're up early," Angie said, coming up beside her, placing a warm hand on Lauren's shoulder.

"Have you ever tried to sleep on top of a watermelon? That's what it's like."

Angie sat down on the slatted porch swing. The metal chains clanked and squeaked at her weight.

Lauren remembered a moment too late that Angie knew how it felt.

Silence fell between them, broken only by the sound of the waves below. It would have been easy—familiar—to close her eyes and lean back and pretend everything was okay. That's what she'd been doing for the past month. They all focused on the now because the future was frightening. But their time for pretense was running out. "My due date is only a few weeks away," she said, as if Angie didn't know that. "The books say you're supposed to be nesting. Maybe we should have a baby shower."

Angie sighed. "I've nested plenty, Lauren. And I've got lots of baby things."

"You're afraid, aren't you? You think something will be wrong with the baby, like Sophie?"

"Oh, no," Angie said quickly. "Sophie was born too early; that's all. I'm sure your baby is strong and healthy."

"You mean *your* baby," Lauren said. "We should turn my room into the nursery. I've seen all those boxes in the laundry room. How come you haven't unpacked them?"

"There's time."

"I could start—"

"No." Angie seemed to realize how sharply she'd spoken. It was practically a yell. She smiled weakly. "I can't think about decorating yet. It's too early."

Lauren saw the fear in Angie's eyes and suddenly it all clicked into place. "The other girl. She decorated the nursery with you."

"Sarah," Angie said, her voice almost lost in the sounds of early summer—the surf, the shore breezes, the birdsong. A pair of wind chimes clanged together, sounding like church bells.

It hurt to see Angie so afraid. Lauren went to her, sat down on the swing beside her. "I'm not Sarah. I wouldn't hurt you like that."

"I know that, Lauren."

"So don't be afraid."

Angie laughed. "Okay. Then I'll cure cancer and walk on water." She sobered. "It's not about you, Lauren. Some fears run deep, that's all. It's nothing for you to worry about. For now that's your bedroom. I like having you there."

"One occupant at a time, is that it?"

"Something like that. Now. Don't you have something to tell me?"

"What?"

"Like that today is your eighteenth birthday. I had to find out from David."

"Oh. That." It hadn't occurred to her to tell them. Her birthdays had always come and gone without much fanfare.

"We're having a party at Mama's."

A feeling moved through Lauren. It felt as if she'd just drunk a huge amount of champagne. "For me?"

Angie laughed. "Of course it's for you. Though I warn you now—there will probably be games."

Lauren couldn't contain her smile. No one had ever thrown her a birthday party before. "I love games."

Angie produced a small, foil-wrapped package and handed it to her. "Here," she said. "I wanted to give this to you when things were quiet. Just us."

Lauren's fingers were trembling with excitement as she opened the gift. Inside a white box marked *Seaside Jewelry* was a beautiful silver necklace with a heart-shaped locket. When Lauren opened the locket, she found a tiny photograph of her and Angie. The left side was blank.

For the baby.

Lauren wasn't sure why it made her want to cry. She only knew that when she hugged Angie and whispered, "Oh, thank you," she tasted the salty moisture of her own tears. Finally, she drew back, wiping her eyes. It was embarrassing to cry so easily, and over a necklace. She went to the porch rail and looked out over the ocean. Surprisingly, it was hard to talk past the lump in her throat. "I love it here," she said softly, leaning forward into the breeze. "The baby will love growing up here. I wish . . ."

"What do you wish?"

Slowly, Lauren turned around. "If I'd grown up in a place like this, with a mother like you . . . I don't know. Maybe I wouldn't be shopping for clothes that could double as parachutes."

"Everyone makes mistakes, honey. Growing up loved doesn't shield you from that."

"You don't know what it's like," Lauren said, "not being loved . . . to want so much from someone."

Angie got to her feet and went to Lauren. "I'm sure your mother loves you, Lauren. She's just confused right now."

"The weird thing is, I miss her sometimes. I wake up crying and realize I was dreaming about her. Do you think those dreams will go away?"

Angie touched Lauren's cheek gently. "I think a girl needs her mother forever. But maybe it will stop hurting so much. And maybe someday she'll come back."

"Needing something from my mother is like waiting to win the lottery. You can buy a ticket every week and pray, but the odds aren't good."

"I'm here for you," Angie said. "And I love you."

Lauren felt the sting of tears. "I love you, too." She threw her arms around Angie and clung to her. She wished she never had to let go.

WITH EACH PASSING DAY, ANGIE FELT HERSELF TIGHTENING. ONE twist of the spine at a time, until by early June she had a constant headache and it hurt to get out of bed. Conlan kept telling her that she needed to see a chiropractor. She'd nod and say, "You know, you're right," and sometimes she even went so far as to make an appointment.

But she knew the source of her problem didn't reside in her bones. It was a heart thing. Every sunrise brought her closer to the baby she'd always wanted . . . and closer to the day Lauren would leave.

The truth was, it was chewing Angie up inside; these two needs of hers couldn't coexist.

Conlan knew this, of course. His recommendation of a chiro-practor was purely out of form, a man's need to find solutions. When they lie in bed at night, as fitted together as long lost puzzle pieces, he asked the questions that mattered. She an-swered each one, no matter how it hurt.

"She'll be leaving soon," he said tonight, drawing Angie closer, stroking her upper arm with his thumb. "She wants to go to Los Angeles early to find a job. The counselor thinks arrange-ments can be made for her to housesit a sorority for the summer."

"Yeah."

"It's the way it has to be," Conlan said.

Angie closed her eyes, but it didn't help. The images were carved into her mind: Lauren packing up, kissing them good-bye, moving out. "I know," she said. "I just hate to think of her being all alone."

Conlan's voice was gentle when he said, "I think she'll need to get away."

"She doesn't know how hard it's going to be. I've tried to tell her."

"She's eighteen years old. We're lucky she listens to us about anything." He tightened his hold. "There's no way you can pre-pare her for this."

"There's a chance . . ." Angie marshaled her strength to finish. "She won't be able to do it."

"Are you ready for that? Last time—"

"This isn't last time. With Sarah, I thought about the baby all the time. I used to go sit in the nursery and imagine how it would be. I'd call her Boo; she'd call me Mommy. I dreamed every night about rocking her to sleep, holding her in my arms."

"And now?"

She looked at him. "Now I dream about Lauren. I see us at her college graduation . . . her wedding . . . then I see us waving good-bye and she's always crying."

"But you're the one who wakes up with wet cheeks."

"I don't know if I can take her baby from her," Angie said, finally daring to voice her deepest fear. "And I don't know how I could possibly refuse. All I know is either way, our hearts get sliced open."

"You're stronger now. *We* are." He leaned over to kiss her.

"Am I?" she said as soon as he drew back. "Then why am I afraid to get Papa's cradle from the boxes?"

Conlan sighed, and for a moment she saw the fear in his blue eyes. She wasn't sure if it belonged to him or if it were a reflection of hers. "The *Field of Dreams* bed," he said quietly, as if he'd just remembered it.

Her father had built it by hand, polishing each bit of wood to a satin finish. He'd said he got the idea from the Kevin Costner movie.

There had been tears in Papa's eyes when he presented the cradle to his Angelina. *I build it*, he said. *Now she will come.*

"Just hold on to me," Conlan said at last. "I'll keep us steady no matter what."

"Yeah," she answered. "But who will hold on to Lauren?"

IT RAINED ON THE SECOND SATURDAY IN JUNE. ALL THE PRAYERS for sunshine had been ignored.

Lauren couldn't have cared less about the weather. It was the mirror image that depressed her.

She stared at herself. The good news was her hair. Pregnancy had given her coppery hair, always her best feature anyway, a new shine.

The bad news was everything else. Her face had begun in the last week to gain weight, and her always apple-round cheeks were edging toward plate size. And forget about her stomach.

Behind her, a pile of clothes covered her carefully made bed. In the past hour she'd tried on every conceivable maternity-wear combination. No matter what she wore, she looked like a soccer mom blow-up doll.

There was a knock at the door. Angie's voice said, "Come on, Lauren. It's time to go."

"I'll be right down."

Lauren sighed. This was it. She went to the mirror and checked her makeup for the fourth time, fighting the nervous urge to layer more color on her face. Instead, she grabbed her purse, slung it over her shoulder, and left the bedroom.

Downstairs, Angie and Conlan were waiting for her. They looked absurdly gorgeous, both of them. Conlan, dressed in a black suit with a steel blue shirt, looked like the new James Bond, and Angie, in a rose-colored wool dress, was every bit his match.

"Are you sure about this?" Angie asked.

"I'm fine," Lauren said. "Let's go."

The drive to Fircrest Academy seemed to take half its usual time. Before Lauren was quite ready, they were there, parking in the school lot.

In an awkward silence, the three of them walked across campus. All around them people were laughing and talking and snapping photographs.

The auditorium was a hive of activity.

At the door, she paused.

She couldn't go in there, couldn't lumber up those bleachers and sit down with all the parents and grandparents.

"You can do it," Conlan said, taking her arm.

His touch steadied her. She looked up at the crowd, then at the decorations strung across the walls.

Class of 2004.

Boldly into the Future.

In what now felt like her other life, she would have been in charge of those decorations.

The gym was full of kids in scarlet satin gowns, their faces scrubbed and shiny, their eyes bright with promise. Lauren wanted to be down there with her friends, a laughing, teasing girl again. The longing was so sharp she almost stumbled. Tonight would be the grad night party; she'd waited years to attend.

Angie took her arm, led her up the bleachers to a seat in the middle. The three of them sat close together, tucked in amid all the other friends and family of the graduating class.

Lauren found David. He stood out from the crowd and

melted into it at the same time. He wasn't even looking up here. He was living the moment, loving it.

It pissed Lauren off that he should be down there, a boy with his whole life ahead of him, while she was here, stuck in the audience, a pregnant girl-woman who'd lost so much.

As quickly as the anger blossomed, it faded, leaving her with the sad longing she'd felt all day.

The noise blurred into one loud, pulsating roar. Lauren balled her hands, hung on to her composure by the thinnest thread.

She couldn't help looking for her mother. Even though she knew Mom wouldn't be here. Hell, she would have missed it if Lauren were graduating.

Still . . . she had this tiny, aching hope that her mother would come back, that Lauren would look up one day and see her.

Angie put an arm around Lauren, pulled her close.

The music started.

Lauren leaned forward. Below, the kids ran for their seats.

One by one the graduates of Fircrest Academy walked across the stage, took their diplomas from the principal, and moved their tassel from one side to the other.

"David Ryerson Haynes," the principal said.

The applause was thunderous. The kids cheered for him, screamed his name. Lauren's voice was lost in the crowd.

He walked across the stage as if he owned it.

When he was back in his seat, Lauren relaxed. She didn't tense up again until they reached the Rs.

"Dan Ransberg . . . Michael Elliot Relker . . . Sarah Jane Rhenquist . . ."

Lauren leaned forward.

"Thomas Adams Robards."

She sat back, trying not to be disappointed. She'd known they wouldn't call her name. After all, she'd graduated last semester, but still . . .

She'd hoped. She'd worked so hard for so many years. It didn't seem right that now she sat up here while her friends were down there.

"It's just a ceremony," Angie whispered, leaning close. "You're a high school graduate, too."

Lauren couldn't help feeling sorry for herself. "I wanted it so much," she said. "The cap and gown . . . the applause. I used to dream I'd be class speaker." She laughed bitterly. "Instead I'm the class joke."

Angie looked at her. There was a heavy sadness in her eyes. "I wish I could make everything okay. But some dreams just pass us by. It's the way life is."

"I know. I just . . ."

"Want."

Lauren nodded. That was as good an answer as any. She leaned against Angie and held her hand as the names droned on.

The ceremony lasted another forty-five minutes and then it was over. The three of them melted into the laughing, talking crowd and moved to the football field, where huge tents had been set up to hold off the rain. So many cameras flashed that it looked like the paparazzi had arrived.

Dozens of friends came up to Lauren, waving at her, welcoming her back.

But she saw the way they wouldn't look at her stomach and the *poor Lauren* in their eyes, and it made her feel stupid all over again.

"There he is," Angie said at last.

Lauren stood on her toes.

There he was, standing with his parents. She let go of Angie's hand and hurried through the crowd.

When David saw her, his smile faded for a split second. Only that, and then he was smiling again, but she'd seen it, and she knew.

He wanted to be with his friends tonight, wanted to do what the Fircrest grads always did on this night—go down to the beach, sit around a bonfire and drink beer and laugh about their years together.

He didn't want to sit quietly with his whale of a girlfriend and listen to her litany of aches and pains.

She stumbled to a stop in front of him.

"Hey," he said, bending down to kiss her.

She kissed him too long, too hard, clung to him, then finally forced herself to draw back.

Mrs. Haynes was looking at her with understanding. "Hello, Lauren. Angie. Conlan."

For the next few minutes, they stood there, talking about nothing. When the conversation fell into an awkward pause, David said to her, "You want to come to the beach after this?"

"No." She found it hard to say the word.

His relief was obvious, but he said, "Are you sure?"

She couldn't even blame him. She'd looked forward to grad night for years. It was the talk of Fircrest. It just . . . hurt. "I'm sure."

They talked for a few more minutes, then headed for the car. It wasn't until later, when they were pulling into the driveway, that she realized that no one had taken a picture of her and David.

All their years together, and there would be no senior grad day photograph.

At the house, Lauren got out of the car and went to her room. She thought she heard Angie and Conlan talking to her, but there was a white noise in her head, so she couldn't be sure. Maybe they were talking to each other.

She sat on the bed, staring at the bedpost for a long time. Remembering.

When she couldn't stand it anymore, she went downstairs and walked out to the porch.

The rain had stopped, leaving a scrubbed, robin's egg blue sky behind.

She stood at the railing.

There, down on the beach below, was a bonfire. Smoke puffed into the air.

It probably wasn't the senior party.

Certainly it wasn't.

And yet . . .

She wondered if she could lumber down the steps to the beach and walk all that way across the sand . . .

"Hey, you."

Angie came up behind Lauren, put a heavy woolen blanket around her shoulders. "You're freezing."

"Am I?"

"Yes."

She turned around, saw Angie's worried face. "Oh," Lauren sighed shakily. Then she burst into tears.

Angie stood there forever, holding her, stroking her hair.

When Lauren finally drew back, shuddering, she saw that Angie had tears in her eyes, too. "Is it contagious?" Lauren asked, trying to smile.

"It's just . . . you're still a little girl sometimes. I take it David is going to the grad night party alone."

"Not alone. Just not with me."

"You could have gone."

"I don't belong there anymore." She pulled free and went to the porch swing and sat down. She wanted to tell Angie that lately it felt as if she didn't belong anywhere. She loved this house, this family, but once the baby was born, Lauren wouldn't belong here anymore.

What had the lawyer said to her?

A baby needs *one* mother.

Angie sat down beside her. Together, they stared down the tangle of overgrown yard to the sandy beach below.

"What happens after?" Lauren asked, leaning forward. She was careful not to look at Angie. "Where will I go?" She heard the fissure in her voice; there was no way she could sound strong.

"You'll come back here. To the house. Then, when you're ready, you'll leave. Con and I bought you an airplane ticket to school. And one to come home for Christmas."

Home.

The word was a dart that pierced deep in her heart. This wouldn't be her home anymore, not once the baby was born.

All her life Lauren had felt alone. Now she knew better. Her mother had been there, and when Mom ran off, Angie stepped in. For these last few months Lauren had felt as if she finally belonged somewhere.

But soon she'd know what truly being alone felt like.

"We don't have to follow someone else's rules, Lauren," Angie said. There was a tinny, desperate edge to her voice. "We can create whatever family we want."

"My counselor doesn't think I should be here after the baby's born. She thinks that would be too hard on all of us."

"It wouldn't be too hard on me," Angie said slowly, drawing back slightly. "But you need to do what's best for you."

"Yeah," Lauren said. "I guess I'll be looking out for myself from now on."

"We'll always be here for you."

Lauren thought of the adoption plan they'd come up with—the letters and photographs and consent agreements. It was all designed to keep the two of them at arm's length.

"Yeah," Lauren said, knowing it couldn't be true.

THIRTY-ONE

ONLAN, ANGIE, AND LAUREN SAT AT THE SCARRED, OLD dining table, playing cards. The music of Angie's youth pounded through the speakers, forcing them to yell at one another. Right now, Madonna was trying to remember how virginity felt.

"You guys are in trouble now," Lauren said, taking the trick with the eight of diamonds. "Read 'em and weep." She slapped down a ten of hearts.

Conlan glanced at Angie. "Can you stop her?"

Angie couldn't help grinning. "Nope."

"Aw, *shit*," Conlan said.

Lauren's laughter rang above the music. It sounded young and innocent, and at that, Angie felt a catch in her chest.

Lauren shot the moon, then got to her feet and did a little

victory dance. It was slow and ponderous, given her stomach, but it made them all laugh.

"Gee. I think I should go to bed now," Lauren said with a wide-eyed innocence.

Conlan laughed. "No way, kiddo. You can't dump us with all those points and then just walk."

Lauren was halfway across the room when the doorbell rang. Before they'd even wondered who it was, the door opened.

Mama, Mira, and Livvy stood there. Each of them held a big cardboard box. They rushed into the cottage, already talking, and went straight to the kitchen, where they set down the boxes.

Angie didn't have to go over there to know what was in the boxes.

Food, frozen in Tupperware, ready to be heated at a moment's notice and served. No doubt each of them had been cooking double dinners for a week.

New mommies didn't have time to cook.

Angie's chest tightened again. She didn't want to go over there and see the evidence of what was coming. "Come on over," she yelled to her sisters and mother. "We're playing cards."

Mama walked across the room and snapped off the stereo. "That is not music."

Angie smiled. Some things never changed. Mama had started turning off Angie's music in the late seventies. "How about some poker, Mama?"

"I hate to take advantage of you all."

Mira and Livvy laughed. Livvy said to Lauren, "She cheats."

Mama puffed up her narrow chest. "I do not."

Lauren laughed. "I'm sure you would *never* cheat."

"I'm just very lucky," Mama said, pulling up a chair and sitting down.

Before Mira got to the table, Lauren said, "I'll be right back. I have to go to the bathroom for about the fiftieth time today."

"I know the feeling," Livvy said, rubbing her own big stomach.

"How is she?" Mira asked as soon as Lauren left the room.

"It's getting close, I think" was Angie's answer. A silent look was passed around the table. They were all wondering the same thing. Would Lauren be able to give her baby away?

"We brought food," Mira said.

"Thanks."

Suddenly the bathroom door cracked open. Lauren ran into

the living room and stopped dead. She stood there, looking pale
and terrified. Water ran down her legs and puddled on the hardwood floor. "It's starting."

"BREATHE," ANGIE SAID, SHOWING HER HOW. *HA-HA-HA.*

Lauren lurched upright in bed, screaming, "Get it out of me."
She grabbed Angie's sleeve. "I don't want to be pregnant anymore. Make it stop. Oh, God, *aaah*—" She flopped back onto the
pillows, panting hard.

Angie wiped Lauren's forehead with a cold, wet rag. "You're
doing great, honey. Just great." She could tell when the contrac-
tion ended. Lauren looked up at her through tired eyes. She
looked impossibly, heartbreakingly young. Angie fed her some ice
chips.

"I can't do it," Lauren whispered in a broken voice. "I'm not—
aaah." She was stiffening up, arching in pain.

"Breathe, honey. Look at me. Look. I'm right here. We're
breathing together." She held Lauren's hand.

Lauren melted back into the pillows. "It hurts." She started to
cry. "I need drugs."

"I'll find some." Angie kissed her forehead, then ran from the
room. "Where's our damn doctor?" She raced up and down the
white corridor until she found Dr. Mullen. He was the doctor on
call tonight; their regular obstetrician was on vacation. "There
you are. Lauren is in pain. She needs medications. I'm afraid—"

"It's okay, Mrs. Malone. I'll check her." He motioned for a
nurse and headed for Lauren's room.

Angie went to the waiting room, which was filled to overflowing. Mira's family, Livvy's family, Uncle Francis, Aunt Giulia,
Conlan, and Mama all stood in the tiny area, taking up too much
space.

Along the other wall, sitting alone in a mustard-colored plastic chair, was David. He looked dazed and scared.

God. He was so young.

Angie stepped into the room.

The crowd turned to her. Everyone started talking at once.

Angie waited. When they finally fell silent, she said, "I think
it's close." Then she crossed the room.

David stood up. He was so pale; he appeared almost translucent against the white walls. His blue eyes held the gloss of un-

shed tears. He moved toward her in jerky, uncertain steps. "How is she?"

Angie touched his forearm, feeling how cold he was. As she looked into his watery eyes, she knew why Lauren loved this boy so much. He was all heart. Someday he would be a good man. "She's doing well. Would you like to see her now?"

"Is it over?"

"No."

"I can't." He said it in a whisper. She wondered how long this decision would haunt him. It would leave a mark, she knew, but most of this day would. On all of them. "Tell her I'm here, okay? My mom is on her way, too."

"I will."

They stood there, looking at each other, saying nothing. Angie wished there were words for a time like this. She felt Conlan come up beside her. His big hand curled around her shoulder, squeezed. She leaned into him, looked up. "You ready?"

"I am."

They made their way through the family and back toward the birthing room. Conlan stopped at the nurse's station and picked up some scrubs.

The minute they walked into the room, Lauren screamed Angie's name.

"I'm here, honey. I'm here." She ran to the bedside and took Lauren's hand in hers. "Breathe, honey."

"It hurts."

It tore Angie up, that kind of pain in Lauren's voice.

"Is David here?' she asked, starting to cry again.

"He's in the waiting room. Do you want me to get him?"

"No. *Aagh!*" She arched in pain.

"That's it. Push," Dr. Mullen said. "Come on, Lauren. Push hard."

Lauren sat up. Angie and Conlan held her upright as she grunted and strained and screamed.

"It's a boy," Dr. Mullen said a few minutes later.

Lauren flopped back in bed.

The doctor turned to Conlan. "You're the father, right? Would you like to cut the cord?"

Conlan didn't move.

"Do it," Lauren said tiredly. "It's okay."

He moved woodenly forward, took the scissors, and snipped the cord. The nurse immediately moved in and took the baby.

Angie smiled down at Lauren through a blur of tears. "You did it." She wiped the damp hair from Lauren's pale face.

"Is he okay?"

The doctor answered, "He's perfect."

"You were a goddess," Angie said. "I am so proud of you."

Lauren looked up at Angie through sad, tired eyes. "You'll tell him about me, right? About how I was a good girl who made a mistake. And that I loved him so much I gave him away."

It cut Angie to the quick, that question, hurt so much that for a heartbeat she couldn't answer. When she did speak, her voice was strained. "He'll know you, Lauren. We won't just say good-bye."

The knowing look in Lauren's eyes made Angie feel like the young one. "Yeah. Right. Well, I better get some sleep now. I'm beat." She turned her face into the pillow.

"Do you want to see your baby?" Angie asked gently.

"No," Lauren answered, and there was nothing gentle in her voice at all. "I don't want to see him."

WHEN LAUREN WOKE UP, HER ROOM WAS FILLED WITH FLOWERS. IF she hadn't felt so terrible, it would have made her smile. From her bed, she tried to match the arrangements to the person. The African violets were definitely from Livvy and Sal. The azalea plant was from Maria. The pink carnations were probably from Mira, and the lilies and forget-me-nots were from Angie and Conlan. The two dozen red roses were pure David. She wondered what the cards said. What did you say to a girl who'd given birth to a baby she couldn't keep?

A knock at the door saved her from the direction her thoughts had taken.

"Come in."

The door opened. David and his mother stood there; both of them looked pale and uncertain.

As she looked at the boy she loved, all Lauren could think about was how flat her stomach was now, how empty. "Have you seen him?"

David swallowed hard, nodded. "He's so small." He crossed the room and came up beside her bed.

She waited for his kiss. When it came, it was over too quickly. They stared at each other in a heavy silence.

"He has your hair," Mrs. Haynes said, walking to the bed. She stood by her son, touched his arm as if to steady him.

"Please . . . don't tell me," Lauren said in a throaty voice.

That silence descended again. Lauren looked at David, and just now, she felt as if he were miles away.

We won't make it.

The realization washed over her. It had been there all along like a shadow in the night, awaiting sunlight to give it form and substance.

They were kids, and now that the pregnancy was past, they would drift toward their separate lives. Oh, they'd try to stay together at their different schools, but in the end, it wouldn't work. They would become what the poets wrote about: first love.

Already David was unsure of what to say to her, how to touch her. She was different now, fundamentally changed, and he sensed that.

"The flowers are beautiful," Lauren said, reaching for his hand. When he touched her, she noticed how cold his skin was.

David nodded.

Mrs. Haynes leaned forward. Very gently she eased the hair from Lauren's eyes. "You're a very brave girl. I know why my David loves you so much."

A year ago that would have meant the world to her. She gazed up at Mrs. Haynes, unable to think of anything to say.

"Well," his mother finally said, drawing back. "I'll leave you two alone." She backed away from the bed and left the room. Her heels sounded like gun blasts on the linoleum. The door clicked shut.

David leaned down again and kissed Lauren. This second kiss was the real thing.

"I signed the papers," he said when he drew back.

She nodded.

"It felt weird . . . just signing him away like that. But we don't have any choice, right?"

"What else could we do?"

He let out a relieved sigh and smiled. "Yeah."

It hurt too much to look at him, so she closed her eyes. "I think I'll go to sleep."

"Oh. Okay. Mom and I are going school shopping anyway. Do you need anything?"

School. She'd forgotten all about that.

"No."

He kissed her cheek then, touched her face. "I'll be back after dinner."

She finally looked at him. "Okay."

"I love you," he said.

It was that, after all of it, that made her cry.

IN ROOM 507, ANGIE SAT IN A THICK WOODEN ROCKING CHAIR, WAITing.

Conlan sat in the chair next to her. Every few minutes he looked at his watch, but he didn't say anything.

"She's changed her mind," Angie finally whispered. Someone had to say it.

"We don't know that," he said, but she heard in his voice that he agreed.

The clock ticked again. And again.

The door opened suddenly. A nurse dressed in orange stepped into the room. She was holding a small blue-blanketed bundle. "Mr. and Mrs. Malone?"

"That's us," Conlan said, rising. His voice was strained.

The nurse walked over to Angie and gently placed the tiny blue bundle in her arms, then she left them alone.

He was beautiful: tiny and pink, with his face all scrunched up like a fist. A few strands of red hair clung damply to his pointed head. His little lips looked for something to suck.

Angie felt as if she were falling headlong, tumbling. All the love she'd been trying to rein in came flooding out. She kissed his velvet-soft cheek, smelled the sweetness of his skin. "Oh, Con," she whispered, her eyes stinging. "He looks just like Lauren."

"I don't know what to feel," Conlan said after a minute.

Angie heard the confusion in his voice, the inchoate pain of a loss he feared was coming, and for once, she was the strong one. She looked at him. "Feel *me*," she said, touching his hand. "I'm steady. I'm here. And no matter what, we're going to be okay."

THIRTY-TWO

LAUREN MADE IT A WHOLE TWENTY-FOUR HOURS WITHOUT seeing her son. She took no chances at all. Whenever a nurse came into her room, she said, *I'm the birth mother; talk to the Malones about the baby*, before the nurse could say a thing.

By the end of the next day, she was feeling good enough to hate being here. The food was terrible, the view sucked, the television hardly got any channels, and worst of all, she could hear the nursery. Every time a baby cried, Lauren had to blink away tears. She tried rereading the USC catalog over and over, but it didn't help.

She kept hearing the high-pitched, stuttering newborn wail. Somewhere along the way she'd started thinking of her baby as Johnny, and she'd sit there, eyes squeezed shut, fists clenched, saying *Someone take care of Johnny. . . .*

She was having a hard time of it, to be sure, but she would have been okay if Angie hadn't visited her last night.

Lauren had been asleep, but barely. She'd heard the highway noise outside and tried to pretend it was the ocean, lulling her to sleep.

"Lauren?"

She'd expected a night nurse, someone checking on her one last time before lights out. But it was Angie.

She'd looked terrible, ravaged almost. Her eyes had been swollen and red and her attempts at smiling were miserable failures. She'd talked to Lauren for a long time, brushing her hair and bringing her drinks of water, until she finally said what she'd come to say.

"You need to see him."

Lauren had looked up into Angie's eyes and thought: *There it is.* The love Lauren had looked for all of her life.

"I'm afraid."

Angie had touched her then, so gently. "I know, honey. That's why you need to do it."

Long after Angie had left, Lauren thought about it. In her heart, she knew Angie was right. She needed to hold her son, to kiss his tiny cheek and tell him she loved him. She needed to say good-bye.

But she was afraid. It hurt so much to *think* about leaving him. How would it feel to actually hold him?

It was nearing dawn when she made her decision. She leaned sideways and rang the nurse's bell. When the nurse showed up, Lauren said, "Bring me my baby, please."

The next ten minutes seemed to last forever.

Finally, the nurse returned, and Lauren saw her tiny, pink-faced son for the first time. He had David's eyes, and her mother's pointed chin. And her own red hair. Here was her whole life in one small face.

"Do you know how to hold him?" the nurse asked.

Lauren shook her head. Her throat was too tight for words. The nurse gently positioned the baby in Lauren's arms.

She barely noticed when the nurse left.

She stared down at this baby of hers, this miracle in her arms, and even though he was so tiny, he seemed like the whole world. Her heart swelled at the sight of him until it actually hurt to breathe.

He was her family.

Family.

All her life she'd been looking for someone who was related to her, and here he was, snuggled in her arms. She'd never known a grandparent, a cousin, an aunt or uncle, or a sibling, but she had a son. "Johnny," she whispered, touching his tiny fist.

He held her finger.

She gasped. How could she ever leave him? The thought made her cry.

She'd promised—

But she hadn't known, hadn't understood. How could she have known how it would feel to love your own child?

I'm not Sarah Dekker, she'd said to Angie only a few weeks ago. *I'd never hurt you like that.*

Lauren squeezed her eyes shut. How could she betray Angie now?

Angie. The woman who was waiting and ready to be the best mom Johnny could have. The woman who had shown Lauren what love was, what a family could be.

Slowly, she opened her eyes and gazed down at her son through a stinging blur of tears. "But I'm your mommy," she whispered.

Some choices, no matter how smart and right, just couldn't be made.

DAVID WAS AT HER BEDSIDE THAT AFTERNOON. HE LOOKED ragged, tired; his smile was faded around the edges.

"My mom thinks he looks like her dad," he said after another of their long, awkward silences.

Lauren looked up at him. "You're sure about all this, right?"

"I'm sure. It's too soon for us."

He was right. It was too soon for them. And suddenly she was thinking of all their time together, all the years of loving him. She thought of their years together; the way he always rambled on about car capabilities and talked nonstop through movies, how he sang off-key and never seemed to know the words; mostly, she thought about the way he always seemed to know when she felt scared or lost and how he held her hand then, tightly, as if he could keep her steady. She'd always love him. "I love you, David," she murmured, hearing the thickness of her voice.

"I love you, too." He leaned forward, pulled her into his arms.

She was the first to pull back. He took her hand, squeezed it.

"This is the end for us." She said it softly. Each word hurt to say out loud. She wanted him to laugh, to take her in his arms and say, *No way.*

Instead, he started to cry.

She felt the burning in her own eyes. She longed to take it back, tell him she hadn't meant it, but she'd grown up now and she knew better. Some dreams simply slipped out of your hands. The worst part was that they might have made it, might have loved each other forever, if she hadn't gotten pregnant.

She wondered how long it would hurt to love him. She hoped it was a wound that one day healed itself, leaving only the palest silver mark behind. "I want you to go to Stanford and forget about all of this."

"I'm sorry," he said, crying so hard she knew he'd take the out she offered. And though that knowledge hurt, it saved her, too, almost made her smile. Some sacrifices had to be made for love.

He reached into his pocket and pulled out a small pink piece of paper. "Here," he said, offering it to her.

She frowned. The paper felt whisper thin between her fingers. "It's the title to your car."

"I want you to have it."

She could barely see him through her tears. "Oh, David, no."

"It's all I have."

She would remember this moment for all of her life. No matter what, she would always know that he'd loved her. She handed him back the pink slip. "Kiss me, Speed Racer," she whispered, knowing it would be the last time.

THE MINUTE ANGIE PASSED THE NURSE'S STATION, SHE KNEW.

"Mrs. Malone?" one of the nurses said. "Ms. Connelly would like to speak with you."

Angie pulled away from Conlan and ran. Her sandals snapped on the linoleum floor, sounding obscenely loud. She shoved the door open so hard it cracked against the wall.

Lauren's bed was empty.

She sagged against the doorframe. A part of her had known this was coming, had been waiting for it, but that didn't make it any easier. "She's gone," she said when Conlan came up beside her.

They stood there in the doorway, holding hands, staring at the perfectly made bed. The scent of flowers lingered in the room. It was the only evidence that last night a girl had been here.

"Mrs. Malone?"

She turned slowly, expecting to see the plump face of the hospital's chaplain. He was the first person who'd shown up in Angie's room when Sophia died.

But it was Ms. Connelly, the woman who'd been appointed guardian ad litem. "She left about an hour ago." The woman glanced down. "With her son."

Angie had expected that, too. Still the pain came fast and sharp. "I see."

"She left you a letter. And one for David."

"Thank you," she said, taking the envelopes.

The guardian said, "I'm sorry," and walked away.

Angie looked down at the stark white envelope. The name— Angie Malone—was scrawled across the front. Her hands were shaking as she took it, opened it.

Dear Angie,

> *I never should have held him.* (Here she'd scratched something out.) *All my life I've been looking for a family and now that I have one, I can't walk out on him. I'm sorry.*
>
> *I wish I were strong enough to tell you this in person. But I can't. I can only pray that someday you and Conlan will forgive me.*
>
> *Just know that somewhere, a new mother is going to sleep at night, thinking about you. Pretending—wishing—that she had been your daughter.*

With love,
Lauren

Angie folded up the letter and put it back in the envelope. Then she turned to Conlan. "She's out there all alone."

"Not alone," he said gently. She knew when she looked in his eyes that he'd expected this all along.

"Too alone, then."

He pulled her into his arms and let her cry.

THEY FOUND DAVID IN THE WAITING ROOM WITH HIS MOTHER.

At their arrival, David looked up.

"Hey, Mr. and Mrs. Malone."

His mother, Anita, smiled. "Hello again."

An awkward pause fell. They all looked at one another.

"He's beautiful," Anita said, her voice cracking only a little.

Angie wondered how it must feel to say good-bye to your son's son. "Lauren has left the hospital," Angie said as gently as she could. "She took the baby with her. We don't . . ." Her throat closed; she couldn't finish.

"We don't know where she went," Conlan said.

Anita crumpled into a chair, saying, "Oh, God," and covering her mouth with her hand.

David frowned. "What are you talking about?"

"She left with her son," Angie said.

"Left? But . . ." David's voice broke.

Angie handed him the envelope. "She left this for you."

His hands were unsteady as he opened the letter.

They all stood there in silence, watching him.

Finally, he looked up. Standing there, crying, he looked so young. "She's not coming back."

It took all of Angie's strength not to cry with him. "I don't think she can." It was the first time she'd dared to say it, even to herself. Conlan squeezed her hand. "She thinks we'd all be better off not knowing where she is."

David reached for his mother's hand. "What do we do, Mom? She's all alone. It's my fault. I should have stayed with her."

They stood there, looking at one another. No one knew what to say.

Finally, Anita said, "You'll call us if she comes back."

"Of course," Conlan answered.

Angie watched them leave, mother and son, holding hands. She wondered what they'd say to each other now. What words could be found on a day like this.

At last, she turned to Conlan, gazed up at him.

Their whole life was in his eyes, all the good, the bad, the in-between times. For a while there, it had seemed that love had moved on, left them behind. They'd lost their way because they'd thought their love wasn't enough. Now they knew better. Sometimes your heart got broken, but you just held on. That was all there was.

"Let's go home," she said, almost managing to smile.

"Yeah," he said. "Home."

. . .

LAUREN STEPPED OFF THE BUS AND INTO HER OLD WORLD. SHE tightened her hold on Johnny, who was sleeping peacefully in the front pack; she rubbed his tiny back. She didn't want him to wake up in this part of town.

"You don't belong here, John-John. You remember that."

Night was falling now, and in the darkening shadows the apartment buildings looked less shabby and more sinister.

She realized suddenly that she was nervous, almost afraid. This wasn't her neighborhood anymore.

She paused, looked back at the bus stop with a longing. If only she could turn around, walk to the corner, and take the bus out to Miracle Mile Road.

But there was no going back. She'd known that when she'd left the hospital. Lauren had betrayed Angie and Conlan's trust; she'd done exactly what she'd vowed not to. Whatever love they'd shown her would be gone now. She knew a thing or two about abandonment.

Lauren didn't belong across town anymore, in that cottage perched above the sea or in the restaurant that smelled of thyme and garlic and simmering tomatoes. Her choices in life had led her here again, inexorably, to where she belonged.

At last she came to her old apartment building. Looking up at it, she felt a shudder of loss.

She'd worked so hard to get out of here. But what else could she afford? She had a newborn son who couldn't be put in child care for months. The five-thousand-dollar check in her wallet wasn't nearly enough. She wouldn't stay long, anyway, not in this town that would always make her think of Angie. Only until she felt better. Then she'd go in search of a new place.

She set down her small suitcase and straightened, arching her aching back. Everything hurt. The Advil she'd taken earlier had begun to wear off and her abdomen ached. There was a sharp, pinching pain between her legs. It made her walk like a drunken sailor. With a sigh, she grabbed her suitcase again and trudged up the weed-infested path, past the black trash bags filled with garbage and the soggy cardboard boxes.

The door creaked open easily. Still broken.

It took her eyes a second to adjust to the gloom. She'd forgotten how dark it was in here, how it smelled of stale cigarettes and despair. She went to apartment 1-A and knocked.

There was a shuffling of feet, a muffled, "Just a sec," then the door opened.

Mrs. Mauk stood there, wearing a floral housedress and fuzzy pink slippers. Her gray hair was hidden by a red bandana that she wore in an old-fashioned style. "Lauren," she said, frowning.

"Did . . . my mom ever call for me?" She heard the pathetic neediness in her voice and it shamed her.

"No. You didn't really think she would, did you?"

"No." Her voice was barely above a whisper.

"I thought you got out."

Lauren tried not to react to the word—*out*—but it wasn't easy. "Maybe there is no out for people like us, Mrs. Mauk."

The heavy lines on Mrs. Mauk's face seemed to deepen at that. "Who's that?"

"My son." She smiled, but it felt sad. "Johnny."

Mrs. Mauk reached out and touched his head. Then she sighed and leaned against the doorframe.

Lauren recognized the sound. It was defeat. Her mother had sighed like that all the time. "I guess I'm here to see if you have an apartment for rent. I have some money."

"We're full up."

"Oh." Lauren refused to give in to despair. She had Johnny to think about now. Her tears would have to be swallowed from now on. She started to turn away.

"Maybe you better come in. It's going to rain. You and Johnny can sleep in the spare bedroom for a night."

Lauren's legs almost buckled; her relief was so big. "Thank you."

Mrs. Mauk led her into the apartment's living/dining room.

For a split second, Lauren felt her past and present collide. It looked so much like her old apartment; same Formica dining set, same shag carpeting. A rose floral sofa was flanked by two blue La-Z-Boy recliners. A small black-and-white television showed an old episode of *I Dream of Jeannie.*

Mrs. Mauk went into the kitchen.

Lauren sat down on the sofa and eased Johnny out of the pack. He immediately started to cry. She changed his little diaper and rewrapped him, but he wouldn't quit crying. His stuttering shrieks filled the tiny apartment.

"Please," Lauren whispered, rubbing his back and rocking him. "I know you're not hungry."

It wasn't until Mrs. Mauk returned, holding two cups of tea and saying, "Are you okay?" that Lauren realized she was crying.

She wiped her eyes, tried to smile. "I'm just tired, that's all."

Mrs. Mauk set the mug on the coffee table and sat in one of the recliners. "He sure is tiny."

"He's only two days old."

"And you're here, looking for your mommy or a place to stay. Oh, Lauren." Mrs. Mauk gave her one of those *poor girl* looks she knew so well.

They stared at each other. Behind them, the sitcom's laugh track roared.

"What are you going to do?"

Lauren looked down at Johnny. "I don't know. I was all set to give him up for adoption, but . . . I couldn't do it."

"I can see how much you love him," Mrs. Mauk said, her voice softening. "And the father?"

"I love him, too. That's why I'm here."

"All alone."

Lauren looked up. She felt her mouth tremble and tears fill her eyes. Again. "I'm sorry. It's the hormones. I cry all the time."

"Where have you been, Lauren?"

"What do you mean?"

"I remember the woman who came for you that day. I stood at my kitchen window and watched you get into her car and drive away, and I thought, *Good for you, Lauren Ribido.*"

"Angie Malone." It hurt to say her name.

"I know I'm just an old woman who sits at home all day talking to her cats and watching reruns, but it looked like she loved you."

"I ruined that."

"How?"

"I promised her the baby and then I ran in the middle of the night. She'll hate me now."

"So you didn't talk to her about it? You just ran off?"

"I couldn't face her."

Mrs. Mauk leaned back in her chair, studying Lauren through narrowed eyes. Finally, she said, "Close your eyes."

"But—"

"Do it."

Lauren did as she was told.

"I want you to picture your mother."

She formed the image in her mind. Mom, platinum-haired,

her once beautiful face beginning to tighten and go thin; she was sprawled on the broken-down sofa, wearing a frayed denim miniskirt and a cropped T-shirt. There was a cigarette in her right hand. Smoke spiraled up from it. "Okay."

"That's what running away does to a woman."

Lauren slowly opened her eyes and looked at Mrs. Mauk.

"I watched you bust your ass for a chance in life, Lauren. You carried home backpacks full of books and worked two jobs and got yourself a scholarship to Fircrest. You came up with the rent when your loser mother spent it all at the Tides. I had *hope* for you, Lauren. Do you know how rare that is in this building?"

Hope.

Lauren closed her eyes again, this time picturing Angie. She saw her standing on the porch, looking out to sea, with her dark hair fluttering in the breeze. Angie turned, saw Lauren, and smiled. *There you are. How did you sleep?*

It was a nothing little memory; just an image of an ordinary day.

"You have someplace to go, don't you?" Mrs. Mauk said.

"I'm afraid."

"That's no way to go through life, Lauren. Trust me on this. I know where the road ends if it starts with fear. You know where it ends, too. In an apartment upstairs and a mound of unpaid bills."

"What if she can't forgive me?"

"Come on, Lauren. You're smarter than that," Mrs. Mauk said. "What if she can?"

"YOU'RE A REPORTER, DAMN IT. FIND HER."

"Angie, we've had this conversation a dozen times. I don't even know where to start. David spoke to all of her friends. No one has heard from her. The guy at the bus station doesn't remember selling her a ticket. Her old apartment has been re-rented; the landlady practically hung up on me when I asked about Lauren. The admissions director at USC said she canceled her scholarship. I have no idea where she'd go."

Angie hit the button on the food processor. The whirring sound filled the kitchen. She stared down into the crumbly mixture, trying to think of something new to say.

There was nothing. In the past twenty-four hours she and Conlan had said everything that could be said on the subject.

Lauren had simply vanished. It wasn't difficult to do in this busy, overcrowded world.

Angie unlocked the bowl and poured the topping over the blueberry mixture. Her sisters swore that cooking was therapeutic. This was her third blueberry cobbler. Any more therapy and she'd probably scream.

He came up behind her, put his arm around her, and kissed the curve of her neck. She sighed and leaned back against him.

"I can't stand the thought of her alone. And don't tell me she's not alone. She's a kid. She needs someone to take care of her."

"She's a mother now," he said gently. "The kid part gets lost in all that."

She turned into his arms, put her hands on his chest. His heart beat beneath her palm, nice and steady and even. Whenever in the past few hours she'd felt dizzy or lost or unsteady, she'd gone to him, touched him, and let him be her anchor.

He kissed her. With his lips against hers, he whispered, "She knows you love her. She'll be back."

Angie could hear in his voice how much he wanted to believe that. "No," she said. "She won't be back. You know why?"

"Why?"

"She's going to think I could never forgive her. Her mother didn't teach her the things that matter. She doesn't realize she's forgiven her mom—or would the second she showed up. She doesn't know how durable love can be, only how easily it gets broken."

"You know what's amazing? You never mention the baby."

"A part of me knew she couldn't do it." She sighed. "I wish I'd told her that. Maybe then she wouldn't have run off in the middle of the night."

"You told her what really mattered. And she heard you. I guarantee it."

"I don't think so, Con."

"I know so. When she had the baby, you told Lauren you loved her and you were proud of her. Someday, when she stops hating herself for what she had to do, she'll remember that. And she'll be back. Maybe her mother didn't teach her about love, but you did. Sooner or later, she'll figure that out."

He could always do it; say just the right thing she needed to hear. "Have I told you how much I love you, Conlan Malone?"

"You've *told* me." He glanced over at the oven. "How long does that thing bake?"

She wanted to smile. "Fifty minutes."

"That's definitely enough time to show me. Maybe even twice."

ANGIE KISSED HER SLEEPING HUSBAND AND ROLLED OUT OF BED, careful not to disturb him. Dressing in gray sweats, she left the room.

It was so quiet downstairs. She'd forgotten that. The silence.

A teenager made so much noise . . .

"Where are you?" she whispered out loud, hugging herself. The world out there was so damned big and Lauren was so young. A dozen bad ends came to her, flashed through her mind like images in a horror film.

She headed toward the kitchen for a cup of coffee. She was halfway there when she saw the box. It was in the hallway, tucked in close to the wall. Conlan must have got it out of the laundry yesterday morning before they'd gone to the hospital.

Yesterday: when everything had been different.

She knew she should turn away from it, pretend she hadn't seen it. But that was the way of her former self, and no good came of not looking.

She went to the box, knelt beside it, and opened it up.

The Winnie-the-Pooh lamp lay on top, cradled in a pink cotton blanket.

Angie pulled it out, held it. The amazing thing was that she didn't cry, didn't ache for the lost baby for whom this lamp had been bought. Instead, she carried it to the kitchen and set it on the table.

"There," she said. "It's waiting for you, Lauren. Come home and pick it up."

Her only answer was silence. Now and then the old house creaked and in the distance the ocean grumbled and whooshed, but here, in this house that had gone from three inhabitants to two, it was still.

She walked out to the porch, stared down at the ocean. She was so intent on the water that it took her a moment to see the girl standing in the trees.

Angie ran down the steps and across the wet grass, almost falling twice.

Lauren stood there, unsmiling, her eyes swollen and red. She tried to smile. Failed.

Angie wanted to throw her arms around Lauren, but something stopped her. There was a look in the girl's eyes that was harrowing. Her mouth trembled.

"We were so worried about you," Angie said, moving a step closer.

Lauren looked down at the baby in her arms. "I know I promised him to you. I just . . ." She looked up. Tears filled her eyes.

"Oh, Lauren." At last, Angie closed the gap between them. She touched Lauren's damp cheek in the gentle kind of caress she'd dared so easily in the past. "I should have told you more about what it was like. It's just . . . it was so hard to think about the day I had Sophie. The few minutes I held her. I knew when you looked into your baby's eyes, you'd be as lost as I was. That's why I never decorated the nursery. I knew, honey."

"You knew I'd keep him?"

"I was pretty sure."

Lauren's face crumpled just a little, her lips trembled and curved downward. "But you stayed with me. I thought—"

"It was *you*, Lauren. Don't you know that? You're part of our family. We love you."

Lauren's eyes widened. "Even after how I hurt you?"

"Love bangs us up a bit in this life, Lauren. But it doesn't go away."

Lauren stared up at her. "When I was little, I used to have a dream. The same one, every night. I was in a green dress and a woman was there, reaching down to hold my hand. She always said, 'Come on, Lauren, we don't want to be late.' When I woke up, I was always crying."

"Why were you crying?"

"Because she was the mom I couldn't have."

Angie drew in a sharp breath, then released it on a ragged sigh. Something inside her gave way; she hadn't realized how tightly she'd been wrapped until the pressure eased. This was what they'd come together for, she and Lauren. This one perfect moment. She reached out for Lauren's hand, said gently, "You have me, Lauren."

Tears streaked down Lauren's face. "Oh, Angie," she said. "I'm so sorry."

Angie pulled her into her arms. "There's nothing to be sorry about."

"Thank you, Angie," she said in a quiet voice, drawing back.

Angie's face softened into a smile. "No. Thank you."

"For being nothing but trouble and keeping you up at night?"

"For showing me how it feels to be a mother. And now, a grandmother. All of those empty years I dreamed of my little girl on a merry-go-round. I didn't know . . ."

"Didn't know what?"

"That my daughter was already too old for playgrounds."

Lauren looked up at her then. It was all in her eyes, the years spent in quiet desperation, standing at her window, dreaming of a mother who loved her, or lying in her bed, longing for a bed-time story and a good-night kiss. "I was waiting for you, too."

Angie felt her smile shake. She reinforced it, wiped her eyes. "And who is this barnacle on your chest?"

"John Henry." Lauren eased the baby out of the front pack and offered him to Angie. She took him, held him in her arms.

"He's perfect," she whispered, feeling a heady combination of love and awe. Nothing filled a woman's arms like a baby. She kissed his soft forehead, inhaled the baby-sweet scent of him.

"What do I do now?" Lauren asked in a quiet voice.

"You tell me. What do you want to do?"

"I want to go to college. I guess it'll have to be community college for now. Maybe if I work for a few months and really save up I'll be able to take classes in the spring. It wasn't what I dreamed of, but . . . things change."

"Even that will be hard," Angie said gently. Harder still would be watching all her friends—and David—go off to college in the fall. She'd lose them all. One by one, they'd go on with their lives. They'd have nothing in common with a girl their age who'd be-come a mother. It would break Lauren's heart.

"I'm used to hard. If I could have my job back . . ."

"Would it help if you had a place to live?"

Lauren gasped; it was a sharp, brittle sound, as if she'd just washed ashore. "Really?"

"Of course, really."

"I wouldn't—we wouldn't have to stay for long. Just until I had enough money for an apartment and day care."

"Don't you understand, yet, Lauren? You don't need day care. You're part of a loud, loving, opinionated family now. Johnny won't be the first baby to grow up in the restaurant, and he won't be the last." She grinned. "And as you might imagine, I could find time to babysit. Not every day, of course. He's your son, but I could certainly help."

"You'd do that?"

"Of course." Angie gazed down at Lauren sadly. The girl looked so young right now; her eyes were full of a hope that seemed brand-new. Angie pulled her into a fierce hug. For a heartbeat, she couldn't let go. Finally, she took a deep breath and stepped back. "You're here just in time. Today is Aunt Giulia's birthday. I've made three blueberry cobblers—which no one except you and Conlan will eat." She reached out for Lauren, and then said quietly, "Come on. We don't want to be late."

Lauren swallowed hard. A quivering smile curved her lips even as she started again to cry. "I love you, Angie."

"I know that, honey. It hurts like hell sometimes, doesn't it?"

Together, hand in hand, they walked across the wet grass and went into the house.

Lauren immediately went to the stereo and turned on the music. It was still set to her favorite station. An old Aerosmith song pulsed through the speakers, rocked the house with sound. She turned it down quickly, but not fast enough.

Conlan came thundering down the stairs, stumbled into the living room. "What the hell's the racket?"

Lauren froze, looked up at him. Her smile slipped. "Hey, Conlan, I—"

He ran across the room and pulled her into his arms. He twirled her around until both of them were laughing. "It's about time," he said.

"She's back," Angie said, patting the baby gently, smiling at the noise. She looked over at the Winnie-the-Pooh lamp on the counter. At last it would light a baby's room. "Our girl's come home."